# A SILENT TIDE

# A NOVEL

———

## WILLIAM E. JOHNSON

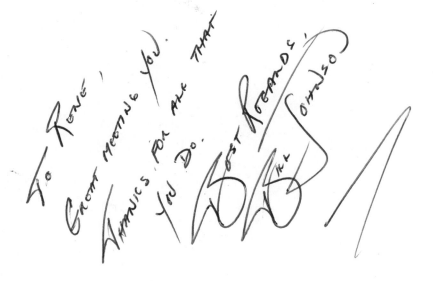

'A Silent Tide' is a work of fiction. Names, characters, and incidents are the products of the author's imagination or are used fictitiously. Any resemblance to actual events or persons, living or dead, is entirely coincidental. With that said, exceptions apply to character Eugene Callis, retired Clerk of the Mathews County Circuit Court who has graciously allowed his name to be used in this book. Green Plains Farm is a non-fictitious locale and much gratitude is extended to Dorothy Long for allowing the inclusion of her home in this book.

This book is dedicated to my dad,

**Anderson Forbes Johnson, Jr. 1927 -2013**

WWII vet, distinguished engineer, phenomenal husband
and father extraordinaire. May I live long enough
and well enough to fill his shoes.

# A SILENT TIDE

---

**PROLOGUE -** March 7, 1927

## BOOK ONE - EIGHTY YEARS LATER

# BOOK TWO - EVIDENCE

# BOOK THREE - JUSTICE

----

## EPILOGUE - FIVE DAYS LATER

----

## 'A Silent Tide'

'Of all the men who sailed and served

On the decks of the oceans wide

Strong are those who live to tell

Their tale of the water's ride.

A lesser song is sadly sung

By those who drowned and died

Their souls interred, forever more

Beneath a silent tide. '

*- The Author*

# A SILENT TIDE

---

## Prologue

## March 7, 1927

Two hours before dawn, a fishing boat loaded with illegal rum slipped quietly into the mouth of a fog shrouded cove on the upper reaches of the Chesapeake Bay. A prearranged signal, from the vessel of two red lanterns hung from hooks on the lee side of the deck cabin, was acknowledged by the pulsing of headlights from the hidden shore and the boat motored slowly to a wharf that emerged from the mist.

After securing the lines of the boat to the dock, the two boatmen on board, one the captain and the other the first mate, both draped in oilskins, came ashore and were met by three men at the end of the dock. Two of the three men were rough in appearance, with the no-nonsense look of longshoremen, short on patience and long on violence. The third man was not of that sort. A long, thick wool coat and a stylish fedora served notice of his rank and his accent spoke of his Chicago roots.

The captain wasted little time. He spoke quickly to the gentleman in the fedora, who, in turn, signaled to his two companions. A delivery truck was backed out on to the dock and the two longshoremen removed the rear canvas cover, lowered the gate and attached a cable winch to the metal rails welded to the bed of the truck. Then, barrel by barrel, the boat's cargo of prohibition-era liquor was off loaded from the hold of the ship and onto the truck whose destination was to the speakeasies of Chicago. An hour of steady labor and the task was done. A final count confirmed delivery of goods as promised and the Fedora removed a small satchel from the cab of the truck. The captain counted the money and handshakes around confirmed the day's success.

The first mate jumped off the dock and onto the deck of the boat to prepare for departure. He walked to the deck cabin, started the boat's engine and waited for the captain who remained on the dock, talking to the man in the long coat.

While the men spoke, the two longshoremen took off the winch and stashed it amongst the barrels of rum. They then secured the rear gate, tied down the canvas cover and moved towards the cab of the truck, eager to be on their way and gone from the stink of the salt marsh and the infernal hum of the bastard mosquito.

The longshoremen reached to open the doors of the truck cab, but both men suddenly stopped cold in their tracks and stared down the gangplank of the pier as it disappeared into the thick fog that blanketed the shore. They had not heard any noise as it was deathly quiet save for the soft lapping of the bay tide against the pilings, the boat and the shoreline. But these men were professionals, well-trained Chicago gangsters, who were able to sense trouble before they could see it. There was danger afoot. Both men could feel it, the premonition being strong, but for them it was too late.

From out of the fog and the darkness and up the worn planks of the dock walked the boots of five hard men, three armed with shotguns and two carrying Thompson .45 caliber machineguns.

The killing was done quick.

The longshoremen died where they stood next to the truck, both gutted at point blank range by dual blasts of 12 gauge buckshot. One of the men holding the Thompson then opened fire, instantly killing the man standing beside the captain, warm in his coat and stylish hat, while cutting down the boat captain himself in the same stream of bullets, satchel of money still in his hand.

Only the first mate who was cornered on the deck of the boat lived long enough to see the faces of his executioners, vile men who lived hard and killed easily. The group of assassins lined the edge of the dock and pointed their weapons at the last surviving smuggler.

"You shouldn't be here, waterman," says one of the men holding the shotgun. "ya friggin' made a big mistake and now yer gonna pay."

The man on the boat stared back with eyes that have seen hell on the high seas a hundred times over. "I'm already payin', seein' as I gotta watch my brother bleed to death on this stinkin' dock. Let me get this boat out of here, take my brother home and give him a proper burial. I won't be back. I'm a Mathews waterman. You have my word. I don't need this stinkin' rum or the trouble it brings."

"Trouble for you, Bub," said the man holding the smoking Thompson, "is that you chose to sell your liquor to the Capone's instead of dealing with us Baltimore boys. And, we just can't cotton to your kind, sailing into our waters and doing business with the enemy, so to speak. Now, if we let you go, what kind of message would that send to Capone and his gang? That we Marylanders are a soft touch and ripe for the pickin'? No, Mr. Mathews waterman, you are not going home today."

Hearing his fate foretold by the same gangster who had mortally wounded his brother, the first mate moved quickly. Pulling a pistol from beneath his oilskins, he blasted two rounds into the machine gunner's chest and then dove for cover behind the deck cabin, grabbing the sawed-off shotgun his brother stowed just inside the doorway.

The return fire from the four killers that remained standing on the dock was without mercy and their onslaught of double aught buckshot and full metal jacket ammo blasted the wheel house to pieces with shards of wood and glass whipping through the air like daggers.

With his pistol in one hand and his brothers sawed-off in the other, the first mate fired away with both weapons, shooting as many times as he could until he could shoot no more. Out of ammunition, his guns dropped from his hands and the waterman collapsed on the deck, as the roar of shotguns and the staccato rumble of automatic weapons fire from the men on the dock pierced the night air.

Bleeding steady and fast from wounds in his legs and chest, the mate lifted his head and gazed over at his brother who, though horribly gutted by machine gun fire, was somehow still alive, begging God not to let him die while his hands grasped feverishly at his intestines that splayed out on the boards of a dock previously stained with the blood of fish.

For the first mate, the sight of his dying sibling was more than he could bear and he rolled over onto his back and fixed his eyes instead on the stars that had penetrated the foggy darkness before dawn's light. It would soon be over.

But fate's work was unfinished that night and even though his own dying breath was well assured and just moments away, the mate suddenly ratcheted to attention. His head rose from his collapsed body like an antenna. His senses were on fire.

He had heard a sound so alien to this hell but so imbedded in his soul that it easily distracted him from the event of his own violent death. His face, once contorted by indescribable pain now bore a look of utter fear, not for his own life or for the life of his brother, but for something far more precious than the lives of two smugglers who had reached the end of days.

Something was terribly wrong and he knew instantly what it was.

His pulse began to hammer as shock and disbelief surged through his veins. How could this have happened? He checked the boat before he and his brother left the dock. The boy wasn't on it, he was certain of it. And he had told him he couldn't come this time. He needed to stay home and help his mother. But oh, how good he was at their game. Hide and seek. It was his favorite. Coils of rope, bundles of nets, sacks of sailcloth and barrels of rum. He could hide for hours amongst it all. Took pride in it, he did. And the youngster loved being on the boat. Couldn't keep him off it. "I'm a waterman, too!" he'd say. And so he was, always by his father's side. Wanting to do man's work. Wanting to be like him.

The mate rolled over to his side and, numbed to the bullet wounds by emotion far stronger than any pain that could be caused by rogue killers, he crawled along the blood covered deck to the open hatchway leading down to the darkened hold of the deadrise.

11

There, sprawled on the deck, his head resting on the hatch cover, the mate again recognized the sound unheard by the ears of gangsters keen only to the noise of their guns.

It was the crying of his nine year-old son.

The mate lowered his head into the hatchway and saw the child directly beneath him, raked with fear and shaking against the ladder. He held his blood stained hand out to the boy and with strength that should have long been expired, said "Son, the sea giveth and the sea taketh away. Remember that and remember who you are. I love you."

And with that, the waterman's body could do no more. Rum and bullets finally did what hurricanes and typhoons couldn't during his thirty years at sea. He died with his eyes open, gazing at the child who held his massive lifeless hand with trembling fingers. The boy who wanted to be like him now stared upward through the hatchway, his dead fathers face outlined by the night sky and by the gathering figures of men with guns.

# BOOK ONE

## EIGHTY YEARS LATER

---

## Chapter One

## Harper's Creek

The talons of the osprey held fast to a small speckled trout while the bird made a final approach to her preferred place of feeding at the mouth of the harbor. Her target was the top of a large, blackened piling that stood four feet above the waterline, a remnant structure of an old wharf that long ago serviced the river boats and fish steamers that once frequented the shores of Mathews County, Virginia.

Fifty years ago, skipjacks full of oysters and scallops bound for the restaurants of Manhattan would tie up two abreast at the wharf, competing for dockage with the pound netters in their deadrise fishing boats which would be loaded to the gunnels with flounder, spot, croaker and striped bass. Hard shell blue crab also thrived in these waters and was the stuff of steamed culinary legend from Boston to Charleston while the sardine-like menhaden was netted in vast volume, processed for its oil with its desiccated remains used for fertilizer in farms across the country. Back then, the world of the waterman was in its prime. The bay was full of bounty, and prosperity was in abundance. Those were truly the times of the high tide.

But prosperity, not unlike glory, is often fleeting and, in time, the fish, the oyster, the scallop and the crab left the bay. The nets became less full, the tide began to ebb and gone were the boats that once overflowed with the best the bay had to give. The well of the harvest had run dry and now, only a hardy few remained to ply the trade of the waterman. The once busy wharf that bore witness to man's capture of nature's good work, had burned to the waterline long ago and was never rebuilt, and the piling that occupied the osprey's attention now stood in silent testament to the bygone days of the feast, charred evidence of a time when the enterprise of the Chesapeake Bay waterman was king.

The osprey landed upon the pilings aged and rotted pinnacle, and ripped into the flesh of its prey while keeping her sharp eyes attuned to the affairs of her mate who stood like a sentinel aside the couple's nest. A well woven hodgepodge of sticks, feathers and sea grass, the nest served as the nursery for the couple's lone chick and was situated between the top of a day marker and the solar light that illuminated the red and green sign boards that directed boat traffic in and out of Harper's Creek Marina.

She ate ravenously, relishing the opportunity to gorge herself without the attention of the seagulls that, like hyenas, excelled at separating the primary predator from their kill. Bothersome birds to an osprey, gulls would often attack her from all sides in hopes of getting the female to release her meal and then, abandoning all pretense of the camaraderie that garnered the catch, they would fight each other like rats over the unlucky fish. Squawking and diving with beak slashing against beak, the fish would be torn to pieces, with the victor, usually the largest of the gulls, feasting on the lion's share of the carcass while the lesser mortals fought over the smaller hunks of meat that remained of the carnage.

Today, however, was an exception to the usual contest and for the moment, the large bird ate in peace for the gulls had no need to ambush a fierce and vicious opponent like a mother osprey on her mission to provide food for her young. On this particular morning, the flock's conniving as to how to satisfy their endless appetite was intently focused elsewhere as a familiar predator of another sort had now captured their attention and an easier go of mealtime was at hand.

Entering the harbor that morning was the *Bay Lady*, a thirty-eight foot fiberglass-over-wood workboat in pristine condition from bowsprit to transom. A classic deadrise design from an era long past, the *Bay Lady* was one of the finest boats of her kind on the Chesapeake Bay. Gleaming white with a Confederate flag posted off the stern, she sounded her horn to announce her return from tending the nets of her Captain, Coles Howard and her decks were covered in fish.

14

As the vessel made her way up the channel, she glided past the two ospreys who were now perched together on the edge of their nest. With their fledgling chick at their feet, both birds watched as the gulls swarmed the fantail of the boat, diving at the culled trash fish and scraps of bait left in its wake as the first mate, Jimmy Jarvis, cleaned the deck from the morning's work.

"Stop fuckin' around, Jimmy and get the lines ready," his captain barked. "You can take care of that bullshit later. I want her tied up quick and these fish off the boat and iced down within the hour. Get some of those jacklegs at the dock to give you a hand. Tell 'em if they work, I'll pay 'em fair. I want her cleaned up and her tanks topped. We got business tonight and I don't want any screw ups. Make sure she's right."

And with that, Captain Coles Howard returned his attention to the *Bay Lady* and expertly brought her starboard to dockside. First mate Jarvis was faithful to the instructions of his captain and the lines were secured within seconds of the boats arrival at the dock. Coles Howard, six and one half feet of third generation waterman, leaped from the boat and walked towards the metal roofed building that served as ships store, wholesale fish market, purveyor of general merchandise and beer hall for the old timers. The sign above the door said "Harper's Creek General Store," but to the locals it was just "Harper's" and for the old watermen, it might as well have been the center of the universe. This is where life took place and if Harper's didn't have it, well most folks said that you just didn't need it.

As he walked towards the old store, the soles of Howard's white rubber boots crunched against the sun bleached oyster shells that served as paving stones around the parking lot of the marina. It was a sound he'd been hearing since birth. He grew up at this dock, knew every inch like he knew his mother's face and had walked many a mile across these shells, first as a barefoot child and later while wearing the white boots that marked the waterman profession of his forefathers. For him, Harper's Marina was home.

His grandfather and his father before him had worked the water all their lives and docked their boats at this very same locale for generations. Howard had worshiped his grandfather and spent many an hour at his side, pulling crab pots, mending nets and cleaning the old man's boat from bow to stern. From his grandfather, he learned the importance of taking care of that which takes care of you. "Forget about your boat and she'll forget about you" the old man would say "and her memory has bad awful timing." A fifth grade education was all he had, but his grandfather was the wisest man in the world as far as the captain was concerned. Dead for twenty years, Howard could still smell his scent in the wind as the old man's mix of Old Spice after shave and Redman tobacco lingered indelibly in his memory.

Howard's older brother and their father had chosen a different path, but for him, the way of the water was something he couldn't resist. It was in his blood, having the freedom to be a man and to do man's work. That's what brought him to it. Hard and dangerous though it was, given that twelve foot waves and sixty knot winds can be on you in a second. But that's when you feel the most alive. That's when you find out what you're made of.

The water was no place for the unsteady or for the uncertain and the graveyards of the local churches were keen testament to those who had tried and failed, at least to those whose bodies could be found. Many more were those who never came back, lost at sea with their stories untold. But dying at sea wasn't a deterrent for him. Better a risk it was to face death on your terms and at the helm of your boat than to face the prospect of no life at all behind a desk; and with all the certainty of time, tide and taxes, a shackled life of pushing paper at a desk wasn't going to happen to Captain Coles Howard.

For Howard, going through the front door of Harper's was like going back in time. Since he could remember, the store had never changed and sometimes he still felt like the seven year old boy who would sit beside his grandfather and the other old watermen who gathered at the store every day of the week, listening to the old men talk while drinking an ice cold Dr. Pepper.

Seating arrangements at Harper's was a carefully orchestrated affair. The younger men would usually stand or sit on one of a number of beach chairs the store's owner collected each year that the tourists would leave behind at the end of the season. The eldest, however, were given the privilege of sitting in the rocking chairs that held center stage in the legendary establishment. Equipped with cushions to comfort the spines of men for whom back breaking work had been a daily affair, the arms of the chairs bore

16

the fine patina of wood made smooth by a thousand rough hands and the rockers themselves were worn thin by many a back and forth made to the tune of politics, weather, fishing, the local gossip of who was cheatin' on who and how much they missed the company of one of their own who passed away not long ago.

In the summertime, the conversation was often muted by the sound of the window unit air conditioners that ran continuously to dampen the intensity of the long bay summer. In the wintertime, however, the men would sit around an old wood stove that glowed red from burning the logs that were stacked in neat rows along the outer wall of the store.

This was always a special time for Howard. The pungent scent of the burning wood added to the already rich character of the old place and seeing the men sitting up close to the warm stove, spinning their yarns and offering their opinions on the issues of the day made him feel like he was part of something special. It was dear to him then and his love for the old store had never diminished over the years. Harper's was his link to the past, a place where he could always go to become immersed in the tradition of the waterman, and he often wondered if he too would one day be one of the old timers sitting around the woodstove with some young kid, perhaps his own grandson, paying rapt attention to the conversations of his elders.

Because it was mid-May, the store's proprietor, Willie Minter, had yet to put in the air conditioners and the windows were wide open, allowing the salt breeze to flow across the counters, shelves and tables that held such merchandise as fishing tackle, rods, reels, line, crab pots, engine oil, repair parts, knives, rope, wheel bearing grease, orange life preservers, bottle openers, laundry detergent, white rubber boots, Dickies dungarees and a variety of dry goods including ample supplies of House of Autry seafood breading and can after can of Old Bay seafood seasoning.

In the back were several glass front coolers with eggs, butter, milk, soda, beer, bait squid and bloodworms. More coolers were up front, old style sliding top units, where waxed cardboard boxes full of clams, crabs, oysters and fish were kept cold and fresh.

Minter usually did his business while standing behind a counter that held a cash register, a display case of Schrade knives, fishing license applications and stacks of free real estate brochures with million dollar waterfront homes adorning the covers. A calendar from 1962 showing a busty blonde holding a can of Texaco motor oil still counted the days from its place of privilege on the same wall behind the counter where Minter kept an enormous rack of spare keys to locks long lost and to boats of former slip owners who haven't been around for decades.

"Willie, you got over a thousand keys there, I reckon, and you don't have a goddamn idea what any of 'em fit," Howard said. "Why don't you just throw all that shit away along with that stupid calendar. Chicks got on one of them bras that make her tits all pointy. She looks like Madonna did in one of them music videos she made."

"Well, I think her tits look just fine," said A.J. Morgan, one of the old waterman seated in a rocking chair next to an old Formica and stainless steel dinette table that held a napkin dispenser, packets of mustard and ketchup, bowls of relish and onions, and a bottle of Texas Pete for the hot dogs that were constant fare for the regulars.

Howard quickly replied, "I can see why you would think her titties look just fine because the last time you saw a pair of tits was the same year as that there calendar!"

The other retirees seated alongside A.J. laughed hysterically while the old waterman blushed at the sexuality of the humor and the fact that Howard's observation had more truth to it than the old man would like to admit. Howard slapped A.J. on the back and hugged the old man. He'd known him since birth and had worked for a spell on his boat. Like an uncle he was to him, as were so many of the other watermen, a brotherhood carved from the wood of ships and the love of life lived on the open sea.

Howard walked to the back cooler, grabbed a single can of ice cold Pabst beer and then helped himself to a steaming bowl of the clam chowder that Minter dispensed from a large pot on an old Sears Kitchenaide stove behind the counter.

"You gonna pay for that?" Minter asked.

"I reckon I have to or else you'll call the house and then I'll really pay for it," Howard said with a smile while reaching for his wallet. Howard was married to Minter's daughter, Ann, and the give and take between father-in-law and son-in-law was part of their daily routine. Minter liked Howard. He was a hard worker who provided well for his daughter. Gave her a nice new home with all the fixings. Howard even bought Minter a new truck for his 70th birthday. All things considered, Willie Minter had no complaints about Coles Howard.

Howard wolfed down the chowder, gulped his beer and then lowered his voice. "Willie, I might be going out tonight, head over to the Bay Bridge, do a little fishing for grey trout. When I come back, I might not be as legal as I should be if you know what I mean. Would you have any heartburn if I lock the gates to the place before I leave so that the Marine Police can't drive in here for a little late night surprise? I'll be back around 4:00 am."

"No problem, Coles," Minter said, "do what you have to. If you need a key, let me know. I've got plenty," Minter said with a smile and a look over his shoulder at the mound of keys hanging on the wall. Howard just grinned, waived his own key ring in return and headed out the door.

# Chapter Two

## Later that same Night

The bow of the *Bay Lady* parted the waters of Harper's Creek as her Captain guided her out of the harbor and into Mobjack Bay. It was 1:00 am, the moon was full and shone like the sun whose light it reflected, with each wave sending the light back to its lunar source with reflections crisp and bright as if the water itself was made of polished glass.

Clearing the day markers that provided a pathway of navigable water out of the creek, Howard gunned the engines and headed east past the New Point Lighthouse and into the waters of the Chesapeake Bay. Howard sipped coffee and checked his cell phone. No message yet. But he knew that it was too early. The calls always came at 2:00 am. Like clockwork. A text message with a single GPS way point coordinate. Once the message was received, he had forty-five minutes to reach the described destination. His point of departure was always the same, two miles south of Wolf Trap Lighthouse. Howard knew he would be there in ten minutes, leaving twenty minutes to spare to get ready to take on another shipment. Howard kicked the door to the boat's cabin and yelled to a sleeping Jimmy Jarvis to get up and get the boarding lines and fender bumpers ready. Tonight, things were going to happen fast and there wasn't going to be time to waste.

Howard reached the departure point exactly on time. He cut off the running lights and waited for the call. Wolf Trap Lighthouse was two miles off but loomed large in the distance, it's silhouette accented by the twinkling lights of the fishing boats that flocked to her base, searching for the schools of angel fish and grey trout that inhabited the waters that surrounded her immense foundation.

"Sport fishermen," Howard sneered, looking off into the darkness towards Wolf Trap, "As if they think they know what fishing really is." He tossed the rest of his coffee into the liquid blackness surrounding the *Bay Lady* and checked his watch. Four minutes to go. Howard paced the deck and looked across the water in all directions. Even with a moon like tonights, as bright as he'd ever seen, Howard could see nothing on the inky horizon, no lights, no boats, nothing. Just open water to the southeast where the lights of the Chesapeake Bay Bridge Tunnel hung above the bay like one long string of Christmas lights, and to the north where there was more open water and then across the bay where Cape Charles anchored the southern tip of the Eastern Shore.

Howard looked again at the time. Two minutes left. Howard unzipped the front of his overalls and checked the pistol in his shoulder holster. A Glock 17 loaded with personal protection hollow points with one in the chamber. One minute till the call. Howard went to the wheel house and ordered Jimmy to get ready to keep a sharp lookout. Sometimes they were miles away when the call came and sometimes their boat was so close they were almost within shouting distance. These people were experts in this business. If they didn't want you to know where they were on the water, they could do it pretty well, Howard acknowledged. Not watermen, but something else, people who knew their business and who were serious about not being found.

Suddenly, the background symphony of water lapping against the hull of the boat was invaded by the mechanical humming of a cell phone. It was time. The text message was as expected, a single way point coordinate. Howard entered it into the Garmin GPS mounted on his instrument panel and brought the *Bay Lady* to life. He fired up her diesels and she was up to full speed in seconds. The screen on the GPS told him his destination was 5.6 nautical miles due southeast. He was heading for the Baltimore Channel, the deep water shipping lane for the container ships that sailed up and down the bay. The destination point was south of the favorite fishing spots of the sunken cement ships, north of the channel entrance at High Level Bridge and far away from any populated shore community. The rendezvous site minimized the possibility of unwanted boat traffic and maximized secrecy for the business transaction at hand. The location was perfect.

The *Bay Lady* did her job well and with her diesels running flawlessly, she covered the distance like a thoroughbred on the home stretch. Howard backed her down a thousand yards from the way point coordinate and guided the darkened ship slowly towards the location.

"Jimmy, get forward. You see lights anywhere near, we move quick." The boat sliced through the water while Howard checked the GPS. Five hundred yards and still the water ahead was empty. The captain could see nothing even though the moon had remained bright, an illuminating co-conspirator along with the cloudless sky and the endless array of stars that pierced the night sky. The *Bay Lady* eased forward. Suddenly, there she was. Two hundred yards away and bathed in moonlight, the vessel was long in the water but low in the transom. A Fountain 42 Lightning. With twin supercharged Mercury 1075's, she was forty-two feet of pure speed. Factory equipped, she could make 110 mph and then some if her captain had the right set of balls and was just crazy enough to see just how fast she could go. The boat was a drug smugglers dream.

Howard put the *Bay Lady* in neutral at a hundred yards out and plugged the red LED signal light into the 15 volt outlet and flashed the lamp twice at the craft, her running lights darkened as were those of the *Bay Lady*. No response. Howard waited an additional two minutes and flashed again. All part of the game. The absence of a immediate response to the first signal from the Fountain was expected. Had he received an immediate reply, he would have moved fast and hard away from the speedboat, as it would have meant that something had been compromised. Tonight, it was so far, so good and finally he received two flashes of a similar red light from the Fountain. Howard put the boat in gear, and, at barely above idle speed, motored over to the speedboat, the Glock pressed against his armpit and ready for action.

As Howard brought the *Bay Lady* alongside the vessel, two people, a man and a woman, stood on the deck of the Fountain. There was a slight breeze over the water and the night chill had both occupants in LL Bean fleece pullovers. The man was a white male, in his forties with a goatee, wearing a Baltimore Ravens baseball hat. The woman was Hispanic in appearance, possibly South American. She said nothing. Only the man spoke.

"You are right on time. I like that. What I don't like is the fact that you are not alone. Who's the kid?" he said, obviously making reference to Jimmy Jarvis who was tossing  mooring lines to the woman who expertly fastened both lines to the bow and stern cleats while Jimmy placed the fenders at appropriate points to keep the boats from bumping each other to the rhythm of the waves that softly brushed against the hulls of both boats.

Howard replied quickly, "He's squared away and knows what will happen if he fucks up. I'll worry about him, you worry about you and your little honey over there and we'll all do just fine." The woman looked at Howard with cold, distrusting eyes. Howard knew she could probably kill him in two seconds if she had the chance. She stood separate and apart from the man with the goatee and close to the cabin entrance, a fact that was not lost on Howard.

"So, first things first," said the goatee. "You should have a lot of money for me, Howard, something around $1,200,000.00, give or take a few pesos. Let's see it. We don't have a lot of time to fuck around."

"It's ready as always," said Howard as he reached down into the opening of the cuddy and removed two navy blue waterproof bags, each about three feet long. Howard placed each bag on the deck next to the cabin. "And the exact amount is $1,214,000.00." Howard added. "The last time I checked, our employers weren't much on the 'more or less' part, or have you forgotten about your predecessor who learned what it was like to go head first into a tree chipping machine."

The goatee grinned. "Oh yes, I remember Diego. So much money, so much temptation. That was indeed unfortunate. Why not you Howard? Aren't you ever tempted to take all this cash and run? It's a lot of money. You can buy a lot of things, women, more drugs. Live life like a real man," the smuggler said as he laughed.

"I am a real man," Howard replied. "Not a drug running piece of shit like you. Now where's my end of the deal. I've got seafood trucks to get loaded and I don't have time to bullshit."

"Ease up, waterman," the man said. "You're no different than me. In the end, it's all about the money, right Maria?" The woman barely acknowledged the reference to her and continued to stare at Howard.

The goatee said, "I've got twenty kilos down below. Heroin. Twice the usual load. Very popular these days. Pack it well so that it doesn't smell like fish when it gets to Baltimore. Any deviations and maybe you end up like Diego!" He laughed again, an irritating high pitched laugh which was beginning to piss off Howard.

"Then bring it up so we can get the hell out of here," Howard said.

The man spoke, "Not so fast, Senor Howard, we follow procedure first. I need to verify receipt of funds. You know the rules, now show me the money."

Howard tossed both bags onto the deck of the Fountain and watched as the goatee opened one bag and then the other. Both bags were packed full of wrapped stacks of one hundred dollar bills. "Count it, it's all there. Just like in each shipment I've done in the past. I'm a man of my word." Howard said.

"And so you are, Mr. Howard. How predictable," said the man.

"I guess I just don't like being fed to tree chippers," Howard said.

The man with the goatee laughed for the last time.

Howard suddenly stepped to the middle of the aft deck of the *Bay Lady*, pulled the Glock and fired one round into the man's face, exploding his jaw, killing him instantly. Howard saw movement to his right. The woman. An AK-47 had come out of nowhere and she had the gun at her shoulder and fired at Jimmy Jarvis. The bullet hit him in the left arm and Jimmy screamed. Howard fired four rounds at the woman, hitting her with three, knocking her off her feet and slamming her body into the lounge area of the Fountain, the assault rifle scattering across the deck that was now splattered in blood.

Howard leaped onto the deck of the speedboat and pumped another round into the bodies of both smugglers. He then threw the bags of money back on to the deck of the *Bay Lady* and went below and brought up four more nylon bags each containing five kilos of high grade Afghanistan heroin and three more bags containing bundles of cash and even more narcotics.

Jimmy remained on the bow of the *Bay Lady*, his face frozen in fear and disbelief at the suddenness and intensity of the carnage around him. The bullet had grazed his left upper arm, and he held a rag to the wound with his right hand.

"Jimmy, get movin' boy," Howard shouted. "We got to get out of here. Grab the bags and get them below now." But Jarvis just stood there. He didn't move a muscle. Clearly lost in the chaos of the unexpected slaughter, the first mate just stared at the bodies on the Fountain, oblivious to the instructions of his captain.

"Jimmy!" Howard screamed. Jarvis finally looked over at Howard, and then looked at the wound. It was minimal and the bleeding had stopped. Jarvis threw the rag to the deck of the boat and picked up the bags of cash and stashed them in the boat's cabin. Howard tossed the remaining bags onto the deck of the *Bay Lady* and Jarvis dutifully stored each one below. He had yet to say a word. Howard looked at Jarvis, as if to give him further instructions but them thought better of it, and decided to finish up things on the Fountain by himself.

Howard dragged both bodies below deck and used mooring lines to lash each corpse to the interior of the cabin. He then went into the head and busted out the inlet pipe and water started to fill the cabin. Howard then opened the engine hatch covers and disconnected the outlet pipes on the heat exchangers and started both engines. Salt water immediately began to flood the engine compartment and the boat started to sink, stern first, as the weight of the twin 1075's and the Chesapeake Bay began to drag the Fountain to the bottom of the Baltimore Channel.

Howard leaped onto the deck of the *Bay Lady*, untied the mooring lines and started her engines. As the two boats drifted apart, both men stared at the Fountain in silence as she first went bow up in a Titanic-like stance and then slipped softly below the surface.

Jarvis spoke first. "What the hell have you done? Are you crazy," he cried, staring at Howard with tears welling up in his eyes.

"Crazy like a fox." Howard growled in return, his eyes boring holes through the soul of Jimmy Jarvis. "They never showed up, you got it? Baltimore still gets their money. We keep it for them, see? We just keep the other money and the heroin for our own investment. They never find out and its business as usual while they go on looking for the guy and his little green card chick who stole their stuff. Just like Diego did."

"Business as usual?" Jarvis shouted. "Are you fucking nuts? This will never work. We won't get away with this. I'm fucking dead. Oh man, why did you do this to me?" Jarvis moaned, throwing his arms in the air while he paced the deck of the *Bay Lady*.

Howard would have none of it. "Do this to you?" he roared. "Who gave you a job? Who got you money for that nice truck and an engagement ring for that pretty little Cassie? Who showed you how to hide your cash and keep things off of the tax man's radar? Who gave you your goddamn manhood and the chance to be something more than some broke crabber living in a rented piece of shit single wide? I did and don't you forget it!"

Howard glared at the first mate from the deck of the boat but Jarvis could do nothing but stare at the water's surface that now bore no trace of the Fountain, her memory lost along with the corpses on board as she found her place at the bottom of the bay along with all the other ships of the ages that have been lost at sea.

Neither man spoke again all the way back to the dock. As Howard brought the *Bay Lady* into Harper's Creek under a moon still full and a sky adorned with the stars that have guided sailors since the days of the Phoenicians, Jarvis sat up front on the bow of the boat, his dangling legs moistened by the bow spray, while the salt breeze flowed across his face, drying both his tears and the blood from a night for which dawn would provide no reprieve.

# Chapter Three

# The Blue Crab


Like many counties in rural Virginia, Mathews has at its epicenter a centuries old historical courthouse green. Built of hand forged brick and dark grey slate roofs, the original courthouse, clerk's office, sheriff's office and jail still occupy a square block in the heart of the village.

Hallowed ground as a memorial to simpler times, the old courthouse stopped dispensing justice some years back when a new and more modern facility was built about a half mile up the highway, away from the businesses that grew up around the original courthouse and the small outbuildings that held the administrative offices that had served the county for over a century. Although no longer in use, the old courthouse still was regarded as the centerpiece of the county and had plenty of vintage architectural company as the rest of the courthouse village hadn't changed all that much since the late 1800s and looked for the most part now as it did then, with restaurants, a pharmacy, a bank, several churches and various store front businesses dispensing hardware, prescriptions, insurance, and things of the sort found on the Main Streets of small towns across the width and breadth of the rural South.

Noteworthy among the local businesses was the office of the town's only physician. An icon to the days when doctors made house calls with black bag in hand and stethoscopes around their neck, Bob Lawson was a disappearing breed.

Born and raised in Mathews, he went to medical school after the Vietnam War, came back home and had been practicing medicine here ever since. His office was on Main Street and he never turned anyone down because they couldn't pay. It wasn't that he didn't need the money; it was just that he'd seen too many men die in Khe Sanh that he couldn't save as a Navy corpsman and he wasn't going to let a buck stand between him and helping someone who needed his services. It was that simple and if his patients unpaid bills brought his bookkeeper to near tears, well that's just the way it was going to be. Doc Lawson was like that, Stubborn on principle, Doc Lawson wasn't going to change, even when it came to his own health.

Known for enjoying large platters of fried foods and gravy over everything, he ignored his cholesterol and eschewed anything having to do with exercise. It just wasn't his way. Instead of running or weightlifting or doing any of the other foolishness that those people do who think they're going to live forever, he instead took numerous walks each day around the block where his medical office was located, while smoking his daily pack of cigarettes and talking to the shopkeepers and passersby who roamed the village square.

Tonight, as he took his evening constitutional and smoked his last cigarette after a long day of treating everything from young Missy's ear infection to Homer Smith's enlarged prostate, Doc Lawson watched as a seemingly endless stream of pickup trucks and Harleys joined him in circling the block, each one looking for a place to park in a courthouse area that was designed for parking when it was just as likely to see a horse and wagon as it was to see a Model T.

Doc Lawson smiled at the activity and filled his nostrils with the pungent scent of steamed crab and real pit BBQ wafting over from the massive exhaust fans that expelled odorous invitations from the bar and grill two doors down. Traffic was heavy for a reason. The Blue Crab was open for business, a Kenny Chesney cover band was inside playing "Summertime" and parking spaces were in short supply.

The Blue Crab was a Chesapeake Bay legend. They opened on May 1st of each year and closed the day after Halloween. On the days in between, customers lined up out the door to get what some say is the best steamed crab and hickory smoked BBQ you will ever eat. Similar comments have been made about their crab cakes, baby back ribs, soft shell crabs, broiled rockfish platters and the all you can eat steamed shrimp special that's been a Blue Crab customer favorite since the joint opened twenty-two years ago.

Founded on a principle that good food ought be prepared by good people, the Blue Crab set a course to become an active player in the community and, over the years, had become command central for the annual flounder and rockfish tournaments held to benefit the local Boys and Girls Club and had sponsored dozens of youth sports programs whose team pictures adorned the walls of the restaurant. It didn't hurt, of course, that the draught beer was always ice cold and that a good band was playing every weekend they were open.

Doc Lawson took a last drag off of his cigarette and made a mental note to pick up a takeout platter of pulled pork and some soft shell crabs that he knew would be on the special's menu tonight. Molly, one of the cooks at the Blue Crab, had been in to see him today and told him that they had gotten in a shipment of the delicacy and that she would make sure that they were fried to perfection for the old physician. Some coarse cut coleslaw and handmade hushpuppies would round things out just right.

Lawson stubbed out the last of his tobacco and headed towards the office door. His staff would be gone but he knew the front door would still be open. He never worried about that sort of thing. He had gone home many a night and had left the door unlocked and sometimes wide open. Not the smartest thing in the world to do but he'd never had anything stolen. In fact, sometimes he'd be at home and someone from the village would call him just to let him know that they'd closed the door to his office and that everything was all right. It's just the way things were in Mathews. People trusted each other. No reason not to. He went in to his office, turned off the lights and grabbed his coat. His appetite made him move with a bit more deliberation than usual and he walked towards the Blue Crab at a brisk pace and said hello to Coles Howard as he stepped through the front door of, in his opinion, the best restaurant in the world.

Howard shook Lawson's hand as he entered the bar and watched as the old doctor tried to make his way to the counter to place his take out order. Might as well have been the President of the United States walking across the floor of the Blue Crab that Saturday night. That old man must have shaken twenty hands before he went ten feet. Every one of them was probably his patients, as were their parents.

"That's one well liked son of a bitch," Howard thought to himself as he sipped his Budweiser, leaned against the wall beside the register near the front door and looked over at Judy who was handling the cash tonight. She was busy running credit cards and keeping things straight.

Howard liked watching her work. They had gone to high school together, even dated for a while and he always enjoyed the opportunity to chat about the old days, even flirt a bit, while she thanked the customers while they paid their bills. Her ample cleavage, well displayed tonight, also drew his attention, and he wondered, just briefly, about what could have happened had he not married Ann Minter. Howard quickly washed that thought out of his head with the last pull on his beer and walked towards the bar to get another.

The bartender, Bobby Howard, had his bottle waiting for him before he even had time to order it. Bobby was his nephew and knew his uncle well. Bobby had worked for him for a spell and it was no secret that his uncle liked two things, a well-kept boat and an ample supply of cold beer. Bobby put the beer on Howard's tab and both men watched as the Chesney band took a break and Chubby Bowen, a local insurance agent, took the empty stage and grabbed the microphone.

"Folks, as most of you know, I'm Chubby Bowen of Bay Insurance and... "

He got no further as someone yelled, "Sit your ass down, Chubby. Unless you can sing like Kenny, get the hell off the stage!" Everyone started laughing and Chubby blushed and sweated profusely. He was dressed in an old navy blue blazer with a Rotary pin on the lapel, a lawn green bow tie, a corn stalk yellow oxford shirt, pleated khakis, canvas tan Sperry Docksiders and was nearly as wide as he was tall.

"Now y'all just hold on," Chubby said. "Tonight I'm here on behalf of the rescue squad and we thought we could use the break to raise a little money for that Jenkins family whose home burned down last week. They got a couple of kids and lost everything so every penny helps. What I thought we could do here tonight to raise some money for this family is to have us a little arm wrestling match. I spoke earlier to Russell Callis about it and he said he'd bet any man two hundred dollars that they couldn't beat his little brother, Randy, fair and square at arm wrestling. Well, Russell's here and says he's got

30

the two hundred and Randy's here and says he'll go for it if any of you out there got the stuff. Randy, is that right?"

Randy Callis stood up from a table next to the stage. "Yeah, that's right," he said and remained standing, eyes scanning the crowd for any man tough enough or stupid enough to take on the challenge.

It was perfectly understandable that most, if not all of the men at the Blue Crab that night were hesitant to step up to the stage. The word "immense" just did not do justice in describing Randy Callis. A six-foot-two waterman, Randy Callis was hauling crab pots at eight years of age and was tonging oysters by the time he was twelve. In the winter, he worked a crab dredge and earned extra money scraping boats at the local boatyards. A couple of years ago, Randy became somewhat of a local hero when he single handedly lifted a diesel engine that had fallen off an engine hoist and was crushing a man's leg. Hard physical work was all he has ever known and he had the arms, the back and the temperament to prove it.

No man stood up to accept Chubby's invitation. Chubby grabbed the microphone and tried to overcome the survival instincts of the men in the crowd by appealing instead to their charitable instincts. "Now come on y'all. I know there are some fellas out there who want to help this family in need. Randy's kind of big and all but he's a real nice young man and I'm sure everything will be just fine. So, let's get someone up here. It's all for a good cause."

Still, no one spoke. Bobby broke the silence by saying "The house will put another two hundred bucks into the pot. Chubby, let's give the winner 25% of the cash. Maybe that'll get someone interested, if you know what I mean." Chubby quickly agreed and soon other people had chipped in and the pot soon stood at eight hundred and fifty dollars. Still, no one wanted to take on Randy.

Chubby was clearly becoming frustrated when suddenly a female voice spoke up from near the front entrance. It was Judy at the cash register. She yelled, "Here's an extra hundred bucks but only if Coles Howard agrees to wrestle Randy!"

31

The crowd went nuts at the suggestion and suddenly chants of "Coles, Coles, Coles!" echoed across the walls of the bar and more money started flying towards Chubby. Now, Coles Howard wasn't a man who coveted the spotlight and he shot a glance back at a smiling Judy who responded with a wink and a squeezing together of her arms, giving him a generous view of her breasts, a message to him that she was not unaware of the direction of his gaze while he enjoyed her company at the register. But, despite his usual reticence for public attention, Howard was not immune to the spirit of the moment and he readily accepted the challenge in good humor. He drained his beer and approached the table occupied by Randy and his brother.

Howard spoke in a loud voice. "Russell, I thought it would be your sister you'd be asking me to wrestle, not your little baby brother. If it was Mary that I'd be arm wrestling, you'd have a better chance of keepin' your money!"

The crowd hooted and howled. Mary Callis was a deputy treasurer for the county and very petite, in stark contrast to her mammoth younger brother. Randy Callis stared at Coles Howard, who was the one man at the Blue Crab that night who garnered his respect, and didn't say anything in return. He just smiled and rolled up his right sleeve while Chubby and Russell quickly cleared the beer bottles off the table. Howard followed suit and soon both men were at the table, right arm to right arm, hands clasped tight.

Chubby acted as the referee. "All right boys, you know the rules. Don't grab nothing with your left hand. First man that touches the other man's hand to the table wins. Get ready, get set....go!"

Like enraged bulls unleashed from their pens at a rodeo, both men exploded as massive amounts of strength surged through the veins that road-mapped the blood rushing to their straining biceps and bulging forearms.

Coles Howard got the jump on Randy right out of the gate. Being the taller of the two men, he enjoyed a height advantage off the surface of the table. The distance from his elbow to his wrist was a good inch longer that Randy's and the additional leverage came to good use.

Coles had Callis' right hand two inches off the table and thought he might make a quick go of it, but Randy Callis had no intentions of losing this fight. Inch by inch, he raised his arm until he and Coles were back at the beginning, all even, and now it was his turn. Howard may have the leverage but nobody in the county had the grip strength of Randy Callis.

Forged by years of handling oyster tongs and crab dredges, Howard felt like Callis' grip was literally crushing his hand, and gradually, Howard's upper right arm got closer and closer to the table. Howard found himself fighting to keep strength flowing to his arm and with the pain so intense, it felt like his hand was going numb.

By now the sweat was flowing in buckets as each man was giving every bit of strength they had as the cheering of the patrons just got louder and louder. Howard sensed though that Callis' horsepower was beginning to ebb and Howard made a tactical decision to fight just hard enough to keep from being pinned and let Randy run out of gas. It was a gamble that paid off. Coles and Randy were soon back at vertical with each man staring the other in the eye, determination written across their faces like letters carved on a tombstone.

Neither man would emerge from this fight as a loser because no other man there that night could have matched these two for sheer physicality and brute strength. But one man had to win and one man did just that. Coles Howard dug deep, and suddenly with a quickness that seemed foreign to a contest that, up to that point, held pace like two elephants, going head to head, each trying to back the other away from a desired mate, he slammed Callis' hand to the table with a force that caused tables to bounce, chairs to teeter and lesser men to question their manhood.

After it was over, the men shook hands, the band retook the stage and Howard headed towards Bobby to get another Bud when he noticed that Jimmy Jarvis was seated alone at the far end the bar, staring at the rows of liquor bottles that stood like soldiers at attention in front of a huge mirror of etched glass.

"Why the long face, Jimmy? You're a rich man," Coles whispered into his ear as he put his arm around the first mate's shoulder. "You should be happy and smiling, not sitting here like some grumpy old shit. You're a young guy. You should be out humping that young Cassie! Now that's what I'd be doing if I was your age!"

Jimmy said nothing as Howard emptied half the bottle of Budweiser in one swallow.

Howard continued on, "How's that little scratch on your arm?" he said.

After a moment Jimmy replied "It's fine," he said, still staring at his reflection in the glass. "I told Doc Lawson I got it caught between the dock line and the piling when I was tying her up. He bought it."

"How's your hand?" Jimmy asked in return. "I thought Callis was going to break it in two. He can't stand you, you know. Always saying around the dock that you pay off the Marine Patrol cops, and shit like that."

"Oh, he's just jealous, that's all," Coles said, "get a better boat, get a nicer truck and the next thing you know, people are saying all sorts of shit about you, right Jimmy?"

Howard laughed and gave Jimmy a friendly nudge but spoke this time in a lower tone. "Now Jimmy, we aren't going to be havin' anybody talking about our little thing, now are we, boy?"

Jarvis just stared straight ahead at the mirror, holding his beer with both hands and said nothing. Howard suddenly reached over and took the bottle out of the hand of his first mate.

Holding the bottle in his own massive paw, Howard said, "She's warm Jimmy. Instead of drinkin', you been thinkin, and that's not a good thing, because there's nothing to think about. Do you understand, Jimmy?"

Jarvis got off the stool and tried to go around Howard and head to the door but, his captain grabbed his shoulder and stared him straight in the eye. "Jimmy, I've got to know that you understand. Look at me, boy. We've got to be straight, you and I."

Jimmy Jarvis paused for a moment, looking blankly into the crowd of the bar. Finally, he said "I've got to go pick up Cassie." He pulled his shoulder away from Howard and left the Blue Crab.

# Chapter Four

## The Fight at the Get 'n Go

Jamal Billups never had a chance.

His mother had him when she was thirteen and went on to have three more kids, all boys just like him. They had no clue who their father was and never knew anything but drugs, alcohol, social services, leaking roofs, bad plumbing and the damp smell of mold and dirt that emanated from the beat up trailers that served as their home throughout the years spent with their mother.

Ultimately, the state intervened and they went to live with their grandmother while their mother drifted on to some other man and to some other life, and Jamal hadn't seen or heard from her in ten years when he stumbled through the front doors of the Get 'n Go at 12:15 to get his second twelve pack of the day. It was a Saturday night and Jamal Billups was on a roll. He was in neither the mood nor at the requisite level of sobriety to comprehend what he was being told by the girl behind the counter.

"What the fuck do you mean I can't buy no beer? I've got the fucking money. Now, I'm going to buy me some goddamn beer!" Jamal said, putting a twelve pack of Natural Light on the counter while leaning against the structure for support in order to offset the effects of a daylong binge of weed, alcohol and his cousin's crack cocaine.

The girl behind the counter at the Get 'n Go that night was Cassie Thompkins. Cassie was eighteen years old and had been working at the local convenience store since she was sixteen. She didn't particularly like the work, but, by now she was used to the routine and she also knew most of the customers who came in, having lived in the county all her life.

When the summer season started, however, then a whole bunch of people started coming into the store that she didn't know, like folks from Richmond or Washington, D.C. who owned vacation homes on the water.

Cassie had never been to any of those places but she knew one thing, they all liked to drink lots of ice cold beer. When the tourists came to town, beer and ice went out the door in equally vast proportions, along with fishing bait of all kinds and gas for their boats. Seemed like all those people ever wanted to do was drink and fish.

Once the season was over, however, things would get back to normal, with the regulars coming in every day, particularly a group of old retirees who would arrive early every morning and drink coffee in the back of the mini mart. Cassie liked that part of her job, watching the old guys pull their trucks into the parking lot like clockwork and get their mugs down from the counter behind the coffee pot. Cassie washed their coffee cups out for them at the end of their morning constitutional and made sure they were clean and ready to go early the next day.

Her boss once told her that washing those mugs made good business sense. Cassie didn't know about that, she just wanted to be nice. The old men always treated her with respect and she just wanted to be kind in return.

Cassie had quit school when she was in the eleventh grade and started working full-time at the store. She had always had a hard time in school and she could never figure things out like math or biology. And foreign languages like Spanish? Forget it. She just never saw the sense in having to learn all that stuff anyway. Never was going to use it and she got blinding headaches every time she tried to keep up with the other students in her class. School wasn't for her. Teachers told her she may have something called a learning disability but her mother and father never came to any school meetings and got pissed off at her every time someone from the school would call or come by their house and ask why she wasn't in class that day. Finally, it all just became too much and Cassie decided that life would be a lot easier if she just started working. Besides, her boyfriend, Jimmy Jarvis, had a good job working for Captain Howard and they were going to get married next year. They would need the extra money to get a house and other stuff, too, so off to work she went.

Her proudest achievement since leaving school was that she had bought herself a two year old convertible Ford Mustang. Bright red with white racing stripes, she loved it and the car was hers at $240.00 a month. Captain

Howard had helped her with some down money and had gladly co-signed the note. Now, when her father came home from the paper mill and started slapping her mother after drinking enough beer for three men, she could drive away from the screaming and the crying in that nice new car. Put the windows down and turn the radio up really loud, so loud that the music drowned out the thoughts in her head, thoughts that wouldn't go away when she was a young girl, locked in her bedroom, hearing the thud of her mother's body slamming against the thin wall of the adjoining bedroom, knowing that if she said a word or tried to come to her mother's defense he would hit her or do even worse, make her touch him like he had made her do so many times before.

She had often fantasized about his death, about killing him and watching him die. Her hate for him was immeasurable but numbness had become her defense and her car and the Get 'n Go her sanctuary. Soon, she and Jimmy would be married and then she would be gone, away from that shack of a home and away from her alcoholic step-father and her pathetic mother who had been beaten so many times that she walked around the house like an abused dog, huddled in the back of its cage, with its eyes on constant surveillance for the slightest movement of a hand or foot, for it always brought pain while hoping against hope for a single act of kindness from her husband that would she knew would never come.

Tonight she was dressed in a pair of tight jeans that Jimmy loved, he said, because it showed off the "cutest ass in the whole county." Jarvis was three years older than Cassie and couldn't keep his hands off her. Cassie had to remind him that he better pay as much attention to working for Captain Howard as he did to taking off her bra or else they'd been having babies while living in a tent! She knew he loved her and that he was just young and young men like sex. Plus, Jimmy was a handsome guy and Cassie was smart enough to know that she wasn't the only game in town and that some of her "friends" would go after him in a minute if they thought they stood a chance of garnering his affections. Cassie knew that wasn't going to happen. Jimmy was faithful and, besides, she did have the cutest ass in the county and looked great in her bikini.

Jimmy was picking her up at 12:30 am, the end of her shift, and she wanted to look great when he showed up. They were going to go out to the beach tonight, just her and Jimmy. She had packed a beach blanket and had put a six-pack on ice in a cooler in her car. Fifteen more minutes and her shift would be over.

But then, in walked Jamal Billups.

"Jamal," Cassie said. "It's past midnight and state law says I can't sell you any beer after twelve. You know that. Besides you're drunk as can be and I can't sell alcohol to an intoxicated person. That's just how it is, now please, just go home."

Billups slammed his hand down hard on the counter surface, causing two teenagers who were in the store checking out the contents of the ice cream display case, to look over at Cassie instead. Having the real good sense to avoid trouble when possible, both youngsters made their way out the front door quick.

"This is bullshit, fucking bullshit!" Billups screamed. "I don't care about no fucking law and I don't care if you think I'm fucked up. You're the one that's fucked up. Now, I'm gonna buy this beer and I'm gonna to walk out of this fucking place and I'm gonna to do it right now." Jamal was shouting at the top of lungs, waving his arms and weaving back and forth, his breath cascading around Cassie in a nostril numbing concoction of cheap beer, stale tobacco and un-brushed teeth.

Cassie had dealt with Billups before and was having none of his stuff. "Jamal, get your ass out of here. I've just lost two customers because of your bullshit and if you don't leave right now, I'm calling the sheriff and he's gonna lock your ass up for drunk in public. Now, leave!"

Billups was too drunk to understand the good sense behind Cassie's suggestion and he continued to press his case, "Go ahead and call the fucking sheriff." He slurred out the words. "I ain't done nothing wrong. You the one that's wrong. You won't sell me any beer because I'm black, that's it. You're just a prejudiced bitch, that's all."

"Jamal, I'm not selling you beer because it's after twelve and you're already drunk. And if I'm such a prejudiced bitch, why do you keep coming in here all the time? Now, go!" Cassie yelled.

Jamal suddenly went crazy. He threw the twelve pack against the wall beside the coffee counter and the beer bottles exploded, sending foam and glass everywhere. He then kicked over a magazine rack beside the counter, and was slamming a lottery ticket dispenser to the floor when Jimmy Jarvis' pickup pulled into the parking lot. Jimmy could see the ruckus from inside the cab of his truck. He jumped out and flew in the store just as Cassie was dialing 911.

Jarvis tried to tackle Billups but missed as the smaller, but quicker Billups dodged his attack and started running towards the front door. But Jarvis was quick too. He turned and chased Billups and this time got his arms around him and both men crashed through the front doors of the store and tumbled to the ground just outside the entrance with Jarvis on top.

Jimmy Jarvis had been an all-district football and basketball star and statistically, was the bigger and stronger of the two but drunk or not, Billups had the fighting experience of a feral tom cat and he caught Jimmy with a left elbow across the bridge of his nose and a right hook that busted his lip open and Jarvis' blood rained down all over Jamal Billups.

Having been unexpectedly wounded, and surprised by the ferocity of Billups, it was Jimmy's turn to do some damage of his own and he started wailing away at Jamal, landing punch after punch with both fists against the flesh of Jamal's head and chest.

Suddenly the night sky was filled with pulsing blue lights as three pickup trucks, with fire department emergency equipment flashing, came speeding down the highway and into the parking lot of the Get 'n Go. Jimmy, like his dad, was a member of the fire department and all the members carried police scanners. Cassie's 911 call that Jamal Billups was tearing up the Get 'n Go and fighting with Jimmy Jarvis, was heard by probably every member of the squad and these guys weren't going to wait for a sheriff's deputy to arrive and let some drunk black guy wreck the place and hurt their friend. Jimmy Jarvis was one of them and each man got out of his truck, ready to take care of business and, tonight, that meant kicking Jamal Billups' ass.

Jamal heard the squealing of tires and the slamming of truck doors and instantly knew he was in serious trouble. Three white men, two with baseball bats, were ten feet away in the parking lot and coming fast when Jamal pulled a knife and put the blade at the throat of Jimmy Jarvis.

"One more step and I'll cut him," Billups screamed at the three men. "I swear to God, I'll fuckin' cut him. Now back the fuck away!"

With the blade of the knife pressing into the flesh of Jimmy's throat and with both combatants covered in each other's blood, more of Jimmy's than Jamal's, the men stopped as instructed. Jamal's eyes flashed wildly back and forth at the three men as he carefully got to his feet. With the knife in his left hand and his right arm around Jarvis's neck, both men moved as one as Billups slowly backed up towards the side of the building that faced a large tract of woods and marsh, putting more and more distance between him and the baseball bats.

Jimmy pleaded with Billups not to cut him and Jamal responded in a low voice, " I ain't gonna cut you, man. It ain't you I'm worried about. Those boys over there are a country nigger's worst nightmare. I'm sorry this happened." And with that, Billups pushed Jarvis to the ground and took off running into a thick stand of loblolly pine and low, dense holly, his dark skin and clothing helping him to disappear into the shelter of the forest and, in seconds, he was gone.

With Jamal and his knife having beat a hasty retreat into the woods, the three men ran quickly over to Jimmy Jarvis and helped him to his feet. Cassie came out and her face was as much covered in tears as Jimmy's was in blood. Everyone then went into the store and Cassie got Jimmy a wet towel and started to clean him up. His lip was busted and he had a small gash across his nose but he was going to be all right. She kissed him and was telling him how proud she was of her 'brave baby' when the Sheriff's Yukon, with lights flashing, pulled into the parking lot.

Serving his fourth term as Mathews County Sheriff, Junior Howard was one of the most popular and well-liked people in the county. Tall and lean of build, with short cut grey hair and piercing blue eyes, he had a no-nonsense approach to law enforcement that went right in step with his reputation for perhaps being a little overly aggressive, some would say violent, in keeping law and order in the county.

In his younger days as a deputy, Howard had killed a local man at a roadside stop. The dead man's family said that Howard had intentionally murdered their son but nothing ever came of it and the people of Mathews didn't seem to mind as they went to the voting booth and gave him their full support in four consecutive elections, with him running unopposed in the last two. Howard was aware of his tough guy reputation and did nothing to quell any talk about him running a tight ship at the Sheriff's department and so what if some dirt bag drug dealer had 'resisted arrest' and got hurt in the process of being taken into custody. That was tough shit as far as Howard concerned. Plus, it was great advertising. Howard wanted the word out on the street that Mathews wasn't some soft target for dope dealers. Bring your drugs here and we will lock your ass up. That was Howard's philosophy and his unofficial campaign slogan when election year rolled around. To him, it was simple. If you obey the law, you'll have nothing to worry about from Sheriff Junior Howard and his deputies.

The Sheriff walked into the Get 'n Go with his gold badge, polished to perfection and gleaming from its place of honor on the left breast of his starched white shirt.

"Where's Billups?" was all he said, barely moving the tooth pick that was perpetually lodged in the far right corner of his mouth. One of the men from the trucks spoke up.

"Fuckin' nigger took off through the woods behind the store. No way we was going to catch him. Too fuckin' quick. He knew we was gonna beat his ass and so he hauled his, he did!" The man laughed and spit into a small Styrofoam coffee cup that already held some of his earlier discharges of tobacco juice from the large wad pressed between his lip and gum. The other men nodded in agreement as the Sheriff turned his attention to Jarvis.

"You let that coon get the better of you, boy," the Sheriff said. "If I had let that happened to me, I'd be hanging my head so far in shame that it would be halfway up my ass by now." Howard was half-joking but also half-

42

serious and to Jarvis, the Sheriff's disapproval felt as sharp and threatening as Billups' knife did ten minutes earlier.

Sheriff Howard cast a quick glance at Cassie and said, "Jimmy, I suspect that you've got better things to do with the rest of tonight than fill out reports about what happened with Billups. He's not going anywhere. He'll wind up at one of his cousins tonight or at his grandmas. In any case, we'll pick him up tomorrow. Come by my office on Monday when you finish working with Coles and we'll get the paperwork straight. Maybe I'll even give you some pointers on how to handle yourself. After all, we can't have Coles Howards first mate getting his ass kicked by some burr headed sack of shit like Billups, now can we?"

The Sheriff grinned at an unsmiling Jarvis and thanked the men in the store for helping out and also thanked Cassie for doing the right thing and calling 911.

He asked Cassie if she wanted him to stick around while she locked up but she said she'd be alright and, besides, Jimmy was here and she didn't think Jamal would cause any more trouble. Cassie thanked the Sheriff for his help and both she and Jimmy watched as he got into his Yukon and drove down the highway.

Cassie took Jimmy's hand and said "Baby, If you want to just go home, I understand, It's been one hell of a night and...."

Jimmy stopped her in mid-sentence and said "Honey, I'm a little busted up but not so much that I didn't notice that you're wearing my favorite jeans. Got some beers in the cooler and the beach blanket?"

Cassie smiled and nodded. "You bet I do," she said.

"Then let's get out of here." Jimmy replied. "Follow me to that spot down off of Haven Beach Road. It'll be private, just you and me."

Cassie kissed him and skipped over to her beloved Mustang, all red and shiny under the convenience store lights. As she walked to her car, she wriggled her ass more than usual because she knew he'd be watching her. He always did. He loved to watch her walk, he'd told her so many times. Like

43

watching two moons rise in the night sky, round and perfect, he once commented as they lay naked on the same beach blanket and while at the same beach towards which she now drove in her car.

She put the windows down and the night air felt cool on her skin. She drove in silence. Tonight, the radio was not on. She had a calmness about her that felt good, that felt right, like everything was suddenly better. She felt like she had the hope that had disappeared so long ago for her mother and there was no need of the music to drown out the thoughts in her head, for tonight was her night with Jimmy. She was in love and they were together. For Cassie, that was all that mattered as she followed Jimmy's truck down Point Hollow Road.

She parked behind him and they walked together, hand in hand, out to the secluded beach, as he'd promised, and made love under a night sky filled with the same stars and the same  moon that two nights earlier, bore witness to the killing of the two drug runners by the sheriff's son. Afterwards, the couple lay bathed in the bright light from the night sky, the details of their naked bodies visible like a black and white photograph in the colorless landscape of moonlit beach. Neither one spoke. They just lay there, silently wrapped in each other's arms, listening to the soft lapping of the waves against the sand of the beach, immune to the whispers of the water and the message of the light.

"Trouble is coming," they said in unison, over and over with each roll of tide and each reflection of moonlight off the water of the bay. Trouble is coming.

# Chapter Five

## The New Lawyer in Town

It was Monday morning and the General District Court for the County of Mathews was in session. On the bench that day was the Honorable Buford R. Mumford and he wasn't going to hear anything further from the defense attorney who had been appointed to represent the defendant who was charged with petty larceny and being drunk in public.

"Mr. Forbes, the court appreciates the fact that you are a former assistant U.S. Attorney and obviously have lots of experience in trying big time criminal cases up there in Washington, D.C. or wherever it is you came from, but we are a small county, and I really don't think the Supreme Court would frankly care whether your client's rights were violated when the sheriff had a little chat with him after he got to the jail without the presence of counsel. Look, everybody here knows that your client is a drunk, and that his daddy was a drunk and so was his granddaddy. And it's plain as day that he tried to steal that pint of Old Crow from the liquor store. So, I'm going to overrule your motions and find your client guilty on the charges of petit larceny and public drunkenness. I'm going to give him sixty days up at the jail. It'll do him some good and I'm not going to impose any fine 'cause he won't pay it any way. Have a good day, Mr. Forbes and please try to remember that we like to keep things simple around here."

And with that bit of business squared away, Judge Mumford asked the Clerk to call the next case, while David Forbes packed up his file, left the courtroom and headed back to his office which was four blocks away.

As Forbes walked along the tree lined avenue that led to the small office he had rented in the old village area, he marveled at the transition that had occurred since he and his wife Karen had finally decided that they had experienced enough of the D.C. rat race and that things needed to change so that they would have more time with their kids and, perhaps of greater importance, more time for each other.

They didn't initially plan on moving to Mathews. Actually, they didn't even know that it existed until they thought that a move to the country was the thing to do. Then they started looking at maps of Virginia and taking day trips down the coast of the Chesapeake Bay.

They found their new home when they first visited the county for the annual Market Days festival that is held religiously every year on the second weekend in September. The two day festival is full of craft vendors, live music and all the crab cakes, sausage sandwiches, hamburgers, and fresh squeezed lemonade that you can eat and drink. There were lots of activities for the family and he, Karen and their two kids, Luke and Katie, had a ball.

They immediately fell in love with the town and purchased a small home on the water with a dock and boat lift. Karen was able to find a job teaching at the local elementary school and David gave notice to the federal government that he was resigning from his job as a drug prosecutor and opened up his own office on Main Street.

"David M. Forbes - Attorney-at-Law" read the sign that hung outside his law office front door, and David smiled every time he looked at it. He just couldn't believe he had made the leap from prosecuting drug cartels at the U.S. Attorney General's office to being a small town lawyer handling almost anything that came through the front door.

His attorney buddies up in Washington told him he was nuts, walking away from a prestigious job with great pay, a great office and great benefits to go work in a small town, not knowing whether the phone would ever ring.

His DEA pal, Simon Epstein, a Jewish guy from Long Island who was tops at monitoring drug cartel operations, however, cheered him on and repeatedly told him that he was doing the right thing.

"Don't listen to those schmucks," he once said over beers at a bar on K Street in Georgetown. "Those assholes don't have the guts to do what you're about to do, step out on your own without a government paycheck as a safety net. Besides, they're secretly glad you're gone. You set a pretty high standard around that office, with all those bullshit long hours you spent preparing your cases. Plus they all want your old office and they really, really want to have Yvonne as their secretary," Simon said with a smirk on his face.

He was referring to Forbes's old secretary at Justice, the ever beautiful Yvonne Jensen. To say her body was perfect would be an understatement akin to saying that the Mona Lisa was just another piece of art because Yvonne was simply beyond perfection in the human sense. She was clearly the stuff of legend.

Around Justice, Yvonne's legs and breasts were the object of constant admiration and attorneys, and their superiors as well, would go out of their way to stop by his office on some false pretense of having to see David when what they really wanted to do was check out the outfit of the day worn by his model-like assistant. Forbes laughed at Simon's observations. "You're right, you know, on both counts. I really feel like I'm doing the right thing for Karen and the kids. And, I wouldn't be surprised if there was a bidding war for Yvonnes's services," he said smiling, while he ordered two more draft Heinekens for he and Simon, who replied, "Bidding for her? With the money she'd bring, you could probably pay off the national debt!" Both men laughed.

This was the one thing that Forbes would miss; the camaraderie with the guys who helped him put the drug lords out of business or at least made it tougher to bring their poison and their violence into the states. David always admired the dedication and professionalism of the DEA, the FBI and the other agents from all the organizations that he relied upon to get the necessary evidence so that he could do his job. He knew he would also miss the power of the office of the U.S. Attorney General and the formality of the United States District Court. But, the hours were long, the kids were getting older and he felt in a sense that he wasn't there for them like he should be. And that those important, precious moments were slipping away as the kids were becoming more and more involved with their own activities and their own friends. David was determined that the memories that his children would have of their childhood would be filled with times spent with their dad, and not with memories of a father who was always at the office.

So they moved, and his initiation into the world of self-employment as a country lawyer and his first days as a practicing attorney in Mathews had been filled with all the wonderment of a kid at Christmas. Each new client was like unwrapping gifts that lie under the tree. You didn't usually know what was in the box, but you always knew it was going to be something good and special and that's how David felt about his new job and what it brought to him every day - it was all good and all very special.

Everyone he had met since he arrived had been most kind and very receptive to having a new lawyer in town and it didn't take long for business to start trickling in. His new secretary, Brenda Pritchett, was a godsend who really helped in getting him acquainted with the local townsfolk and up to speed in the legal community. For years, Brenda had worked for a local attorney who had passed away some time back and she was looking for employment when David and Karen moved to town.

The timing was perfect, and although Brenda was the antithesis of Yvonne in the looks department, she was every inch her equal in getting the work out in an organized fashion. Plus Brenda was a 'from here', the colloquialism that distinguished multi-generational Mathews citizens from 'come here's', a sometimes less than complimentary term used to describe those who move here from outside the county.

As a 'from here', Brenda knew everybody in town and from her thirty plus years working for her former employer, she also knew everybody up at the courthouse and David quickly became introduced to the Judges, to the Clerks and to all the other attorneys in town.

Brenda also knew how to handle the typical business that came through the front door of a country law practice. She could type a basic will in nothing flat and put together a simple real estate closing like nobody's business. Letters got out in a timely fashion to the courts in the criminal and traffic cases that David was appointed to and the files were always in order.

It helped that Brenda got along well with not only him, although he knew she viewed him as something of a curious anomaly - this big city lawyer hanging his shingle in her hometown - but that she also got along well with Karen and the kids who were always coming by the office after school. When the front door of his office opened at around three each day and he could hear their voices and their footstep as they ran down the hall to his office, David knew that he had made the right call. This was life as he envisioned it should be, and so it was, like a dream come true.

David was a block away from his office and could see his nameplate hanging from its wrought iron bracket atop the door frame, when the late morning sounds of slow moving traffic and leaves rustling to the movement of a soft bay breeze was suddenly muted by the screaming of police sirens as cars full of sheriff's deputies came flying down the street, turning right and heading east towards the beaches. He slowed his pace and watched as these vehicles were then soon followed by a rescue squad ambulance and a fire department jeep.

Something big had happened, probably a bad accident, David thought, as he turned his attention back down the street and continued his walk back to his office when he saw Brenda walking towards him, feverishly smoking a cigarette and talking on her cell phone.

"I can't believe it, I just can't believe it, this is so terrible, oh my God," she exclaimed. Brenda was as much talking to David as she was to the person on the other end of the phone.

David said, "What are you talking about, what's going on?"

"Oh, David, it's bad," Brenda said, putting away the phone. "It's Jimmy Jarvis. He's dead. Two kids found him at the beach. They think he was stabbed to death. Oh, this is so terrible."

David didn't know what to say. He didn't know who this Jarvis guy was but Brenda knew him well enough to be obviously upset.

"Who were you talking to?" Forbes asked.

"It was Gail at the Clerk's office. She called me when she heard the news. She also told me that the magistrate has issued warrants charging Jamal Billups with killing Jimmy. That's what the sirens were all about. The sheriff's department is heading out to bring him in."

She pulled deeply on her cigarette and looked at David. "You don't know this town, but I do. This is not going to be good. Jimmy was a really well

49

liked kid. Everybody loved him. On the other hand, Jamal Billips is as black as they come and isn't worth a damn. When the news gets out that Jimmy is dead and Jamal Billups did it, there's going to be hell to pay, I assure you. And God help Billups when they catch him. Jimmy worked for the Sheriff's son, Coles Howard, as a mate on his boat and knew most of the deputies. When they catch him, oh my, they will tear him apart!"

Forbes took Brenda by the arm and led her back to the office. He told her she could take an early lunch but she opted to stay close at hand. The office phone was beginning to ring off the hook as news spread around the county that Jimmy had been murdered by Billups.

David went back into his office, hung up his jacket and emptied the contents of his briefcase on his desk. He took a long drink from the water bottle parked on the sill of the window that looked out on Main Street and watched from the window as shopkeepers and townsfolk gathered in clusters on the sidewalk, all of them obviously talking about the crime, with some crying and others visibly angry, the conversations shrouded in a seriousness that spoke volumes about the enormity of the murder and the loss of Jimmy Jarvis.

David got up from his chair, walked down the hall and out the front door to the sidewalk, water bottle in hand, to get a better view of the situation. He took another drink and looked up and down the street. From this vantage point, he could see more and more people queuing on the sidewalk as a fleet of pickup trucks started rolling down the street, filling every parking place in town as their occupants started gathering at the tarmac aside the fire department building where the fire engines, sparkling clean and perfectly maintained, were parked that day.

Forbes stood in silence, taking it all in. "Popular white kid gets murdered by unpopular black guy in a small southern town. This isn't going to be good, just like Brenda said," he thought as he turned and went back in to his office.

---

Years later, whenever David was called upon to recall that day, he spoke of a fact that escaped his usual attention to detail, something that didn't enter his mind as his stood in front of his office on that day in May in 2007. Amidst all the commotion of sirens and the news of the tragedy, and while observing the human drama unfolding on the street corners of the old courthouse village, David had failed to notice that there wasn't a single black face to be found on the streets that day. Not one. Brenda's prophesy was indeed foretold the minute the ink was dry on the felony warrant charging Jamal Billups with first degree murder. Hell was going to be paid for the death of Jimmy Jarvis, of that there was no doubt. And for the first time in memory, doors were locked, drapes were drawn and certain people stayed home.

# Chapter Six

## The Manhunt for Jamal Billups

Within an hour of the discovery of Jimmy's body at Haven Beach, a team of deputies from the Sheriff's office had assembled in the parking lot of a post office just off of route 660 on the western side of the county and were busy putting on SWAT tactical gear, loading shotguns and feeding clips into M-4 assault carbines.

Moments earlier, the Sheriff and his lieutenant, Jake Carter, had gone to Billups' grandmother's house looking for Jamal but the man wanted for the murder of Jimmy Jarvis was nowhere to be found. The old woman claimed he hadn't been there all night, but the Sheriff wasn't buying it. He knew these people would lie at the drop of a hat to protect one of their own and that the only way to control 'em was through the fear of God itself and if the look on her face was any evidence of his success, then he had achieved his standard by a wide margin when the Sheriffs' boot kicked the door off its hinges as he and Carter burst into her house armed with 12 gauge shotguns.

Howard and Carter tore her home to shreds looking for both Jamal and the knife that killed Jimmy Jarvis, and, although the old woman had retreated in silence to a corner of the kitchen and covered her mouth with both hands as they did their work, her eyes bulging in sheer terror as every door was kicked open and every piece of furniture in the old house was turned over and their contents emptied on the floor.

"He leave a knife here?" Carter hollered as he approached the woman from the direction of the small living room from where a plastic-covered couch, her one prized piece of furniture, lay overturned on the floor beside the busted remains of an old chiffarobe and what was left of the family Bible, its pages now torn from its worn leather binder and spread across the room like dried leaves from an old tree.

The old woman answered the lieutenant's question by shaking her head side to side as fast as she could, all the while trembling with raw, gut-wrenching fear.

"Goddamn it, stop lying to me you fucking whore!" he yelled. "You know where he is, he was here last night! Tell me where he is right now or I'm gonna beat your black ass, so help me!" Carter raised his right arm as if to strike the woman, when Howard stepped in.

"Back off Jake. She ain't gonna tell us anything, are you Miss Billups?" The Sheriff grinned at the woman who had pressed herself hard against the kitchen counter. Howard then moved closer to the woman, her light gray dress darkened by the stains of her fear soaked sweat that now beaded on her ebony face like droplets of cold, dark rain.

"Your kind never does talk, do they now?" asked the Sheriff. "Don't matter what on earth you folks do, whether it's killing a white man or killing each other, it's just fine as sunshine as far as y'all's concerned, now ain't that right Miss Billups?"

Paralyzed by the nightmare that had become her home, she couldn't have answered his question if she had wanted to and just stared wide-eyed at the Sheriff, trembling uncontrollably as surge after surge of pure adrenaline rushed through her veins.

"Ain't that right?" he suddenly screamed and the woman performed the impossible, compressing herself further and further into the corner of the kitchen, her body seemingly melting into the wall, trying to shrink herself away from the body of the sheriff who was now just inches from her own.

Howard pressed even closer to the old woman, and putting his face next to hers, he softly whispered, "Miss Billups, you people can lie all you want, but we gonna catch Jamal and when we do we're gonna kill him just like he killed Jimmy Jarvis. Yes, ma'm, we gonna kill him good. No comfy jail cell for your bastard grandson 'cause that would just be too easy. Besides, fucking no-count like him would think it's a Holiday Inn compared to this trash dump. Now, you listen here, Miss Billups, if I find out you been lying to me or if you talk to anyone about our little chit- chat here today, I'm gonna come back here and burn this pile of sticks down to the ground with you in it, you hear me, Miss Billups? I might even let old Carter here have his way with you first, if you know what I mean. Carter's not too particular and who knows, you might even enjoy it."

The Sheriff then backed away from Jamal's granny, told Carter to grab the shotguns and then headed out to the Yukon. As the old woman watched the two men leave the kitchen, gather their guns and walk out the front door, her knees buckled and she slid to the floor, her legs splayed akimbo on the one-hundred year old wood of the old home. She didn't dare leave the kitchen as she could still hear them talking in muffled tones on the front porch, but seconds later she heard the slamming of car doors and found the courage to peek through the kitchen window just as the Sheriff's Yukon roared out of the rutted sand driveway and headed west towards the state road.

Knowing them now to be gone, and having somehow gathered the strength to rise off the floor, she slowly started to repair the damage done with beads of sweat now joined by tears of relief. She went into the living room and righted the couch. Then she slowly picked up the torn pieces of the family Bible and held the old book in her lap as she sat down on the sofa that was adorned in a needlepoint pattern of roses and ivy. Her church had given it to her on her sixtieth birthday and she protected her treasure by keeping it covered in clear plastic slipcovers since the first day the Rev. Covington and two deacons from the church brought it to her home.

She never had the kind of money to buy something like that for herself and no dirt was ever going to get on that beautiful sofa as long as she lived. What money she ever did have, she used it to raise both her kids and her grandkids. She had worked hard all her life, cleaning rich peoples' houses and sittin' for old folks. She was proud of the fact that she had never taken a dime of welfare in her life. The old woman didn't believe in it, having always thought that welfare was just slavery done different, that's all. She always told her kids that if you give a person free food, then they won't have to achieve nothin' in order to eat. Welfare and dope was the same thing to this granddaughter of slaves. Both took away a person's desire to do hard work, and if the black man don't do hard work, the bible tells us that he ain't never gonna be free. That's what the Reverend Covington says every Sunday, that hard work will set you free.

As she sat on her beautiful plastic-covered sofa and shuffled the torn pages back into the old Bible, she closed her eyes and began to softly sway back and forth. The old woman then began to moan, her arms wrapped around her body, hugging herself tight as she started to wail in a loud, aching voice, the sound echoing off the lemon yellow walls and pale white ceiling of her living room. She started to sway harder and harder, from back and forth to then round and round, clutching herself tighter and tighter as if exorcising the memories of the last hour from her soul, the plastic slipcovers now slickened with the tears that rolled off her cheeks and the dampness of the perspiration that soaked her dress.

Unable to further summon the necessary strength to sit upright, she fell from the sofa to the floor and curled up in a fetal position, hugging the Bible to her breast and praying to God that Jamal would be all right. She cried and prayed until she could cry and pray no more, and then laid there, still and unmoving amongst the shattered remains of the chiffarobe and the other earmarks of the Sheriff's success, staring at the lone item undisturbed by the onslaught. It was a small crucifix hanging above the doorway to the front porch. Overcome by exhaustion and with the image of the statue in her mind as the last thing she saw, she closed her eyes, said a last prayer for Jamal and fell asleep.

———————

Back at the post office parking lot, Sheriff Howard conferred with the deputies who had been dispatched to question the various members of Billups' extended family as to any knowledge they had as to Jamal's whereabouts. As expected, they all claimed that they hadn't seen him since the fight at the Get n' Go and the Sheriff began to wonder whether Billups had more sense than the Sheriff was giving him credit for.

He thought out loud to the law enforcement officers who surrounded his Yukon.

"You know, Billups may be as dumb as they come but that boy has always had the survival instincts of a New Point marsh buck," Howard said, a reference to the deer that inhabited an area at the southern tip of the county that were well known for their ability to elude the hunters table.

The Sheriff continued with his analysis, pacing on the gravel parking lot as he spoke. "By now, that boy knows that Jimmy's dead and that we're lookin' for him. He also knows that we'd go first to his grand mama's, so I'm not too surprised we didn't find him there and he for damn sure ain't gonna go to his cousins, neither. No, he's gonna go where he thinks we won't, someplace he thinks we won't think about but it'll be someplace that he's been to before, some place he's comfortable with, where he knows the lay of the land and all that shit."

The Sheriff paused for a moment with his thoughts and then became irritated at the group's silence. He yelled at the gathering.

"Well, don't any of you assholes have any idea where he might be? Can't sit around here all goddamn day!"

Matt Robins, one of the deputies spoke up. "Sheriff, I think I might know where he is. I ain't certain but there's a good chance he's over at Green Plains Farm."

Green Plains Farm was a legendary six hundred and fifty acre estate located on the North River in Mathews County, just downstream from the Auburn plantation once owned by John and Yoko Lennon. The Sheriff looked at his deputy in disbelief. "Now what the fuck would a shithead like Billups have anything to do with Green Plains?"

The deputy stammered a bit and then spoke to the Sheriff while staring at the ground and shuffling his feet. "Well, Jamal and I were sort of like friends growing up. Not good friends," the deputy quickly added, "but we knew each other 'cause every winter, I went with my granddaddy when he used to go over to Green Plains and help the caretaker butcher the hogs that they raised over there. Jamal's great grandfather was one of the caretaker's helpers and lived in a small one room house beside the stables and the hay barn. After a while, Jamal and I would get tired of watching the killin' and the

56

butcherin' and we'd go play in the hay barn. We'd climb up into the hayloft and stay up there for hours at time. Sometimes we'd spend the night out there, sleeping in the straw while the men stayed up late in the evening, putting the meat in the smokehouse and drinkin' whiskey. Jamal used to say he could live in that hayloft forever and givin' that he was living with his mother at the time and all the hell that brung, I believed him."

The deputy was still staring at his shoes when he looked up and said, "That barn is still there and I'll bet he's up in that hayloft right now, sir, scared to death."

The Sheriff said nothing in response and motioned for Carter to walk with him over to the front porch of the post office and away from the crowd of deputies that now were fully outfitted in SWAT gear and armed to the teeth.

"Carter," Howard said, "I think it'd be best if Jamal's buddy over there didn't go along for the ride down to Green Plains. Send his ass back to the office and tell him to sit tight. Second thing, I'd be really happy if Mr. Billups didn't make it out of that hayloft. The last thing I want today is a live body being taken into custody. Think you can handle that?"

Carter smiled and stared over the Sheriff's shoulder as pickup truck after pickup truck came roaring down route 660 carrying a dozen men dressed out in Realtree camouflage, with each vehicle packed tight with high-performance four-wheelers outfitted with shotguns, crossbows and plenty of ammunition.

The lieutenant looked back at his Sheriff and said, "Give me and these boys a ten minute head start and you won't have nothing to worry about." The Sheriff stared hard at his second in command, and replied "You got fifteen and don't fuck it up."

# Chapter Seven

# Green Plains Farm

The fluttering wings of a barn swallow woke Jamal Billups and he sat upright in the hayloft, his head aching and banging like a drum from his fistfight with Jimmy Jarvis. "That white boy sure could hit, but his best was nothing like the beatin' them other boys would have done with those baseball bats had they got a hold of my black ass" he thought.

Jamal ran his fingers through his wiry hair and inspected the blood on his clothes from the fight the night before. "Damn, I am fucking covered in this shit," he spoke aloud and felt the knife in his pocket press against his leg as he rolled to his side and looked over the edge of the straw covered loft and down at the old Massey Ferguson tractor he used to ride on with his beloved great-granddaddy.

Billups smiled as he remembered his great-grandfather, as a short stocky man with no front teeth who loved to laugh, drink peach flavored moonshine and eat the smoked meat that came from roasting whole pigs for hours on end in deep earthen pits lined with heated rocks and charred burning hunks of aged hickory and apple wood.

The old man could play a blues guitar too, Robert Johnson style, and Jamal would hang out with him for hours on the front porch of the old man's place at Green Plains and listen to him pick an old Sears Roebuck guitar and talk BBQ like nobody's business. Johnson's "Cross Roads Blues" was Jamal's favorite tune and his great-grandaddy could play it without missing a beat, "Old school, shit, for sure." he thought, languishing in the memory. What he wouldn't give for five more minutes of that old man's sweet, wonderful love.

Happy to be back in the safe haven of the loft, Jamal stood, stretched and brushed off the straw that stuck to his clothes and then walked over to the side of the loft and looked out the air vent at the apex of the loft ceiling and stared at the pastures that were bright green with the lush grass that fed the dozen or so thoroughbreds that called Green Plains home. Jamal could see the stables at the far end of the pasture and was thinking about going over to see the horses when something caught his attention and he ran to the other end of the loft and looked out the other vent at the far end of the barn.

Off in the distance, in the direction where the driveway entrance to Green Plains met the state highway, Jamal could hear the sound of engines getting louder and louder. Four-wheelers, almost a dozen of them, suddenly appeared at the edge of the woods that bordered the western end of the estate that fronted the highway and they were coming fast in the direction of the hay barn.

At that moment, every hair on his entire body stood on end. He looked at the blood on his shirt, felt the knife in his pocket and knew they were coming for him.

Jamal's mind ran wild. "Something fuckin' happened to Jimmy," he thought. "He was fine when I pushed him down and ran. What the fuck happened? All this ain't about me bustin' up the Get'n Go and trading punches with that boy. This looks like bad shit. I don't know what kind of shit it is but whatever it is, I am for damn sure gettin' blamed for it."

He didn't have time to ponder his own questions as the four-wheelers were covering ground quick. From his vantage point in the loft, he could see the men operating the machines. All of them white, all of them dressed in camo and all of them carrying weapons. Not a sheriff's uniform anywhere.

"Jesus, Jesus, Jesus!" Jamal thought as he jumped to the floor of the barn when suddenly the door facing the oncoming four-wheelers splintered, pierced by an arrow that missed his head by inches, impaling itself into the wall at the far end of the barn.

Jamal ran to the doorway opposite the direction of his attackers and made a decision to try to make it to the main house which was about two-hundred yards away.

He took off, running towards the old southern mansion that stood three stories above the North River, its waterfront portico a harbinger for the legions of country gentry who had been arriving by river craft to the old estate since before the Civil War. The field side entrance, towards which Jamal now ran, was adorned by several acres of old growth trees, and beautiful well-nurtured gardens bordered by scalloped brick walls and several small outbuildings that once held ice brought by river steamers but now held the lawnmowers, weed eaters and other equipment of the yard men who manicured the lawns and gardens surrounding the 'Big House' as it was known to the bevy of slaves who had worked the farm before the Civil War.

The noise of the engines of the four-wheelers grew louder as the machines got closer. Jamal's feet barely touched the ground as his legs carried him across fields once blackened by the warm blood of freshly slaughtered hogs.

"He's heading for the house!," he heard one of them yell and instantly the machines roared even louder as the men cranked on the throttles and headed in his direction. He turned his head to look over his shoulder and saw a man level a cross-bow at him from sixty yards away. Billups could hear the whoosh of the arrow as it soared past him and disappeared into a well mulched thicket of mountain laurel and english holly.

He was thirty yards from the house when he finally ducked behind the edge of the scalloped brick wall that bordered the garden and ran low behind the wall towards the moss-covered brick of the walkway that led from the garden to the staircase at the entrance to Green Plains.

Jamal heard the four-wheelers slow down and he looked over the top of the wall and saw that at least six of the riders had dismounted. He heard a voice command, "No guns, just the crossbows. I don't want no shooting at the house." and knew it came from that asshole Jake Carter who had arrested him on numerous occasions in the past, and who always managed to slip in a punch or two in the process.

He watched as they grabbed their crossbows and started running fast towards the gardens. Jamal left his cover behind the centuries old brick wall and sprinted down the walkway, hitting the staircase at full speed, taking the steps two at a time. Now a more visible target as he came out from behind the cover of the brick wall, three arrows immediately came flying in Jamal's direction and shattered just inches from his body as they hit the impenetrable two-hundred year old brick of the old estate, the broken shafts of the arrows raining down on the mansion's porch of inlaid slate and mortar.

Jamal prayed at light speed for an unlocked door and his prayers were answered as his hand turned the knob and the solid oak doors opened to the immense foyer where Presidents had once stood in their visits to Green Plains. Hurling his body across the threshold, he felt a moment of relief when suddenly an arrow from a cross bow slammed into the back of his right thigh, sending screaming pain down his leg that brought Jamal to his knees. Billups looked down at his wound and at the shaft of the arrow that stuck out five inches from the back of his leg. Bleeding bad, he tried hard not to panic. Jamal had been in the old house before with his great-grandfather and knew there was an old basement staircase down the hallway. Maybe if he could get there, maybe he could stay alive.

Billups pulled himself up and limped as fast as he could into the main foyer of the mansion. He then turned right, and headed down the hallway that led to a suite of rooms consisting of a dining room, a library, an office and the main living room, a cavernous area with a spectacular view of the other mansions that dotted the shoreline of the North River.

Halfway down the hallway, blood streaming from his leg, Jamal heard the men enter the home and knew he didn't have time to make it to the basement staircase. He pulled his body into the room immediately to his left, locked the door, moved to the side opposite the door and grabbed an antique sword from a coat of arms that hung above the fireplace that kept warm the thousands of books that filled the shelves of a massive library.

Shaking from both the loss of blood and the sheer terror of the lynch mob that had pursued him into the mansion, Jamal held the sword out in front of him like a warrior of old and could hear the movement of bodies on the other side of the door as the blood from his wound puddled on the heart-of-pine floors. The pounding of his heart sounded like the beating of a hundred drums as the seconds passed, each one an eternity, until he heard the handle to the door move back and forth as someone's hand tested the lock and saw the light blotted at the bottom of the door from the presence of boots.

61

Then, his heart stood still as his fear froze him as solid as thousand year old ice. They had found him.

Somewhere in the house, a clock began to chime, once, twice and then a third time when the door exploded open and six men in camo stormed into the room. Jamal was attacked from opposite sides and the sword went flying from his hand. Viciously kicked and unmercifully beaten where he fell, he was then dragged from the library and then down the hall and then to the main foyer where the men took him out the entrance facing the water and threw him down the steps where he landed in a mangled heap at the foot of the stone staircase.

His leg numbed from the pain and his mind nearly blank from the loss of blood, Jamal could do nothing more than just look up at the posse who now stood over him, each one armed with a crossbow and staring down at him with nothing less than pure homicidal intent.

One man spoke up. "I'm gonna do it. Jimmy was my best friend and this fucker's gonna pay." The other men nodded their consent and backed away, watching as the designated executioner shouldered his crossbow and pointed the weapon at Jamal, who just laid there, wallowing on the edge of consciousness as his blood ran onto the ground of Green Plains.

The man put his finger on the trigger of the bow and said "Goodbye, asshole," when suddenly a female voice yelled "Stop!! What are you doing! What the hell is going on?"

The men paused from the execution and looked up from where they stood. The voice came from a third floor window atop the mansion. Dorothy Hughes, owner of Green Plains, and master of all things within her domain, looked down from her vantage point above the mayhem. She held a rifle in her hand and spoke with unquestionable authority.

"That man is Jamal Billups and I know he's wanted for the murder of the Jarvis boy. I also see that he's very much alive and can easily be taken into custody. You with the bow, put it down now!" The man who was the object of her instruction first looked at his partners and then complied, pointing the weapon at his feet and stepping back from Jamal who was now lying on his back and smiling like a fool. Clearly delirious from the loss of blood, he later recounted that he thought that an angel had suddenly appeared that morning like right out of the Bible stories his grandmother had read to him as a kid.

Ms. Hughes commanded further, "You with the orange hat and you standing next to him, yes you," she spoke to the two men who stood to the left of Jimmy's best friend. "Pick him up and bring him up the steps and into the house. You two stay with him until the Sheriff arrives. No other man is to step foot into my home, now do it."

Again, the men complied and Jamal was carried up the steps and into the front hallway. "You other men, now get off my land! I'll be down these steps in less than thirty seconds and if I find a one of you here, you will surely get what you were going to do to him. Now, move!"

The arrival of Ms. Hughes at the foot of the staircase was simultaneously met with the sound of engines starting on the four-wheelers that were parked at the far end of the garden. She walked, rifle still in hand, towards the two men who stood watch over Jamal, and bent down over the wounded man.

"I remember you when you were a little boy," she said, "running around here all the time with your great-granddaddy. You loved the loft then, so I'm not particularly surprised that you came here now." Billups smiled weakly at the soothing voice as Ms. Hughes stood up, walked to the kitchen and came back with a towel. "You!" she commanded again to the man in the orange hat, "Press this against the wound on his leg and don't move until an ambulance gets here." The man stared at the rifle in her hand and quickly did as he was told.

She then walked to the hallway entrance that overlooked the gardens and looked down the mile-long driveway above which floated the effervescent dust of the four-wheelers as they left the property per the commands of its mistress. She had called 911 from a phone in the third floor room and knew that her beloved Green Plains would soon be overrun with law enforcement officers and as she sat down on the front steps of the estate to await their arrival, she leaned the rifle against the stone columns that accented the front of the entranceway, and picked up the tip of one of the arrows that had shattered against the thick brick front wall of the mansion.

She held the razor sharp broad head in her fingers, the arrow tip sharp and menacing, and gazed at the trail of blood that began at the front steps where Billups was hit by the arrow and made a mental note to get a cleaning company out here first thing in the morning. She then stood up and walked down the steps as vehicle after vehicle started coming down the driveway. She smoothed the front of her blouse, touched up a strand of hair that had fallen across her forehead and met the Sheriff's Yukon as it came to a halt at the at the foot of the front porch.

"Why Sheriff Howard, so nice to see you again," she said politely in her cultured Virginia accent as she held out her hand. "Mr. Billups is in my foyer and despite the efforts of some characters who trespassed on my property, he's alive for the moment. I trust that doesn't displease you." Dorothy awaited his response as she watched her reflection dance on the polished surface of the Sheriff's Ray Ban sunglasses.

"Why, not at all, Miss Dorothy. Not on all." said the Sheriff in return, surprised by the firmness of her handshake and hiding well his displeasure as to Jamal's being alive despite his instructions to Carter. "These men did good work in apprehending Mr. Billups and we're just very glad that you weren't hurt by this man."

Dorothy said, "Sheriff, I've known Jamal since he was a young boy. He was of no danger to me. But I'm not so sure I can say the same about those two over there," making reference to the two men in camo who by this time had made their way out the front of the house and were talking to a similarly attired Lt. Carter at the far edge of the driveway next to the gardens.

"Looked like a lynch mob, if you ask me," she continued on in a firm, confident voice. "Had I not poked my head out the window and pointed my Daddy's old squirrel gun at the head of one of the fellows who just high tailed it off my property, Jamal would undoubtedly be dead right now, no doubt about it."

Sheriff Howard shifted his toothpick from one side to the other and said "Well, they're just good old boys who lost one of their childhood friends. They're a little emotional right now, a bit over excited perhaps, and that's all. I can't say that I blame them. Now you just let us do our job and everything will be fine. We'll be out of your hair in just a few minutes."

Dorothy declined further comment as she and the Sheriff turned and watched as Jamal was taken out of the house and down the steps on a stretcher. As he passed, he looked over at her and mouthed the words "thank you," too weak to speak them aloud. She was close enough to briefly hold his hand and then he was gone, whisked away by the waiting ambulance. She turned as if to say something else to the Sheriff but thought better of it and watched in silence as the caravan of police cars followed the ambulance up the driveway and off her land.

She went back into the house and walked down the hallway to the main living room where she poured a small glass of excellent sherry. "White men hunting a black man with bows and arrows," she mused as she took a sip of the fine sweet wine and watched through the floor-to-ceiling windows as the reflection of the mid-morning sun set the water of the North River on fire with its brilliant hues of yellow and orange. She pondered the complexity of it all, nature's beauty versus man's inhumanity and thought of the razor-sharp broadhead she held in her hand just moments ago.

She finished her sherry, straightened the antique ivory clip that held in place her long brown hair and then walked across the hallway to inspect the damage in the library. She loved the old room. It was her father's favorite and she had many fond memories of him sitting at the huge mahogany desk that occupied center stage in the library, listening to him talk on the phone to some important person, discussing the affairs of big government and big business. She put the items on his desk that had been disturbed by the ruckus back into their proper place and returned the sword to her family's coat of arms above the fireplace, being careful not to tread in the small pool of Jamal's blood that had begun to dry on the old mansion floor made of wood honed smooth by the hands of slaves.

# Chapter Eight

## Breakfast at Patty's Diner

David arrived at his law office at 6:45 a.m. the morning after Billups' arrest, briefly checked his emails and then walked the two blocks to Patty's Diner for his morning coffee and breakfast while thinking about the events of the day before.

The nightly newscast of the previous evening featured interviews with Sheriff Howard and a helicopter's view of the Green Plains Estate where Billups was captured. In his comments to the press, the Sheriff praised the good work of the citizens who helped to track down Billups and thanked them for risking their lives in order to bring Billups to justice for the murder of Jimmy Jarvis.

The broadcast also featured interviews with some of the local townsfolk who talked mournfully about the loss of Jarvis, and the interviewer, a petite blond with the even toned voice of talking heads everywhere, ended the broadcast with a commentary as to what the murder had done to upset the image of Mathews as being a quiet country community known for its safe streets and low crime rate. The local daily newspaper also featured the story in its morning headlines, announcing the killing of Jarvis and the arrest of Billups from the window of the vending machine in front of Patty's and it was of no surprise that everyone inside was reading the paper and talking about the capture of Billups at Green Plains.

Breakfast at Patty's, a traditional morning gathering spot for the locals, had become David's regular routine since his arrival in Mathews. He felt comfortable in the place, which was an old drugstore that had been outfitted with a more modern kitchen, and now dispensed eggs, pancakes, bacon, hash browns and hot coffee at twenty-five cents a cup. You could eat at the old soda counter which still had the original chrome ringed spinning stools covered in 1950s orange vinyl or you could sit at any one of the tables or in the booths that lined the wall next to the store length windows that looked out on to Main Street.

Thanks to Brenda, David was practically on a first name basis with most of the customers at Patty's who seemed to accept him as a breakfast time regular and he felt very much at home on those mornings when he either grabbed a seat at the counter between a couple of burley watermen or was invited to share a table with the bank manager, doctor or owner of a local business establishment. He had even been asked to join both the Rotary Club and the Lions Club. This was life as he dreamed it could be when he and Karen decided to leave the brutal pace of David's former job and seek a better place to raise their kids, and to find more time for each other.

This morning, as David was offered a seat at a window booth with the owner of the local funeral parlor and the broker who ran a real estate office two doors down from David's law office, the conversation was predictably about the killing of Jimmy Jarvis and how sad it was that big city crime had come to Mathews. From the booths to the tables to the stools at the counter, the talk of the diner flowed without boundaries as most, if not all of the customers discussed the murder. There was also more than one comment about how blacks were senselessly killing each other in the cities and now had killed a good country boy like Jimmy for no reason at all.

From the tabletop conversation and from his own reading of the paper, David knew that Jimmy's body had been found at the beach at the end of Point Hollow Road and that he had been repeatedly stabbed. David also read that Jimmy had been an all-star athlete at Mathews High School and since he was just twenty-three, he was still probably in good physical condition when he was killed. As he sipped his coffee and shoveled in his eggs that were scrambled soft to perfection, he said to his tablemates, "You know, guys, this Jarvis kid appeared to be in really good shape. And, ...ah...since there is plenty of room usually to run on a beach, whoever killed him had to get pretty close to do it. Billups may not be the killer at all because he would have been the last person Jarvis would have welcomed that night out on that beach. In all actuality, Jarvis knew his killer well and trusted him enough to allow him to get close. Consequently, the killer was probably white."

Forbes knew he had said the wrong thing the moment the words left his lips. The funeral director's forkful of waffle dripping in maple syrup stopped in mid-flight as he stared at David in disbelief as the analytical commentary flowed from the lawyer seated across from him in the booth.

Others within hearing distance also ceased delving into the generous portions that kept them coming to Patty's morning after morning and glared at David whose unfamiliarity with local ways hung over his head like a bright, blinking neon sign. Even Chrystal the waitress, who was Patty's daughter, froze with her pot of coffee over at the next table and could not have looked at Forbes with more incredulity if he were an alien from Roswell.

Finally the real estate broker broke the silence. "Well, ah, Mr. Forbes, you're not suggesting that someone here in the, ah, community killed Jimmy, are you?"

David was struggling to come up with the words that would ease his way out of the hole he had dug for himself in the last sixty seconds when the silence was ended by the booming voice of Sheriff Junior Howard from two booths down towards the back of the diner.

"I'll answer that question," Howard said, "As it seems our new lawyer appears to be at a momentary loss for the tools of his profession!"

The Sheriff stood up and walked towards David who was still seated in the booth. No one spoke a word and not even the ceaseless diner bustle of utensils touching plates pierced the moment, the only audible intrusions being the air slicing whir of the ceiling fans and the grainy impact of the Sheriff's boots against the surface of the diner's well-waxed floor of black and white tile.

"Weren't no white man that killed Jimmy Jarvis, Mr. Washington lawyer," the Sheriff said, his voice heard by every ear in the diner. "Billups stabbed that young man three times in the chest and I've got that bastards knife with Jimmy's blood all over it to prove it. No, sir, no white man did this crime so you take your goddamn opinions and your family and get the hell out of here!"

The Sheriff raised his voice and placed his right hand on the grip of his pistol to make sure there was no doubt in David's mind, or in the mind of any other customer in Patty's that morning, as to who he was and what he could do.

"I'll make no secret of it!" the sheriff continued on to his morning audience. "You people visit here, then you move here and first thing you know, you think you're some kind of goddamn Christopher Columbus, discoverin' us for the first time or some shit like that. Well, we've known who we are for a long time and we don't need you or your kind telling us who we are or what we need to do. Now you got any questions you want to ask me, lawyer man?"

David stared back at the Sheriff, somewhat uncertain as to what to say or whether it would be best not to say anything at all. Forbes opted for simplicity and responded, "No, Sheriff, I don't have any questions. Thank you for being very clear and direct. I appreciate that."

The Sheriff laughed and sneered, "You don't appreciate shit. You think we're all just a bunch of country dumb-asses that don't have enough sense to come in out of the rain."

Howard turned to the young waitress, gave her a ten and told her to keep the change. With a toothpick lodged squarely in the corner of his mouth, he then returned his attention to David, and stared intently at the new attorney.

"It's a fool's errand to try to mess with who we are, Mr. Forbes. You remember that now, you hear?" Howard nodded to the undertaker and the real estate broker in the booth, politely said "y'all have a nice day" to all within earshot and left in his Yukon heading down Main Street in the direction of the Courthouse.

Silence remained in the diner even after the Sheriff's vehicle went up the road and it seemed to David like years passed before the first word was spoken or the first impact of fork on plate pierced the emptiness and brought the noise of the diner back up to its usual breakfast time volume. Forbes and his tablemates limited their remaining moments together by talking about the weather while he ate and drank faster than usual, sadly eager to get away from the coolness that had overtaken the diner and get back to the office.

David was admittedly shaken by the Sheriff's comments at the diner as he knew they reflected an unavoidable sentiment that found safe harbor in the minds of many that he met since moving to the county. For some, outsiders were an unwelcome species, the general sentiment among the 'from here's' was that people who moved to the county always seemed to want to change something about the place once they got here. They were always saying that Mathews needed this or needed that and how much better it would be if such and such were done a different way.

David knew he bore the 'come here' label but the simple truth was that he just wanted to be accepted in the community and didn't want to change a damn thing about any of it. All he wanted was for his wife and children to have a home here and to feel comfortable. But try as he might, he knew he was not one of them and that there would always be a dividing line, a difference that was indelible, one of birthright that no amount of earnestness could ever create or overcome.

David was walking back to his office with his thoughts in tow, when his cell phone buzzed. It was Brenda. "Where are you?" she said. "I just left Patty's. I'm one block away. What's up?" he said. Brenda replied, "You need to get back here, grab your jacket and briefcase and get up to the courthouse. Judge Mumford's office just called and they want you up there first thing this morning."

"What's the deal with the Judge?" David said.

"I'm not sure," Brenda replied, "But I spoke to Gail and she thinks that you're going to get appointed today to represent Billups on the felony charges of murdering Jimmy Jarvis. If that happens, oh brother, this office is going to get nuts, no doubt about it."

David hung up the phone as he was at the front door of his office and when he walked in, Brenda had his jacket and briefcase already waiting for him on the small couch in the front lobby. She took a cigarette out of her small paisley covered cigarette case, and grabbed the lighter that perpetually stood duty at the right corner of the desk calendar that bore the inked markings of dozens of phone numbers and shadings of corners that tattooed the days of the week for the month of May. She preceded David out of the office and lit up her cigarette the second she was on the sidewalk.

Forbes spoke first. "You know those things are really bad for your health," he said making reference to the cigarette in her hand.

Brenda replied, "No shit. You don't think I know that? Or maybe you really do think we're a bunch of country dumbasses who don't know enough to come in out of the rain." The secretary laughed as a look of shock and surprise passed over her boss's face. "You didn't think I'd hear about you and the Sheriff over at Patty's?"

David stammered, "That was just a few minutes ago, how the hell did you hear about that?"

Brenda took a drag on her cigarette, exhaled a cloud of gray, smiled the smile of someone with superior information and said, "cell phones, baby. This is a small community. News travels fast, real fast. Get used to it."

She then paused, looked him in the eye and asked, "You're going to take that case, aren't you?"

David responded, "If appointed, I'll have to take it. I'm not going to turn it down, if that's what you're asking."

"No, I'm not saying that," Brenda said. "It's just that some people around here aren't going to like the lawyer that represents Billups, that's all. You've done well to move here and get the business that we have now. I'm just worried that if you take this case, you will lose some clients, that's all. People can be pretty shitty sometimes."

David tried to speak reassuringly. "Look, we'll be fine. Besides, if Billups is as guilty as people say he is, then it should be a relatively simple case."

"What do you mean *if* he is guilty as people say he is?" Brenda exclaimed. "Billups *better* be guilty because if he didn't do it, I'm not sure some folks around here would be real happy about you trying to find out who really *did* do it."

71

By now, Forbes had his jacket on and was turning to walk up the sidewalk, briefcase in hand. "Brenda, relax. I'll take the case, do some investigation and represent Billups the best that I can. Now, how bad can it get?" David said with a disarming smile, while walking backwards away from Brenda.

She smiled in return, "I think you've been here too long already," she said.

"Why's that?" he yelled from up the sidewalk.

"Because you're already acting like a country dumbass!" she yelled back affectionately. David laughed at the right on target remark, waived and headed up Main Street to the Courthouse.

---

David's arrival at the courthouse that morning did not go unnoticed by the two men who occupied the corner office in the Sheriff's department that was adjacent to the building that housed two court rooms, a small detention facility and the Clerk's offices for both the Circuit and District courts.

One of the men, Sheriff Howard, stood at his office window and watched through the blinds as David walked, briefcase in hand, through the front doors of the courthouse. The Sheriff continued to stare out the window after David entered the building and spoke aloud to the other guest present that day.

"Judge Mumford is appointing that new lawyer to represent Billups," he said. "I tried to convince him and the Commonwealth's Attorney, Archibald Hudgins, to get one of the local jacklegs on the case but Arch said that he called all three of 'em and every one of 'em begged off, givin' some reason or the other why they couldn't do it. They just scared that's all. Can't say as I blame them, but I'm worried about this new guy. He isn't going to be like the others. Hell, they'd go see Billups one time and not open their file again until they show up in court to plead him guilty. No, this fellows going to be different, I'm afraid. He could end up being a problem."

The sheriff then turned from his office window and stared at the man seated across from his desk in one of the two leather covered chairs that were a gift from Mothers Against Drunk Driving as a sign of their appreciation for his long record of DUI convictions.

"Get your goddamn boots off my desk" he commanded and with one swipe, knocked the feet of his son, Coles Howard, off the corner of his walnut desk and then sat his massive frame down in the large chair behind the desk that was centered between two flag poles, the one on the left displaying the flag of the Commonwealth of Virginia and the one on his right displaying the flag of the United States.

Numerous plaques of professional achievement covered the wall behind him and well over a dozen pictures of him with numerous elected officials that adorned the remaining walls in his office announced to all who entered his office that the Sheriff was a man who knew his business, and more importantly, knew the right people to get things done.

"This Forbes fellow will be asking a lot of questions, you can count on it," he said after he got settled in his chair. "And he's going to be asking a lot of questions about you and Jimmy, you can count on that too. I want you to cooperate with him to a point. Be courteous but don't give him anything he doesn't ask for. Remember, we got Billups with a knife, both covered in Jimmy's blood and a motive for him to want to cut Jimmy up. That's all a Mathews jury will need to hear to send that niggers ass away forever. You understand? In other words, don't screw anything up. You've fucked things up enough already. But if we keep it simple, everything will turn out just fine. Think you can handle that?" the sheriff mockingly inquired of his waterman son.

"What about Cassie?" replied Coles Howard. "Sooner or later, Forbes is going to learn that she was dating Jimmy and that she was a witness to all the bullshit that went down at the Get n' Go. He'll talk to her for sure. What the hell is she going to say?"

The Sheriff smiled knowingly and replied, "Cassie's a good girl who knows she better keep her mouth shut. She knows you had a little chat with Jimmy at the beach that night and that's all she knows. However, I suspect that Cassie will have very little recollection of that chat. In fact, I'm right sure that she won't have any memory of it at all"

"What the hell did you do this time?" asked Coles of his father.

"I just reminded her about how ungrateful her daddy would be if she came to the rescue of that son of a bitch," the Sheriff said, moving his toothpick like a conductor waived his baton. "And that the next time she called 911 about her father beating her mother, we just might be a bit delayed in responding to the call. I also assured her that the Sheriff's department would be appreciative of her assistance and would make sure that an apartment for her and her momma would be coming their way, just as soon as the trial was over and Billups was convicted. I have no doubt that we can count on her cooperation."

"You are one piece of shit," replied Coles, grinning at his father.

"Me?" the Sheriff replied laughingly. "You're the one that gunned down those two dirt bags and made off with all that money and product. You and your brother and your perfect crime bullshit. You should have told me about it first."

"You would have nixed it and you know it," said Coles.

"Maybe, maybe not," said his father. "All I know is if it doesn't pan out, they won't be coming for me. They'll be coming for the both of you and we can't let that happen, now can we? If that lawyer man ties you to Jimmy's death, your brother's business associates will tie you to the missing cash. That would be bad news for you, Coles. Real bad news."

"It won't happen." Howard's son replied. "Donnie smoothed everything out. They think that shithead running the boat took their stuff and disappeared with his little Chiquita. Besides, we sent all the cash we owed 'em in the last seafood run to Baltimore. If we were thieves, why would we make sure they got their one point two million? To them, we're just some good old

74

boys trying to make a livin'. They still trust us. In fact, the next run is already in the planning stages. So relax, Pop."

"'I'll relax when that nigger's ass has been convicted and hauled off to prison." the sheriff said. "In the meantime, call your brother and make sure he knows what's going on down here and tell him to call his mother. He doesn't talk to her enough and she worries about him. You know how she can be, now get out of here. I've got other things to do besides clean up your mess."

Coles stood, left his father's office and headed to his pickup, a silver 2007 Dodge Ram crew cab with a Cummins diesel and four wheel drive. As he approached the vehicle, Coles dialed a number on his cell phone and a voice answered, "34th precinct, how can I help you?" to which Coles responded "Donnie Howard, please." The voice at the other end said "Hang on. I'm putting your call through." And thirty seconds later, Donald Howard, Senior Investigator - Narcotics Division - for the 34th precinct for the City of Baltimore answered the phone.

# Chapter Nine

## The Lawyer and the Client

Following his capture at Green Plains, Jamal Billups was hospitalized overnight and then released to Mathews County deputies the following morning who transported him to the county jail where he was booked and formally served with the warrants charging him with the murder of Jimmy Jarvis.

Upon his arrival at the jail, Billups declined to make any statement to the investigator assigned to the case. Noting that 'nothing' I'd say make any damn difference in how y'all think any way,' he exercised his right to counsel. Because of the numerous rumors floating around the jail that the white inmates had placed bets as to how long Billups would last in general population, the alleged killer of Jimmy Jarvis was placed in solitary confinement and that's where he was when David Forbes arrived at the jail to interview his new client.

When David entered into the public reception area at the jail, he presented his photo I.D. and his Virginia State Bar card to the officer at the front desk, went through the metal detector and then walked down a long hallway of light gray cinderblock walls and a perfectly shined floor of dark blue tile. He stopped at a solid steel door at the end of the hallway and was reading a sign that said something about no firearms beyond this point when a buzzer sounded and the door opened to a central foyer monitored by a main control room identifiable by the large panes of darkened glass that dominated the wall on the right side of the room.

A female African-American correctional officer was standing by a doorway to his left as he entered. "Are you Billups' attorney?" she asked.

"I am," Forbes replied.

"He's in the first room on the left once we go down this hallway," she responded. "Once you go into the room with Mr. Billups, I'm going to lock the door behind you. When you finish your business with Mr. Billups, just tap on the door. I'll be right across the hallway and I'll hear you. Any questions?" she asked, smiling.

"Nope," David said. "Thanks for the briefing. I may be here awhile. I hope you don't get too bored waiting for me to come out."

"Oh, boredom suits us just fine around here, Mr. Forbes." she said with a smile. "Boredom means that the inmates are playing nice and we like that a lot. You just take your time."

David nodded his thanks again and walked into the room where seated in a small green one-piece plastic chair and dressed in orange jail house pajamas, sat Jamal Billups.

Neither man spoke until the officer closed and locked the door.

Jamal said, "You my lawyer?"

David responded, "I am. My name is David Forbes. Here's my card. The court appointed me to represent you on the murder charge against you involving Jimmy Jarvis. We have a preliminary hearing coming up soon and we need to get prepared. You're in a lot of trouble and I want to go over with you what your legal rights are and what procedures will be followed in your case."

"Man, you can just skip all that bullshit," Jamal said, cutting David off before he could say another word. "I've been arrested before. I know what my rights are and all that shit. I just know I didn't kill that Jarvis boy. These charges are bullshit, man, total bullshit."

Jamal reached over for the crutches that were leaning in the corner next to the small desk that separated him and David, placed a crutch under each armpit and started walking around in the small interview room that held the two men.

"Fucking leg hurts bad, man," Billups said. "They won't give me nothing for the pain except some fucking Tylenol. I got shot with a goddamn arrow. Can you believe that shit, a fuckin' arrow! Like I was some goddamn

77

deer! You got any pull around here, man? I could use something to get rid of this pain, and who the fuck are you anyway? I been livin' in Mathews all my life and never heard of no David Forbes."

"I'm somewhat new in town." David said. "Moved here about six months ago. My office is down the street from the drugstore. I used to practice up in D.C., mostly drug prosecutions and that sort of thing."

"What were you," Jamal asked, "The fuckin' FBI or some shit like that?"

"Something like that," David replied. "Actually, I was an Assistant U.S. Attorney. We prosecuted a lot of cases that the FBI investigated."

Jamal kept pacing around the room on his crutches while he looked suspiciously at his lawyer. "A prosecutor! Ain't you supposed to be on the other side of shit like this? I don't want any prosecutor to be my attorney. By the way, how many brothers did you send away when you were doing this U.S. Attorney shit? I'll bet it was a lot."

"It was." David answered. "I prosecuted lots of brothers because lots of brothers in D.C. were selling lots of drugs and killing lots of brothers and sisters in the process. It's how it was up there. Now I'm down here, on the other side, representing you."

Jamal started to respond but it was Forbes' turn to cut him off. Growing impatient with his new client, David decided to be blunt and got right to the point.

"Mr. Billups, let me be upfront with you," his lawyer said. "I've already looked at some of the reports from the Sheriff's office and you're in a world of trouble. You get into a fight with Jimmy Jarvis at a convenience store. You pull a knife and threaten to cut him in front of numerous witnesses. The next morning, his body is found at the beach with multiple stab wounds. When you are arrested later that day, your clothes are covered in his blood and a knife is found in your pocket that is also covered in his blood. That, my friend, is one fucked up set of facts. Now, we can spend our time listening to you ramble on about who you do or don't want as your attorney. Or, we can spend our time trying to get your ass out of this mess. It's your call, pal. Frankly, it doesn't matter to me one way or the other but it should matter a hell of a lot to you. Now what's it going to be? If I were in your shoes, to use your words, I would suggest, that we "skip all *your* bullshit" and start working on your case. What do you say?"

Jamal stopped pacing and stared at the floor. When he looked up at David, his eyes were tearing up and his mood had grown somber. "Man, I didn't kill him. I swear to God, I did not kill that boy."

David challenged his new client. "Oh yeah, well there's a bunch of evidence that says otherwise. Jarvis' blood was all over your clothes. A knife in your possession was covered in his blood. Hell, you even threatened to kill him in front of three witnesses!"

"Shit, those white crackers would lie at the drop of a hat," Jamal said.

David countered quickly. "Maybe they would but you don't even deny that part of the story. Who's to say you didn't drink more after you left the store, that you got more and more pissed off at Jarvis and then hunted him down and stabbed him to death out on that beach. Doesn't seem like too much of stretch for a Mathews' jury to reach that conclusion, now does it?"

The lawyer's sharp attack on Jamal had him pressed back into a corner of the interview room, leaning on his crutches and staring intensely at his attorney.

"Man, whose side are you on?" Jamal asked incredulously.

"Yours, dumbass," David replied. "But we got some bad facts here that we need to overcome. Now let me guess, after the fight, you drank more, got completely fucked up, then passed out and don't remember shit until you woke up in a hay barn at Green Plains Farm."

"That's about it," Jamal said.

"And I'll bet there were no witnesses to corroborate your story that you didn't go anywhere near that beach after your fight with Jarvis at the store. True?" David asked.

"Yeah, after I got out of the woods I went to my cuz's house," Jamal replied. "No one was home but I found me some beer in his fridge. I drank what beer he had and walked until I got to Green Plains. That's all I remember."

"Didn't see anybody?" David asked

"Not a soul," Jamal said.

"Why didn't you just stay at your cuz's house?" his lawyer inquired.

"Cause he and I don't sometimes get along" Jamal explained.

"Like when you steal his beer?" quizzed David.

Jamal grinned and replied, "No, like when I'm tappin' his woman. He got pissed last week when he learned I was messing with Shantee."

"Shantee?" asked David

"Yeah, his girlfriend Shantee Jarvis," responded Jamal

"Any relation to Jimmy Jarvis? David inquired.

"No, she black. Jimmy Jarvis is white. I thought you knew that," Jamal said.

"I did. Just checking. What's your cousin's name?" David asked

"Lester Billups," Jamal said.

"And where does Lester Billups live?" David asked.

"Up on Route 14, about two miles from the store."

David probed further. "If Lester was pissed at you for messing with Shantee, why did you go there instead of just going home? You lived with your grandmother didn't you?" he asked.

"Yeah," Jamal said.

"So, why didn't you just go home?" Forbes asked.

Jamal looked at his feet and responded, "I knew there was no liquor there. My granny don't let no alcohol in the house."

David challenged Jamal again. "Okay, I get that. But, why didn't you at least go there first to get some clean clothes, take a shower, something? You were covered in blood, man."

Jamal continued to stare down at the floor. He responded, "I was too fucked up and didn't care. I just wanted to get somethin' to drink. That's why I went to my cuz's house. I don't like going home all fucked up no how. My granny don't like it."

"How much did you drink at your cuz' house?" David asked.

Jamal replied, "I didn't drink nothin' at his house. I took it and left."

"What did you take?" David asked.

"Two quarts of Miller beer," Jamal replied.

"Drink it all?" David asked.

"Every drop," Jamal responded.

"How long did it take you to get to Green Plains?" David asked.

"I don't know. A couple of hours maybe. I can't really remember," Jamal said.

"And you never went near the beach?" David probed.

"Never," Jamal said.

David continued. "Why did you go to Green Plains that night?" he asked.

Jamal started shuffling around on his crutches."Just wanted to, I guess," he said.

"When's the last time you been there?" David asked.

"Oh, man, it's been years," Jamal said.

"So, why go there that night? Why not go somewhere closer to home?" David pressed.

Jamal stared at the small light fixture in the ceiling and replied, "I don't know, man. It's nice out there. I used to go there a lot as a kid. I guess I just wanted get away from shit."

"What kind of shit?" David countered. "To a lot of folks, it's going to look like you're hiding out, trying not to get found."

Jamal shrugged his shoulders. "It's what I did, man. I don't know what else to tell you."

David leaned back in his chair and clasped his fingers behind his head. "Let's see. No witnesses as to your whereabouts after the fight. You're covered in the victim's blood with a possible murder weapon in your possession and then you go to a place where you haven't been to for years. You're not helping me much, Jamal."

Jamal again leaned back into a corner on his crutches but this time stared David in the eye and said" I didn't kill him, that's all I can say. And if I did kill him, then I must be goddamn Superman."

"Why do you say that?" David asked.

Jamal replied, "Get me a map of the county and I'll show you why."

David tapped on the small glass window of the interview room door and the officer appeared as promised. Within minutes, a county map was procured and Forbes spread the map out on the desk while Jamal placed his crutches against the wall, took a seat at the desk and asked his lawyer for a pen.

Jamal spoke first. "Look. Here's where the fight with Jimmy took place. For you dumbass 'come here's' this place is called Wards Corner."

David smiled at the remark and watched while Jamal took his pen and marked the area with a blue "X." Jamal continued with his presentation.

"Now, pay attention Mr. Prosecutor, here's the beach where Jimmy's body was found." Again, Billups took the pen and marked the area with same mark that showed the location of the store.

"All the way over here is Green Plains Farm," he then said, "and this here is where my cuz lives." Jamal marked both locations with the blue pen.

Jamal put the pen down on the desk and looked at David. "That beach is a good five miles from the store. Green Plains is six miles in the other direction. If all this bullshit they be saying about me is true then that means I walked five miles to a beach, killed some dude and then walked eleven miles in the other direction. All the while being all fucked up? Besides, how the hell I'm I supposed to know he's at some beach anyway? I don't have no cell phone and don't have no car. See what I mean, man? This don't make no sense."

Billups continued on. "Look, lawyer man. You're a good guy. I can see that. But you got to understand. I didn't kill Jimmy Jarvis. I've known that boy since he was a kid. I'm older than him but I seen him around, watched him play football, you know what I'm saying? I ain't got nothing against him and I ain't gonna kill no one over a damn fist fight. We just messin' around that night, that's all. Hell, if those cracker fools not shown up with their big ass trucks, lookin' for some nigger's ass to kick, I probably wouldn't be in all this fuss. I'm not saying that Jimmy wouldn't be dead, I'm just saying they wouldn't have a reason to be blaming it on me. Besides, I had no cause to do something like that no how. I read the newspaper. Stab a boy to death like that? No way, man. That's some evil shit. I ain't like that. You can ask anyone who knows me. Ain't no other black man did it either. That kind of killin'? That's white man's bullshit or maybe it was one of them Mexicans that do all that landscaping shit. You wait and see. Besides, that Jarvis boy's ass was stabbed at the beach and we country niggers don't hang out at no beach. No coloreds allowed and all that shit. We don't ever go near the fuckin' beach, man. Never."

83

David sat in his chair with the map in front of him and, for the first time, began to get a different take on Jamal Billups.

Jamal leaned forward and looked at David. "Man, look, you're new around here but you got to understand somethin'. This is Mathews County. I didn't do any of this shit but I'm smart enough to know my black ass is all but convicted. I just hope you're one good motherfuckin' lawyer, cause it's gonna take all you got to get me out of this."

"All I've got is what you're going to get," David replied. "Now I've got to get back to my office." Forbes then stood and grabbed his file from the desk along with the county map.

As his lawyer prepared to leave, Billups struggled to his feet, grabbed his crutches, and pleaded with David. "Help me, man. I don't want to go to prison for the rest of my life for something I didn't do."

Forbes placed his hand on Jamal's shoulder, smiled and said, "If you didn't do it, the only place you're going is back to your granny's."

David then tapped on the glass to get the officers attention but before she arrived, he turned back around to Jamal and said "Let me ask you a question. Why would someone want to kill Jarvis? By all accounts, he was a well-liked, clean cut young guy. High school star athlete, engaged, kind of kid you'd want living next door."

"In other words, someone not like me?" quipped Jamal, smirking after the remark.

"My thoughts exactly," responded David who couldn't help but smile at the friendly joust with Jamal.

Both men laughed as the comment helped to take the edge off the moment.

Jamal, still smiling, shook his head and said. "I can't answer that but let me ask you a question. Why *do* most white people kill each other?"

David paused for a moment, frankly surprised by the astuteness of the question and then responded, "For passion or for money, I would think."

"My thoughts exactly," Jamal said parroting David's earlier remark. Forbes liked Jamal more by the minute. The guy had an intelligence and a wit that was sharper than his initial appearance would indicate.

Jamal continued. "No way a big guy like Jimmy Jarvis was stabbed to death by an ex-girlfriend, a jealous boyfriend or some stupid shit like that. So I think we can get rid of the passion thing. That leaves us with the money thing. Root of all evil, so says my Granny. What do you say Mr. Prosecutor man?"

"I'd say your Granny is one smart woman," replied Forbes as the officer opened up the door and escorted him back up the hallway to the lobby where David gathered his keys and his ID at the front desk and left the jail.

# Chapter Ten

## Lunch with Karen

When Forbes had first arrived at the jail, he had parked away from the other cars in the far end of the jail parking lot, an old habit he had developed years ago when he bought the first true love of his life, a 1986 Porsche 911 SC.

The last remnant of his bachelor days, David had hung on to the car despite Karen's proddings that he needed something a little more kid friendly. He just couldn't bring himself to say goodbye. Plus, she still looked great and handled like she was brand new. David tossed his files in the passenger seat, pulled out of the lot and headed back to his office, putting the Porsche through her paces along the single lane roads that crisscrossed the county, enjoying the freedom to really drive the car as opposed to the endless crawl of bumper to bumper traffic on I-495 which was a daily affair up in D.C.

As Forbes downshifted into a curve and then accelerated into the straightaway of a narrow single lane road of curving charcoal gray asphalt bordered by fields of soy and corn, his thoughts returned to the small interview room where he had just met with Jamal.

The evidence pointed to guilt, didn't it? Victim's blood, a weapon, threats to wound, witnesses and a dead body found shortly thereafter. At Justice, David had gotten convictions on far less evidence than this. But something was sticking in the lawyer's craw.

Maybe it was the geography. After all, Jamal's point about the distance made some sense. Or maybe it was just Jamal himself. David had prosecuted numerous homicide cases but somehow Billups just didn't seem to fit the profile of someone who would commit the degree of violence that led to the death of Jimmy Jarvis. Jimmy died a horrible death, obviously killed by someone either in an uncontrollable rage or by someone used to killing, someone comfortable with it. But the Jamal he just met didn't fit into either category. Hell, he didn't even come across as someone who could kill or would kill. Fight at the drop of a hat? Sure, but commit murder, and particularly, a homicide as vicious as the one that killed Jimmy Jarvis? As Forbes saw it, the chips just didn't fall in that direction.

But, if not Jamal Billups, then who did it and why?

In the minds of most folks in the county, David's client was all but convicted and Forbes knew that evidence to the contrary would be hard to come by because there was no doubt that both the Sheriff's department and the community in general would be resistant, to say the least, against any investigation based upon any theory that lead to a conclusion that Jimmy Jarvis was killed by someone other than Jamal Billups.

Forbes knew that Jarvis was engaged to marry that Cassie girl who managed the Get n' Go where the fight took place. Maybe her parents or an ex-boyfriend had a beef against Jarvis and wanted him dead. But why a knife and why at a beach? Murders like that were almost always by gunshot and at the home of the victim or the assailant. The 'passion thing', as Jamal phrased it, didn't make much sense.

That left the 'money thing', but Jimmy was just a mate on a fishing boat. How much of a 'money thing' could he get caught up in while working on a fishing boat that would be enough to get him killed in a small town like Mathews? Perhaps when he had the opportunity to interview Cassie Thompkins and the fishing boat captain that Jimmy worked for, maybe things would begin to clear up a bit.

When David hit a long stretch of straight road that served as the dividing line between large stands of loblolly pine, he grabbed his cell phone from the console of his car and called Brenda.

Knowing from caller I.D. that David was on the phone, she answered, "So, is he guilty?"

David replied "Maybe, maybe not."

"Oh, god," she replied, "the 'maybe not' part scares the hell out of me."

"Relax," he said. "A lot of work needs to be done. We'll see how it all comes together. In the meantime, I've got a question for you. Who did Jimmy Jarvis work for? I think I read something about it in the paper but I can't remember."

Brenda replied, "He was a mate on Captain Coles Howard's fishing boat. Been working there for a couple of years. Great job for a young guy. Coles is one of the best commercial fishermen around. Makes good money and probably paid Jimmy well. And I'll bet Jimmy did a great job for him. It's so sad."

"Yes, it is. Do you know this Coles Howard?" replied David.

"Of course, I do!" Brenda said, not hiding for one minute her feigned affront that David would think that there was actually someone in the county who she didn't know. "He's a second cousin on my mother's side. Want to meet him?"

"Sure. Any date and time that's clear on the calendar is fine with me," David said.

"I'll set something up," Brenda said. "Probably best to see him down at the docks. He keeps his boat at Harper's. I'll call him this afternoon and get it on the books. I'm sure he'll be happy to talk to you about Jimmy."

"I'll also need to interview the Cassie girl who works at the Get n' Go. I'll bet you know her, too." David said.

Brenda replied, "You know I do but good luck getting in touch with her. I heard she quit her job at the store and isn't answering her cell phone. I guess losing Jimmy the way she did was just too much for her to take. I do know that she lives with her parents. Let me call out there and see what I can set up."

"Thanks," Forbes replied. "You know, you really do a great job."

"I know," Brenda replied, laughing. "Are you coming back to the office?" she asked.

"Ultimately, but first I think I'll stop and grab some lunch with Karen at the school," he said. "Would you please call her and give her a heads up that I'm on my way? I should roll in just about when her class goes to lunch."

"With that crazy car you drive, it shouldn't be a problem." Brenda answered. "I'll call her right now."

David signed off with a 'thanks', tossed the phone into the passenger seat and, six miles later, pulled into the parking lot of the school with minutes to spare. Karen was waiting for him when he arrived and together they walked down the hallway towards the cafeteria, weaving their way around the multitudes of lunch bound elementary students going in the same direction.

Greetings of "Hi, Mrs. Forbes" occurred every few feet and were accompanied by the upward stares from dozens of young eyes at the tall man in the suit walking beside their teacher.

"Is it always this busy?" David asked his wife, "and this noisy?"

"No," she replied. "Sometimes it's even busier and noisier but its lunchtime and the kids are excited. Give it an hour and it all quiets down until the buses come to pick them up at the end of the day."

David showed his admiration, "I don't see how you do it. All these kids. All day long. And you say I'm nuts to do what I do. I'd go crazy if I was here every day, all day"

Karen replied, "Oh you say that now but think about it. Don't you feel special when you teach Luke or Katie how to do something new, like how to throw the football, or fix something or figure out some math problem? It feels good, doesn't it? Now, take that feeling and multiply it twenty-fold. Look around you. There are lots of little opportunities to feel that special, to use your words, every day, all day."

Karen smiled and looked up at her husband who bent down and gave her a peck on the cheek, "You're something special, you know that?"

David's wife blushed  because her husband's spontaneous display of affection had its own set of witnesses in the form of about twenty second graders lined up to go into the cafeteria who all said in unison, "Ohh, Mrs. Forbes...He kissed you!"

Karen said with feigned admonishment, "David, don't do that here!"

David smiled at the kids in the line who were staring and giggling at the kissing couple. Several of the kids inquired, "Who's that Mrs. Forbes, who's that?

"This is my husband, David," Karen said. "He's Luke and Katie's Daddy."

"Ohh," they said in unison. "Are you a teacher, too?" one of them said.

"No, I'm a lawyer," he responded to which the chorus of young voices again went "Ohhh."

Temporarily sidelined from her role as third grade teacher, Karen quickly went back into character, told them that they had all been very polite but now it was time to be quiet and wait for the cafeteria attendant to escort them into the lunchroom, and she wanted all of them to show Mr. Forbes just how polite they could all be.

Upon that instruction, they all stood still while one little girl silently waived 'bye-bye' as David and Karen walked over to the food counter, helped themselves to the salad bar, grabbed a couple of bottles of water and headed back to Karen's empty classroom for a few minutes of quiet time.

"So, did you see him?" She asked.

"Go see who? Billups?" David said between forkfuls of salad greens dripping in Caesar dressing.

"No, the Easter bunny," she replied. "Of course I mean Billups. Who else would I be talking about? It's all everyone is talking about around here. And they all know that you're representing him. It's kind of weird. Everyone's talking about it, but no one's talking to me about it. Know what I mean? I feel like I'm out of the loop, kind of distant from things. I'm not sure I like it. I

90

was starting to feel like I was a part of things around here, a new school year, a new batch of kids and now there's whispered conversations in the hallway that stop whenever I get near. I wish you hadn't taken that case, is what I guess I'm trying to say. That's horrible isn't it? I shouldn't feel that way but I do. But I know its not fair to you. You're doing what you love to do. But sometimes I just wish the job came second and we came first, that's all."

Karen finished speaking and just sat there looking at David. She hadn't even touched her lunch.

"But baby, what the hell do you expect me to do? I can't turn down a court appointment. Plus, this is a big case. Puts me in the spotlight and right on the map. You can't buy that kind of advertising. C'mon girl," David said with a smile, "The whispers will eventually stop, and the case will become old news soon enough. Plus, ask me what I did yesterday."

"Okay. What did you do yesterday?" Karen said, asking the question begged.

"I signed up to coach Katie's soccer team," David proudly announced.

"Soccer," his wife said. "What do you know about soccer?"

"Not a damn thing but I didn't know anything about making little babies either until I met you," he said playfully. "Nothing like a little on the job training." David grinned at his own remark and continued to plow through his lunch.

Karen grinned back, "You're bad."

"Just reacting to your more than ample inspirations, baby," he replied, with a mock exaggerated stare at her breasts as he shoveled in another forkful of salad

"Now you're getting really bad!" his wife said as she reached over and touched his hand.

"Is he guilty?" she asked.

"Why are we talking about the case again?" David asked. "I thought you wanted me to put the job second and family first?"

"I do but I just had to ask," she replied. "Some things have happened up at the high school. Two boys got into a fight. One was black the other white. White kid was wearing a shirt with a confederate flag. There's also been a bunch of pushing and shoving, some threats over cell phones and stuff like that. There's talk of cancelling the football game. I'm just really concerned that some of this could roll over on Luke and Katie. I just don't know what I would do if either of them got hurt because of something like this."

"You mean because I'm Billups' attorney?" he said.

"Of course that's what I mean," Karen answered. "David, please forgive me. I'm a mom. Don't get mad because I worry. I love you guys so much. If anything were to happen to any of you, I couldn't live with myself."

Forbes tried to be reassuring. "Baby, these things never get personal. Remember the Gonzalez trial about that drug kingpin that executed Epstein's partner in that sting off the coast of Belize? Those Columbian assholes swore they would kill everyone associated with his arrest and prosecution, but nothing ever happened. If ever there was a case that was going to get personal, that was it. But it never did, and neither will this one. We'll be OK. You'll see, trust me."

"David," his wife replied. "I do trust you. But this is a small town. Hell, it seems like everybody is everybody else's son, daughter cousin, aunt, uncle something or the other. I'll be glad when it's over."

"Me too," David said, "and it will be soon."

The bell rang signaling the end of the lunch period. Karen spoke, "Oh well, quiet time is over, brace yourself for the invasion," and then they came, kid by kid, little pairs of feet marched into the classroom and obediently took their places at their assigned desks, with most of them staring at David and again waving 'bye-bye' as he whispered "See ya, kids!" as he, in turn, waved to Karen and left the room carrying both empty salad trays back towards the cafeteria.

"What a difference a lunch bell makes," Forbes thought to himself as walked down a  hall that was now quiet and empty, except for a few kids making a last minute mad dash from the bathroom to the classroom. David made a right hand turn into the cafeteria and walked towards two large grey trash receptacles that were located at the far corner of the cafeteria, next to a large counter area where tray after tray of half eaten lunch offerings were scraped and placed on a conveyor belt that fed into a large commercial dishwasher at the rear of the cafeteria kitchen.

As David approached the counter he was greeted by a pleasant faced African-American male, about fifty-five years of age wearing large black horn rimmed glasses and a goatee with his silver and black whiskers braided in two long strands that extended about two inches below his chin.

"You must be Mr. David Forbes?" the man said.

"I am, and you are?" David asked.

"I'm Terry Covington. I'm the Senior Custodian around here. I saw you walk in earlier with Ms. Forbes plus I seen your picture in the paper when you was appointed to represent Jamal. So I kinda knew who you was. It's nice to meet you. Let me take those from you," the custodian said, reaching out for the trays that were in David's hands.

"It's nice to meet you, too, Terry," David said handing both of the trays to the custodian.

"Ms. Forbes is a real nice lady," Terry commented, "and the kids like her a lot. If they didn't, I'd know. I hope she likes it here."

"She does, Terry," Forbes replied, "We both do and so do our children and I really appreciate you asking. That means a lot."

"We'll, I thank you and don't you worry about her or your kids," Terry said. "There ain't nothing that goes on around her that ol' Terry don't know about first. So don't you worry 'bout nothin' at all."

"Terry, I thank you again, but what would I have to worry about? I'm afraid I'm a little lost in all of this," David said, not quite sure what to make of this Covington fellow or what he was saying about the well-being of his kids.

"Just ask your wife. She knows," The man said, dumping the salad containers into the large trash bins and then placing the trays on the conveyor.

"She knows what?"

The custodian looked David in the eye. "About how people around town are talking about the killing of the Jarvis boy, and about the fact that it's her husband who's defending the nigger that done it."

Forbes must have stared wide-eyed at that last remark because Terry laughed deeply, and said "Don't be so shocked, Mr. Forbes, by what I say. If I didn't think you was a good man. I wouldn't be talking to you like this right now. But you is a good man. I know how things go around here and how people talk. Been livin' here all my life. Let your wife know that ol' Terry won't let her kids out of my sight long as they in my school. She has my word on it."

David just stared at the custodian like he was something out of a movie. How does he know all this stuff?

Terry laughed again and David thought, 'Am I that obvious?' Then the custodian reached for a towel hanging off one of the trash bins, wiped off his hands and reached into his shirt pocket, pulled out a business card and handed it to David. It read:

*The Rev. Terrance N. Covington*

*First African Assembly of God,*

*Rt 660, Cardinal Virginia.*

The custodian straightened his shoulders, deepened his voice a bit and said, "Mr. Forbes, I'd be most honored if you'd please bring your family to our church next Sunday, as my personal guests. Now, I know what you're thinking and you're right, you probably will be the only white folks there," Terry laughed again and said, "but that's a good thing. We are a loving people and you and your family will feel right at home. Plus, it's our annual Deacon's Day Celebration as well. Your kids like fried chicken and homemade ice cream?"

"They sure do," David replied. "You know that's right!"

"Then they'll really feel right at home!" Terry said with a broad smile. He held out his right hand and David accepted his handshake which was warm and firm. Terry then placed his left hand on the attorneys shoulder and locked his eyes onto David's.

"You be sure to come now," he said "it's important that you understand who we are and to know that Jamal did not kill that boy."

"I take it that he's related to you somehow," David replied.

"He's my nephew, Mr. Forbes and I've known him since he was a baby. He's had his share of run-ins with the law, but he's no killer, Mr. Forbes. No sir. Whoever killed that Jarvis boy still walks among us. Like Mephistopheles, sir, he walks among us and we need you, Mr. Forbes to do God's work. We need you to find the devil who heinously slayed that child and bring him to justice. Will you do that for us, Mr. Forbes?"

David was mesmerized by the cadence of the minister's delivery. He's heard a thousand closing summations by the best trial lawyers in the business but had never heard one who could hold a candle to this custodian. Forbes finally mustered some words and said "I'll do all that I can. We'll be there next Sunday."

"I know you will," the custodian responded. "By the way, Mr. Forbes, are you a man of faith?"

"I guess so, Terry" David replied, "but, I'll confess that sometimes it's hard to come up with an answer to that question that answers all the other questions that seem to crop up along that same subject line, if you know what I mean."

"I do know what you mean, Mr. Forbes," Covington replied. "Your question was asked like a man who genuinely recognizes the benefits of judgment truly deliberated. It's an art becoming lost more by the day, I'm afraid. In any event, we will have to talk more at a later time. I'd be interested in what you have to say. Yes, sir, I'd be very interested indeed. Perhaps the answers that elude us today will become ever more clear to both of us as time moves on. Mr. Forbes, you have a good afternoon."

# Chapter Eleven

## Captain Coles Howard

"How's lunch?" was the first thing Brenda asked when David came through the front door of the office. 'Interesting' was all he could say in reply as he walked down the hall and tossed his files on his desk and reached for the bottle of water that was on the window sill from earlier that morning.

"Have you ever heard of a Terry Covington?" David shouted to Brenda from his office down the hall.

Brenda got up from her desk and started walking in his direction, "Are you talking about Terry Covington the custodian up at the school or are you talking about," Brenda paused for a moment to deepen her voice and spoke in a lower tone, "the Reverend Terrance Covington who pastors the black church in Cardinal?"

David laughed at Brenda's good natured impersonation of the man he met for the first time just moments ago. "Both, I think. I met him today in the cafeteria. He's an interesting guy."

"Terry's all right," she replied. "He and I went to high school together. He means well and he's really into his religion. In a good way, I mean. He pastors a nice church and they have a great choir. You should go over there sometime."

"Funny you should mention that," David replied. "He invited Karen and I and the kids over to their annual Deacon's Day Celebration next Sunday. I think we'll go."

"Did he tell you that he's Jamal's uncle?" she asked.

"In fact, he did," David answered, "And he is adamant that his nephew did not kill Jarvis."

"We'll, at this point, you can't really expect him to think otherwise," Brenda noted and then asked, "I guess you heard about the stuff going on up at the high school."

"You mean the fist fight between the black kid and the white kid?" Forbes asked. "Karen told me about it over lunch. Something about a confederate flag on a t-shirt. Sounds like stupid kid stuff to me. It'll all die down. Give it a little time and people will forget and move on."

"I hope you're right but I don't know about the forgetting part," Brenda said as she walked back up the hallway to her desk and reached for her cigarettes and her lighter. "My granddaughter is a junior up there and she says things are really tense especially because Jimmy's funeral is this Sunday and the memorial service is to be held at the school auditorium. She told me that there's lots of stuff going around on cell phones like photos of Jimmy with a confederate flag in the background and text messages being forwarded from phone to phone saying that no blacks better come to the funeral or they'll get their asses kicked. Stuff like that. It's bad."

"And, by the way," she added as David followed her back up the hall to the law office lobby, water bottle in hand, "Don't get too settled in at your desk. You won't be there long."

"Yeah, why's that?" David replied as he shuffled through the pile of mail on the corner of Brenda's desk.

"I called Coles Howard like you asked and he called me back when he pulled into the dock. He wants to see you today at 3:00 pm down at Harper's Creek Marina. The time was clear on your calendar so I said okay. Was that okay?" she asked.

"Sure," David replied. "I've never been to Harper's Creek Marina, but I'm betting this Coles Howard fellow won't be hard to find."

"Oh, you're right there," she noted. "He's a big guy with a big boat and a big ego. He's easy to spot, no doubt about that. But then again so are you."

"Why do you say that?" David asked after he pulled his *Car and Driver* magazine from the stack of law firm letters and legal periodicals that were the daily fare from the postmaster.

"We'll, given that guys in shirts and ties driving Porsches don't pull into Harper's every day, I'm pretty sure the two of you will find each other real quick. Maybe he'll even take you for a boat ride," she said smiling while she took a long drag off her cigarette, standing on the sidewalk just outside the front door of the office.

David shook his head and smiled back. "I swear," he said, "a jailhouse visit with Jamal Billups, lunch with my wife in a school full of kids, a bizarre conversation with a black minister who's also a cafeteria custodian, fist fights over confederate flags and now a meeting with a boat captain down at a marina. What a day. How much crazier can it get?"

"All I can say is welcome to Mathews," Brenda replied as she crushed out her cigarette and came back to her desk to answer a ringing phone.

---

When David pulled into the parking lot at Harper's Marina, his first thought was that this was one of the prettiest places he had ever seen in his life.

The sky that afternoon was azure blue, the water of the creek a deep green and the oyster shell parking lot a mixture of chalk and pale gray. The crab pot markers attached to the dozens of pots stacked up on the dock were painted in stripes of orange and yellow and the cedar siding of the old store displayed weathered hues of gold and red. White was the color of choice for the deadrise fishing boats that were tied up along the dock and also for the boots the men wore who were loading waxed cardboard boxes of freshly caught fish into the back of a refrigerated seafood truck.

The scene was completed by the row of seagulls perched along the top edge of the sign that said 'Harper's Creek General Store'. For any book about the Chesapeake Bay, this was the picture for the front cover, no doubt about it.

David got out of his Porsche and walked towards the seafood truck and read the signs on the side of the cab doors which said 'Howard's Seafood, Mathews, Va.'

"Can I help you?" asked one of the men as he stacked a box of fish onto the back of the truck.

"I'm looking for a man named Coles Howard." David responded. "Is he around here anywhere?"

"Coles? Nah. We ain't seen him all day," the man responded quickly in the thick, clipped brogue of the Chesapeake Bay waterman. "He went out early this morning before the sun was up to go mermaid fishing over on the Eastern Shore. I'm guessin' the mermaid fishin' must be pretty good 'cause he ain't come back yet. And who might you be so I can tell 'em who's been asking about 'em when he gets in?"

David struggled to understand what the man was saying in the unfamiliar accent. To him, it was like listening to a foreign language. Ultimately, he said, "I'm David Forbes. I'm an attorney in town. My secretary, Brenda, told me we had an appointment at three o'clock. Maybe I misunderstood something. Here's my card. Would you please give it to him when he gets back from . . . uh, where did you say he was again?"

"Mermaid fishin' on the Eastern Shore," said the man.

"Well, okay, when he gets back, ask him to give me a call and . . . ." David stopped in mid-sentence and realized he had taken the bait hook, line and sinker.

Forbes didn't think he had ever turned a deeper shade of red in his life than the color he was blushing right now. He was a 'come here' for sure. As an added reminder of his unfamiliarity with local ways and his total inability to understand the comments of the man loading the fish, he could hear his two helpers laughing hysterically on the other side of the vehicle.

The man who first spoke to Forbes took off his gloves, held out his right hand and said, "I'm Coles Howard. Hope you don't mind us fuckin' with ya a little bit. It's just our way of being friendly. You can tell a lot about a man by the way he can take a little ribbin', don't ya think, Mr. Forbes?" Coles laughed and gave David a strong, hard handshake.

Howard kept on talking. "It's nice to meet ya, Mr. Forbes. Ya know, your secretary, Brenda, is my cousin and she's been workin' for lawyers for many a year and I have great respect for what y'all do so I want ya to know that there's no hard feelings that you represent the no-good bastard who killed Jimmy, no hard feelings at all. Now, how can I help you?"

David heard Coles' hint loud and clear that he was only so welcome here at the dock and the lawyer knew he had limited time to get what information he was going to get, if any.

"Brenda told me that Jimmy worked for you," David said.

"That's right. He did work for me for almost three years. He was the first mate on my boat and did a damn good job, which is a far sight more than you can say about that worthless son of a bitch you got as a client. I know him, too. He ain't worth shit and never has done a goddamn thing worth doing in his whole life." Coles said as his huge arms tossed another fifty pound box of fish into the back of the truck like it was instead stuffed full of feathers.

As he reached for the next box of fish on the dock, Coles paused in his labors and spoke again. "Let me ask you something, Mr. Forbes, why is it that your client had to kill a good boy like Jimmy? If he had to kill somebody, why didn't he just kill one of his own kind? I mean that's what they do best, ain't it? Make babies, do drugs and kill each other? Hell, I ain't ever seen nothing like it in my whole life. And Jimmy was getting ready to get married. Man, you got your hands full with this one, Mr. Forbes. I don't envy you one bit. Now what else do you need to know?"

"I hate to show my ignorance, but what exactly does a first mate do," David asked.

"Well, that's not an ignorant question at all Mr. Forbes. I respect ya for askin' it." Howard replied. "Most 'come heres' act like they think they know what fishin's all about when what they know ain't worth shit. I mean it's okay if you want to call it 'fishin' when you put a little worm on the end of a hook, or burn up fifty gallons of gas to catch two fish like those dickheads do during rockfish season, but when it comes to real fishin' and I mean fishin' to make a livin' and support your family, well that's a different thing all together. My boats over there," Coles said as he motioned in the direction of the large fishing vessel tied up at the dock.

"C'mon, I'll give ya a guided tour, maybe even show you the mermaid rigs we use over on the eastern shore," Coles said with a wink back at his workers who again got a laugh at David's expense and went back to loading the boxes of fish into the back of the truck.

David and Coles walked down the dock to a gleaming white workboat tied starboard to dockside. "Here she is," Coles said, "the '*Bay Lady*'. Jimmy loved her and it shows. On my boat, Jimmy did everything I did except handle the money and sign the checks. He had her ready to go first thing in the mornin' and had her cleaned up at the end of the day with lots of man's work in between. I'm a poundnetter and tend three sets of nets off New Point. I also do some crabbing on the side and run a nice little soft shell business. There's lots of work that needs to be done every day. Nets need to be tended and repaired, crab pots need to be baited, set and checked, plus ya gotta keep up with your peeler pots and pounds, and your boats need to be kept runnin', Then you got to deal with seafood buyers who don't want to pay you nothin' for your catch and while all that's goin' on, then you got to deal with the goddamn marine police who are always trying to tell you how to do something that they could never do themselves. Bunch of government assholes, if ya ask me," Coles said as he spat into the water alongside the boat.

"But getting back to your question, Mr. Forbes," Howard said, "Jimmy loved doing all of it. He made no secret of it that someday he wanted to have his own boat and to run his own business and that's what he should want to do. See, my wife and I could never have no children so I always kinda looked after Jimmy, made sure he learned right, if you know what I mean? By the way, are you hungry Mr. Forbes? I could use a cup of chowder right about now. You ever been in Harper's General Store?"

"No, I can't say that I have," David replied.

"Well, you's in for a real treat," Howard said. "I'm buyin' today, Mr. Forbes. C'mon in and maybe meet some of the fellas."

As David and Coles stepped off the dock and started walking across the parking lot towards the store, David asked, "Can you tell me how much Jimmy was paid for the work that he did for you?"

Coles turned and stared at David in mid-stride, "Now, what bearing would that have on why that asshole killed Jimmy, Mr. Forbes? Jimmy worked his butt off for what money he had and I frankly don't see how that's any of your business."

"I don't mean to be intrusive," David said trying to be careful not to overstep his bounds. "Just a routine question. Let me be blunt. I can see that a lot of what goes on here is a cash business and I suspect that there is a sizable difference between what cash is received and what is actually declared on income tax returns. I don't care about that. I'm just trying to understand whether someone besides Jamal Billups had a reason to kill Jimmy Jarvis. Money is always something that you look at in almost every case, but, frankly, it's hard to see how it would be a factor here. So pardon my question. I don't mean to unnecessarily pry into Jimmy's financial affairs. I'm just trying to do my job."

"You think Jimmy was killed by someone other than that black bastard, Mr. Forbes?" Coles asked.

"I don't know, Mr. Howard," David replied. "Billups denies killing Jimmy. At this stage of the game, I'm just trying to gather all the facts, that's all. Again, I'm just trying to do my job."

"Jimmy was an honest boy, Mr. Forbes," Coles replied, squinting at David in the blaze of the late afternoon sun. "His tax returns will tell the tale. Look, we work a lot in cash around here like you said. But it's hard to put a number on how much Jimmy got paid regular because mother nature don't

103

give you any guarantee when you go out on the water. Sometimes she's kind to you and loads your boat with fish. Sometimes she takes a different view of things and kills every hand aboard with a single swipe of wind and wave. Jimmy made enough to keep above water and to have some hope of a future as a waterman which is more that I can say about a lot of the other waterman around here. Hard way to make a livin', Mr. Forbes, hard way to make a livin'. Think you're getting a little ahead, when suddenly your motor breaks down or a Nor'easter comes through and sends your riggin' halfway across the bay or some asshole up in Washington passes a new regulation that makes the life of a single goddamn sea turtle somehow more important than a man's right to earn a livin'. Don't make no sense at all."

The men were about thirty feet from the front entrance to Harper's when David took notice of an old weather-beaten one-story building next to a broken down dock on the other side of the creek from Harper's General Store. On the front porch of the dilapidated structure sat an elderly man in a rocking chair. Above the porch was a barely legible sign that said "Walter R. Taylor and Son Seafood."

"What's the story on that old place?" David asked Coles, nodding in the direction of the building across the creek.

"Oh, that's Walter Taylor's establishment," Howard explained. "It used to be a store like Harper's here but he ain't run it for many a year. He's just a worn down waterman, old and bitter. He sits over there all day long in that there rockin' chair. From sunup to sundown. Hardly ever moves."

"Is it my imagination or is he staring at us?" David asked.

"Oh, he' staring at us all right," the captain explained. "More to the point, he's probably staring more at me than at you. See, old man Taylor's got a bit of a grudge against my family. As I'm sure you know, my daddy is the county sheriff and some time back, when daddy was a deputy, he pulled over Taylor's son for drunk drivin'. Taylor's boy tried to fight daddy and ended up getting shot. The old man claimed that daddy outright murdered his son. That wasn't true, of course. Taylor's son was an out of control hard case who could drink ten men under the table. That old man never could come to grips that his only kid was a fuck up and blames daddy to this very day."

"How long ago was his son killed?" David asked.

"Oh, about thirty-five years ago," Coles responded.

"Man, that's a long time to hold a grudge," Forbes noted.

"Time passes slowly around here Mr. Forbes," Howard said, "and for that old man, I guarantee you that to him, it seems like it only happened yesterday."

'Unbelievable,' David thought as his Bass loafers hit the steps of Harper's for the first time and both men walked through the door of the old store.

"Coles," yelled one of the old timers. "I see where the VMRC has got this new regulation that . . . ." when, suddenly, the old man stopped talking in mid-sentence when he realized that Coles was not alone but had some guy with him wearing a shirt and tie.

About six men were in the store that afternoon, including the proprietor, Willie Minter, and they were all looking at David, who paused at the front entrance and wondered whether he was breaching some ancient right of privilege by even being in the store in the first place.

"Come on in, Mr. Forbes, don't be shy. These old farts won't hurt you none," Coles said as he walked past the counter where Minter was stocking boxes of crab pot zincs and culling rings.

"Boys, this gentlemen here is Mr. David Forbes," Coles said by way of introduction. "He's the new attorney in town who Brenda works for and he represents that asshole that killed Jimmy. Mr. Forbes asked if he could come on down here and ask some questions about Jimmy and I thought we ought to oblige him with that request. By the way, Mr. Forbes, do you like clam chowder and I mean real clam chowder? Not that crap that comes in a can, but real chowder? Willie, get the man a cup of chowder."

Minter nodded and did as instructed by his son-in-law and ladled out a large Styrofoam cup full of the steaming soup from the large pot on the stove behind the counter. The store clerk then gathered up a plastic spoon,

105

some napkins, and two packets of saltines and placed the soup and its accompaniments on the Formica table where two of the retirees were already sitting.

Coles grabbed a chair by the table and said "Sit on down, Mr. Forbes. Chowder is on me today." David complied and sat down at the table, nodded at both of the retirees and said "How are you today?" Both men nodded back to Forbes but neither man said a word in reply.

Coles went to the tall coolers at the back of the store and grabbed two ice cold cans of Pabst beer and walked back up to the table. He sat down in the chair across the table from David, opened both beers, placed one in front of David and kept one for himself.

"Here's to ya, Mr. Forbes" Coles said and took a hefty draught from the can. David followed suit with a gulp of his own and then took spoon in hand and tasted the chowder for the first time.

"I can honestly say that this is the best chowder I have ever had," David said, "simply delicious."

"Hear that boys?" Coles said in a loud voice, "Best he's ever had! Now ain't that some shit. Best the man's ever had. Willie, you ought to win some sort of prize for that there chowder of yours. Maybe even get you on one of them cookin' shows on TV!" Coles laughed, took another long pull from his can of beer and then leaned forward and spoke again to David from across the table.

"Now, Mr. Forbes, not to be discussin' business while you be eatin' the best chowder you've ever had, but let's get back to your little theory that maybe someone else other than that there nigger client of yours killed Jimmy. I'd be interested in hearing about that theory."

David paused before responding to Coles' request. He had learned his lesson at Patty's and bought time with another spoonful of chowder and was considering another sip of beer when Howard took advantage of the lull in the conversation and announced again in a loud, booming voice, "Did ya know

106

that boys? Mr. Lawyer here thinks that Jamal Billups is an innocent man." Coles laughed again, drained his beer and crushed the can with one hand.

At that moment, David knew he was in trouble and for the second time in less than thirty minutes, he had again taken the bait hook, line and sinker.

Howard got up and went back to the cooler and got himself another can of Pabst. All eyes were on him as he walked back to the table, but, this time, Coles took the chair right next to David's.

No one in the store said a word.

The Captain opened his beer, took a long drink from the can and spoke again, this time in a deep whispering voice, his face just a foot away from David's ear.

"Ya know, Mr. Forbes, I got to make a confession. I lied to you earlier today, about respecting lawyers, that is. Truth is, I can't stand any of ya. As far as I'm concerned, you're all a bunch of blood-sucking leeches that ain't never done an honest day's work in your whole fuckin' lives. But ya get a couple of college degrees and a law license and suddenly ya think you're tough shit. And when ya get tired of playing lawyer, then you become a judge or worse yet, a goddamn politician and that's why things are so fucked up everywhere you go. It's because you worthless motherfuckers are in charge and you don't know a goddamn thing."

Forbes didn't dare respond as Coles swallowed half the can in one gulp, wiped his beard and slid his chair even closer to David. He continued to speak while Jamal's lawyer sat frozen in his chair.

"And now here you are, sitting at the same table where Jimmy used to sit, drinkin' his beer and eatin' his chowder. You know what Jimmy used to say to Willie all the time, Mr. Lawyer? 'Best chowder in the world, Mr. Minter, best chowder in the world', over and over again. Jimmy never had a bowl of it without paying' a compliment to my father-in-law over there. Polite and respectful Jimmy was, but he can't be polite and respectful anymore because he's dead!"

107

And with that Coles slammed his right hand down on the table with such force that David's half empty cup of chowder spilled over and his barely touched can of beer flew two inches in the air before it too landed sideways causing David to start grabbing at some napkins to wipe up the mess while his table mates just stared at him in silence.

Coles wasn't finished. "You know what's the best I ever had, Mr. Lawyer Man? Jimmy Jarvis as a first mate. Yes, sir, that's the best I ever had. And I don't care what bullshit that coon head has been tellin' you over at the jail, that rat bastard client of your's killed Jimmy in cold blood out on that beach. And now you've got the balls to come here with your lawyer questions about how much Jimmy was paid and accusing us of tax evasion and shit like that?"

Howard looked around at the old men at the table and the others who stared at David from the rocking chairs just a few feet away.

"That's right, tax evasion!" Coles yelled to his audience. "This man said as much right out there on that dock just a few minutes ago, now ain't that right, Mr. David Forbes, Attorney-at-Law?"

Forbes was beaten, and he knew it. He pushed the soiled napkins that were soaked with spilled chowder and beer into a small pile in front of him on the table and said to no one in particular, "I think its best I leave."

He then stood and turned to Minter and asked what he owed him for the chowder and beer. From behind him he heard the sound of another dinette chair sliding against the worn wood floor of the store and knew that Coles had stood up as well.

Howard spoke next in a low whispered tone. "Mr. Forbes, I told you that the chowder was on me when we first walked in here. I guess your memory has gotten little fuzzy in the last few minutes. Must be a lot on your mind." Coles was now so close behind David that he could feel his breath on the back of his neck. David didn't dare turn around.

Minter broke the silence when he spoke his first words since David walked into Harper's.

"It's on the house," he said.

David mumbled a muted "thanks" in Minter's direction and then walked out of the store, opened the door of the Porsche and collapsed in the front seat, visibly shaken. "Jesus Christ," he said to himself, "I've been in prisons, jails, nasty bar fights in my college days, sting operations with the DEA and Marine Corps boot camp but I've never felt fear like that. What the hell is going on and what have I gotten myself into?"

David was lost in his own question and didn't notice as he pulled away from Harper's that his exit from the iconic establishment was watched closely by the old man in the rocking chair across the creek.

Of all the things said by Coles Howard that day, the waterman was wrong in his assumption that it was he who was the focus of the elderly waterman that afternoon. It was actually the lawyer who held the attentions of Walter Taylor.

Like the Rev. Terrance Covington, Walter Taylor too believed that the devil still walked among us, but for Taylor, his devil was the man who had taken his only son. Deeply religious just like his late wife, Taylor was convinced that Providence had answered his prayers and that this attorney had been summoned by the Good Lord himself to do His work. It was David Forbes who was going to bring his son's killer to justice, of that Taylor had no doubt. And for the first time in thirty-five years, the old waterman ceased his daily vigil on the front porch of his old store, went inside, and closed the door.

# Chapter Twelve

## The First African Assembly of God

"Mommy, why do I have to wear a dress?" David and Karen's nine year- old daughter, Katie, said in a loud voice. She was standing just on the hallway side of the threshold of her parent's bedroom that was located on the second floor of their two story home on Gwynn's Island.

"My friends at school say that when they go to church they get to wear shorts and flip-flops and t-shirts and I don't understand why I have to wear this dress!" she said again with greater emphasis as she pulled at the shiny black belt that accented the lavender dress and formed a perfect match with her new pair of patent leather black shoes.

Karen paused while putting the finishing touches on her own attire, then turned to her daughter and said, "Because this is a special day. We are going to a different church and we are going to look nice. Besides I'm wearing a dress, too," she said, striking a models pose and flashing a theatrical smile as she knelt down to readjust her daughters unwanted belt back to its appropriate position.

"I don't care," her daughter replied with defiant hands on hips. "Savannah says she doesn't have to wear a dress when she goes to church!"

"Maybe when you go with Savannah to her church, you can dress that way. But today, you are going to wear this dress. And that's all I want to hear about that," Karen said as she stood and surveyed how pretty her daughter looked, all dressed up in her beautiful dress with a pout the size of Texas located smack dab on the middle of her face.

David was watching the scene play out while he was shaving in the master bathroom, when suddenly he leapt into the middle of the bedroom, jumped on the bed and started singing "Put on a happy face," badly imitating the venerable Broadway show tune.

110

Karen started laughing and Katie yelled "Daddy, stop it!" which just made her daddy sing it louder.

David then jumped from the bed, landed on his knees right in front of his daughter, spread his arms and said, "Who's the prettiest little girl in the whole world?"

Katie could resist no more. She broke out a smile and said, "I am!" and got wrapped in her daddy's arms as a reward.

Forbes held his daughter out at arm's length and said, "You know what your problem is, kid?"

A father and daughter ritual for years, Katie quickly replied on cue, "Yep. I know my daddy loves me and I'm too damn cute!"

Karen said "Katherine Marie!" in mock indignation of the mild use of profanity that had been a forgivable sin since Katie and David had first started the wordplay some years ago.

Katie giggled, knowing she had again gotten away with a saying a bad word, but that was an allowed part of her traditional exchange with her daddy. She gave him a big hug to which he said "Now get your butt downstairs. We'll be out of here in a few minutes."

Katie scampered down the hall, took a right turn down the staircase and was immediately replaced at the bedroom doorway by thirteen-year-old Luke.

Dressed in khakis, docksiders and a blue oxford shirt, the teenager was holding a yellow necktie in his hands and had a look of total frustration on his face.

"Dad," he said, "Will you tie this thing? I can't friggin' get it right and its pissing me off."

"Luke, watch your mouth," David said, while tying his own tie in front of the mirror.

"So," Karen commented, "Your nine-year-old daughter can say 'damn', but your thirteen year old son can't say 'friggin' and 'pissing me off'?

"Yep," David said while maneuvering the final loop to complete the knot in his blue and red striped regimental tie of Italian silk.

"Well, that doesn't make sense," his wife said. "What's your standard then, the younger the kid, the more profanity they can get away with? With the way you see it, I guess it's okay then for a six-year-old to tell someone to 'go fuck themselves'?"

"Mom!" Luke said at the unusual display of obscene language coming from his, well, mom. He loved watching his parents hash out an issue.

"No. Not at all," David calmly replied, knowing that Luke was memorizing every word to replay this parental event for years to come.

"The difference is that when Katie says it, she's being cute and knows she has mommy and daddy's permission to say that one word, but only on cue."

"Luke, on the other hand, is speaking spontaneously and feels he has the right, at the ripe old age of thirteen, to use whatever words he wants to use, profane or not. That's wrong. And besides, like Mark Twain once quipped," David said while dropping his voice into the deepest southern accent he could muster, "The boy knows the words but can't carry the tune. Profanity from the mouth of a thirteen-year-old just comes out all wrong. Like P Diddy trying to sing opera."

"Or you trying to sing beat up old show tunes," Karen said smiling, acknowledging by the comment that David had made his point and had flavored it with a teaching moment for Luke as well.

David smiled back at his bride and motioned over to Luke who was still standing in the doorway, watching the intellectual passion play that Luke would appreciate in years to come as one of the many facets of the love between his mother and father.

Luke joined him at the dresser and David's heart swelled as he and his teenage son stood side by side in the mirror. David untied his own tie and both started from scratch.

"Now, the art to tying a tie begins with putting the skinny side on the left and the fat side on the right, with the skinny part about half as long as the fat side. Got it?" David looked over as Luke did as instructed. Father and son nodded at each other in the mirror as David continued on.

"The next part is cool. Turn the tie over so it's upside down, or in other words, seam side up so you can see the label on the fat side." Again, Luke did as instructed and waited for the next step.

"Great," David said, inspecting Luke's work in the mirror.

"Now, time for the critical step number three," his dad said in a deep voice. Luke grinned at his old man and watched carefully.

"Let's make an X by crossing the fat side under the skinny side," David said. Luke followed his father's direction and made the X with the two ends of the tie.

"Now, holding the X together with the thumb and forefinger of your left hand, and, using the fingers of your right hand, fold the fat part back over the X. Notice that the seam side is now on the inside." Luke nodded up and down, and looked back at his dad for the next step.

"Now, keeping your left hand where it is, take the fat end back up through the top of the X and put it through the loop you just made and pull it down a little bit to start to form the knot." Again, Luke followed his dad's every step. David looked over at his son.

"Last step." David said. "Switch hands. Take your left hand and hold the fat side of your tie up near the top. Pinch it a little bit between your thumb and middle finger and use your forefinger to form a little channel right in the middle of the tie, like this."

David leaned over so that his son could see up close the critical final maneuver. "Keep the fingers of your left hand where they are and with your

113

right hand, slowly pull the skinny end until, what do ya know, a perfectly tied tie appears on the neck of the world famous Lucas Anderson Forbes."

Luke stared at himself in the mirror. His tie looked just like his Dad's did every morning when he went to work.

"Wow, that's friggin' awesome," he said.

"I thought I told you to watch your language," David said, both of them just staring at themselves in the mirror, with Luke's perfectly-tied tie hanging around his neck like an Olympic medal.

"Hey, Dad?" Luke said.

"Yes, son," David replied.

"Maybe, if I teach you to sing, maybe you can teach me to cuss." Luke said. "If you did, that would be friggin' awesome. 'Cause, you really suck at singing!"

Luke ducked a playful backhand from his old man and ran laughing out of the room and followed his sister's path down the stairs.

"He's your son, no doubt about that," Karen quipped from the hallway beside the door to Luke's bedroom where she had gone to retrieve his blazer that she tossed to him like a quarterback making a handoff to the star tailback as Luke scooted past his mom and left both of them with the sound of his shoes descending the stairs two at a time.

"Only the good parts, baby. Only the good parts." David replied, "Now let's herd these kids up. It's time to go to church."

———————————

114

The First African Assembly of God called home a small wood frame church located in the Cardinal area of the county and on this Sunday, its parking lot was packed with cars.

David gave up looking for parking in the church lot and finally found a place to park Karen's 4Runner on the soft, narrow shoulder of the road that fronted the church which was bordered on both sides by deep ditches that were constantly called to duty, draining the water that inundated the county during times of heavy rain and particularly during the hurricane months of August and September.

As the family made its way towards the church, they were joined in the parking lot by a host of people all dressed up in their Sunday finery. Karen leaned down to Katie and whispered, "I don't see many people wearing shorts and flip-flops here today," to which Katie said nothing in muted thanks for her mother's good advice earlier that morning because she, too, saw the little girls who were in her class at school and they were all attired in beautiful dresses with their hair braided to perfection.

"Hi Katie," said one little girl with a wave.

She was wearing a sapphire blue dress adorned with a pale yellow bow. In her hair was the blossom from a magnolia. The child was standing next to someone who appeared to be her grandfather.

Without waiting for a response, the little girl walked over, gave Katie a hug and asked "Are you coming to my church today?" Katie replied, "I guess so, am I Dad?"

David responded "Of course, we are. That's why we're here, silly." And then the little girl said to David, "Can Katie sit with me and Grandpa, please, please, please?" David replied "Sure, if it's okay with your Grandpa," he said more so to the tall black gentleman who now stood at his side, holding a Bible in his right hand and wearing a slate gray shark skin suit and a tie trimmed in vertical stripes of mauve and alabaster. His shirt was ivory, his shoes were spit shine black and he looked great.

"Of course, it's fine with grandpa" said the older gentleman. "Why don't you two run, I mean, walk on in and I'll be in momentarily. And don't forget to save me a seat!" he requested as the two little girls took off, hand in hand, in the direction of the sanctuary.

"Your daughter is precious," said the old gentleman. "I'm Lester Diggs. That's my granddaughter, Keysha."

"She's precious as well and that dress is beautiful," Karen said. "That's our daughter Katie and by the way we're Karen and David Forbes. And this is our son Luke. It's really nice to meet you."

"And you as well," Lester Diggs said. "I'm one of the church deacons. Reverend Billups told me he had invited you and we are glad you are here. Please allow me to walk you inside. I'll help y'all to find a seat. Sometimes it gets a little crowded in here."

As they made their way towards the church, Deacon Diggs looked over at Luke and said, "And how are you today young man?"

To which Luke replied, "I'm fine, sir."

"Sir?" Diggs replied. "Did I hear you say 'Sir'? My goodness, you don't hear that kind of respect much anymore. Mr. and Mrs. Forbes, whatever you both be doin', keep on doin' it cause any young man that knows to say the word 'Sir' is a young man that's on the right track. Yes indeed he is."

Karen smiled at the compliment and gave her son a hug as they reached the steps to the church entrance.

"Don't do that, Mom!" Luke said as he shrugged away from his mother. "Half the football team is standing over there," he said in reference to a group of tall, powerfully built young men who had assembled at the foot of the steps and were helping the elderly and some wheelchair bound parishioners up the steps of the church.

Diggs noticed Karen's gesture and overheard Luke's comment to his mother.

"You know why these boys are so big and strong?" Diggs said to Luke with a big smile on his face. Not waiting for an answer, Diggs said "Because they gets lots of hugs from their mamma's!"

Luke just stared at Diggs which made the old man laugh. "Smile, boy! You are loved! It's a glorious thing, love. God's gift to all of us. Yes it is. Now let's see if we can find y'all a seat."

The four walked up the steps to the old church, its steeple topped with a plain white cross that adorned the surface of an otherwise cloudless, bright blue sky. They entered into a small foyer area and were promptly greeted by an usher that gave each of the visitors a small paper pamphlet that announced the annual Deacons Day Celebration and outlined the itinerary for the service and for the festivities that were to follow.

Diggs whispered into the ear of the usher, who immediately turned to David, Karen and Luke and said, "Mr. and Mrs. Forbes, welcome to our church. Please follow me." The usher turned and walked under a curved archway that marked the entrance to the left aisle of a sanctuary that was constructed with a row of pews on the left, a row of pews on the right, and a long row of pews down the middle.

As David, Karen and Luke followed the usher up the aisle, people turned and stared with curiosity at the new arrivals.

Pastor Covington was accurate in his prediction. They were the only white people in the church and the further up the aisle they walked, the more curious David became as to where they would be seated because the sanctuary was packed with parishioners and he couldn't see a seat anywhere. But the usher saw or knew something otherwise because he walked with the measured pace and confidence of someone holding season tickets to a Yankees game, causing David to sense that their presence here today had all of the accoutrements of a finely orchestrated affair.

His suspicions were confirmed when the usher finally showed them to their seats. They were smack dab in the middle of the front row, three seats together and right beside Katie and her little friend. Lester Diggs came in from the right hand aisle and took his seat beside his granddaughter.

A finely orchestrated affair, indeed. The old man smiled at David as he sat down in the pew, opened his Bible and focused his attention on the scripture before him.

Luke nudged his Mom and whispered, "Look, they've got a band over there." Karen looked to her left and sure enough, over in the far corner of the sanctuary was a four-piece band that consisted of keyboards, a set of drums and two guitars.

"That's cool," Luke said as he continued to stare over at the band thinking to himself 'what kind of church has a band?' Karen likewise directed David's attention to the collection of instruments and David was about to whisper his own commentary on the presence of the band when suddenly the doors opened on both sides of the elevated stage at the front of the sanctuary and members of the choir came out wearing flowing white robes accented in blood red velvet trim.

One by one, they filled the rows of seats behind the pulpit. They were followed by the Reverend Covington and a stunningly beautiful woman attired in an amazing dress that harbored what looked like every color under the sun.

Once everyone had assembled, Reverend Covington approached the pulpit and the church suddenly became as quiet as a cave. He began to speak.

"Brothers and sisters, let us thank God for this beautiful day and for his mercy in allowing us, his children, to spend time together in the midst of his bounty and his benevolence. For this we are grateful and we thank thee God for thy goodness. Can I hear an 'amen'?" the Reverend Covington asked of his flock.

The congregation replied with an 'amen' of their own but the Reverend was far from satisfied with the intensity of the response.

Again, but this time with a sharpened tone that pierced every corner of every pew, the Reverend asked, "Can I hear an 'amen' people!" to which he received an even more enthusiastic response in return. But, it wasn't enough for the man of the cloth.

118

"One more time!" he commanded "and I want to feel it this time. I want to feel it in my heart. I want to feel it in my soul and I want you, the good people of this church, to feel it in every inch of your body, and in your heart, and in your soul but most of all, and I surely mean most of all, I want the good Lord to feel it. Now people, can I hear an 'amen'?" at which the crowd roared back with an 'amen' intended to crack the walls, chip the paint and no doubt turn the cross atop the church into a giant galactic antenna that would transmit their message far into the heavens.

The Reverend Covington smiled as the voices of his congregation reverberated throughout the church and said, "Well, I guess everyone's awake now," and the congregation nodded and smiled in return, laughing together at the entertaining result of their collective good work. The pastor knew his job.

He began, "Ladies and gentlemen, we welcome all of you here today to our annual Deacon's Day Celebration. The Good Lord has blessed us with a most bountiful day and for that we are most grateful. Looking out from my humble post behind the pulpit, may I say that all of you look so fine today. The ladies look so beautiful and their gentlemen so handsome. And look at all these little children, dressed up so nice and behaving so well. We are so blessed here today to have with us some special guests to our church. Mr and Mrs Forbes and their two nice young children are with us today. Mr. Forbes is the attorney who is helping brother Jamal in his time of need. Mrs. Forbes teaches at the elementary school and I see her and their two nice children Luke and Katie every day, so please take time after the service to introduce yourselves to these wonderful people and show them your love. Because that's what it's all about - God's love and our love for one another. Do I hear an 'amen'?" to which a response was enthusiastically received.

The reverend continued on. "Now, I know that most of y'all are thinking about eating all that good food that our wonderful sisters have been preparing all morning long, but, first, we got a good service planned for today and now I'm going to take a seat and ask Sister Judy to take the pulpit, Sister Judy?"

Reverend Covington sat down and watched as the lady in the multi-colored dress approach the pulpit. She looked over the congregation, paused for a moment and then, she closed her eyes and bowed her head.

Nobody moved a muscle.

Suddenly in a strong firm voice, with eyes still closed, she began to sing, *a capella*, the opening verse of 'Amazing Grace.' Perfect in tone and spellbinding in its effect, she gradually increased the tempo of her words until she reached a crescendo, her voice filling every crack and crevice of the First African Assembly of God when suddenly she stopped, opened her eyes, raised her arms to the sky and said "brothers and sisters, raise your voices in song!"

On her command, the remaining members of the chorus stood as did the congregation. The band kicked in with the opening refrain of 'I'm Coming Home' and the church was suddenly saturated in the words and music of the old negro spiritual that had been saving souls and giving hope since before the Civil War.

David and his family were mesmerized. People all around them were singing and clapping in cadence with the beat of the band and joining in was just not an option. Soon, they were swaying in time with the rest of the congregation to what was some of the sweetest singing they had ever heard.

When the song was over, the Reverend Covington retook the pulpit and administered the morning's service wherein he spoke "of the love that was in everyone and the need to recognize love as the force that one could always call upon to defeat the devil that was in all of us, that devil that makes us do the things we know we ought not do."

To David, it was classic fire-and-brimstone material but there was something different about this service, this church, and these people. There was a realness here that often eluded him at so many other religious services that now seemed like cheap seats by comparison. In the stadium of God, this was a skybox suite for sure.

Maybe, he thought, it had something to do with the enthusiasm of the congregation, the frequent 'amens' and the 'Praise Gods' that peppered the Reverend's call for obedience to His word. Maybe it was the color of their skin. Maybe it was something else. At one point, several women started walking up the aisles, waving their arms in the air, and repeatedly thanking God to the rhythm of the many hymns that were sung during the sermon. For

David, it was also part history. From slavery and segregation to the KKK and the brutal murder of Martin Luther King, this church and these people have seen a lot, been through a lot. Hell for them didn't lack for definition or example. Their religion was all too often their only hope, like a life preserver tossed to a man overboard on a pitching sea; it was their one last chance at a desperate salvation.

When they sang these old gospel songs and listened to the words of the minister at the pulpit, they were singing and hearing the words of a people who truly stood unique in the eyes of history. There was a stark and undeniable continuity here, a link from centuries past to the present, from slave ships, chains and whips to a small church in rural Tidewater Virginia in 2007 that most other churches and most other religions can't begin to claim. These people believed in their God. This sanctuary was their place of refuge. Of that, there was no doubt.

Once the service concluded, the Reverend announced that refreshments would be served in the meeting hall that was located at the back the church. Rising with the rest of a hungry congregation, David, Karen and Luke walked with Lester Diggs and watched as the two little girls scampered off to join the other children playing on a small swing set beside the church. Reverend Covington met them at the doorway to the meeting hall.

"Well, Mr. and Mrs. Forbes," he said, "I trust the service was to your liking?"

"Very much so," David replied. "It was excellent in all respects. We greatly appreciate the invite."

"It has truly been our pleasure," the Reverend replied. "Now, please follow Brother Diggs here. He'll help y'all to fill your plates with some of the best food you'll ever eat."

The Reverend's representations about the menu were right on target. In the meeting hall were several large folding tables that were covered in a veritable cornucopia of the finest eating the South had to offer.

Platters of fried chicken and the best fried fish the Chesapeake Bay could produce were accompanied by sides of corn on the cob, spoon bread, fried okra, deviled eggs, collard greens slow cooked in fatback, stewed tomatoes with black eyed peas, red beans and rice, sweet potato casserole, iced pitchers of sweet tea and jugs of kool aid for the kids. Buckets of homemade strawberry ice cream rounded out the fare. Life was good.

His appetite having ramped up a bit since he turned thirteen, Luke's eyes nearly fell out of his head when he viewed the feast before him. Diggs was standing behind him and watched the boy become mesmerized as he gazed over the incredible array of delectable goodness laid out before him.

"Pile it high, son," said the Deacon. "These ladies around here will get mighty upset if there's a square inch on your plate that ain't covered in food."

He then turned to David and Karen. "Y'all help yourselves. I'm going to step outside and get the girls in here so that they can get a seat at the table too so that we can all eat together."

And so they did. They were joined at the table by the Reverend Billups and by a never-ending stream of well-wishers who came over to thank David and his family for coming to the service and for helping Jamal. David had never felt more welcome anywhere, at anytime, than he did here today. Truly, comfort was the shared status quo.

After three trips to the food table, it appeared that Luke had finally gotten his fill and the family Forbes soon decided it was time to go. They said their goodbyes and were just leaving the back door of the church annex when a short, thin woman in her seventies walked up to David and blocked his path. She wore a thin grey cotton dress, clutched a small purse in both hands and stared into his eyes with a gaze that stopped him cold.

"I'm Jamal's granny," she said. "I've raised him since he was a young boy, and I want you to know that he did not kill that Jarvis boy."

"Jamal has mentioned you several times." David responded. "It's nice to finally meet you."

"I said," she repeated herself while ignoring the returned greeting, "that he did not kill that Jarvis boy. Do you believe that, Mr. Forbes? Do you believe that Jamal is innocent of murdering that young child?"

"Mrs. Billups, I am going to do everything I can for your grandson," Forbes said.

"Mr. Forbes," she replied, "Everything you can do, can never be enough if there is no certainty in your heart."

She then reached out with one hand and gripped him tightly on his forearm and said, "I spoke to him yesterday. He trusts you. Now, you need to trust him. Look in your own heart, Mr. Forbes and you will find what you need. I shall pray for you every day, sir, that your path to settin' Jamal free is clear and certain."

The old woman then released her grip and gliding past him like a vesper, dark and whispery grey, she disappeared into the large gathering that continued its assault on the tables of food that never seemed to empty.

---

"Well, kids, what did you think about that?" Karen asked of Luke and Katie as the four of them made their way out of the meeting hall and across the now half empty parking lot to their car.

"That was great," Luke said "I'm stuffed" and punctuated his announcement with an enormous burp.

"Jesus Christ, Luke!" said David.

Luke counted with a "Hey, watch your language, Dad, we're in a church parking lot!"

Karen cut off David before he could respond and said, "So, Katie, what did you think of today?"

Katie said, "I liked it a lot. I want braids and beads in my hair like Tanya and I want to invite her for a sleep over and I want to start going to this church 'cause they're really nice and I want you to make fried chicken like they do and I want . . . ."

Karen smiled and exclaimed "Okay, okay we get the picture. Did you have a really good time?"

"Yes, I did," her daughter said.

"Aren't you glad you wore your dress?" her mom asked.

To which Katie replied, "Yes, I am."

Karen looked over her shoulder at Katie who blew her a kiss and mouthed the words "Love you Mommy." Karen smiled in return and turned her attentions to her husband.

"So, Mr. Forbes, what did you think?" she asked.

David pondered his response as he started the car and headed north on Route 660 and then took a right on Route 14 to head back to the courthouse. "It was great. That's all I can say. It was great. I'm glad the kids were here. It's not something most white kids ever get to see. Or white adults for that matter. Have you ever been to a black church service?" he asked his wife.

"Nope," she said "You?"

"Me, neither," David responded. "Kind of crazy in a way, when you think about it. I can't quite sort it all out. Same God, same religion. But white folks go to their church and black folks go to theirs. Oh, well. I guess that's just the way it is and probably always will be. And by the way, what the heck is going on up here?"

Karen followed David's eyes down the highway and saw that the intersection at the courthouse was blocked off by law enforcement vehicles with blue lights flashing. David's SUV was the fourth car in line and his immediate thought was that it was a roadblock. But no cars were moving through, and David finally saw the reason why.

From down Main Street came a hearse and David knew instantly that it was carrying the body of Jimmy Jarvis. His funeral was today. The hearse was followed by several limousines carrying family members, a fire engine and then by an endless parade of pickup trucks heading to the cemetery.

David and Karen said nothing. Luke spoke up first. "Everyone at school said there's going to be a fight if any black person showed up at the funeral."

His father said, "Luke, that's probably just talk. Kids say a lot of things they don't really mean." Karen was about to add her comments when David put his hand on her leg and mumbled "Hang on. This should be interesting." Karen looked at David and he nodded in the direction of the man in uniform walking up the shoulder of the road towards their car.

Sheriff Junior Howard approached the passenger side of the vehicle and Karen put her window down accordingly.

"Morning counselor, Mrs. Forbes. Sorry for the little delay. Jimmy's funeral is today as you can see. I don't expect you'll be going, but that's understandable all things considered with you being busy and all with your Sunday morning activities and such. By the way how was your lunch?"

"Lunch?" David asked.

The sheriff shifted his tooth pick from left to right and said "Yes, your lunch down at the colored church in Cardinal with the right Reverend Covington presiding. I know you were there. Seen your car in the parking lot."

"Lunch was just fine, Sheriff, thank you for asking," and David left it at that.

Forbes wasn't opposed to a little verbal judo with the sheriff, but not now, and not with Karen and the kids in the car, And particularly not after the Sheriff delivered his little message that he knew where David had been earlier that day. As innocuous as their morning activities had been, it was still a warning that the Sheriff kept a close eye on what went on in his county.

From the brevity of David's reply, Howard knew that he had gotten his message across and said no more. He tipped his hat to Karen and walked back to the squad cars that were beginning to pull away now that the funeral procession had passed.

David and Karen said nothing as they watched the Sheriff walk back up the road. Breaking the silence, Karen said, "That guy gives me the creeps. I hope he leaves us alone. Is he one of the good guys or one of the bad guys?"

"I don't know," David replied. "I honestly don't know. There are so many questions flying around that I don't have the first clue how to answer but I'll say this, something tells me that a day of reckoning is coming. I know I'm sounding a little biblical and maybe it's because Reverend Terry did a good job of getting everyone all jacked up this morning, but I swear, something's coming. I can feel it. I just hope I can keep it away from you, from all of you," he said with a nod to the kids in the back seat.

"You'll do just fine," Karen said. "I have all the faith in the world in you. I mean that."

"Thanks," David said in return. "I appreciate that because something tells me I'm going to need all the help I can get."

# BOOK TWO

## Evidence

---

## Chapter Thirteen

## The Defense Begins

In the final days leading up to the preliminary hearing, David was still at a loss as to how to put together a plausible defense for Jamal Billups.

Despite whatever credibility Billups may initially have had with his 'Superman' theory that time and distance made it impossible for him to have killed Jimmy Jarvis, the evidence against his client was still staggering and it was beginning to be a foregone conclusion that a Mathews jury would easily ignore any argument that Billups was innocent on that theory alone. To defend Billups, David would need more legal ammunition than that, but evidence favorable to his client was in short supply.

The prosecutor, Archie Hudgins, had been more than gracious in allowing David to peruse his investigation file and to make copies of anything he wanted and those documents were now spread out before him on his conference room table.

He had the autopsy report, the death certificate signed off by Doc Lawson, and an analysis of the blood found on Jamal's clothing and on the knife he had on him when he was arrested. As expected, the blood was Jimmy's

He also had typed reports of law enforcement interviews with the two boys who found Jimmy's body at the beach, the interviews with Cassie

Thompkins and the interviews with the three guys who came to Jimmy's rescue after the fight.

There was also a disc of digital photos showing Jimmy's body at the beach and of his pickup that was found at the beach access parking lot. Plus, there was an inventory of the contents of Jimmy's truck and what was found on Jimmy's body both of which revealed nothing other than the sort of things you would expect to find on the person and in the truck of a twenty-three year old country boy who lived in Mathews County.

The autopsy revealed that Jimmy died of three stab wounds to the chest, with cause of death listed as severe internal bleeding consistent with numerous punctures to the lung and heart.

Forbes made a note that there were no defensive wounds on Jimmy's body referenced in the report, meaning that Jimmy, for one reason or the other, had little time or little inclination to react to his attacker.

The autopsy report did make reference to a preexisting small laceration to Jimmy's left upper arm that had a bandage on it when Jimmy's body was found on the beach. Other than that, there were no bruises, scratches, or other marks on his body other than the wounds to his face that he had received in his brawl with Billups earlier that evening.

One surprise in the evidence was that the autopsy report revealed the presence of semen in Jimmy's underwear and also a substance consistent with vaginal fluid, the source of which David was certain was Cassie Thompkins.

After he finished reading the autopsy report, David's eyes went back and forth over the photos of Jimmy's body lying on the beach which showed a white male lying face up on the sand. He was dressed in a pair of white cargo shorts and wore a light green short sleeve shirt decorated in a fine print of small, pale yellow swordfish. His clothes were covered in large splotches of dried blood and his eyes were wide open. On his feet was a pair of well-worn tan Sebago's and on his left wrist was a large cheap silver-colored watch. Two feet from his head, lying upside down in the sand, was a sun bleached pale yellow "Brew Thru" baseball hat. The bandage from the preexisting wound identified in the autopsy report was partially visible from just underneath the shirt sleeve covering his left upper arm. The area around his body was spotted with large clumps of darkened sand, stained a blackish-red from the blood that had poured onto the beach from the wounds in Jimmy's chest.

It appeared from the other photos in the file that Jimmy's body was recovered approximately two-hundred yards to the left of the parking lot where his vehicle was found, but it was impossible to tell from the photos whether any footprints were visible in the dry sands of the beach in the vicinity of the crime scene or in the crushed, sandy gravel of the parking lot. In any event, there was no report in the prosecutor's file of any footprints being found at either location nor was there any mention in the reports prepared by the Sheriff's office that a footprint analysis had been performed at the scene.

Adding to the pile of missing forensic evidence was the absence of any tire tread analysis that may have provided clues as to whether any other vehicles were present in the parking lot around the same time as Jimmy's murder. Also missing was any fingerprint analysis of Jimmy's truck, a particularly critical factor that certainly would be a part of any modern crime scene investigation. All in all, the prosecutors file was not exactly what David was used to seeing from his years of working with the FBI.

Forbes's attentions went back to the pictures of Jimmy's body lying on the beach. He picked up another photo of Jimmy, this one taken from a newspaper article about his murder that showed a very much alive Jimmy Jarvis holding up the winning fish at the Blue Crab Restaurant's annual flounder fishing tournament.

"Handsome kid," David thought. "He was big, too."

Forbes's mind drifted back to the analysis he had so carelessly announced out loud at Patty's diner that memorable morning after Jimmy's body had been discovered at Haven's Beach.

'What the hell was Jimmy Jarvis doing two hundred yards out on a beach, presumably alone except for his killer, in the middle of the night? And why were there no defensive wounds?'

Nobody was going to stick a knife in a big guy like Jimmy Jarvis without getting the fight of their life unless the killer was able to get up real close and Jimmy wasn't expecting it, that's for sure.

And that rules out Jamal Billups, doesn't it?

Jimmy knew that Jamal was packing a knife from their close encounter earlier that night, so there was no way he was going to let Billups get anywhere near him again. The only way Jamal could have pulled this off was if he killed Jimmy while he was either asleep or passed out drunk out there on that beach and, for David, it was just too much to believe that the Jamal he met for the first time several weeks ago at the jail was enough of a cold blooded killer to commit a crime like that. But, if not Jamal, whoever did this had to be someone who Jimmy knew well and trusted enough for them to know where he was that night and well enough for whoever it was to let them get up so close.

Who fell into that category? Cassie, for one, but plunging a knife three times into the chest of guy the size of Jarvis takes a hell of a lot of speed and power. Plus, David had handled enough contract murder cases in his career to know the difference between the work of a rank amateur and the surgical precision you see from a knife welded in the hands of an experienced professional.

In his opinion, the wounds to Jimmy's body fell into the latter category. They were positioned tightly together, separated by no more that ¾ of an inch and were grouped approximately 3 inches below, and slightly to the left, of the left nipple. To David, this indicated that all three penetrations were done at lightning fast speed, one right after the other. Bam, bam, bam! And, it had to have been done so fast that Jimmy never had time to move. Who kills like that? Not Cassie Thompkins, that's for sure. And not Jamal either. Whoever did this murder is very comfortable with a knife, and, in all likelihood, has killed before. And, more importantly, they knew Jimmy.

David laid the photos down on the conference room table, took a swig from his bottle of water and walked up to the front lobby of his law office. It was early Saturday morning and the phones were quiet. Karen had taken the kids to go see her parents up in Springfield for the weekend, and

David had some time to himself so he came up to the office to put in a little extra work on Jamal's case.

He sat down in one of the two Chesterfield leather chairs in the front lobby and looked out the window at the early morning pedestrian traffic going up and down the sidewalks that bordered Main Street. From his vantage point, he could see folks going into the small bakery that just opened up across the street and coming out with bags of the freshly baked items of the day along with cups of steaming hot, fresh-brewed coffee.

Forbes had taken up the habit of also patronizing the small shop after it became clear that his morning presence at Patty's among the locals was perhaps not as welcome as it once was. Several trips to the venerable establishment after his encounter with the Sheriff were met by a diminished presence of hospitality and David decided that it was best to accept it as the way things were and to simply move on; a decision which, in the long run, proved to be less traumatic than David expected given that the almond croissants and the double espresso lattes from the little bakery across the street were just as good as anything he could get on the streets of D.C.

Karen experienced a similar change in atmosphere at the school with her fellow teachers, and with some of the parents of her students, but thankfully, summer vacation kicked in just in time and, with the kids out of school, the social impact of David's representation of Jamal Billups became less of an issue and Karen spoke less of whether the move from D.C. had been the right thing to do. David knew that the move to Mathews had been the right thing to do but quietly conceded that his acceptance of the appointment to represent Billups had not been without its negative consequences.

Brenda was sadly right when she said earlier that "people can be pretty shitty at times." Two local business owners had withdrawn as clients, new business had noticeably declined and David's Porsche had been keyed from the front fender to the rear quarter panel about two weeks ago. He made a report of the damage to the Sheriff who just sneered and said, "Ya can't have it both ways, Mr. Forbes. If you want to be loved around here, best you stop saying that Billups didn't kill Jimmy. You see, I heard about your little visit to Harper's. And, what the hell were you doing attendin' a service at that killer's church on the same day as Jimmy's funeral? We're a small town Mr. Forbes and we take care of our own. You and your family, sir, don't seem to want to be on that list. Have a nice day."

David tired of his social surveillance of Main Street, so he got up and walked back to his conference room and stared again, for the one hundredth time it seemed, at the stacks of reports and photos that covered the table. He sat down in one of the Windsor chairs that surrounded the table and was studying the photos of Jimmy's body when he decided to call his buddy Simon Epstein at the Drug Enforcement Administration. Simon loved two things, women and his work, and David knew that if he answered the phone this early on a Saturday morning, it was a good chance that he would not be in bed with his latest girlfriend but in front of his array of computers at DEA.

Simon picked up the phone on the third ring and knew it was David from caller I.D. "Only a guy who's not getting laid calls another guy this early on a Saturday morning. What's the matter, Karen tired of the same old thing already?"

"She's out of town, you dumb yid, and look who's talking. How's life in the big city?" David said affectionately to his old DEA pal.

"Same shit, different day, you gentile schmuck," replied the agent. "Before you get to the reason why you called, I have to tell you about Yvonne's attire of the day; that is, her attire yesterday. It was nothing short of spectacular. She was dressed in a thigh high ivory dress, with a matching jacket, and a low cut white blouse with enough cleavage showing to stop traffic out on K Street. I was over at your old stomping grounds, so I just had to check in and make sure she's doing ok, if you know what I mean," Simon said in reference to David's famously beautiful secretary at his former office in D.C.

"Yeah, I know what you mean. She could make the sun shine on a rainy day," David quipped.

"And then some!" replied Simon. "Now, how are you? I hear you got yourself appointed to a little murder case down there in Happyville. I didn't think those kind of crimes were supposed to happen in the land of the greener grass. Nothing like jumping in with both feet, Kimosabe. Whatcha got going on?"

David said, "Young, well-liked white guy got stabbed to death. Older, not-so-well-liked black guy is charged with doing it."

"Did he do it?" Simon asked.

"I don't know." David responded. "I'm in the process of figuring it all out. There's lots of forensic evidence tying him to the crime but there's some other things going on that make it complicated. In other words, I don't think the case is as clear cut as our local prosecutor thinks it is. But I've got my work cut out for me. What's going on up in your neck of the woods?"

Simon said, "Usual stuff. Drugs, money, and violence. The holy trinity at its worst. The more drugs, the more money, the more violence. It never fucking ends. You would have thought that all of this Homeland Security stuff would have put a dent into it but it didn't do a goddamn thing. Planes, boats, submarines, carrier pigeons, or some asshole's rectum. Hell, they always find a way to get it in. In fact, some top notch Mexican drug gangsters, the Los Zetas, apparently like to use the Chesapeake Bay to move their shit around. I came across bits and pieces of encrypted email and cell phone traffic a month or so ago about a shipment that went missing down your way. I guess someone didn't show up when they were supposed to and it must have been a shit load of cargo and a hell of a lot of cash. We keep an eye on their operatives who run distribution networks out of Miami and Baltimore and they were pretty pissed off."

"Well, if I see any Mexican drug lords running around town, I'll let you know. Married yet?" David said, changing the subject.

"Married? Me? And deprive the women of the world of my fabulous charm and Jewish sense of humor? Not to mention my legendary bedroom reputation for not letting the ladies down, if you know what I mean. Of course I'm not married! Too many women in this town to give up for just one, except for someone like your Karen of course."

133

"Or perhaps Yvonne. Every time you'd see her in my office, your eyes looked like they were about to explode!" David said to which Simon replied "Just like another part of my anatomy!"

David was shuffling through some of the file documents while he spoke to Simon on the phone. Suddenly he spotted something in one of the Sheriff reports that caught his attention.

"Hey, Simon. I'm at the office and something just came up. Let me call you later."

"Shalom," said the agent. "You take care of yourself David. Keep in touch.

"Will do, old friend. Be good and I'll talk to you soon."

David hung up and focused on the single piece of paper that he held in his hand. It was a typed report of an interview with the two boys who found Jimmy's body. The report had been prepared by Dep. Matt Robins of the Mathew's Sheriff's Office. David knew Robins and always like how he presented himself in court. He was a professional, straight-talking officer who appeared to like his work and did a good job at it. David had read Robin's report before but this time he paid closer attention to the statements the boys made about what they had observed at the scene when they first saw Jimmy's body.

Robins had done a thorough job of interviewing both boys and had asked them repeatedly to try to remember everything they could about what they observed when they came upon Jimmy's body at the beach. Predictably, both boys were upset at first and their recollections of the event initially were emotional and consisted of only the most basic of details. But Robins pressed on and was able to get more and more facts out of both boys and, when asked if they recalled ever seeing anything around the area where Jimmy's body was found, one of the boys finally said that he thought he remembered seeing a pair of shoes and some empty cans of beer. Robins asked the boy if he could recall any additional facts about the shoes or the cans but the boy could only remember sparse details, such as that there was a pair of shoes (he couldn't recall what they looked like), some beer cans (he couldn't recall how many) or how close they were to Jimmy's body ("Maybe ten feet or so. I can't really remember," was what the boy said in the report).

David quickly scanned all the photos and the rest of the reports prepared by the other members of the Sheriff's office who participated in the crime scene investigation at the beach, and there was no mention of finding a pair of shoes or a bunch of beer cans at the scene in any of the other reports and none of the photos showed a pair of shoes or any cans of beer at the scene.

He remembered that the toxicology results that accompanied the autopsy report showed that Jimmy had a post mortem blood alcohol content of .12, but Jimmy had been seen drinking beer at the Blue Crab right before the fight at the Get n' Go which could possibly explain the presence of alcohol in his blood-stream. Plus, people leave shoes and such on the beach all the time, as well as empty beer cans, so what the boys saw at the beach that morning could have nothing to do with this case. On the other hand, it could be a critical factor in finding out what happened to Jimmy Jarvis that night. And if the boys really did see a pair of shoes and some beer cans near the body, why didn't the shoes or the beer cans show up in any of the photographs and why weren't they mentioned in any of the reports? David made a mental note to interview Robins and the boys himself and see if he could fill in some of the missing pieces of the Deputy's report.

As important as this evidence could be, however, David knew that the most critical witness in this case would be Jimmy's girlfriend, Cassie Thompkins.

Brenda had tried to call her to set up an interview but, as she had told him earlier, the girl was apparently no longer working at the Get n' Go and her cell phone had been disconnected. David knew that his only option was to go see her at her parent's house where she lived and hope that she would be willing to talk. Cassie Thompkins was probably the last person to see Jimmy alive before he was killed and was the best person to ask why he would have gone to the beach that night after leaving her house and perhaps why someone other than Jamal Billups would want him dead.

According to the report prepared by the sheriff, Cassie was with Jimmy when the Sheriff left the convenience store that night after Jamal had fled into the woods following his fight with Jimmy. She said that Jimmy took her home right after the fight and then told Cassie that he was feeling tired from all the bullshit with Billups and just wanted to go home. Cassie said he never told her he was going to the beach and the last time she saw him alive was in her parents driveway. Of interest, though, was that she made no mention that the pair apparently had sexual intercourse at some time after the fight and before he was murdered.

David knew then what he had to do. He looked at his watch, gathered up all the photos and the report detailing Cassie's interview and stuffed them into a legal size leather portfolio. He left the conference room, walked across the hallway to his office, grabbed his car keys and retrieved an ice cold bottle of water from the fridge in the small kitchen in the back of the hallway. He locked up the office, got into his car and drove to Haven Beach.

# Chapter Fourteen

## The Storm at Haven Beach

There were two other vehicles in the parking lot when David arrived at Haven Beach. One was a Ford pickup truck, the other was a Land Rover. Together they were a study in contrasts, as different as the county itself.

The Ford was a rough looking, beat up affair with items of fishing gear and old pieces of mail scattered across the dashboard and a large Igloo cooler in the back bed situated amongst numerous empty beer cans, crumpled up empty packs of Marlboro cigarettes, two old tires, a dented gas can and at least a dozen discarded plastic containers of Quaker State motor oil.

The Land Rover on the other hand was waxed to perfection with nary an indication that anything other than kid gloves had ever graced its perfectly appointed leather interior.

Looking around the beach, David guessed the truck belonged to the fellow with a full head of gray hair and a week's worth of whiskers who was tending two fishing poles located about fifty yards to the right of the parking lot that were held upright by PVC rod holders buried deep in the coarse sand that gathered at the water's edge.

That bit of deductive reasoning left ownership of the Land Rover to the only other people at the beach that morning, a young couple who were tossing tennis balls to a pair of Labs who were swimming in the water further up the beach, about a hundred yards to the right of the owner of the pickup.

Forbes took in the scene. It was a bit overcast, the sky a mix of soft gray and muted yellow, pierced now and then by the golden rays of a sun trying to work its way into the mornings mix of tone and hue. The tide was low and the pale green water had retreated to expose vast expanses of smooth sandbar and the grassy beds that served as the nursery for so much of the marine life that lived in the bay, especially the famed blue crab.

David heard the couple yell something about dolphins and looked over in their direction and saw them pointing to a small pod of the large creatures swimming about three hundred feet off shore, their large gray bodies arcing in almost perfect unison as they dove for the baitfish in the surrounding waters while guarding their calf who playfully mimicked his parents while swimming in the protective nursery at the center of the group.

In the sky above, a solitary osprey kept an eye on the water's surface for her daily catch while a flock of brown pelicans, like a squadron of planes patrolling the beach, flew left to right just inches above the gently rolling surface of the Chesapeake Bay. The breeze was blowing soft but steady, with its warmth punctuated now and then by a touch of cold air that caused David to look east and he could see the gathering thunderheads that meant that rain that would soon intrude on his morning visit to where Jimmy was killed.

David reached over to the passenger seat of the Porsche and took the crime scene photos from his portfolio. He could see that the Land Rover was parked in almost the same spot as Jimmy's pickup had been on the night of the murder. He looked to the left of the parked vehicle and then started walking in the direction of the spot where Jimmy's body had been found. David had a good idea of the locale from the photos in his hand but soon learned that even without the photos, he would have found the crime scene without any difficulty at all.

Two hundred yards from the parking lot, in the exact spot where Jimmy Jarvis's body had been found, was a cross made of white PVC pipe that stood approximately three feet tall with its base buried deep in the cold, wet sand like the rod holders of the old fisherman at the other end of the beach. Attached to the cross were dozens of weathered pieces of paper, mostly handwritten notes, with their inked remembrances bleached away by the searing sun or stained and made unrecognizable by the rains that had fallen since the written tribute was placed at the memorial to Jimmy Jarvis. Some retained their readability because the visitor had put the note in a plastic sandwich baggie. These David read and he was instantly taken by the emotion that emanated from the prose and poetry of Jimmy's friends and family.

In addition to the handwritten notes, there were numerous mementos left by people who obviously cared deeply for Jimmy. Several NASCAR souvenirs were scattered about the cross. There was also a Brew Thru hat, just like the one in the crime scene photo, which had been attached to the center of the cross with a nylon wire tie. Located just above the hat was a photo of Jimmy that had been protected against the elements by being stuck inside a clear CD case that was wedged between the hat's brim and the cross. A small confederate flag had also been attached to the very top of the cross with remnants of yellow crime scene tape that had been discarded on the beach. About a dozen empty Corona bottles stacked neatly against its base completed the memorial which reminded him of the crosses that you sometimes see while driving down the highway that mark the locale of a tragic automobile accident where a loved one had passed.

David reached for the CD case and carefully removed it from behind the brim of the hat. He paused while he studied the photo. This was one well-liked young guy, he thought. Lots of family and friends. It was just so tragic that he had to go so young and with so much life left to live.

Holding the photo in his hand, Forbes began to feel a bit like an intruder and he looked around to see if anyone was taking an interest in his presence at the tribute to Jimmy when the CD case suddenly came open in his hand. Feeling that he was desecrating hallowed ground, David immediately tried to shut the case but could feel that something was wedged in the case, behind the photo that was causing it to pop open. He looked into the container and saw that a piece of paper had been folded and placed behind the photo in the back of the case. David's curiosity overwhelmed any reluctance he may have initially had to viewing its contents and he slowly unfolded the paper.

What he saw in his hand was an ultrasound photo of a tiny unborn child that identified the patient as one Cassie Thompkins. The date on the ultrasound was approximately eight weeks after Jimmy's murder. The child had to be Jimmy's and he died not knowing he was a father. "Jesus Christ, she's pregnant. Cassie Thompkins must be shattered," David thought. "I wonder how many times she's been to this memorial, stood where I'm standing right now and cried her eyes out over the husband she'll never have and the father her child will never know. Crazy."

Forbes placed the ultrasound photo back into the CD case, made sure it was shut tight and carefully wedged it back behind the brim of the hat. He got up, brushed the sand off his jeans and looked up at the sky. The storm clouds he had noticed moments earlier had been aggressive in their approach and now hovered ominously overhead. Dark and menacing, they announced their arrival with an initial salvo of huge droplets of rain and strong gusts of a chilling breeze, and David knew he had just seconds to find cover before all hell broke loose. He clutched his portfolio, took a last look at the memorial and trotting back to his car, he was just able to get in and shut the door before the sky exploded with relentless buckets of rain and percussive blasts of thunder and he could feel his car getting rocked by gale force winds.

"This, no doubt, must be a Nor'easter," he thought making reference to the legendary storms that can do as much damage as a Category One hurricane and can descend upon the Chesapeake Bay without a moment's notice.

Driving was futile and so he decided to wait out the storm and watched as the rain drenched couple and their equally soaked pair of labs made a beeline for their Land Rover as did the fisherman who tossed his rods and gear into the back of the ancient Ford and then leaped into the front cab of what was clearly a home away from home for the old man.

The couple in the Land Rover decided to make a run for it, so they backed their vehicle out of the parking lot and were soon quickly out of sight in his rear view mirror, lost in a thick curtain of shale gray pouring rain.

David stayed put and looked over at the one remaining vehicle in the parking lot and could see a soft glow emanating from the cab of the truck and guessed that its occupant had just lit up a cigarette and also had made the decision that he too would wait out the storm. And so, there they sat, the lawyer in his Porsche and the old fisherman in his pickup, their drivers bearing witness to nature's harder hand at work, her force and power on majestic display as sky and sea quickly melted into one indivisible force, a black swirling cauldron of wind and water.

In short order, the storm increased in its intensity. The rain became devilishly random in its approach and now attacked his car from all sides like so much watery buckshot propelled by the relentless  seventy mile an hour winds that seemed intent on removing him and the car from the beach, like an animal scratching an irritating pest off its fur. Rain, wind and thunder presented themselves like nothing David had ever seen in his life and he could hear the roar of the surf as the waves grew taller and bolder in the teeth of the fury and pounded the sand with such ferocity that the Porsche vibrated with each barrage and he began to think that the couple in the SUV made the right call.

The onslaught seemed like it would never end but in time the murderous clouds exhausted themselves, the sun began to punch holes in the sky and an eerie calm settled across the water as the storm moved on to do her damage elsewhere. After the rain stopped, David stepped out of his car and noticed that the air had a scent to it that he couldn't quite describe.  It was the smell of oxygen refreshed, the sweet perfume of a beach honed clean by an abrasive mix of wind, water, salt and sand. Forbes learned that day that despite the destructive power of what had just passed, it left in its wake a beauty in its passing, a purity in and of itself that can only be achieved when a high powered storm etches its mark on a small stretch of beach on the coast of the Chesapeake Bay.

He nodded to the driver of the pickup who had rolled down the window and, with a practiced hand, expertly flung a spent beer can into the rear bed of the truck. David then walked behind the pickup, across the parking lot and in the direction of where Jimmy's body had been found and immediately knew something was wrong. As he walked along the beach, he noticed that the landscape had changed, the small dunes that had rippled the waterfront had been flattened by the raging wind and tide and the cross was nowhere to be seen. David stopped walking in the storm drenched sand and stared at the emptiness before him, trying to take it all in. Moments ago there was a great tribute to a young guy. Now there was nothing. Forbes walked all around the exact spot where the memorial once stood in a vain attempt to find the cross, to find some remnant of the love of Jimmy's family and friends. But he couldn't see anything. The hat, the CD case, the messages, even the beer bottles were gone. Everything was lost, either blown into the marshes or swept out into the bay. Nothing was left. Nothing.

David was giving up hope and was about to retreat back to the parking lot when something caught his eye. About forty feet from the where the cross had once stood, he saw something reflect the glare of the sun that was wedged amidst a large cluster of salt grass. It was the CD case. David knelt down and picked it up and by some sheer act of blind luck, Jimmy's photo and the ultrasound were still in the case. He brushed off the sand, put the case in his pocket and headed back to the parking lot.

His was the only car still there, the pickup having left right after David had walked out to where Jimmy had been stabbed three times in the chest by someone he knew and trusted. He started the Porsche, headed back up the rain soaked beach road and took a left on Route 645. It was time to see Cassie Thompkins.

# Chapter Fifteen

# Cassie Thompkins

As torrents of rain pounded their cadence into the metal roof of the porch on the back of her parent's trailer, Cassie pulled the old afghan she found in the closet around her shoulders, took a long drag off her cigarette and watched as the wind, from the same storm that had pulled Jimmy's cross from the sands of Haven Beach, formed small whitecaps on the flood waters that had invaded the salt marsh that bordered the backyard of her parents' home in the Perry area of Mathews County.

Cassie loved a storm. Ever since she was a little girl, she always liked to look out the window and watch them approach over the horizon, clouds all big and gray. The wind usually came first and then the rain. Lightning and thunder were her favorite parts. She found it exciting the way the sky would light up bright as day, especially at night, when a big bolt of lightning would strike and then she would wait for the rumble of the thunder.

Her grandfather had told her that if she counted the seconds between the lightning strike and the thunder blast, she could figure out how far away the lightning bolt was when it hit the ground. He said it was all about the speed of sound or something like that. She couldn't remember now what he told her, but she could remember as a little girl she would have her nose pressed to the glass and would count out loud the number of seconds after each bolt of lightning until she heard the roar of the thunder. She didn't know what it all meant but that was all right. She would just shout out the number of seconds and her grandfather would smile and say, "You done good, little scooter, you done good." 'Scooter' - that's what he called her. No one else did, and she hadn't been called that in many a day. Her grandfather passed when she was ten, and since then, she still counted the seconds after each bolt of lightning but now she kept the numbers to herself.

Cassie looked at the spent butt in her hand and cursed herself for smoking. She leaned over the side of the chair she was sitting in and crushed it out in an old sand filled Maxwell House coffee can that had been on the porch

143

for as long as she could remember. Both her mother and her step-father smoked, and she just fell into the habit right along with them. They objected at first but in her family, smoking seemed as natural as breathing, and in time the dissention went away and packs of cigarettes from the cartons she used to bring home from the convenience store were hers for the taking.

She'd been smoking since she was fifteen but now she was pregnant with Jimmy's baby and was trying so hard to quit. She placed one hand on her stomach and softly rubbed her womb as tears began to form in her eyes. She promised herself that one day she would stop crying but that day had yet to come and not one came and went yet where tears weren't part of her daily routine. Especially since she had quit the store. She loved working there, but she just couldn't take it anymore. The stares, the questions, the whispered comments behind her back. It was all just too much and when Coles Howard had told her he was paying off her Mustang and suggested that she stay home for a while after the funeral, she decided it was the thing to do. Besides, her mom and step-dad, who she called 'Tommy' didn't care. In fact, Tommy even encouraged it which was odd in a way given that he couldn't go five minutes without reminding Cassie and her momma who paid most of the bills around the house.

She also knew that Howard had spoken to Tommy right after Jimmy had been killed. He had come by the house and Tommy had told her to stay inside while the two men spoke beside Howard's pickup in the front driveway, each drinking a beer from the cooler in the garage that Tommy kept perpetually stocked with iced-down cans of Budweiser. Howard and Tommy had known each other for years, but were never beer drinking pals. Since Jimmy's death, though, they seemed to have gotten a bit more friendly and hardly a week went by without Howard driving down the long, rutted sand driveway to have a beer with Tommy and, she knew, to make sure Cassie knew he was keeping an eye on things. His message was clear, as was the talking to she got from the Sheriff after they found Jimmy's body at the beach. And they had to know she was pregnant. She had told her mom who in turn told Tommy, and she had no doubt that Tommy had told Howard. What a mess. She was so scared and so afraid that at times she thought her nerves would make her explode. She would shake so hard when she thought of that night on the beach with Jimmy. She was terrified about her baby's health as

144

there was no way all of this stress could be good for something so tiny like what she saw on the ultrasound.

She pulled the afghan even tighter around her shoulders and again began to cry, softly speaking Jimmy's name as tears rolled down her cheeks. She instinctively reached for the pack of cigarettes on the small weather-worn table next to the rocker but stopped short of her intended destination thinking not yet, not right now, maybe never again but she knew she wouldn't make it. She didn't have it in her to quit. Too much was going on right now. It was all too much.

The storm had dissipated, and she watched as the sun started to work its way through the clouds. A great blue heron had already staked out its territory at the edge of the marsh and was getting set to feed on the buffet of small minnows and crabs that the storm had left behind in its wake when the post-storm calm was disturbed by the barking of Tommy's hunting dogs which almost always meant that someone was coming up the driveway.

Cassie got up from the chair, and walked through the back door of the trailer. She took a quick peek into her parent's bedroom and saw that her mom was still sleeping and then walked to the living room and looked out the front screen door. Coming down the long, rutted sand lane to their home was a small silver car and Cassie knew instantly that it was the lawyer for Billups. She recognized the car from seeing him drive it around town. Being the new lawyer, he kinda stood out. He had also stopped into the store on a few occasions. He seemed friendly and all at the store but, seeing him now coming down the driveway, Cassie didn't know what to do.

Starting to shake again, she shut the door and looked out the blind to the one window in the small living room that faced the front yard and watched as the car pulled up next to her Mustang. The visitor got out, and, instead of walking immediately up the front steps to the porch, he walked slowly around the red convertible. Cassie could see that he was checking out her car which made her feel good in some small way that someone besides herself appreciated one of the very few things she had that was hers and hers alone. He then turned towards the trailer and Cassie ducked away from the window and leaned against the wall. She could hear his feet walk up the front steps of the porch and, although she knew it was coming, she still jumped when he knocked on the front door.

She was only several feet from where the lawyer stood on the porch but she made no move to open the door. He knocked a second time and Cassie still didn't move. "If I don't answer the door, he'll go away," was her thinking and it appeared to achieve some measure of success as she noticed that he didn't knock a third time.

But he didn't leave, either. Forbes was still there, walking back and forth on the front porch, his shoes making a soft shuffling sound on the salt treated two by sixes that composed the small wooden landing at the top of the steps to the trailer. Soon, however, the sound of his shoes stopped and Cassie figured the noise she'd hear next would be him walking down the steps and out to his car, but she was wrong.

"Cassie Thompkins!" said a loud voice from the other side of the door. "I'm David Forbes, I need to speak with you. I completely understand that you probably do not want to speak with me. If I was in your shoes, I would feel the same way. I also know that you know that I represent Jamal Billups who is charged with killing your boyfriend, Jimmy. And I take no offense if you hate me because of who I represent, but I do need to talk to you about what happened that night. Please believe me, I don't want to cause you to suffer anymore than you already have. I promise I won't take long. If you would please just give me ten minutes of your time, I'd be most grateful. It won't take any longer than that, I promise." David paused. The silence hung like sheets of lead in the air.

After a minute of no response from Cassie, he spoke again. "Look, I've got a pretty good idea that you're home and probably standing just on the other side of this door. You want to know how I know? That's one nice ride sitting out in the driveway. I used to see it all the time when you were working up at the store and I can tell you love it because I don't think I ever saw a speck of dirt on it. I'm a car guy myself and I notice that kind of thing and I'd bet good money that Cassie Thompkins doesn't go anywhere unless she's behind the wheel of that Mustang. Now, can we please talk? I won't take long, I promise. Besides, I'm starting to feel a little foolish talking to some door when I know there's a young lady standing just on the other side who has

146

something to tell me about what happened that night. Cassie, please open the door."

Cassie stood there with her eyes closed, still hoping he would leave. He sounded nice and genuine and there was a part of her that wanted to talk, and that was precisely what she was afraid of, that she would trust him, that she would tell him what happened and that was something she knew she could never do.

A minute passed when finally the lawyer spoke again. "Cassie, I'm going to leave my card on your front porch. You can call me if you change your mind. But I wanted to tell you that I know you're pregnant."

The comment ripped through Cassie like the flash of the lightning bolts she would count as a child.

David continued on. "I went to the beach this morning and saw the cross in the sand. I opened the CD case that had Jimmy's picture on the cover. I shouldn't have done it but I did and I'm sorry. I saw the ultrasound that you put in the case. This storm that just passed, I was at the beach when it hit. The cross got destroyed and all the stuff on it was gone when I went back to look. The only thing I could find after the storm was the CD case with Jimmy's photo and the ultrasound.  I kept it and I'm going to leave it here with my card. It's yours and you should have it. I know that you've been to that cross many times and probably cried your eyes out each time you went."

"I also know you're a whole lot lost right now," he continued."You have to be. You're pregnant and the child's father was murdered right out there on that beach. The date on the ultrasound puts your pregnancy right around the day of the murder. I know you and Jimmy had sex that night. The autopsy report said there was semen in his underwear. I know you told the sheriff that you and Jimmy drove straight here after the fight at the Get 'n Go. But you and I both know that's not completely true. After the fight, the two of you had sex somewhere, and I doubt it was out here in your parent's front yard. The autopsy also showed that Jimmy's body had a fairly high level of alcohol at the time he died. The sheriff's report says he only had a couple of beers at the Blue Crab before he came to pick you up at the store which tells me he drank some more sometime after the fight and before he was

147

murdered. The boys who found Jimmy at the beach claim that they saw a pair of shoes and some empty beer cans lying in close proximity to his body. Jimmy died with his shoes on. I'm willing to bet that those empty cans belonged to Jimmy. Now, I'm wondering if you might be able to tell me who the shoes belonged to?"

The question begged for the answer that Cassie knew she couldn't give. She closed her eyes even tighter as she remembered finding her shoes on the front porch after one of Howard's now frequent visits to have a beer with her step-father.

The lawyer spoke again. "Look, I know you didn't kill Jimmy but I think you have some idea who did and we both know it wasn't Jamal Billups. If you want, call the Sheriff and get his permission to talk to me, I don't care, but Cassie, please, we need to talk."

Moments passed and still facing a closed door, David felt like he had exhausted his best efforts and turned to walk down the steps when the door opened and Cassie Thompkins walked out on to the front porch. With one hand clutching the afghan, she ran the other through the long strands of blond hair that had stuck to her tear stained cheeks and said in her born and bred Chesapeake Bay accent "I don't need to call the Sheriff to get his permission to talk to you, I can talk to anyone I want."

"I know you can," David said, looking up at Cassie from where he stood on the steps leading down from the porch. "I didn't mean anything by that last statement. If it offended you, I apologize."

"It's okay. I know you didn't mean nothing by it. I guess I'm a little sensitive these days," Cassie said as she impulsively reached for the pack of cigarettes that never left the pocket of her jeans.

David held out his hand and said, "I'm David Forbes. I've already introduced myself to the door. It's nice to meet you in person."

Cassie smiled and took his hand and said, "I'm sorry for the way I acted. I'm just not used to all this and, uh, can you wait here a second? I'll be right back."

And in thirty seconds, she was true to her promise with a cigarette in hand from the pack she had left on the back porch. "I know I shouldn't be doing this, smoking I mean. I'm gonna quit. It's just hard right now," she said while taking a long drag.

David said nothing, took a few steps up towards the porch and reached over for the CD case that he had placed on the porch railing moments ago. "Here. This is yours. I'm sorry this is all I could find" he said as he handed her the small plastic case.

Cassie took it and looked down at the photo of Jimmy in the case while she spoke to David. "Look, I appreciate you coming out here and bringing this to me. It means a lot, it really does. And I know you're just trying to do your job, to help Jamal and all but I can't talk to you. I just can't. And you really shouldn't be here. Tommy should be home any time now and he's got a temper that's real bad. He's my step dad and he won't like it one bit that you're here."

David asked, "Why should he care if I just want to ask you a few questions, no harm in that, is it?"

Cassie took another drag off of her cigarette and looked up at Forbes. The tears were filling her eyes again, and David thought he saw something else besides loss and sadness on the face of Cassie Thompkins.

Fear.

She spoke again, "It's complicated. Tommy's become real good friends with the Howards. Coles is here a lot. I just can't talk to you and you really need to leave right now. Please."

David said, "Can't talk to me or won't talk to me? There's a difference I think."

"Mr. Forbes, please don't ask me any more questions. You just don't understand and you really need to go," she said when suddenly her attention was diverted as she looked straight over David's left shoulder and down the lane. Her prediction had come true.

149

Driving towards the trailer, through the soggy sand and the standing water in the old rutted driveway, came Tommy in his pickup. Dog-tired from his third shift stint at the mill, Cassie's step-father skidded to an abrupt halt beside his faded grey two car garage, jumped out of his truck and slammed the door to a F250 covered in light brown streaks of wet sand and mud.

Dressed in steel toe Redwing boots and grease stained Dickies overalls, the man covered his ground in long, angry strides as he made his way to the front steps of the porch where stood David Forbes.

"Who the fuck do you think you are?" were the first words out of his mouth.

David responded as calmly and diplomatically as he could. "I'm David Forbes. I'm an attorney. I just stopped by to ask your daughter a few questions, that's all." David reached into his shirt pocket, took out one of his business cards and reached out to hand it to Tommy when the man, tall, lanky and full of bad temper, suddenly grabbed David's card bearing arm with a vise-like grip and threw him off the steps of the front porch, slamming the lawyer back first on the crushed gray stone of the parking lot at the bottom of the steps.

Dazed and shocked by the unexpected attack, David rolled over to his side and managed to get to his hands and knees when he heard Cassie scream, "Tommy don't!" a plea which was ignored when her step-father unleashed a thunderous kick to David's ribcage that sent the lawyer back over on to his back, holding his chest and writhing in pain.

Forbes managed to look up and through eyes welded near shut from the pain rolling across his body like plow shares across soft soil, saw Tommy standing over him, his face contorted into a well-defined mask of rage and violence with both of his fists balled up tight for round three if it came to that.

David didn't move.

"You listen to me, asshole!" Tommy said, his beet red, unshaven face forming a frame of violence around coal black eyes filled with anger and hate.

"You don't need to tell me what your name is or what you do for a livin', you understand me? I know who you are! You're the lawyer for that nigger bastard who killed Jimmy! You got no business coming here, you got that? This is my land! I pay the bills around here. And I got two 'No Trespassing' signs out at the end of that there driveway. What's the matter? Can't you fuckin' read? You stay the hell off my property and stay the hell away from my daughter, or I will have you arrested and put in jail along with that nigger client of yours. Now get in your fancy, fuckin' car and get the fuck outta here!"

Cassie's step-father backed up and watched as David struggled to his feet, grimacing in pain and holding the side of his chest that bore the brunt of Tommy's boot. The fall to the ground didn't hurt him too bad but the assault to his chest was a different story altogether. The kick had been well-delivered, and Forbes knew several ribs had probably been fractured in the process. He wanted to make some sort of parting gesture to Cassie but thought the better of it, and, instead, he turned away and slowly, silently made his way to the car. David opened the driver's side door and slid carefully into the front seat of the Porsche, breathing in shallow gasps as each lungful of air sent knife-like pain screaming across his ribcage. As he left the house and drove up the rutted gravel path, he tried to keep Cassie in his rear view mirror as long as he could, but Tommy had her up the steps and inside the trailer before he even had the Porsche turned around in the driveway.

———————

Back inside the house, Tommy's foot found purchase for the second time that afternoon when he kicked in the door of the small, cramped room at the end of the hallway that served as Cassie's sleeping quarters in the old trailer. It was no bigger than a walk-in closet and Cassie had run there immediately after she got inside because she knew that she was going to get what she had seen her mother get so many times before.

As far as her step-father was concerned, talking to Forbes was an unforgiveable sin. Cassie had been repeatedly warned by him and the Sheriff not to talk to nobody about Jimmy and it wouldn't matter to Tommy how many times she told him that she didn't tell that lawyer nothing or how pregnant she was with Jimmy's baby, seeing Forbes on his front porch was enough evidence for Tommy that his step-daughter needed reminding that nobody meant nobody.

When the bedroom door blew off its hinges from the force of his boot, Cassie retreated across the top of an old worn futon that served as her bed until her movement was blocked by a wall covered in stacks of plastic storage containers that held whatever possessions she had in this world. Tommy straddled the futon and backhanded Cassie so hard that she spun a complete revolution and fell like a figure skater who had missed her landing in the corner of a world she despised.

Her head reverberated from the impact like the Claxton of a bell and she momentarily lost her vision, seeing only shadows of movement in shades of black and gray, while her ears tried to sort out the screaming and yelling that had suddenly doubled in its intensity and which was so loud that it seemed to permeate every pore of her skin.

Cassie focused hard on regaining her senses and saw that her mother had emerged from her own room and had her arms around Tommy's neck and was pulling him out of Cassie's bedroom and into the narrow hallway that separated her own hell from that of her daughter's. Cassie's mother was an alcoholic and apparently Tommy's screaming mixed with the vibration of the trailer from the impact of Cassie's body against her bedroom wall was enough to awake the woman from the effects of her nightly routine of drinking enough cheap box wine fortified with generous doses of Aristocrat vodka until she could forget who she was and who she lived with. It usually took a lot for her mother to get where she needed to be and on most nights, she drank to where she would pass out and Cassie had to carry her to an empty bedroom while Tommy did similar damage to himself out in the garage, drinking endless cans of beer to all hours of the night.

For Cassie, it was the same thing every day and every night. Hell from a bottle at the end of a rutted old driveway. Jimmy was supposed to be her way out but now he was gone and Cassie watched as Tommy turned and pushed her mom down the hallway, both arms flailing away as he repeatedly slapped her, yelling and screaming all the while. She was a veteran of this war. She knew her enemy. She didn't move or say a word as the blows came. She simply let him hit, again and again, until the blows stopped coming.

And then she stood up, as she has done so many times before, removed the gown she was wearing and walked naked down the remainder of the hallway, disappearing into bedroom while her husband walked lockstep in close pursuit. She always rationalized that it would keep him from hitting her further, and it would keep him away from Cassie. And it seemed to work, or so she thought as this toxic mix of abuse, acceptance and submission did indeed calm the waters, leaving a stoic peace of sorts in its wake that was an acceptable bargain to Cassie's mother. Afterwards, Tommy would always exit the trailer for the drunken solitude of the garage, and she would be left alone to bathe in the warmth of her wine and vodka.

Cassie got up off the futon, walked down the hallway and picked up her mother's gown off the floor. Tossing it on the small couch in the living room, she then grabbed her keys off the kitchen table and ran down the porch steps to her beloved Mustang.

On far too many occasions as a young girl, she had to stay in the house and listen through the paper thin walls of the old trailer as her step-father received his sexual reward for keeping short the beatings he was inflicting on her mother. But no more, now she could fly like the wind and fly she did. With the top down, she drove for over an hour, letting the wind dry her tears and clear her head from the nightmare of her afternoon. She saw a corner of the subpoena poking out from the cars console where she had stuffed it the week before when Sheriff Howard had brought it by the house. The preliminary hearing was on Monday.

"Just keep things simple, Cassie, and you and that precious baby of yours will do just fine," was what he'd said when he handed her the paper. "Keep things simple, my ass," she thought. What he wanted her to do was lie like hell and lie she would cause right now she had no choice. But one day the lying was gonna stop and she, her baby and her mother, if she could convince her to leave, would be gone from here. Far, far away from all of this. She would get help for her momma and raise her baby like Jimmy would want her to.

Cassie parked the car at Haven Beach and could see that the storm had done its work just like the lawyer said. The fact that the cross was gone struck her in an odd way, one that she didn't expect. It was like Jimmy himself

153

had sent her a message, telling her to move on, or even more so, and that was to do what's right.

She stared off into the steel blue skies over the Chesapeake Bay and with her hands firmly gripped on the steering wheel, she promised herself that one day, she would do exactly that. She took one last look at the spot where she and Jimmy had made love that night, the same spot where he was killed moments later and tightened her grip on the wheel. "So help me God, those bastards are going to pay," she said aloud to the audience of sand, sea and wind that blew softly down the beach. "So help me, God."

She then roared out of the parking lot. Back to the trailer she would have to go, but her days there were numbered, she promised herself, Jimmy and their child. And as she drove back to the hell that lay at the end of that rutted sand road, she knew that it was a promise she was going to keep.

# Chapter Sixteen

# The Preliminary Hearing (part one)

Three days after his encounter with Tommy's boot, David's ribs still burned with pain and he grimaced slightly as he gathered up his files and walked the three blocks to the courthouse for the preliminary hearing in the Billups murder case.

The purpose of a preliminary hearing was to determine whether there was evidence rising to a level sufficient to find probable cause that Jamal Billups had murdered Jimmy Jarvis as charged in the warrant. Most of the time, these hearings were more of a formality than anything else and Forbes knew, as he walked to the courthouse that Tuesday morning, that Judge Mumford would find the evidence sufficient to certify the case to the Mathews County Grand Jury who would then, undoubtedly, return an indictment against his client.

Jamal would not be testifying on this day, but David had gone to see him in the jail and had briefed him as to what he could expect during the hearing. His client was no longer using crutches to get around but had become despondent and seemed resigned to the fact that he was going to be convicted and spend the rest of his life in prison for a crime he still denied having committed.

As he approached the courthouse green, Forbes could see that the case had predictably gathered more than the usual attention given to the court's criminal docket. Around the court entrance, numerous townspeople were milling about, a few of whom were David's old tablemates from his previous life as a breakfast customer at Patty's Diner. However, the vast majority of these onlookers were not realtors or bankers. They were, instead, men of tanned, leathery skin and worn calloused hands. Shod in their white rubber boots, standing tall as one in the hot morning sun, stood the watermen of the Chesapeake Bay.

Once inside the courthouse, Forbes found that there was an equal number of people in the lobby and he had to weave his way to the courtroom doors which he found guarded by Deputy Matt Robins.

"Mr. Forbes, how are you today, Sir?" said the hulking young deputy.

"I'm fine Deputy. Are we open for court today?" David said with a smile.

"We are but the Judge ain't on the bench yet. It should only be a few minutes more. You need to see your client before things get started?"

"No. I met with him yesterday and he's as prepped as he needs to be for this sort of thing. By the way, I read the reports you prepared in this case and you do good investigative work. In my former career, I handled a lot of cases with the FBI. They could use a good investigator like you. If you ever need a reference, you just let me know."

Robins' large face flushed like a cherub at the compliment and he thanked David profusely for his offer.

The lawyer spoke again. "I was really impressed with the detail level of your report, particularly the observations by the two kids that some beer cans and a pair of shoes were found near the body. Funny thing that they didn't show up in any of the crime scene pictures. What do you make of that?" David asked, all the while focused like a laser beam on Robins' face, on guard for the reaction he hoped would come.

It did. Robins tried to hide his reaction to the lawyer's inquiry but poker wasn't his game and his face quickly became an anxious mask of hidden honesty and knowledge unrevealed. Robins stumbled in his response and was saying something along the lines that kids probably didn't remember things right when a rescue of sorts appeared in the form of the court clerk who opened the door from the inside and whispered to the clearly nervous deputy that the judge would be on the bench in about five minutes and that he could start letting folks into the courtroom.

Robins averted his gaze from Forbes who knew that he had just gotten all he was going to get from this Deputy who quickly busied himself with his bailiff duties.

David approached the clerk and, after making sure that the Billups' matter was the only case scheduled for the afternoon docket, took sole occupancy at the defense counsel table and started to arrange his papers for the impending hearing. Judging by the number of witness subpoenas that had been issued by the Commonwealth's Attorney, David figured that Archie Hudgins would call no more than four people to testify, them being Sheriff Howard, Doc Lawson, Cassie Thompkins and one of the witnesses to the fight at the Get 'n Go.

At this stage in the game, the prosecutor clearly held the upper hand and David didn't expect a lengthy case since the Commonwealth needed only to show a sketch case for the Court to find probable cause.

His trial materials in order, David spun around in his chair and observed the crowd that was gathering in the courtroom. Not unlike the First African Assembly of God, the courtroom was designed with two rows of wooden benches divided by an aisle in the middle down which now walked Archie Hudgins, files in hand, with Sheriff Howard at his elbow. Forbes walked over to his adversary for the obligatory handshake and then walked back to his counsel table, stopping briefly to talk to Sherry Wilton, the reporter for the local weekly whose office was directly behind his and who enjoyed a beautiful view of the old courthouse green. David liked Sherry. Always friendly, she covered everything from garden club bake sales to supervisor meetings and was clearly enjoying the opportunity to report on something with a little more meat on the bone.

"Got your pencil and paper ready to go?" he asked.

"Ready and rarin' to go," she replied with smile.

"Make me look good now," he said good naturedly in a conspiratorial whisper.

"Now, how could I ever do anything but make you look good?" she said with another smile and a wink.

David returned a smile and started to turn his attention back to his papers when the figure of Coles Howard standing in the back of the capacity courtroom crowd caught his eye. The two men briefly made eye contact until David heard the telltale knocking on the door to the judge's chambers that signaled the arrival of Judge Mumford.

"All rise!" came the command from Lt. Jake Carter who had positioned himself directly beside the clerk who was seated to the left of the judge.

"The Mathews County General District Court is now in session, the Honorable Buford R. Mumford, presiding. All persons having motions to make, pleas to enter and suits to prosecute come forward and you shall be heard. God save the Commonwealth and this Honorable Court. There will be no talking while court is in session. You may be seated."

And upon that command, Judge Mumford took his seat in a high-backed leather chair as did the persons in the courtroom, and after the shuffling of feet and the rustling of clothing had finished, the old jurist cleared his throat, swore in the court reporter and began the case.

"Madam Clerk, it appears that we only have one matter on the afternoon docket and that's the case of *Commonwealth v. Jamal Billups*. I see that Mr. Hudgins and Mr. Forbes are both present at counsel table, so I'm assuming that both the prosecution and the defense are prepared to go forward today, is that correct, Mr. Hudgins?"

"Yes sir."

"And for you Mr. Forbes, are you and your client prepared to go forward to today?"

"Yes sir, we are."

"All right, I'm assuming that there are no motions for a continuance. Are there any other motions or other matters that the court needs to take up before we bring in the accused and begin with the presentation of the evidence?

"No sir," said both attorneys in near unison.

"Fine, then, ah, Lt. Carter would you please bring in Mr. Billups and seat him beside his attorney."

Carter nodded affirmatively to the judge, and then made similar motion with his head to two deputies standing next to a secured door on the other side of the courtroom. One of the deputies spoke briefly into a small microphone attached to his duty shirt and within seconds, the door opened revealing a light grey concrete block wall that served as the backdrop for the shackled figure of Jamal Billups.

Wearing an orange jumpsuit, Jamal walked into the courtroom with cuffs on his hands, cuffs on his feet with a chain joining the two that jingled with a steady cadence as he shuffled from the doorway towards his attorney's table with both arms firmly in the grasp of the two Deputies.

In David's opinion, Jamal's despondency had gotten worse and he looked, and acted, like a man who had given up hope. His braided hair had been shorn off since their initial interview and he sat at counsel table with his hands folded in his lap, his dark, sad eyes staring into the crevasse between his knees.

Jamal's arrival into the courtroom caused a brief murmur to erupt from the onlookers in the gallery and Judge Mumford banged his gavel and exclaimed, "The bailiff just said there will be no talking while court is in session and the court is in session. I am clearly aware that this case has folks a little excited and I understand that but the next person who talks during this hearing is getting escorted out by the bailiff and I mean it." He finished with a menacing glare directed at the folks in the gallery and then addressed the attorneys.

"Now that we have Mr. Billups in the courtroom can we proceed? Mr. Hudgins, do you need to make an opening statement or can we just get right to the evidence?"

The prosecutor, having just heard the not so thinly veiled preferences of the Judge, declined to make an opening statement as did David who had no intention of making one anyway. For the most part, this was the prosecutors show and Judge Mumford just made it perfectly clear that he expected an expedient presentation of the case.

"Alright then, call your witnesses to be sworn. Mr. Forbes, I don't expect you'll be putting on any evidence, is the Court correct in that assumption?"

"The Court is correct, sir."

Judge Mumford looked over at the witnesses that had been led to the front of the courtroom by a one of the bailiffs and prepared to administer the oath. As predicted, there was Doc Lawson, Sheriff Howard, Cassie Thompkins and a man that from the witness subpoena on file from the clerk's office, David took to be Jason Callis who was at the Get' n Go.

"Now, everyone who's gonna testify, raise your right hand. Y'all swear to tell the truth, the whole truth and nothing but the truth, so help you God?"

After all the witnesses noted their duty to follow the court's oath, Judge Mumford ordered the witnesses to go out into the hallway and not talk about the case until they were called to testify. As the four were led to the back of the courtroom by one of the deputies, Billups whispered to David, "I'm scared, man. What the fuck are all these people doin' here? This is like some lynching getting ready to happen or somethin'. Man, this is fucked up."

David put his hand on his client's shoulder and tried to assure him that the hearing was not going to last long and that soon he was going to be back in his cell, but all he received for his assurances was a mumbled "I don't know, man" in response from his client.

Forbes paused for a moment, reached into his briefcase, pulled out a legal pad and a pen, slid them across the counsel table to his client and said, "Here, listen to what these folks say and take some notes. You can help me and help yourself."

But, Jamal didn't look up. He just shook his head, picked up the pen and started doodling on the empty sheet of paper.

"Ok. Mr. Hudgins," Judge Mumford, said, "Call your first witness."

"Your Honor, the Commonwealth calls Jason Callis."

The witness, who appeared to be a young man in his early twenties, walked into the courtroom and took a seat in the witness stand to the right of the judge.

Archie Hudgins began his direct examination. "All right son, tell the court your full name."

"Jason Michael Callis."

"And how old are you and where do you live?"

"I'm twenty-four and I live with my parents next door to your mother's house in Cobb's Creek."

The prosecutor cleared his throat and then asked the young man what he did for a living to which he responded that he had graduated last year from the Apprentice School at the Newport News Shipyard and worked there as an engineering associate.

"Did you know Jimmy Jarvis?"

"I did. I've known him my entire life. We grew up together and played football together in high school. My girlfriend and I used to double date all the time with him and Cassie. We fished together, hunted together, and worked in the volunteer fire department together. We did everything together until that son-of-a-bitch over there killed him!"

Callis' comment brought murmurs of agreement from the crowd and David was out of his seat objecting at the very same time Mumford's gavel was hammering down fast and hard on the small round wooden gavel rest that protected the surface of the bench from calls to order that required some attention getting from the old Judge.

161

"Young man," the judge scolded, "Not another word like that in this courtroom, you understand me? Or else you'll spend some time back in the holding cell until you learn what and what not to say in a court of law. Am I clear?"

"Yes, sir," responded the witness who was staring bullet holes through the head of Jamal Billups who, in turn, said to Forbes in a low voice, "I told you man. You don't know these folks, I do. I'll never make it, that's for damn sure."

The prosecutor continued on with his questions. "Now Mr. Callis, where were you at approximately 12:30 am on Saturday, May 12, 2007?"

"I was on my way home from eatin' crabs over at my cousin's house when I got a call on the scanner that Jimmy was getting attacked by Billups over at the store."

David rose from his seat. "Judge, I'm going to object to the answer given by the witness as to his characterization of the facts per the call on scanner. First, the call itself is hearsay and second, his answer is a characterization of the facts received over the call and not an exact recitation of the call itself, which is inadmissible anyway. That's my objection."

Archie Hudgins rose to give his response but was waved back into his chair by Judge Mumford. "Mr. Forbes, The witness is just trying to tell us why he went to the store, that's all. I'm sure we'll all hear more evidence about what exactly took place that night. Your objection is overruled. Let's move on, can we?"

As David retook his seat, Jamal, with pen in hand muttered under his breath, "They don't like you either and don't you forget that."

Hudgins continued with his direct examination.

"Tell us what happened after you heard the call on the scanner."

"I went to the store, pulled into the parking lot and saw Jimmy on top of him," he said pointing to Billups. "They were on the sidewalk right in front of the door, fighting. Both of em' were throwing punches at each other.

Jimmy's nose and lip looked like they were bleeding pretty bad and Jamal had blood all over his shirt."

"What happened next?"

"Well, two of our friends that also had scanners in their truck got to the store at about the same time and we all then jumped out and ran over to the fight. We got about ten feet away, when he," pointing again over at Billups, "pulled out a knife and put it at Jimmy's throat. He told us that if we came any closer, that he'd cut him. He was all wild-eyed and stuff and we froze 'cause we believed him. He got up and made Jimmy get up and they backed away from the front of the store and towards that side that was next to the woods. I could hear Jimmy begging him not to cut him. Once he got around to the other side, he pushed Jimmy down and took off running into the trees. We tried to follow him but there was no way we'd ever catch him. We came back to the store and waited with Cassie until the Sheriff arrived. That's about all I know."

"That's all the questions I have of this witness, Judge."

"All right, Mr. Forbes, your witness."

David stood up and approached the podium located between the counsel tables.

"Thank you Judge. Mr. Callis, you've known Jimmy all your life, correct?"

"Yeah, that's right," said the witness, now fidgeting in his chair and clearly not comfortable with being cross-examined by the lawyer representing the man charged with murdering his best friend.

"You guys played football together, correct?"

"Yes sir."

"And I believe you played on the same team that made it to the finals of the state championship, correct?"

"Yes, sir."

"That's quite an accomplishment for you and Jimmy. I didn't know Jimmy but I heard he was quite an athlete."

"He was. Best linebacker in the state as far as I was concerned."

"And, I assume, still very strong and very fast, even a couple of years after his playing days were over, true?"

"Yes, sir. We still lifted weights together a couple of times a week. He was in great shape."

"Jimmy was on top of Jamal when you first arrived at the store that night, true?"

"Yes, sir"

"And when you first arrived, you didn't see Jamal with a knife in his hand or a weapon of any sort, now did you?"

"No, sir."

"In fact, from what you could see, the two were engaged in a fist fight, without any weapons involved whatsoever until you and your friends pulled into the parking lot that night. Isn't that correct?"

"Yeah, I guess so."

"Now, when you and your friends got out of your trucks, what were you going to do?"

"Break up the fight. Help Jimmy."

"Okay, that's understandable. Now, by breaking up the fight, how were you three going to do this? I'm assuming that you guys were going to pull the two men apart, something like that?"

"Yeah, something like that."

"You and your friends weren't going to attack Mr. Billups in the process now were you?"

"No, sir, not unless he attacked me first."

"Did my client ever attempt to attack you or one of your friends that night?"

"No."

"Then can you tell us why you grabbed a baseball bat out of your truck and carried it with you as you approached the storefront?"

"Personal protection, that's all."

"You weren't going to use it on Mr. Billups in order to help Jimmy were you?"

"Not less I needed to, I guess."

"Did you think you needed it given that you had four guys against one guy. Seems like you guys had the upper hand by a long shot at that point."

"Never know. I was just being careful, that's all."

"Fact of the matter is that Mr. Billups didn't pull out that knife until you walked over carrying the baseball bat you took out of your truck, isn't that right?"

"Maybe. I don't know. It was dark out."

"True. But the fistfight was taking place right outside the front door. Plenty of light out there to see what was going on, wasn't it?"

"Maybe."

"But the first time you saw a knife that night was when Jamal told you not to come any closer, true?"

"Or he'd cut Jimmy. Yeah that's true."

"But he never cut Jimmy did he?"

"Not then but later he for damn sure did."

"You believe that Jamal Billups killed Jimmy, don't you?"

"I sure do. He done it. No doubt about it."

"No doubt in your mind."

"None."

"Again, you've known Jimmy all your life."

"Yep"

"Have you ever heard him say anything about bad blood between him and the defendant?"

"No. I can't say that I have."

"Any prior fights between the two that you're aware of?"

"Not that I know of."

"As Jimmy's best friend, are you cognizant today of any reason whatsoever that Jamal Billups would want to kill Jimmy other than because of the fight that night at the store?"

"No."

"You've told us how you and Jimmy hunted together, played football together, still lifted weights together and how he was still in as good a shape as he was back in his playing days. Have I summarized your previous testimony correctly?"

"Yeah."

"Then I have one last question for you Mr. Callis."

"Ok."

"How is it that a former all state linebacker who's still in excellent condition gets stabbed to death by a five foot, nine inch tall drunk black man in the middle of a wide open beach where's there more room to run then he ever had on a football field? Doesn't make any sense to me. Does it make sense to you, Mr. Callis?"

The witness didn't have time to answer as Archie Hudgins' objection to the question was quickly sustained by Judge Mumford who sent a quick and not so subtle glare over at Jamal's attorney.

After David advised that he had no further questions for the witness, Callis was excused from the witness stand. Forbes then glanced around the courtroom and saw Karen standing near the doors at the back of the courtroom. As husbands and wives can often do, they sent their love to each other without saying a word. David smiled and turned his attention back to his papers spread out on the table in the courtroom. "She never comes to these things but she came to this one," he thought to himself. "Crazy how things work sometimes."

Jamal was looking at his lawyer and said in a low voice, "What the hell are you smiling about? Nothing funny about this shit. That cracker lied his ass off. He had that bat in his hand because he was going to beat my head in. Lying fool. You had him on the beach thing, though. Is that why you're smiling?"

"No," David answered. "My wife's in the back of the courtroom. Seeing her here made me feel good, that's all."

"She come to see the nigger get hung, too, huh?"

"Yep," David replied sarcastically. "She even brought a picnic basket with fried chicken, potato salad, green beans and lemonade. Everything we white folks like to eat and drink at a colored man's hanging."

"Sorry man," Jamal said, regretting the comment. "Didn't mean nothin' by it."

"I know," Forbes said, "Neither did I. Now, let's get focused for round two."

167

# Chapter Seventeen

## The Preliminary Hearing (part two)

"Your Honor, the prosecution calls Dr. Robert Lawson as our next witness."

In less than thirty seconds after one of the bailiffs whispered into his microphone, Doc Lawson walked through the rear doors to the courtroom and strode directly to the witness stand. He was acquainted with the layout of the courtroom, having testified on many an occasion in his years of practice although he couldn't recall whether he had ever done so to such an audience as rapt as this one appeared to be.

On this day, he wore pressed tan khakis, a pair of coffee brown Rockport tassel loafers, a dark blue blazer, a white oxford shirt and a tie adorned with alternating stripes of the navy blue and orange of his beloved University of Virginia. He carried a thin manila file that presumably held what medical information he had on Jimmy Jarvis.

Once the physician was seated, Archie Hudgins asked his first question.

"Would you please tell us your full name?"

"Dr. Robert Allen Lawson."

"And what is the nature of your employment, sir?"

Judge Mumford interjected, "For Christ's sake, Mr. Hudgins, we all know who Doc Lawson is and what he does for a living. Just get to what he knows about this case and forget about all this "what he does for a livin'" business. You got any problem with that Mr. Forbes?"

David stood up. "Not one bit, your Honor. Sounds great to me."

The lawyer smiled to himself as he sat back down. Big city attorneys just don't know what they're missing. The pile of bucks at the end of the day may be stacked a little higher but the practice of law just doesn't get any better than this.

As Forbes settled in his seat, he looked over at Jamal who was doodling away on his legal pad. He was drawing something and David leaned over slightly to get a better view and saw that it was a small ship with masts and sails. Waves and simple caricatures of seagulls rounded out the scene. The drawing was childlike, but there was talent there, crude but present nevertheless. David refocused his attention as Archie Hudgins moved on to his next question.

"Dr. Lawson, Jimmy Jarvis was a patient of yours is that correct?"

"Yes, sir. I've been his doctor since he was born. I've known him his entire life."

"On the morning of May 25th, 2007, did you have the occasion to see Jimmy Jarvis?"

"I did. A deputy had come to my home that morning and said that a body had been found at Haven Beach. He told me he had seen the body and that it was Jimmy Jarvis. I drove out there immediately and saw Jimmy's body lying in the sand."

"And what did you do once you arrived at the scene?"

"Well, it was clear to me that Jimmy was deceased, but I still checked his vitals as a matter of record. He was fully clothed in a shirt and a pair of shorts, both of which were covered in blood, mainly on the left side where I could see that he had apparently been stabbed at least three times."

"And where were these wounds exactly on his body?"

"Approximately four to five inches below the left armpit and about three inches to the left of his nipple."

"Were these wounds caused by a knife, in your opinion Dr. Lawson?"

"Well, that might be a question best answered by the Medical Examiner in Richmond, but since you asked it, my answer would be, yes. I've treated a number of knife wounds in my career and saw a bunch in the service. The wounds I saw on the body of Jimmy Jarvis that day were clearly caused by a knife of some sort. Not a doubt in my mind."

"Were the wounds of a sufficient degree of severity to cause death?"

"Yes sir, in my opinion. They were very close in proximity to the heart and lung. Probably one of the worst places for a man to get stabbed. They were lethal wounds."

"Based upon your examination, did you find any other cause as to the death of Mr. Jarvis other than the knife wounds you've just described to the court?"

"No sir. In my medical opinion, that's what killed Mr. Jarvis."

"Thank you, Doctor. I have no further questions, your Honor."

Judge Mumford rotated his chair in David's direction and said, "Okay, Mr. Forbes, your witness."

"Thank you, Judge. Dr. Lawson, Jimmy has been your patient since birth, correct?"

"Yes, sir, I've known the boy since he was an infant."

"Treat him on a regular basis?"

"I would best describe Jimmy as an infrequent patient. In other words, he came to see me when he had to, which isn't unusual since he was a young fellow without any health issues. Guys like Jimmy don't get regular checkups. I'd see him if he had the flu, or when he'd get injured playing football, stuff like that."

"When you examined Jimmy's body at the beach, did you notice any other wounds or injuries to his body that morning?"

"I did. His face was bruised up a bit and there was some degree of swelling around his mouth and eye, He also had two small lacerations, one to the right side of his nose and the other to his upper lip."

"I am assuming that you have received some information about this case from law enforcement that Jimmy had been in a fight with my client earlier that evening, is that true?"

"Yes, sir, that's correct. I commented on the facial injuries at the scene and Lt. Carter told me that, in fact, the two men had an altercation the night before in the parking lot at the Get n' Go prior to the stabbing at the beach."

"Were his facial injuries consistent with a fist fight?"

"I would say so. They were the typical stuff you see after a fistfight. Like I said, small lacerations to the lip and nose area, some facial swelling, that sort of thing."

"Would these facial injuries also cause Mr. Jarvis to have experienced a certain amount of bleeding?"

"Certainly. Busted noses and lips typically bleed profusely at first but they clot quickly. I would hasten to guess that Jimmy did lose some blood during his fight with your client but not much. And, if I may add, when I saw Mr. Jarvis at the beach that morning, there were no traces of blood on his face that I could see."

"Which would be consistent with him having cleaned up a bit after his fistfight with Mr. Billups at the store. Correct?"

"Correct, assuming that's what took place."

Forbes liked Doc Lawson more and more. He was quick on his feet and he wasn't going to be led down any blind alleys while testifying. David continued.

"Doc, when you first got to the beach that morning and saw Jimmy's body, who else was there besides you?"

"Sheriff Howard and Lt. Carter were standing next to Jimmy's body. Lt. Carter was taking pictures if I recall correctly. There were two other deputies present as well. They were standing in the parking lot and were marking off the area with yellow crime scene tape."

"Did you see Deputy Robins at the scene that morning?"

"I saw him that morning but not at the scene. He was the deputy who came to my house and told me about finding Jimmy's body at the beach."

David shifted the topic of his cross examination quickly.

"Doc, you had seen Jimmy in your office the day before his body was found at Haven Beach, correct?"

The physicians answer was a predictable "Yes," but for the first time David swore he saw Doc Lawson flinch on the witness stand. A subtle change at best but it occurred, nevertheless. For the briefest of moments, his expression flickered, his gaze slightly shifted, and his body position adjusted, all happening in the microseconds between the question asked and the answer given.

It was also the first question asked by David that the doctor didn't readily provide all the information that was going to be requested in the predictable cross-examination that was sure to follow.

"Doctor, why did Jimmy come to see you that day?"

Archie Hudgins was out of his chair. "Your Honor, I object. This is irrelevant testimony. We're here today about a murder case where the cause of death is as clear as day. What medical care this fine young man received one day, two days, three days or whenever before the day of this heinous killing has no bearing whatsoever on whether defense counsel's client murdered Jimmy Jarvis. Counsel is fishin' in the pond of the irrelevant and is wastin' the courts time in the process."

Judge Mumford took off his bifocals, rubbed his eyes and looked down at Forbes from the bench. "Mr. Forbes, as we all know, this is a serious case and I'm inclined to give you a certain amount of leeway here today in

173

cross-examining the witness for the prosecution, but where are we going with this line of testimony?"

"You Honor, the autopsy report and Dr. Lawson's own notes show that Jimmy had an injury to his upper arm which required medical treatment from the witness the day before he was killed. My questions to the witness will simply regard this one visit. I need to make sure that Jimmy wasn't involved in a prior physically violent encounter that may lead to a person other than my client having a motive to kill Mr. Jarvis. I promise I'll be brief in my line of examination. Couple of questions, that's all, Judge."

"All right, ask 'em and be quick about it."

"Why was Jimmy in your office that day?"

"Mr. Jarvis came in with a laceration about two inches long on his upper right arm. The skin was broken and there was some minor tissue damage. I sewed in a couple of stitches, applied some antibiotic ointment and gave him a tetanus shot. I put on a bandage and sent him on his way."

"Did he tell you how he came to be injured?"

"Yes, he did." Again, the physician flinched.

"And what did he tell you?"

"He told me he had gotten his arm caught between the dock line and the piling when he was tying up the boat he works on." Doc Lawson paused for a moment and then said, "The wound looked consistent with his version of events, if I may add."

"Mr. Forbes," said Judge Mumford, "has your curiosity as to this issue been satisfied by the witnesses' answers to your questions?"

David looked directly at Doc Lawson and said, "Yes, sir, it has."

"The court is so glad. Now do you have any questions for him or can he get back to his office? We only have one doctor around these parts and he needs to be doing other things than sitting in a courtroom all day."

174

"Judge, I have just a few more questions for Dr. Lawson. If I could have just a moment to review my notes, I might be close to wrapping this up."

"Take all the time you want Mr. Forbes. Justice is nothing if not patient," said the old Judge, casting stones of sarcasm amongst his words as he reached for his pitcher of water.

As David looked over his notes on his legal pad one more time, he couldn't help but again gaze over at Jamal who was still working on his sketch that now displayed an armada of small boats sailing across a yellow, legal pad sea.

It was then that something about Jamal hit him like the boot kick from Cassies step-father. His client was drawing with his left hand.

Forbes quickly scanned the police reports and noticed that the witnesses at the Get 'n Go all said Jamal had the knife in his left hand when he was holding it at Jimmy's throat. David looked over again at Jamal who was doodling away, oblivious to the wheels spinning inside the mind of his attorney. Given the location of the wounds, it would almost be impossible for them to be inflicted by a left-handed assailant.

The attorney reeled. "Could it really be this fucking simple?" he thought. He buried the thought away for the time being and focused on wrapping things up with Doc Lawson.

"Last question, Doc. While you were at the scene, you didn't happen to notice a pair of shoes and some beer cans lying in the vicinity of Jimmy's body, did you?."

"No, sir, I can't recollect that I did."

"Thank you. Judge, I have no further questions for this witness."

Judge Mumford swiveled back over in the prosecutor's direction. "Mr. Hudgins, I think we've gotten all we need to get out of Doc Lawson, can he be excused?"

"Yes, sir, he can. The prosecution has two remaining witnesses, Sheriff Howard and Cassie Thompkins."

"Fine. As I suspect that Sheriff Howard may be on the witness stand for some time, let's take a fifteen minute recess. Court is adjourned until 2:30 p.m. Counsel, may I see both of you back in chambers?"

"Yes, sir," said both attorneys as they walked past the bench and through the side door held open by one of the bailiffs.

---

"Grab a seat, Archie," the judge said. "You too, David. You don't mind if I call you David, do you? We usually drop down a rung or two on the ladder of formality back here. Helps to take the edge off things in the heat of battle, so to speak. Anybody care for some coffee, water, that sort of thing? Gail will be happy to get you some of either, if you care for any. Hell, if this doggone hearing were over and it was anywhere close to five, I'd be offering y'all some of Scotland's finest, but it's a little early in the game for that sort of thing."

Judge Mumford continued on, having settled himself into the chair behind his chamber's desk with his hands folded in front of him like a child saying grace.

"Now, David, you got yourself quite a case here. You're a good lawyer and all, but things are looking a bit tight for your client, if you know what I mean. I'm not going to be the judge that handles the actual trial. Y'all will be in the good hands of Judge Byrne when that time comes, but just on what I'm seeing and what I've read in the papers, it's murder one and life in the penitentiary for your client if a Mathews jury gets a hold of this case. Have you boys talked about a plea agreement? Spare the county some expense and all? I'm sure Archie would knock some time off, if your client would oblige us all by not putting everyone through this, if you know what I mean. You do know what I mean, don't you Mr. Forbes, I mean, er, David?"

"I do, sir." he replied.

176

"Well, that's a good start. Now then, it seems to me like you two men need to be doin' some talkin' and negotiatin'. After all, it's what we lawyers do, isn't it? Damn, I wish it were closer to five o'clock. With a little taste of that eighteen year old McCallan in my closet over there, we could resolve this case right here and right now. What do you say, gentlemen?"

"Can't do it, judge." David said.

"And why not, Mr. Forbes?" the judge exclaimed. "You know your client is as good as gone once those twelve jurors hear this case!"

"Because my client didn't kill Jimmy Jarvis," David said as he stood up. "He's an innocent man, and I'm going to prove it. Now if we're through, I'd like to get back to counsel table."

"You go do that, Mr. Forbes. We'll see you in the courtroom directly," said the judge, signaling to Forbes that the prosecutor was obliged to stay while David was obliged to make his exit from chambers.

# Chapter Eighteen

# The Preliminary Hearing (part three)

Once everyone had assembled back in the courtroom, Archie Hudgins turned towards the bailiff at the courtroom door and said, "Deputy, ask Sheriff Howard to come in please."

As with Doc Lawson, Howard was through the door quickly and approached the stand like he was McArthur retaking the Philippines.

Once settled in the witness chair, the Mathews County Sheriff wasted little time in securing control of the proceedings. He didn't even wait for a question. He just sat down, opened his file and spoke directly to the judge.

"Mornin' your Honor. On May the 25th of this year, I was having my breakfast up at Patty's when I got a call that a body had been found by one of our deputies over at Haven Beach. I got in my car and went immediately to that location. I was joined there by Lt. Carter and another deputy who secured the scene while the lieutenant and I conducted the investigation. The body was that of Jimmy Jarvis. I've known him since he was a kid. He was lying on his back and his chest area was covered in blood. He was clearly dead, but we called Doc Lawson to come over as a matter of protocol."

"With as little disturbance to the body as possible, I unbuttoned Jimmy's shirt and was able to see what looked like three knife wounds on the left side of his chest. That's where all the blood had come from. We then searched the surrounding area for any evidence of what was clearly a homicide. No weapon was found at the scene nor were we able to acquire any other evidence either from the beach area where Jimmy's body was located or from his truck which was parked in the parking lot. We checked it for prints and that sort of thing but nothing turned up. We did take photographs of where we found Jimmys body and of the truck and I've got a set of 'em right here if your Honor would like to see 'em."

Judge Mumford looked over at the prosecutor and said, "Mr. Hudgins, despite present appearances, the Sheriff is technically your witness. Are you movin' these photos into evidence?"

"We are, Judge. If they could be so marked as Commonwealth's Exhibit number one, I'd be most obliged."

"They are so marked as Commonwealth's Exhibit One. You may continue on Mr. Hudgins or Sheriff Howard, however it is that we're doing this today."

The prosecutor shrugged and Howard continued on.

"Your Honor, the night before Jimmy died, I received a 911 call that Jimmy and the defendant, the one sitting over there next to his lawyer, had been in a fight and that the defendant had pulled a knife on Jimmy and had threatened to kill him. Some boys from the Fire Department heard the call on their scanners and were able to get to the scene before me, but the defendant took off running through the woods and nobody could catch him. When I arrived, everyone was back inside the store and Miss Cassie, Cassie Thompkins that is, she's Jimmy's girlfriend, was cleaning some blood off of Jimmy's face with a towel. I talked to Jimmy and the witnesses and confirmed that Jamal Billups, the defendant, was, in fact, the other person involved in the fight."

"I am very familiar with the defendant and know his legal history as well. I know that he was born and raised in Mathews, doesn't have a driver's license, has a lot of local family and, by all accounts, was very intoxicated the night of his encounter with the victim. Seeing as the defendant wasn't much of a flight risk to leave the county and given the fact that it didn't seem like there was going to be any more trouble that night between the two, I told Jimmy to come see me on Monday, after the weekend, to fill out a report. When I left, it was just Cassie and Jimmy at the store and Cassie was locking things up for the night. That was the last time I saw Jimmy alive."

"Continue, Sheriff," Hudgins asked.

"After we found Jimmy's body at the beach, we assembled a tactical unit composed of deputies and state troopers at the intersection of Rt. 660 and East River Road where we knew the defendant had a number of relatives livin'. We had initiated and completed a search of several homes occupied by family members when we received information that led us to believe that the defendant may be hidin' out in one of the barns at Green Plains Farm over on the North River. Lt. Carter assembled a small group of men on four wheelers and they were able to flush the defendant from his hiding place and capture him before he was able to cause harm to any more of our citizens."

"When he was captured, the defendant had blood all over his shirt and we found a knife in his pants pocket that was covered in blood as well. We had 'em both tested at the lab. Blood matches were found for both Jimmy's blood and the blood of the defendant on the shirt of the decedent and on the knife. I had the knife analyzed and it was found to be a perfect match for the fatal wounds that killed Jimmy Jarvis. Got the lab results right here and got the shirt and knife in a bag over on Archie's desk," he said pointing over at the prosecutor who held aloft two clear plastic bags, both marked with yellow evidence stickers that clearly contained clothing and a knife of approximately five inches in length.

Archie Hudgins rose from his seat at counsel table. "Your honor, the Certificates of Analysis from the Division of Forensic Sciences up at the state capital have been duly filed at the Clerk's office and we provided copies to Mr. Forbes."

"You received the Certificates, Mr. Forbes?" the Judge asked.

"'I did, sir. No issues with the filings your Honor, but if I may have a moment, I would like to briefly examine the items in the bag. If your honor please, it will only take a minute."

After receiving a "Suit yourself, Mr. Forbes" from Judge Mumford, David walked over to the prosecutors table, picked up each bag and viewed the bloodied shirt of Jimmy Jarvis and the weapon that killed him, a stainless steel kitchen knife smeared with dried dark red blood from tip of blade to end of handle. Forbes held the bag with the knife aloft and examined it closely in the fluorescent glow that emanated from the ceiling lights of a courtroom that was now packed with onlookers. He returned the bags to the prosecutor's desk and sat down next to his client who immediately grabbed his arm and whispered urgently in his ear.

"That ain't my knife, man."

Forbes turned in his seat and looked at Billups, "Tell me that again?"

"That ain't my knife. No way, no how."

"How did it get your blood on it then?" David whispered back.

"You know damn well how it got there. Fuckin' Sheriff put it there. After one of his lynch mob put an arrow in my leg, there was enough of my blood pouring out of me to cover fifty knives. That ain't my knife, that's all I'm sayin'."

Billups shook his head and said, "Man, oh, man, they done got me set up right." He stopped talking and stomped his uninjured leg hard on the floor causing two of the deputies to move closer to counsel table.

David motioned them back with a quick 'he's all right' which in turn caused Judge Mumford to inquire, "Mr. Forbes, is there an issue with your client that needs to be addressed by the court?"

"No, sir, we're fine or rather, I mean, he's fine. We're ready to proceed." David turned away from Jamal and focused his attention back to the front of the courtroom when he caught the eye of Sheriff Howard who stared back with the look of a man who knew the content of the conversation the lawyer just had with his client.

"Mr Hudgins," Judge Mumford asked, "Do you have any more questions for the Sheriff or rather does he have anything else he'd care to add to this proceeding?"

"Several more questions, your Honor. Now, Sheriff, when and where was the knife in this bag found?"

"I found it myself in the right pocket of the cargo pants the defendant was wearing at the time he was captured at Green Plains. I searched him immediately upon my arrival at the premises and before he was taken out to the ambulance. I found the knife that is in that there bag. I removed it from his pocket and placed it in the bag where it is right now. It was covered in dried blood when I found it just like it is right now. I've never taken it out of the bag since. I transported it myself to the state lab and picked it up last week and it's been maintained in my evidence locker ever since, along with Jimmy's shirt that I packaged in a similar manner at the beach where he was murdered. Only one person has a key to the evidence locker and that person is me."

"Last question, Sheriff, did the defendant ever make any statement to you about this horrible crime?"

"No, sir. He was barely conscious when we removed him from Miss Dorothy's residence and never said a word all the way to the hospital in Gloucester. Once he was out of surgery, I went to go see him again at the hospital. He was awake when I approached, and I asked him if he would care to make a statement about what happened to Jimmy Jarvis."

"And what was his response?"

The sheriff said, "He told me to go fuck myself."

"He say anything else?"

"No that was it. I read him his Miranda rights and left his hospital room. Since then, neither I, nor any member of the Mathews County Sheriff's Office has had any contact with the defendant except to transport him for this hearing."

"I have no further questions for the Sheriff at this time."

"Your witness, Mr. Forbes," said Judge Mumford.

David rose from counsel table and approached the witness. "Sheriff, when you arrived at Green Plains exactly where did you first see the defendant?"

"He was lying on the floor of the foyer just inside the entrance way to the mansion at Green Plains."

"Anyone else in the foyer with my client at that time?"

"Yes, many people in fact. Several of Lt. Carter's men were there along with the team of deputies who accompanied me to the scene. Three or four state troopers showed up along with some rescue squad folks, as well. It got kinda crowded real quick."

"Was Ms. Hughes present, or rather Miss Dorothy as you previously referred to her?"

"She was there for a few minutes. I suggested that she wait outside while we finish up our business and she complied. I think she went out on the front steps but I'm not completely sure. I just know she left the immediate area as I requested."

"How soon after you arrived did you search my client and find this knife?"

"I searched the defendant immediately upon my arrival as per protocol. It was the first thing I did in order to make sure that the area was safe, that any evidence at the scene was not contaminated and so that the chain of custody did not become an issue. I found the knife during my search of the defendant's person just like I've already testified to."

"Who else saw you remove the knife from the defendant's pocket?"

"Everyone that was there, I suspect, but, then again I haven't had cause to make inquiry. Perhaps you can call them up here one at a time and ask them yourself. I will tell you that I immediately bagged the knife, removed it from the premises and locked it in the console of my police vehicle and then locked the car."

"Was Dep. Matt Robins the first officer on scene at Haven Beach?"

"No. Lt. Carter and I were the first officers on scene. Robins was the duty officer on patrol that morning and was only a mile or so from where the boys lived when the call came in. He went directly to their house and took the initial report from the two youngsters who found Jimmy's body at the beach.

He called it in and I instructed him to go get Doc Lawson immediately and drive him over to the scene."

"You've read his report I presume?"

"You presume right. I read all my deputies reports, counsel."

"Did you note the comments by the boys that they saw a pair of shoes and some beer cans near to where Jimmy's body was found?"

"I did and there was no evidence of that sort when Lt. Carter and I arrived at the scene."

"Did that strike you as somewhat odd that the boys would remember specific items such as these in their statements to Robins but that no evidence of their presence would be found by you or Lt. Carter?"

"No, sir, not at all. People leave things on the beach all the time. Sneakers, flip-flops, beer cans, chairs, hell, you name it. No shortage of that kind of stuff on the beaches around here, that's for sure. I have no doubt that the boys probably saw something, it just wasn't where they thought it was. Kids are like that. They get real excited and time and distance gets all screwed up, and I wasn't going to search five square miles of beach for something that had no bearing on this investigation. All I can say is that there were no such items found anywhere in the vicinity of the crime scene."

"Did you ever bring the boys back out to the beach to show you where they say they saw the shoes and the beer cans?"

"No, sir, I did not. Them kids been through enough that day and I wasn't going to put them through any more. Besides I was kinda busy with a manhunt at the time and I wasn't going to stop until that murderer next to you was captured and that's what I did."

"But the shoes and the cans may have some bearing on whether someone else was with Jimmy that night out on Haven Beach, true? Someone else who perhaps might be a witness to all of this?"

"Look Mr. Forbes, you can throw out all the theories you want. It wouldn't matter if the kids said the shoes and cans were a foot from Jimmy's body. All I can say is that nothing of that sort was there when Carter and I arrived at the scene and he and I got there damn quick. If I had found them, I would have bagged them as evidence. You can count on that, sir. I know my damn job."

Judge Mumford interrupted the cross examination. "Mr. Forbes, not to cut you off, but this is a preliminary hearing, not a trial with a jury in the box over there. And it seems to me that at this juncture, the Commonwealth has well met its burden. I mean we got cause of death by way of fatal knife wounds that appear to have been inflicted by the knife found on your client's person that was covered in the blood of both the decedent and your client, with the event of death occurring shortly after a fist fight between the defendant and the decedent during which your client held a knife at the throat of the decedent and threatened to cut him. You know. Ma Mumford used to always say that my brother was the smart one, but am I missing something here? I mean, unless you have something critical that the court needs to know, I think we've heard all we need to hear from this witness. Right now, you're sort of running down rabbit holes, sir."

The judge rested his case and the silence in the courtroom hovered around David like cold, damp fog. Forbes turned from his place of attack at the podium in front of the witness stand and walked back to counsel table. Billups was staring down at his notepad, the fleet of sailboats crossed out of existence by an angry pen welded in the hand of man for whom hope had truly become lost.

David turned to the bench and said, "I'm done, Judge. Thank you."

"Very good. Now, Mr. Hudgins, can this witness be excused?"

"Yes, sir he can and we have one more witness. That's Cassie Thompkins and she should only take a few minutes."

"All right, let's get her in here and get this over with."

# Chapter Nineteen

# The Preliminary Hearing (part four)

Cassie Thompkins crossed paths with Sheriff Howard as they changed places in the courtroom. She couldn't bring herself to look him in the eye but could feel the cold steel of his stare stabbing through her skull with all of the intensity of the thrusts of the knife that killed the father of her child. Her pregnancy was beginning to show and she placed one hand over her small, protruding abdomen as she walked slowly to the witness stand.

The prosecutor asked his first question. "Ma'am, please tell the court your full name and where you live?"

"My name is Cassie Lynn Tompkins, and I live with my parents over on Winter Harbor Road."

"Ms. Thompkins, I'm going to ask you some questions about the night that Jimmy died. I want to apologize in advance for any discomfort that this may cause you."

"Oh that's all right. I'm okay with it, I guess. I'm fine really. What do you want to know?" Cassie was clearly nervous and cast a quick eye over at David who returned a reassuring smile to a witness who was smart enough to know she had reason plenty to be scared.

"Did you see Jimmy the night before he was killed?"

"I did. He came by the store to see me. I was getting ready to close up for the night when Jamal came in and wanted to buy some beer. He was really drunk and it was after twelve, and I couldn't sell him any beer even if he wasn't drunk. I told him as much and he got real mad and threw a twelve-pack against the wall and beer and glass went everywhere. Jimmy showed up right when that happened and they commenced to fighting right out in front of the store. I called 911. Some of Jimmy's friends picked the call up on their scanners and showed up before the cops did. They jumped out of their trucks and started coming towards Jimmy and Jamal. Jason Callis had a baseball bat that I guess he grabbed from the back of his truck. I was still in the store when I saw Jamal get behind Jimmy with a knife and move towards the side of the store. I couldn't see anything after that. Next thing I saw was Jimmy walking back around to the front of the store. Jamal was gone. They said he ran off into the woods."

"Tell us what happened next?"

"Jimmy came into the store, and I got a fresh towel and cleaned him up. He had a split lip and his nose was busted up some. He was bleeding kinda bad but I got that to stop. Then Sheriff Howard showed up, asked a few questions and told Jimmy to come see him on Monday. Then the sheriff left and me and Jimmy went back to my place."

"What did you do there?"

"Nothing. We just sat in his truck in the driveway and talked for a while. I asked him if he wanted to do something, and he said he was tired from all the ruckus that night and just wanted to go home. I asked him if he wanted to come in for a while and he didn't want to do that, either. He and my step-dad don't get along so good. So he left. That's the last time I saw him alive."

David noticed that Cassie's answers to the prosecutor's questions were directed to some far off corner of the courtroom as she never once stared in his direction as she responded in a voice that was as divorced from emotion as her answers were from the truth.

"Do you know why he went to the beach after he left your house?"

"I have no idea," she said. "He probably just wanted to be alone for a while. Jimmy loved that beach. He grew up there. We went there all the time with our friends and . . . ."

And then the damn broke. Tears came flooding down Cassie's face as her steady tone gave way to uncontrollable sobbing. She was done trying to hold on. The bailiff came over with a box of tissues while Judge Mumford motioned to his clerk to take a few moments to console the witness.

During the brief stay in the proceedings, David stood up and gazed around the courtroom which was still packed with dozens of onlookers. Karen still occupied her seat at the rear of the courtroom. The couple exchanged raised eyebrows that signaled mutual agreement as to the intensity of the moment and Forbes was about to turn his attention back to the matters at hand when he noticed a familiar figure sitting close to his wife.

It was the old man he'd seen on the front porch across the creek from Harper's Marina, Walter Taylor. He hadn't seen him earlier and guessed that he had come in after the hearing had gotten underway. Then something strange happened. The old man smiled and David swore he was staring directly at him when he did it. Nothing wrong with that of course, but odd, kind of like the man himself.

Forbes turned back around when he heard Archie say, "Judge, I have no more questions for this witness," and handed Cassie Thompkins over to the defense for cross-examination. David grabbed the black leather portfolio that held his legal pad and approached the dark wood podium that stood before the witness stand.

With pen in hand and a courtroom full of muted anticipation, he looked into the eyes of Cassie Thompkins who this time stared not off into the neutrality of some far off part of the courtroom, but rather fixed her gaze squarely on the face of the lawyer who suffered in silence the beating he received three days ago at the hands of her step-father just as she also suffered in silence the truth as to who killed Jimmy Jarvis.

David opened the binder and the hand written examination points on the yellow pad leaped out at him like angry yellow jackets defending a disturbed nest as he prepared to ask his questions.

The semen in the decedent's underwear.

Her pregnancy and the ultrasound.

Howard's visits to her step-father after the murder.

The beer cans.

And the shoes found at the beach by the two boys. The shoes. They both knew they were her shoes. Left at the beach the night Jimmy was murdered. After they had made love. After she had seen him get repeatedly stabbed by someone she knew well and hated with every inch of her soul, well enough to obey every command she had received since, hated enough to never, ever forget.

The lawyer repeatedly clicked his ball point pen which sounded to him like cannon fire in the silence of the moment, and then looked up from his legal pad and stared back into the eyes of Cassie Thompkins who had not wavered in her gaze which was still directed solely at David Forbes.

The message from her look was clear and unequivocal. Wrapped in silence, she said in muted voice, "Ask me anything you want and I shall tell you the truth."

He paused and then began his cross-examination. But for all of the questions that needed to be asked, not one left the mouth of David Forbes that day in the Mathews Courthouse. Instead, in his mind, David asked Cassie each and every question that was jotted down before him in blue ink on pale yellow paper and though not a word passed between them in the courtroom that morning, she responded clearly and unequivocally, uttering cold, hard truth and telling him everything he needed to know about how the father of her child and man who was to be the savior from the hell of her daily existence was stabbed to death out on Haven Beach that night. And then they were done. Forbes closed his portfolio and secured his pen to the inside pocket of his suit coat. David knew that one day, Cassie Thompkins would tell her story in open court, but that day was not today.

"Your Honor, I have no questions for this witness," he said and returned to his seat beside Billups, who quickly whispered, "What the fuck you mean you got no questions for that chick. I got about ten thousand. She knows I didn't kill that boy. What the hell are you doing? You givin' up on me? Goddamn, I can see that right now. You're giving up on me. You ain't any better than any of these other crackers."

David whispered sternly back to his client, "I'm not giving up on anything. She wasn't going to tell the truth up there and you know it. At least, not yet. Now, you do your job and I'll do mine."

"Sure. You do your job and I'll do my job. Ok, fine. I got just one question. I know what you supposed to be doing but what's my job?"

"Keep drawing and stop whining. Think you can handle that?"

Billups didn't have time to respond as Archie Hudgins stood up and addressed the court.

"Your Honor, that concludes the Commonwealth's case. I don't believe Mr. Forbes intends to present any evidence. If that's correct, I move to certify the charge of murder in the first degree to the Mathews County Grand Jury for the return of an indictment against the defendant. I'll coordinate with Mr. Forbes on the setting of a trial date if your Honor, please."

Judge Mumford looked at Forbes and said, "You intend on puttin' on any evidence here today on behalf of your client?"

David responded, "No, sir. And we note no objection to the motion of the Commonwealth to certify. I'll concede that they have met their burden at this juncture."

"Very well," the old jurist said. "The charge is hereby certified to the Mathews County Grand Jury and this hearing is adjourned." Mumford brought his gavel down to emphasize the finality of the moment and exited through the door behind the bench, no doubt heading for the best Scotland had to offer.

Two deputies escorted Billups away from counsel table and through the side door back to the detention area. David shook the prosecutors hand and walked back through the throng of people that were going in the same direction when he saw Karen standing just outside the rear doors of the courtroom. As he headed her way, Forbes noted that Taylor was nowhere to be seen.

"Some hearing, huh" he asked as he gave his wife a brief peck on the cheek.

"You can say that again," Karen replied. "What happened up there with that Cassie Thompkins girl? The way you were preparing for this case last night, I thought you would have had her on the witness stand for an hour. But, no questions? What's up with that? Not your usual style."

David responded "Not the usual case, either. Just a decision I made trying to fit all the pieces together. I'll have my day in court with her again. She and I both know that. For a number of reasons that I can't get into right now, I think I made the right call up there. Time will tell."

"I hope so. By the way, what's on your docket for the rest of the day, counselor? Your wife has a reception to attend later this afternoon for a teacher who is retiring up at the high school. All the punch and cake you can eat and she would be very happy if her handsome attorney husband would go with her. It would give him an opportunity to meet some of the folks her wonderful wife works with so that they can see that he's a great guy and not some monster because he represents the most unpopular man in town. Think you can find some time in your busy day for little ol' me?" she said with a seductive wink that signaled the reward that would surely follow after the kids went to bed.

Being no fool, despite the opinions of perhaps many that day to the contrary, Forbes quickly said, "Absolutely." and agreed to meet at the high school in about an hour. After their goodbyes, David went to see one of the bailiffs and asked to see his client for a few moments before he was transported back to the jail.

––––––––––––

The attorney was escorted back to a small holding cell equipped with a stainless steel commode and a narrow concrete bench on which sat Billups who was secured by handcuffs, footcuffs and a waist chain that was padlocked to a metal u-bolt attached to the bench.

David waited until the solid steel door to the cell clanged shut and then turned to his client.

"What do you mean that knife isn't yours?"

"That's not my knife, man. I swear to God it ain't."

"Evidence says otherwise." Forbes responded matter of factly. "It's got your blood all over it and it's got Jarvis's blood all over it. Forensics says the blade pattern of the wounds found during the autopsy matches the blade of that knife within a reasonable degree of scientific certainty. And the Sheriff has testified that he took it out of your pocket when he searched you at Green Plains."

Billups blasted back, "Fuck the sheriff and fuck that reasonable scientific certainty bullshit. I don't give a damn how many lies that sheriff tells. That ain't my fuckin' knife!"

"Ok, settle down. Let's chat," David said assuming a more passive, reassuring tone. "Let's take this step by step. When you were captured at Green Plains, did you have a knife on you?"

"I did," Billups responded.

"Where did you have it on your person?"

"It was in the left pocket of my pants. I was wearin' cargos and I kept in the lower pocket," Jamal said

"How did you know you had the knife with you that day?"

"When I woke up that morning in the hay loft, I rolled over to look down at the floor of the barn. When I did, I could feel it in my pocket," he said.

"Once you began running from the barn to the house, did you ever throw it away or lose it to your knowledge?"

Billups looked up at David, "No way. I don't think it would've have fallen out of that pocket and I for damn sure didn't throw it away."

192

"Why didn't you throw it away?" Forbes asked.

"First of all, I had no reason to because I had no fuckin idea that Jimmy had been killed. Second, even if I had heard about it, I wasn't the one who did it and third, because it's a damn nice knife," responded Jamal.

"Damn nice knife?" David asked, raising his eyebrows.

"Stainless steel spring action Kershaw," Jamall said with a touch of pride. "Cool as they come. That piece of shit in that bag was some kitchen knife, probably came from the Sheriff's own house. His wife's probably wonderin' where the fuck it is right now. And a fixed blade at that. Who the fuck would walk around with something like that in their pocket?"

"You remember being searched by the Sheriff in the foyer at Green Plains?" David asked.

"No, sir." Jamal replied shaking his head. "Last thing I remember was an angel from above holding a rifle and drawing a bead on the head dude of the lynch mob who was about to shoot an arrow into my chest. I was some fucked up by that point. I don't remember shit after that."

"Let's talk about witnesses," David said. "Anybody you know ever see you with that 'cool as they come' knife you claim you had?"

"Hell no," Jamal said emphatically. "You don't go flashin' that kind of shit around unless you want to see it get ripped off, and people do that shit all the time. Brother gets all fucked up and next thing you know, he wakes up and half his shit is gone. Drugs, money, jewelry, a gun, cell phone, Ipod, picture of his mama. Shit, people don't care. Steal anything from anybody at any time. Can't trust no one and no one knew I had that knife."

"How long you had that knife?" David asked.

Oh, 'bout a year or so."

"I don't suppose you got a receipt lying around, do you?"

"Oh, sure. It's folded up all nice and neat and sittin' right next to my well-kept checkbook, and you know what they say about us black folks and our checkbooks. Sir."

David shook his head and looked down at Jamal. "My friend, this is not good. Your blood. His blood. Blade matches wound, a sheriff who will testify that he took it from your pocket and you don't have a single bit of evidence to present that the knife in that bag wasn't the knife you held at Jimmy's throat the night before he was killed other than your own testimony."

"And they ain't gonna believe me no how. We both know that. Am I right?" demanded Jamal.

"Maybe so, hard to say right now," responded his attorney.

"Hard to say, my ass. We both know it's true," Jamal said. "Hey, what about fingerprints, man, I mean, sir. I haven't heard anything about that kind of shit. If I held that knife, shouldn't there be one or two on there somewhere?"

"None found, so says the forensics lab in Richmond and they're one of the best in the country. We used to use them all of the time when I worked at Justice. Just blood smears. Lots of blood smears. Yours and his." David shook his head and then said, "By the way, I took notice that you're left handed."

"I am. So what? What's that got to do with anything?"

"Maybe nothing. But for a left-handed person to stab Jimmy where those wounds were located, they would almost have had to come at him from behind. On an open beach and given how strong Jimmy was, I doubt that could happen. Maybe one stab wound but not three. No way. The more likely scenario was an attack from the front and for that to happen, particularly when you take into account where the wounds were located, the killer would have to be someone who carried the knife in his right hand. And, Jimmy had to know the person, and trust him, to allow him to get that close. And we both know that person wasn't you."

"Cassie knows that, too. Doesn't she, sir?" His client asked.

194

"Yes sir, she does." David answered. "Of that I have little doubt."

Jamal said, "Ah, I was wonderin' if you'd do me a favor next time you get to talk to her?"

"Sure," David replied, thinking in his mind that if he did, it for damn sure wouldn't be at her home given the hospitality he received just a few days ago from her step-father's boot, "Name it."

Jamal paused for a moment and then said, "Please tell her I didn't mean all that shit I said to her in the store that night. I was just all fucked up and pissed off that I couldn't get no more beer. Cassie's always been nice to me and I been in her store on many a day when I didn't have no business buyin' more beer. She's told me to leave before and I just always left 'cause I knew I could always find someone to buy it for me. I don't know what happened that night. I guess I just lost it. I knows I drink too much but it's just what I do every day. Get my money from workin' some chicken-shit job and spend it all on beer and liquor. Hell, half the time, if I didn't have my Granny, I probably wouldn't even stop drinkin' to eat. She always makes something for me to eat 'cause she knows how I am."

Jamal stopped for a moment to hang his head and then continued to speak while he looked down at the floor of the holding cell. "Man, I wish to hell I'd been home with her that night. God knows I've wished it so many times since I been thrown in here. If I hadn't been out drinkin' and smashed that twelve pack against the wall that night, Jimmy and I wouldn't have commenced to fightin'. He'd probably still be alive and I wouldn't be in here."

"And sir?," Jamal asked, looking up at David with tears in his eyes as he jerked the chains on his hands and feet to emphasize how locked in he was, "This here shit is gettin' real old."

Forbes looked back at his client, "Jamal, I'm doing the best I can," he said as he stood up to leave. "All I can say is that the truth usually comes out in these cases. It's just sometimes hard to know exactly when that moment will be. But I'm not stopping until that moment is at hand, you can count on that. I gotta go. I'll talk to you later."

"You take care of yourself, lawyer man. And, ah, one more thing," Jamal said firmly to his attorney, "I need you alive if I'm ever gonna get out of here."

Puzzled by what his client just said, David looked over his shoulder as he was pressing the buzzer to be escorted back to the lobby of the courthouse. "Jamal, I'm not going anywhere. Why the 'need you alive' comment? That was a strange one."

Billups replied, "Cause I can tell by the way you been suckin' in your breath every time you stood up and every time you sat down in your chair that you got your ribs worked over real hard. Probably got a few of 'em broken. I can tell cause I knows how it is. Someone beat you up because you my lawyer. Am I right?"

Both men looked at each other in the cold dim light of a cell that smelled of concrete, stale urine and pine scented disinfectant.

"Yes," replied the attorney who said nothing more, nodded to the deputy who opened the door and walked down the detention area hallway, briefcase in hand, each step bringing a wince of pain and more importantly, an appreciation for the perceptiveness of the innocent man who was his client.

# Chapter Twenty

## The Championship Season

After David left the holding cell at the courthouse, he stopped by his office to check in with Brenda, and, once he had signed off on some letters and pleadings, he followed through on his promise to Karen and soon was wheeling his Porsche into a parking space marked "Visitors" that was next to the front entrance of the Mathews High School.

After checking in at the front office and receiving directions to the cafeteria where the reception was being held, David turned left out of the office door and walked down a hallway of polished hardwood floors that emanated a warm honey glow in the soft ambiance of the florescent lights embedded in the ceiling of the old school. The floors themselves were original equipment, part of the initial architecture that still remained from when the building was first constructed in 1939.

"They certainly keep things neat as a pin around here," he said to himself as he walked alone in a hallway empty of the usual traffic of students and teachers. It was the week before school began and no students were present, only teachers, administrators and support staff getting ready for the year ahead. The hard surface of the wood floors gave David some company, however, as he was accompanied by the sound of his heels echoing off walls lined with dark blue metal lockers that bore the markings of years of combat with the multitudes of students who, for nine months out of the year, called them home to textbooks, notebooks, laptops, backpacks, lunch bags and anything else they could cram in to the small enclosure before they slammed the doors shut, spun the combination locks and headed off for class, home, playing field or wherever.

Polished wood soon turned to well waxed linoleum and this, coupled with the sound of talking and laughter, told David that he had reached his destination. He found himself standing next to Karen in the cafeteria, holding a slice of yellow cake covered in white cream cheese icing that advised him in red lettering that he was about to eat the "Happ" from "Happy Retirement."

Turning down a dixie cup of cold lemonade, David opted instead for a bottle of water that he grabbed from an ice-filled cooler alongside a long table adorned with a pale green tablecloth that was covered with the rest of the cake, several gallons of ice cream, napkins, plastic forks and over a dozen brightly wrapped gifts and cards brought by the visiting teachers who extended best wishes to one of their own.

Karen and David made the rounds and in the space of about fifteen minutes he was introduced to most everyone present and if there was any animosity afoot about his representing the killer of Jimmy Jarvis, he certainly didn't sense it that day. Everyone was as kind and warm as they could possibly be and they all had something positive to say not only about Karen but also about their kids and that made him feel great. Their kind words affirmed once again his strong belief that leaving Washington was the right decision for a lot of excellent reasons, not the least of which was that it is hard to beat having your kids in a school system so small that all the teachers know who they are.

David was still at Karen's side when she became engrossed in a conversation with another teacher about standardized testing procedures. It all sounded Greek to him, and boring Greek at that, so David wondered off by himself and soon was standing, water bottle in hand, before a large framed photograph hanging on the cafeteria wall.

In big gold letters at the top of the photo were the words "1983 Virginia High School Group 'A' State Champions." Across the bottom of the photo ran small lines of text that spelled out the names of the forty-two young men seated in the picture, all wearing numbered football jerseys, and smiling broadly no doubt because of the large gold trophy that sat center stage between two of the largest of the team members who were seated on the bottom row of the gymnasium bleachers where the photo had been taken.

"That was quite a team we had back then," David heard someone say and he turned around to meet a tall man standing next to him who had short gray hair and wore blue jeans, cowboy boots, a moss-green chambray shirt and a dark brown suede blazer.

"I'm Mike Adams. They say I'm the superintendent in charge around here. But some days, well, I'm not so sure. That can be a pretty headstrong bunch over there at times," he said with an easy smile and a nod over his shoulder in the direction of the teachers and administrators who were still milling around the cake and the familiar green of the Gatorade drink cooler, no doubt borrowed from the athletic department, that still held an ample amount of lemonade to quench the thirst of the steady stream of well-wishers coming and going out of the cafeteria.

David responded with a firm handshake knowing that the man in front of him was Karen's boss and good impressions were the order of the day.

Adams quickly put him at ease. "You know, your wife is one of the best hires I've made in years. She is a true professional. Very well-respected by her peers and truly loved by her students. That's a combination you don't see every day. In other words, don't get any bright ideas about going anywhere. Your wife has a job here for as long as she wants it, and we hope that's for a very long time."

"I appreciate that Mike. She loves it here and so do our kids," David said.

"Well it shows, that's for sure," replied the superintendent.

Adams paused for a moment as he turned away from David and gazed at the team picture that had moments ago had drawn the lawyer's interest. The superintendent lowered his voice. "I heard about your car getting keyed and I've also heard some of the predictable racist crap that some folks just can't help themselves saying about Jimmy's murder. I knew Jimmy, of course, and taught him, too. I also taught your client although it wasn't much because he never came to class but that's neither here nor there. What's done is done, I suppose, although it's kind of hard to believe that Jamal would ever kill somebody. He just never struck me as that sort. In any event, it's funny how things and people for that matter don't change all that much here in Mathews. No matter where you go around here, there always seems to be a link to the past that's just hard to break."

Adams glanced over at David and added, "I know that because I've lived here all my life."

199

He continued, "Take this photograph, for example. As I'm sure you know, Jimmy played football here and his team almost won the state championship but a last minute field goal sent the trophy over to a team from Roanoke, and we had to ride the bus home with a second place finish as our reward. The 1983 team in this picture is the only state champion we've ever had and if you look at the boy holding the trophy on the right, you might see somebody you'll recognize."

David looked closely and the resemblance struck him immediately. Coles Howard at age 16 or so.

"Yep, I thought you might pick him out of the lineup," said Adams studying the change of expression on David's face.

"I understand you got acquainted with Coles over at Harper's Store. A.J Morgan is my uncle on my mother's side so I heard all about it. Coles is something, all right. He was something, too, on the football field. Played lineman on both sides of the ball. He never missed a down, was fast as a cat and could hit like a truck."

"From what I've seen of him," David responded, "he looks like he could slap on the pads right now and still do some damage out there on the field. He's one big guy."

Adams smiled, "Yeah, I guess he is, but I'll say this, as big and fast as he was, he wasn't a better player than his older brother."

"Older brother?" David inquired.

"Yeah, Donny Howard," Adams said. "He was a senior and Coles was a junior when this photo was taken. Donny didn't have his younger brother's size or speed but he brought a different skill set to the game when he ran out on to the field."

"Oh, yeah, and what was that" asked David.

Adams turned, looked at him and said, "Meanness. Pure and simple. Donny Howard didn't just hit a player to stop 'em, he hit to hurt 'em. Everytime. No doubt about it. I don't think Donny ever played in a game where somebody from the opposing team wasn't carted off the field with a broken something or the other. And that boy never blinked an eye, never helped a player up, and never willingly took a knee when a player went down on the other team. Had to threaten to take him out of the game," he concluded with motion towards the team photo.

"And which one is he?" David asked with a nod.

"Why he's the one sitting next to his brother," Adams said. "He's the other boy holding the trophy. Yep, there they sit. Donny and Coles. The Howard boys together in their moment of glory."

"I certainly know where Coles works," David responsded, "but how about Donny, what does he do for a living?"

"Donny?" Adams said rubbing his chin. "I haven't talked to him in years, but I keep in touch with his family. He went into law enforcement, same as his old man."

"Where does he work, do you know? David asked.

"I do. Last I heard he was working as an undercover narcotics investigator for the Baltimore City Police Department. Been doing it for years."

"Baltimore?" David said to himself more than in response to Adams.

"Yep. And with a profession that no doubt is well suited to his disposition. God help any drug dealer that crosses his path. Donny Howard with a badge and a gun would be a force to be reckoned with, that's for sure."

Adams checked his watch and said "Well, I've enjoyed our conversation but I best get back over to the cake table and join in the festivities. If I can ever be of any help to you or your family in any way, please let me know."

The two men shook hands and, once again, David was standing alone, facing the photograph but this time he was staring into the dark eyes of a high school football player holding on to a trophy won hard on the gridiron twenty four years ago and wondered what that young man knew now about a certain drug boat that recently went missing off the coast of Mathews and about another young football player named Jimmy Jarvis who got stabbed to death because he might well have known something about it, too.

David was still lost in his musings when Karen appeared at his elbow and whispered with a nudge, "What's a girl got to do to get a little attention around here? You're standing over here just staring at this old football picture. What's the big deal? Memories of your old playing days coming back to haunt you?"

"Something like that," he responded. "Sorry for straying from the crowd," he quickly added.

"That's all right. C'mon, let's say our goodbyes and get out of here. I know you've had a long day. I'll tell you what. How about dinner out tonight? Maybe some shrimp and barbeque at the Blue Crab, a cold beer or two? My treat. I'll round up the kids. Meet you there around five-ish?"

"Sounds perfect, maybe even better than perfect." he replied and as they started their exit from the cafeteria, David paused just briefly before he left the cafeteria to cast one more glance at the framed photo that had so held his attentions just moments before.

"Baltimore," he said once again to himself. "I've got to call Simon. He'll know who this guy is." David got a second nudge from his wife, "Stop that," she said.

"Stop what?" he asked, once again was surrounded by the echo of footsteps as they walked the polished wood of the long hallway that led to the front entrance of the school.

"You know what I mean," Karen said. "Stop drifting way. I can see it in your eyes. Something's going on in that head of yours, I know it. You've got that look like you used to have when you were working with Simon. Anything going on I need to know about? You know, we moved here to get away from that sort of thing."

202

David smiled at his wife. "Everything's fine. Just a quick thought about today's hearing crossed my mind. That's it. It's all good, as they say."

"It better be," Karen responded. "See you at five."

# Chapter Twenty-one

# A Walk with Doc Lawson

David returned to his office, unloaded his files from the preliminary hearing and placed them in a thick cardboard banker's file box that sat atop a small lateral cabinet in his office that held his legal research files and other materials on the Billups case. He made a mental note to call Simon about Donny Howard and then tried to focus on the correspondence and pleadings on his desk from other legal matters that were demanding of time that David knew was in short supply.

The case was eating him alive. He knew it but something was wrong about the facts, about Billups, about the brothers Howard, about Cassie, about everything. Forbes struggled to keep his attention on the other cases at hand until a reprieve came when five o'clock rolled around and David said good night to Brenda and headed up the block to the 'Blue Crab.' He could smell it before he could see it and, thankfully, tables were in ample supply as it was a Monday, the weekend tourists were gone and the band was off until Friday night.

David wasn't in the place more than a minute before Karen and the kid's arrived and they were seated by a pretty waitress wearing a 'Blue Crab' t-shirt at a long wooden table that was covered with a sheet of the restaurants trademark brown paper that would soon be stained from butter dripping off the Old Bay seasoned steamed shrimp and from the sauce of their legendary hickory smoked pork ribs.

Refreshed from the cold beer that was soon in hand, David smiled as he took it all in. Luke and Katie were drawing on the paper with the complimentary crayons left by the waitress and Karen was eyeing him over the top of her own mug of beer that was so thick with frost that you could write on it.

In fact, she had done just that. With her fingernail, she had etched across the front of the mug the words "I love you."

David spotted the message, quickly etched his own response "I love you, 2" and they both smiled in silence as they watched their kids doodle.

Life was good and soon got better when the food arrived and everyone started digging in. At center stage was a wooden cutting board with a rack of St. Louis style baby back ribs surrounded by two pounds of steaming spiced shrimp. A platter of roasted ears of corn on the cob smothered in herb butter, a small serving dish of collard greens accented with bits of Vidalia onion and some of the smoked pork that held center stage at the table and a large paper plate full of corn bread dotted with pieces of bacon and made with whole kernel creamed corn rounded out the feast. Paper towels became the order of the day and the waitress soon arrived with another welcomed round of beer and sweet tea without even being asked.

"Coming back down to earth, counselor?" Karen asked.

"Yeah, Daddy," Katie said, "Mommy said you've been in one of your mooooods."

"Kate, hush," Karen said tossing a mommy glance at her youngest from across the table.

"Honey, I said no such thing," she continued with a loving but sarcastic look back at her husband

"Yes, she did. She said it twice. Once in the kitchen and once in the car. She said it one time with a bad word, too," declared the nine-year old with one hand over her mouth, hiding a grin as wide as the Mississippi.

"Busted," David said to his wife who was looking more beautiful by the moment.

"So, what are you going to do? Spank me?" she said with a grin.

"Maybe so. Sounds like to me you've been a bad girl," David replied with a wink.

"You have no idea," Karen winked in return.

"Ohh, Daddy's going to spank mommy. This should be fun!" Katie said.

"That's not what they're talking about," Luke mumbled at his sister while he put the finishing touches on a race car he had drawn on the one remaining area on the brown paper table cloth that wasn't tattooed with the evidence of their meal. "You are such a child," he added in order to emphasize a difference in maturity as only a thirteen-year-old can to a nine-year-old sibling.

"Mommy, he called me a child," Katie pouted to Karen, while pulling on her mother's sleeve with a sauce stained hand, indifferent to the fact that she was doing a good job of proving her brother's case.

"Well honey, he's right in a way but I think that you are more of a 'young person' than a 'child', don't you think so too Luke?" his mom inquired with a not so veiled directive as to how her question better be answered.

"See, I'm a young person, not a child," Katie said indignantly to her brother.

"Whatever," Luke replied as he colored in the flames shooting out of the massive exhaust pipes on his brown paper car.

Karen shot him a look that did no good and decided to return her attentions to her husband who was watching the whole thing play out to its wonderful and predictable end.

"He's growing up, Baby," David said with a shrug.

"In more ways than one," his wife responded. "I think maybe you and he need to have a little talk."

That got Lukes's attention. He looked quickly up at his dad who looked back at him and then David looked at Karen and said, "Honey, you are absolutely right on all fronts. I agree completely."

"Son," David said sternly while turning to look at Luke, "we need to have a man-to-man talk."

He then paused briefly and added, "Right after we order some mile high chocolate cream pie!"

"Now you're talking," said Luke with a big smile and a high five to his Dad.

Karen shook her head at David who had a grin that matched his son's tooth for tooth. Giving way to the moment, she surrendered to the good time being had between father and son, grateful that David was back to, well, being David.

Fifteen minutes later, dinner was over. David paid the bill, kissed his wife and kids goodbye and walked back down the block carrying a styrofoam box with leftover shrimp and ribs that would soon find a place of honor as tomorrow's lunch in the office refrigerator.

The shops along the sidewalk were closed and early evening pedestrian traffic was non-existent except for the lone man walking towards David at a slow pace, smoking a cigarette.

It was Dr. Lawson.

The two men met midway on the block and warmly shook hands.

"Evening counselor. By all appearances it would seem that the members of the Forbes family dined rather well this evening, yourself included," said the old doc as he made a motion towards David's tie that was now adorned by a rather large stain from the herbed butter sauce.

"Aw, shit," David said has he held up the tie for close inspection. "An expensive one, too, and a Christmas gift from my mother-in-law, at that."

"That's all right," the doctor said. "I know the feelin'. Happens to me all the time. Wife says I have the table manners of a Neanderthal and makes me keep a couple of spares at the office just in case."

"That's a good idea, Doc," David replied. "Looks like I need to follow your wife's advice myself."

"Smart woman, Estelle, if I may say so myself. By the way, David," Lawson said, "You did a good job in court today. I like the way you ask your questions. Direct and to the point. You obviously prepared well for your day in court. Some lawyers I've met from the witness stand don't seem to understand that part of their case."

"Well, thanks, Doc. I appreciate your kind comments," David responded.

"Call me Bob, please. Everyone around here calls me Doc and that just pisses me off. Makes me feel like I'm some ancient codger carrying around a dusty beat up black bag on some old TV western like *Gunsmoke* or some shit like that."

"Bob, it shall hereinafter be," David said with a smile.

Lawson took a long drag off his cigarette and looked at David. "Think you got something on the 'beer cans and shoes' thing? I remember the question." he asked.

David responded, "Maybe. Hard to say. The two kids who first found Jimmy at the beach initially told Deputy Robins that they also saw some beer cans and a pair of shoes lying near his body. It was mentioned in Robins' report but the Sheriff denies that there were any such items anywhere around and nothing of the sort is shown in any of the photographs. I've tried to call the homes of both boys. I never got a return call from one of the families and the other boy's mother told me that if I tried to talk to her son, that she would have me arrested. What for I don't know but, as you can expect, there hasn't been much outpouring of support from the community for my side of the case."

"Of that, I have no doubt," Lawson said. "I park near your car on most days so I've seen, ah, the most recent indicator of your new found popularity. Goddamn idiots. Some people just don't know when to grow up. Not much you can do about it, though. I guess that's just how it is," the physician commented with another exhale of smoke added for emphasis.

"It is that and then some," David said in response, paused and then added, "Bob, there was one question that I wanted to ask you today that I didn't."

"And what question was that, David?" replied Lawson as he stubbed out the last of his cigarette in the potted plant located in front of the drugstore that for over thirty years had served as a repository for his spent tobacco.

David made his next comment carefully with a close watch being made on Lawson's face. "It was about the wound to Jimmy's arm," said the attorney.

Lawson avoided Forbes' gaze and reached into his shirt pocket for another cigarette. He pulled out a fresh Marlboro, tamped it on his wrist, locked it between his lips and fired it up with a click and a flash from a stainless steel Zippo lighter bearing the red and gold crest of the United States Marine Corps.

"What's the matter? Didn't like the answer I gave you?" asked Lawson.

David responded, "Oh, no, I liked your answer just fine. There was just one little problem with it."

"And what was that, David," Lawson responded, still looking anywhere else but at the lawyer standing in front of him.

"It wasn't true. You and I both know that, and I'm beginning to believe that some other folks in that courtroom this morning probably knew it too." David's comment lingered in the air like a diagnosis of terminal cancer as he awaited the doctor's response.

Lawson shot a quick, narrow-eyed glance at David, but said nothing. He turned and started to slowly walk back down the block from whence he had come. After he took several steps, Lawson paused and motioned over his shoulder for the lawyer to walk with him.

David quickly caught up to the aging physician and, for a while, the two men walked in silence, basking in the soft ethereal glow of an early

209

evening moon that was rising like a phoenix over the public library that held station on the other side of the street until finally Lawson spoke.

"You know, I didn't lie on the stand today, but I don't take offense at what you said. My testimony was medically accurate in that his wound could well have been caused by a rope burn from a mooring line as Jimmy described to me that day in my office."

"But . . . ." Forbes said, begging additional commentary from the aging doctor.

"But the shape and characteristic of that rip across his arm brought back a lot of memories, mostly bad ones at that. I'd like to forget most of 'em to be quite honest, but, I'll tell you, David, when I tore off that makeshift bandage that Jimmy had put on his arm and saw that wound for the first time, it was like I was back at the battle of Khe Sanh in '68."

Forbes said nothing. He just watched while Lawson took another drag off of his cigarette. The physician continued on.

"I was a Navy Corpsman assigned to the 26th Marines. Khe Sanh was a hell of a fight and boys were getting shot up something awful. Head wounds, disembowelments, limbs taken off, burns. Shit, everything. Hell, you name it, I saw it. I tried to fix 'em up as best I could but so many men died 'cause they needed more than I could give them out of a medic bag. Anyway . . .," he said as he paused to draw a breath and wipe away the beginnings of a tear, ". . . there was one wound that I saw more than any other during my entire time over there."

"And what kind of wound was that?" David asked.

"Light flesh wound from an AK-47. Treated 'em all the time. You couldn't get through the day without somebody getting nicked somewhere or the other. Commonplace stuff for a medic in those days"

Lawson looked over at David. "When I pulled the rag off that he had wrapped around his arm, I swear that was the first thought that went through my head. Goddamn flesh wound. But the rope explanation had some plausibility to it and the bullet thing went out of my head as quick as it came in. Thought it kind of silly at the time. Maybe I dismissed it too quick. I don't know."

The aging physician stubbed out his cigarette and instinctively reached for another when he scolded himself and put the pack back in his shirt pocket. "Smoke too many of these damn things as it is. Been telling the wife for years that I'm going to quit. Maybe I'm just too much of an old fool to know any better."

Forbes was speechless. Lawson looked at him and smiled. "You best get that BBQ in the fridge before it spoils and get home to that wonderful family you have. You're a lucky man, David. But I suspect you already know that. You strike me as the kind of fellow who knows what's important in life and what's meaningless bullshit, if I may be so bold to say."

David was still at a loss for words but if the old physician was expecting him to say something, he certainly didn't show it. Doc Lawson put his left hand on the lawyer's shoulder and gave David a firm handshake with the other. "You take care of yourself and please be careful. In the opinions of some, you may be doing too good of a job for your client. You have a good evening."

And with that, the two men parted company on the sidewalk with David headed towards his office and Doc Lawson headed towards another cigarette, lost in the fog of memories of comrades who had died and the tragic truth that a round from an AK-47 had once again left its mark on a patient of his who he couldn't save from the wounds of a war that were yet to come.

# Chapter Twenty-Two

## An Old Waterman's Tale

The next day, after David finished his morning docket of misdemeanor traffic cases over at the courthouse, he walked back to the office and was greeted by Brenda as he came through the door. She was standing next to an open filing cabinet beside her desk. "Good morning," she said with files in one hand and a cup of coffee in the other. "You're back earlier than I expected."

"Yeah," David said, "It was a quick morning. Couple of guilty pleas. Court didn't take long at all."

Brenda shut the filing drawer and said, "Well, that's good because you've got company waiting for you in the conference room. A man by the name of Walter Taylor's here. He was standing at the front door when I showed up at 8:15 am. God only knows how long he'd been waiting there before I arrived. I told him that that you probably wouldn't be back till around 9:30 a.m. or so but then he said the strangest thing."

"What was that?" David asked

"He said that he's been waiting thirty-five years for this appointment and if he had to wait a few minutes more that would be fine with him. He's really old and I think he's a little off his rocker if you know what I mean," Brenda added with a whisper and a wink.

David remembered seeing Taylor on the front porch of his old store from across the creek at Harper's and his conversation with Coles Howard about Taylor's belief that then Deputy Howard had murdered his son. He also remembered that Taylor had attended the preliminary hearing and had smiled at him from the back bench in the courtroom. He grabbed a pen and a legal pad and said, "Well, you can't fault a man for wanting to be early for an appointment. I'll go see what he wants."

David walked into his conference room and saw an elderly gentleman sitting slightly stooped over in one of the brown-leather, cushioned chairs that surrounded his oval-shaped conference table made of dark maple. The visitor was dressed in faded denim overalls and wore an old, gray work coat with papers of importance known only to him stuffed in every available pocket. His weathered hands rested on the top of a hand carved cane of red oak topped with a small metal likeness of a duck's head made of well-worn tarnished brass. On his head was an oil stained Washington Redskins ball cap. On the table in front of him was a folded up piece of what appeared, at first glance, to be a page from an old newspaper, its small type faded against the yellow pale of the paper that had been worn and weakened by age like the man who had brought it into the lawyer's office.

David sat down beside his visitor, held out his hand and said, "Mr. Taylor, I'm David Forbes. It's nice to meet you."

Taylor smiled at David's greeting, displaying elderly gums missing half their teeth and took David's hand into his own. His grip was warm and soft. "I know who you are," the old man said in the accent of a lower Chesapeake Bay waterman. "I read about you in the newspaper and I seen ya over at Harper's. I'm Walter Taylor and it's nice to meet you as well."

"So how can I help you, Mr. Taylor?" David asked.

The old man sat upright, looked straight at David and said, "Mr. Forbes, I'll get right to my business. The sheriff killed my son, and I want you to do all that you can to get him convicted of doing it. I'm not a rich man, but I'll see that ya get paid for your time. That's why I'm here, to ask ya to do that for me."

David said nothing to Taylor of his conversation with Howard and was beginning to think that Brenda's assessment of Taylor's mental faculties may have more credence than she knew.

"Mr. Taylor, first let me say that I am truly sorry for the loss of your son. I have a son myself, and I can't imagine your grief. Now, can you tell me when this murder took place?"

"The sheriff shot him thirty-five years ago, two months past. August 7, 1972 to be exact," said the old man.

David continued to be patient with his elderly guest and said, "Mr. Taylor, you know that it's usually the job of law enforcement officers and the Commonwealth's Attorney to look into these sorts of things. I assume that some sort of official inquiry took place into the facts and circumstances leading to your son's death."

Taylor leaned forward until his chin was just inches above the veined arthritic knuckles of his hands that were locked together atop the brass handle of his cane and said sternly, "You're not listening, Mr. Forbes. I said that the *sheriff*, when he was a *deputy*, shot my son. Nobody did nothin'. They took his *word* for it. He has gotten away with killin' my boy and I want you to put an end to it." Taylor leaned back in his chair and stared at Forbes with eyes filled with certainty and resolve.

David asked his next question even though he knew the answer was a foregone conclusion, "Were there any witnesses?"

"Only the Good Lord himself, Mr. Forbes," was Taylor's response.

David looked down at the blank page of his legal pad and rolled the tips of his unused pen back and forth between the thumb and forefinger of each hand. He finally looked up at Taylor and said, "Mr. Taylor, I'm not sure how I can help you get justice for your son. This shooting took place a long time ago. From what you tell me, there were no witnesses. No forensic evidence was preserved, you can bet on that. Plus, I'm assuming that there will be some sort of record that an official inquiry or investigation was conducted and that no evidence was found of any wrongdoing. Maybe if we know something now that wasn't known then, we could do something but absent that I just don't know what I can do for you. The bottom line is that I don't want to tell you that I can do something when I can't." David stopped talking, laid the pen on the legal pad in front of him and waited for Taylor to respond.

At the other end of the table, the old man, who had lost his son, closed his eyes and paused for a moment while his hands slowly massaged the handle of his cane. He finally looked up at the lawyer, smiled and said "Would you like to see a picture of my boy?"

Without waiting for David's response, Taylor's right hand, wrinkled like old parchment, left the cane and reached for the crumpled old newspaper article that lay before him on the table. He unfolded it and handed it to David. The article showed what appeared to be a high school graduation picture of a handsome young man in his late teens. The writing below the picture was his son's obituary.

Taylor began to tell his story. "Thirty five years ago, Sheriff Howard was a deputy when he shot and killed my son. He murdered my boy out on Knights Wood Road, pretty near to where they say that colored boy killed Jimmy Jarvis. Howard said my son attacked him after he pulled him over for drinking and driving. That was a bold-faced lie. There was no truth to it."

David challenged the old man, "How do you know Howard was lying?"

Taylor suddenly sat erect, pounded his cane on the floor and responded angrily, "Because no unarmed twenty-five year old man who's lived in the county his whole life is going to attack an armed deputy."

Forbes countered. "Mr. Taylor, with all due respect, unarmed country boys getting killed by law enforcement officers in small towns, particularly after they've been drinking, isn't exactly news. They get drunk, they get pulled over, they get argumentative, things get out of hand, they get to fightin' and bad things come about as a result thereof. Sad, of course, but it does happen."

"Mr. Forbes, I know my son did not attack Howard that night."

David took a deep breath. The ramblings of this old man who clearly could not get over the loss of his son were starting to wear a little thin. He tried hard not to let it show and asked, "Again, Mr. Taylor, how do you know this?"

"My boy's name was John Anderson Taylor. We took to calling him Johnny. His mamma named him after her daddy. She died soon after he was killed, couldn't take losing her only child. It was too much for her. Now

215

Johnny liked to take a drink now and then and when he did, sometimes he would drink more than he should, raise a little ruckus and because of that, Johnny ended up gettin' arrested a time or two. Drunk in public, disturbing the peace, that sort of thing. He'd go to jail for a few days, sober up and then come on home. It was no big deal to him if he had to go to jail. He was used to it. Besides, Johnny knew most of the people up at the jail, anyway. So, what I'm trying to tell you is that he had no problem with it and he had no reason to attack Howard. But Howard had plenty reason to want him dead."

"And why was that?" David asked.

"Johnny told me that Howard was turning his back while some watermen from over in Guinea were helping to unload shipments of cocaine out in the Mobjack Bay and taking it by a skiff over to a dock on the East River. Taking bribe money from 'em, he was. Johnny found out about it, ran his mouth a little bit and got killed for it and the deputy that killed him is now the goddamn sheriff!"

Forbes looked square at Taylor, "You got any proof of that other than what your boy told you?"

"Nope. Don't need none. Got plenty of proof already"

David put his pen down and said, "If you've got plenty of proof, I'd like to see it because what I've seen and heard here today isn't going to do it for you, Mr. Taylor. I'm sorry, sir, I've heard a nice story and all but you haven't made out a provable case in court of law"

Taylor reached over and slowly retrieved the faded newspaper clipping lying on the table in front of David, folded it carefully and put it in the lower right pocket of his coat. He again situated both hands on the top of the cane and stared with tired, rheumy eyes at the lawyer on the other side of the table.

"I'll show you all the proof you need, but first I need to ask you to do me a favor"

"And what is that Mr. Taylor?"

"I need ya to give me a ride home." Taylor replied. "I can't drive. Doc Lawson took my license from me some years back. Said it was for my own good and for the good of everyone else out on the road, including him I suppose."

David looked at his watch and immediately regretted doing it. The figure before him was a worn-out old man who just wanted some closure on the death of his child. Who could blame him? Whatever else was on his calendar for the morning would just have to wait.

"Sure, Mr. Taylor," David said."I'll be happy to give you a lift. Just tell me where you need to go."

Taylor's eyes brightened a bit and said, "Just down to Harper's. I'm right across the creek from the store. You seen me over there. That's where I live." And then he asked, "Are we gonna go in that sporty little car of yours I seen you in over at Harper's? I ain't never rode in something like that."

David couldn't help but smile at the old man and said," Mr. Taylor, one ride home in a Porsche 911 coming right up."

Taylor said nothing in response. He just grinned his toothless grin, looking like a kid on Christmas morning.

David continued on and said, "Look, I'm parked around back. You go out the way you came in and I'll meet you out front."

He then helped Taylor to his feet and walked him down the hallway to the front foyer. David said, "Brenda, I'm going to . . . ."

She cut in, "I know, I heard . . . .come with me Mr. Taylor."

As David reached for his keys and grabbed his cell phone, Brenda turned, took a couple of quick steps back down the hallway and whispered, "You know what they say about no good deed going unpunished."

David threw both hands up in the air, one was holding the keys to the Porsche and the other one holding the phone, and whispered back, "I know, I know but something tells me this is going to be too good to miss."

David pulled the 911 around to the front of the law office on Main Street and watched as Brenda carefully helped the old man get situated in the passenger seat. The grin hadn't left Taylor's face. He ran his left hand along the leather bolsters of the seat and said, "Wow, this is some fancy car. I'll bet it goes fast." David fastened his seat belt, "Mr. Taylor, fasten that seat belt of yours and we'll see just how fast she *can* go!"

"Fine by me, Mr. Forbes. At eighty-nine, I can use all the thrills I can get!"

Hearing that, David smiled in return and he made sure that Walter Taylor got his wish. Two miles south of the courthouse, with a straight line of open highway and not a car in sight, David put the accelerator to the floor and when he hit 125, he finally let off the accelerator, downshifted to fourth and looked over at Walter whose eyes were riveted on the ribbon of asphalt that was flying beneath the floorboards of the 911.

"How did you like that, Mr. Taylor?" David yelled to the old man over the noise of the engine.

"That was some mighty fine driving Mr. Forbes. I thank you for that," Mr. Taylor shouted back.

"It was my pleasure, Mr. Taylor, my pleasure," David responded as he brought the car back down to something less than reckless driving. Taylor then gave David directions on how to get to his side of Harper's Creek which took David down a rutted old road of sand and clay, the terminus of which was the beat up old building that David had first seen from across the water when he had his memorable visit to Harper's Creek General store.

Both men got out of the silver Porsche and soon stood on the salt-bleached planking of the front porch of the old store where sat the rocking chair in which Taylor had kept his daily vigil for so many years.

218

"This is my home," said the old man while resting one hand on his cane and the other on the back of the rocker.

"Used to run a seafood business here, same as that one across the creek," he said with a nod towards the bustling concern on the other side of the water.

"After Johnny got killed, I kinda lost my taste for it. Losing him took a lot out of me, I reckon, just like it did to my wife. Sold most of my riggin' some years back. Now all I've got is that small deadrise out there at the dock."

Taylor made a motion with his hand that took David's eye to a forlorn looking old wooden boat that was tied up at the end of a dock littered with rusted crab pots and the remnants of tattered nets that haven't caught a fish in many a day.

David looked back over at Taylor and noticed that his eyes were tearing from the memories of better days that just wouldn't let go.

The old man spoke, "You know Mr. Forbes, I've been a waterman my whole life. Worked hard for it, I did. Had to really 'cause I had no choice. We lost our father when I was nine years old so I quit school in the fourth grade and I've been workin' the water ever since. I crabbed, tended nets for pound netters, did a spell as a deckhand on the menhaden steamers sailing out of Reedville, done a bunch of gill nettin', Hell you name it, I done it. I took whatever work I could find and not the first word of complaint ever was heard from the mouth of Walter Taylor I can tell you that for a fact. We had to eat. No work, no food, simple as that. Besides, I had two younger sisters at the time so my momma had her hands full."

The old man paused as he stared off into the distance. "They're all dead now," he said, his hand rubbing the back of the rocker while he spoke.

David asked, "What happened to your father?"

Taylor shifted his gaze to the open water that lay beyond the mouth of the creek. "My daddy was a waterman and times were hard back in the Twenties. You did what you had to do to get by and Daddy and his brother made extra money by running liquor up the bay. One time, they were meeting some fella's from Chicago at a dock up in Maryland. It was late at night. I had hid on the boat before they left home. Daddy didn't know I was on board. I thought they was just going out fishin'. I was asleep in the hold down below when I was woke up by the sound of gunfire and men screamin'. They had been ambushed by a gang from Baltimore. I poked my head up through the hatchway and saw that we was tied up at a large dock. There was a bunch of men on the dock standing next to a big truck. They all had guns. They had shot two men who were lying next to the truck and had killed a third man who was laying face down on the dock behind the truck. My Uncle was lying beside him, holding his intestines in his hands. He had been shot up somethin' awful and was covered in blood. I could hear him crying as he lay on the dock behind the truck. My father was still alive and was standing on the boat up at the bow. He was saying something to one of the men on the dock who was holding one of them tommy guns you see in the movies. I couldn't exactly hear what daddy said, but then I saw my father pull out a pistol and shoot the man he was talkin' to in the chest. Then, I watched as the other men shot my daddy so many times that he bled to death right then and there on that workboat. He died while I was holding his hand, and I miss him somethin' terrible to this very day. He was finest kind."

Forbes was incredulous, "My God. What happened to you?"

"They pulled me out of the hold and threw me on the deck of the boat next to Daddy. I thought they were going to shoot me, too. I guess they didn't have the stomach to kill some kid over bootleg liquor, so they dragged my uncle's body off the dock and threw him onto the boat. He was dead by then. And then they untied her lines, and pushed her off. One of the men said 'He'll never make it 'cause a Nor'easter was comin'.' Right he was about the storm but they was wrong about me not makin' it. I took the helm and got her out of the creek and into the bay when that storm hit us about ten mile south of where daddy was shot and she blew somethin' terrible. I pushed and pulled my father's body and my uncle's body into the hold of the boat and then held on to the wheel for dear life while the sea tried to kill me too. I guess the Good Lord had other plans, and, somehow, the boat and I made it home in one piece. I was nine years-old then, and I've been a waterman ever since."

David was stunned into silence by the old man's tale. All he could say was "That's one hell of a story."

"Yeah, I guess it is in a way. Sometimes though I wonder whether it was the best thing for me to have sailed out of that storm. Yes, sir, sometimes I truly wonder." At that, Taylor moved around to the front of the chair, took a seat while David grabbed a small folding beach chair that was leaning against the salt bleached plank wood wall of the old front porch and sat down beside his host.

After the old waterman got situated in his rocker, Taylor spoke again. "Mr. Forbes, as you can see, I'm an old man and I probably don't have much time left. I give thanks for every day I wake up and I'm right thankful to be with you here today. You have a nice office up there in the courthouse. You know, I went to grade school with a lawyer who used to practice in that very same office years ago. Patrick Trusch was his name and he was some kind of smart, book smart if ya know what I mean. He lived just down the road from my family's house in New Point. His daddy worked with my daddy on the water and he and I used to play together as kids all the time. Back then, we went to school in a one-room school house. We'd play games like jacks and kick the can and marbles in the school yard. You ever play marbles, Mr. Forbes?"

"Can't say that I have Mr. Taylor."

Taylor smiled again, forming deep canyons in skin that looked like cracked leather in the shadowy cast of the old porch. "Kids don't play like they used to, Mr. Forbes. Nowadays they stare at TV's, smoke dope and have sex with each other. It don't make sense. Damn near un-American. Kids don't have no chores like they used to neither. And people wonder why everything has 'Made in China' stamped on it. Bunch of ignorant fools, if you ask me. I was helping my daddy on his boat from the time I could walk and I do mean from the time I could walk. It was hard work but we liked it. To us, it was fun. I think that's the difference between then and now. These days, folks don't want to work hard for nuthin'. They want it all just handed to 'em, like they somehow deserve it without havin' to earn it first."

221

Taylor was clearly in his element and continued on, "You know, I've been thinkin' about it Mr. Forbes and I know now that I was born too late. Yes, sir, I was born too late. I wasn't meant to see all this. My time, I truly believe, was in the early 1800's, workin' a harpoon on the great whaling schooners just like my grandfather did as a boy. Sailed out of Nantucket at the age of fourteen and traveled from the Atlantic to the Pacific looking for whales, he did."

Taylor looked over his shoulder and pointed to the top of the doorway to the old store. Resting on two galvanized hooks was an old wooden harpoon tipped with a ten inch spear head made of blackened steel.

"See that?" he said. "That's a whaling harpoon that once belonged to my grandfather. When I was a kid, I'd take that harpoon out every day and pretend that hay bales were whales. I got to be pretty good at throwing that harpoon. I could hit the mark every time."

The old man smiled at the memory and kept on with his tale. "My grandfather died before I was brought into this world, but my daddy did a good job of rememberin' his stories and they was some good ones. One thing my grandfather always used to say was that you could tell a lot about a man by how well he kept his hands on the oar of the whalin' boat when he's got five tons of pissed-off harpoon stuck whale swimming right at 'em."

Taylor paused briefly and then looked David right in the eye, "My question to you Mr. Forbes, is how well do you think you can keep your hand on your oar, the one you're holding right now, sir?"

"Keep my hand on the oar?" David responded. "You've lost me a little bit, Mr. Taylor."

"Lost you?" Taylor exclaimed laughing. "Mr. Forbes, I'm talking about your case! The reason I asked you that question is because you got five tons of pissed-off whale swimming at you right now yourself. I came to see you this morning because I don't think you know it yet. Or maybe you do. Am I making any sense to you, Mr. Forbes?"

Taylor said nothing more and looked over at David sitting in his beach chair, while the westerly breeze from Harper's Creek blew across the faces of both men, stirring the pale green strands of marsh grass that bordered the old store.

David was lost by the cryptic prophesy of the old waterman. He really didn't know what to say. He looked over at Taylor who sat before him like an oracle, hands still folded upon the brass duck head handle of his cane and staring him dead in the eye. He awaited David's response.

The lawyer finally spoke, "Mr. Taylor, and would you mind if I called you Walter. Is that okay?

"That's fine with me, Mr. Forbes, and I'll call you David if that suits you"

"That suits me just fine as well. Now Walter, I'm new around here. I don't know a lot of the local folks or much about the history of Mathews, but I'm getting the feeling that there's a bunch of things going on around here that no one wants people to know about or talk about. I mean, God knows, most folks I run into don't want me asking questions about anything other than when can Jamal Billups plead guilty to murdering Jimmy Jarvis so that all of this can just come to a quick and predictable end. Not to repeat your question to me, but is any of this making sense to you, Walter?"

Taylor leaned forward in his rockin' chair and said, "It makes a lot of sense to me David because I've lived it once before. I've seen everything you're seeing now. Want to know somethin' else?"

David nodded at the old man and said, "Sure. What's that?"

"Coles Howard killed Jimmy Jarvis just as sure as I'm sitting here," Taylor said in a matter of fact tone.

Forbes was stunned by Taylor's allegation and his head swam in disbelief while a pair of seagulls tore a small peeler crab to pieces at the end of the dilapidated dock in front of the old man's store.

223

The lawyer leaned back in his beach chair and said to Taylor, "Well, I interviewed Coles Howard and he gave me the distinct impression that he'd be the last person on earth who would want Jimmy dead. Said he was a great employee. Appeared to think of him as a son of sorts."

The old man was quick to respond, "He's a lying bastard if there ever was one. He's trying to *fool* you. David, listen to me. Now look over there," Taylor said, motioning with one hand towards Harper's Marina. "Big, nice boat, big, nice house just up the road, new trucks. Man, you don't get all that from catching croakers and tending crabpots. Coles Howard and Jimmy were doin' a lot more than fishin', that's for damn sure. Look, I sit over here all day long. I watch the boats come in, and I watch 'em go out. I know what they catch and how much they get paid. Done it all my life. Now I don't know how to use no fancy computer, but I do know how to count boxes of fish and bushel baskets of crabs. Something went wrong somewhere, and Jimmy got caught up in it. He was killed to keep him from tellin' anybody about it, same as what happened to my boy."

"Tellin' anybody about what?" David asked of the old man. "Look, Walter, everything you've pointed out can be easily explained. Banks lend money every day so that people like Coles Howard can buy a home, a new boat, trucks, invest in new equipment, and that sort of thing. It happens all the time. If anything is going on over there that's illegal, it's probably the under-reporting of income Howard makes from his seafood business which I suspect is the kind of thing that goes on all the time around here. I got that much already. What I'm not getting is why Coles Howard would kill Jimmy Jarvis over some IRS shenanigans. I mean, hiding some of your income is a common practice in a cash business. Why kill Jimmy over that? It makes no sense."

Taylor squinted at David and said, "It does if there's big trouble comin' from how you got the money in the first place. Howard's kind of money weren't comin' from no fishin' and he weren't getting' it from no bank, I'll bet you on that. Most likely drugs, if you ask me. I think he got greedy and made a mistake. It would be in Cole's nature to do somethin' like that. Always wantin' more and thinkin' he can get away with doin' anything that he wants being that his daddy is the sheriff. But this time, he bit off more than he could chew. I think he pissed off some people who don't give a rat's ass who his father is and he couldn't trust a good kid like Jimmy Jarvis to keep his mouth shut. So he killed him. Simple as that. End of problem. That's how Coles Howard would see it. Clear as day to him."

David still wasn't convinced. "Why do you say it's drugs? This is a small town. Hard to believe there's big money in any drug business going on in Mathews. Harder still to believe you could pull off a drug smuggling operation without half the county knowing about it, the way folks talk around here"

Taylor pounded his cane on the boards of the old porch and said, "It ain't about 'around here'. It's about getting' it to where it needs to go. You really don't know a damn thing about the seafood business, do you?"

"See those trucks over there?" he said pointing over to Howard's fleet parked next to the general store.

"Every week, those trucks go to Baltimore, Chicago, Washington, New York City and Boston, packed with ice and seafood. You can hide most anything you want in those trucks and nobody's ever gonna know. Cash, drugs. You name it."

The old man continued to press his case, "And I'll tell you something else. I sit out here all day, but I don't sleep all that well neither. In other words, I'm up a lot at night, too, and I'd see things that ain't right. Coles Howard, he and Jimmy, they'd be going out at night. Sometimes, I'd be up when they'd come in and I ain't never seen no fish come off that boat, just some seabags that Coles and Jimmy would take off the boat and throw in the back of Coles' truck. Now why would they be goin' out at night? They for damn sure ain't out there tendin' pound nets and pulling crab pots at night. No sir, David Forbes, they be doin' something else other than fishin' and that's what got Jimmy killed, I'm certain of it."

David became curious, "Do you recall the last time they went out in the boat at night?"

Taylor said, "I can't be one-hundred percent certain but I'm almost sure it was the night before Jimmy Jarvis was killed out on that beach."

"Jesus Christ," David said his mind racing back to his conversation with Simon over the weekend, "Have you told anybody about this?"

Taylor laughed again. "Man, you don't get it. Tell who? The goddamn sheriff?"

"How about the Commonwealth's Attorney?" David asked.

"Hell, no. The Sheriff and him been friends since high school. You couldn't trust Arch Hudgins to scratch his own ass without getting the Sheriffs permission first. He won't do shit about any of this. That's why I came to see you," Taylor said keeping his gaze locked on David.

The attentions of both men were momentarily interrupted by the sounding of a ships horn from out in the channel. It was the *Bay Lady* coming in from her morning's work and both men watched as Coles Howard brought her expertly to the dock with a new mate on board who was busy getting her lines tight and her gear stored away.

As the gleaming white workboat tied up at her berth, Taylor said, "My father used to always say that 'the sea giveth and the sea taketh away'. In fact, those were the last words he said to me before he died up at that dock in Maryland. Daddy was a fine waterman and a good man who got caught up in something he couldn't get out of. Same thing happened to Jimmy Jarvis."

"Smugglin' then and still smugglin' now," said the old man, shaking his head. "Funny how some things don't change much on the water."

Then, Taylor slowly rose up from the old rocker, lifted his cane in his right hand and, like Moses with his staff, he pointed its brass handle at David and said, "I'm an old fool. Of that, there is no doubt. But you will do well to recollect my words to you today, Mr. Forbes. Thirty-five years ago, Sheriff Howard shot and killed my son in cold blood. Thirty-five years later, his son did the same thing to Jimmy Jarvis. Your colored client, sir, is an innocent man. The sea giveth and the sea taketh away, David. You remember that."

And with those as his parting words, Walter Taylor went inside, shut the door and left David standing alone on the front porch, next to the rocking chair that was still moving from the old man's exodus from David's presence.

David placed his hand on the back of the chair, stopping its motion, and slowly rubbed the old wood while absorbing the lingering proclamations of the old waterman.

"What if the he's right," David thought to himself. "What if Howard had something to do with the missing drug shipment that Simon spoke of Saturday morning. And what about his brother Donny working vice for the Baltimore PD. The timing of it all is just too uncanny to ignore particularly given Taylor's observations about Howard's nighttime activities the night before Jimmy died. That Howard's standard of living appeared to be a notch or two above where it should be if he were just selling seafood was also a factor. Plus if he did hijack that drug shipment, Howard would have plenty of motive to make sure that Jimmy Jarvis kept his mouth shut. You rip off the Zetas and they will kill you. No doubt about it."

Forbes took the keys to the Porsche from his pocket, stepped off the front porch of Walter Taylor's home and was heading to his car when something made him pause and look in the direction of Harper's.

There, on the bow of the *Bay Lady*, stood Coles Howard and there was no doubt he was watching David's every step as he walked towards his car from Taylor's home.

The two men locked their gazes onto one another and it became clear to David that he was looking at the man who had stabbed Jimmy Jarvis to death that night out on Haven Beach. He didn't have all the evidence it would take to prove his case, but, first and foremost, he once was prosecutor and a prosecutor he would become again. In time, the evidence would come and he would prove his case, of that he held no doubt.

Across the creek, unbeknownst to David, Coles Howard was having an epiphany of his own. He knew the story Taylor had told the lawyer and could sense by the way Forbes was acting that the old waterman may have gotten into his head, maybe even got him to believe his tall tales from long ago. This David Forbes could become dangerous if he got too inquisitive and started asking more questions then he should things that weren't any of his business. Coles Howard was going to make sure that didn't happen.

The standoff continued. And as one man walked to his car and the other stood at the helm of his boat, both men sent predictions to the other from across the waters of Harper's Creek.

From David Forbes came the promise, 'I know what you did and I will bring you to justice.'

From Coles Howard came the reply, 'You are not one of us and I will kill you if you try.'

For both men, the hunter and the hunted, the lines were drawn, the stakes were set and the chase was on.

# Chapter Twenty-Three

# The Fight at Market Days

In his gut, David agreed with the old waterman's take on things, but as he drove back to his office, the lawyer in him began to question whether he could prove any of this. Forbes knew that there was a big difference between what you believed and what you could prove in a court of law. Convincing twelve jurors that Coles Howard killed Jimmy Jarvis was going to take a hell of a lot more evidence than he had.

David knew that the first place to start was with the money. 'Follow the money' was a time tested adage at Justice, and he could think of no reason why it would not work here.

His first thought was to issue a subpoena for Howard's business records and his tax returns, knowing that the waterman would probably fight like hell to keep from disclosing this information but he had to start somewhere and Howard's financial records were as good a place as any.

Secondly, he would go to the clerk's office and search the land records for mortgages, notes, and financing statements. Like Taylor said, it takes a lot of money to buy big boats, new homes and new trucks. If Howard borrowed the money, he would have a mortgage recorded on his home and, perhaps, financial statements recorded on his boat or on any of the trucks used to haul his seafood.

But Forbes knew that even if he could somehow prove Howard was laundering thousands of dollars more than he was receiving in income from his seafood business, he would still be hard pressed to prove that the money came from an illegal drug operation and that Jimmy Jarvis was killed because of it. The IRS would have a field day with that kind of information and could raise all the hell they wanted to, but it wouldn't carry much weight in a murder case.

David needed to prove that the money came from trafficking in narcotics, and right now, that evidence was non-existent. Despite everything that Taylor said and saw, the fact was that there wasn't one shred of proof that showed that Coles Howard was involved in drug trafficking and if David issued the subpoena for Howard's financial records, he would have to show that they were material to the case and, right now, he wasn't sure he could meet that burden.

The bottom line was that David's initial enthusiasm for Taylor's theory began to wane as logic and evidentiary principle began to intrude into what was previously a solo performance of pure, unencumbered instinct. It was at that moment David went back to his Saturday morning conversation with Simon. He reached for his cell phone and called Simon as the Porsche ate up the road heading back into town. He got his voice mail.

"Simon," he said," This is David. Look, you mentioned something when we spoke on Saturday about a missing drug shipment down in my neck of the woods. I need to talk to you about that. Call me. It's important. Thanks." David hung up, parked the Porsche and went into the reception area, passing Brenda who was on the phone.

He went back to his office, grabbed his tape recorder and quickly dictated a subpoena request for all of Howard's financial and tax records. He ejected the tape, grabbed his water bottle and walked back up to Brenda's desk, dropping the tape on her desk and heading back out the door.

"Hold on a minute," Brenda said when he had one foot out the door. "What's up with you. Your house on fire or something? You look like a man on a mission."

"I think I'm on to something. I'm heading up to the courthouse. I'll be back in about a half-hour or so," David replied.

"Well, cool your jets, cowboy," Brenda said. "The person on the other end of the phone is some guy named Simon Epstein. Says you two worked together up in Washington. You want to speak to him?"

"Simon! Why didn't you tell me he was calling?"

"Because you flew in and now you're flying out. You're up to something, I can tell. Did that old coot get you to believe his tall tales?"

"We'll talk about him later. Please see if you can get to that tape as soon as possible. I'll take Simon's call back in my office," David said as Brenda responded with a rolling of her eyes at the tape that landed on her desk.

David went back to his office, settled in his chair and grabbed the phone. "That was quick," he said to his friend.

"Well, I was on another line when you called but you certainly got my attention," Simon said. "What's going on down there, David? Did you see some Mexican drug lords walking down Main Street in Happyville?"

"Simon, this murder case of mine has taken on some new twists," David said. "It's hard to explain but I've received some information that some watermen down here may be involved in drug smuggling and I'm not talking about some weed now and then but serious shit, bringing large amounts of narcotics in on workboats, packing it into fish containers and shipping it in seafood trucks to New York, Baltimore, Philly, Boston, wherever. The evidence, frankly, is thin and if I went into detail as to my source, you'd think I'm nuts but I swear to God I think I'm on to something, particularly about this missing drug shipment you told me about."

The lawyer continued."There's a big 'maybe' that this shipment went missing the same night that the kid who got murdered here in Mathews went out on a workboat suspected of being involved in a drug smuggling operation. I need some details about the missing Los Zeta shipment. Date, time, location, how it was hijacked, stuff like that. I also need to know chain of command and who their contacts are here in Virginia. I know I'm no longer cleared for this intel, but my client's life depends on me finding out the truth of who killed this Jarvis boy, and the more I dig, the more it points towards something more than just bad blood over a fist fight at some damn convenience store. I need your help, man."

"David," Simon said, "I'll tell you what I can and probably some of what I shouldn't. Now, this is confidential shit so do what you do so well and keep your mouth shut or I won't give you any more newsflashes on how well Yvonne is maintaining her reputation, if you know what I mean."

"Sworn to secrecy with a blood oath and secret handshake," David replied. "Now, what's up?"

"I'll dig around in our files and get you some more detailed stuff later on but right now this is generally what we know," Simon answered, "We intercepted a number of communications from a Mexican cartel, the Los Zetas, with cells operating in Miami and Baltimore. Although it's hard to piece it all together, it appears that something was lost that was being transported by boat off the coast of Mathews. From what we can gather, the boat just disappeared and there must have been a substantial shipment on board because the Zetas seem pretty pissed."

"How long ago did this happen?" David asked, his senses now on full alert at Simon's reference to Baltimore as a cartel contact point.

"About two months ago, give or take a day. Again, it's hard to say. Our info is limited. These guys are pros and they don't go around posting their shit on Facebook. But, I can say that the time period that I just gave you was when all the chatter started about the missing shipment. I also know that your victim was murdered about the same time. I've been following the newspaper coverage of your case on line."

David took another long pull from his bottle of water. His pulse was pounding and his mind was swirling at light speed from the gathering evidence that was linking Coles Howard faster and faster to a possible drug smuggling operation. The old man just may be right.

"Simon, is there anything else you know that you're not telling me?" David asked his DEA pal.

"David, why would I hold info back from you? You may be out of Justice but you're still a federal prosecutor at heart. Besides I couldn't ask for a better pair of boots on the ground. Keep your eyes and ears open and let me know if you hear anything. Okay, compadre?"

"I'm happy to be your guy in Happyville, Simon," David replied.

Simon paused, cleared his throat and then asked, "Uh, David, you don't know anything about this that you haven't told me, do you?"

"Not yet," David said. "But I may have something soon. I'll explain later after I pursue some leads down here."

Simon's tone suddenly changed and he spoke forcefully to his old friend and said, "David, you listen to me you *schlep*. If you know something about this Los Zetas business, you tell me first before you do anything on your own. You know how these operations go down. Things can get complicated fast and sometimes you can't see all the angles. Besides, these fuckers don't play and they will kill you quick."

"Relax old pal. I know my limitations," David said reassuringly.

"No, you don't and that's what scares me," Simon responded. "You hear anything you even think might pertain to this, let me know immediately, okay dude?"

"Done deal. Married yet?" David said, abruptly changing the subject.

"Of course not," Simon smugly replied. "Too many women in this town to give up for just one, except for someone like your Karen of course."

"I'll make sure to tell her you said that," David replied

"You take care of yourself David", the agent said, "Call me now."

"Will do, old friend," Forbes responded. "Be good and I'll talk to you soon."

———————————

David hung up the phone, picked up a dart on his desk and threw it at the board on the other side of his office.

"Could all this be linked together?" He pondered. "A Mexican drug cartel, cells in Miami and Baltimore, a boat with a lot of drugs missing out in the bay, all happening around the same time as Jimmy's murder?"

David launched another dart at the board while he continued on with his mental analysis of Simon's revelations. "This is crazy, though. It's just too much to believe that a couple of local guys would be involved with a Mexican drug cartel. But, what the hell were Howard and Jimmy doing going out at night and what if Howard's financials show a huge discrepancy between income and expenditures? And what if Howard did in fact kill Jimmy, why else would he kill him but to keep from getting killed himself. Simon was spot on when he said the Zetas don't play. If Howard ripped them off, they would kill him and every member of his family in a New York minute. If they did steal that shipment and Jimmy talked, Howard was a dead man and he knew it."

David took another swallow of water and said aloud, "As they say, you just can't make this shit up."

His mind went back to the subpoena for Howard's financial records. If there was a hornet's nest out there, this was one way to kick it for sure, David thought. The old man was right. Killing Jimmy makes sense if there's big trouble comin' from how you got the money in the first place and ripping off a murderous Mexican drug cartel was about as big a trouble maker as you were going to find.

David's thoughts also shifted to Karen and the kids. What if there is a connection? Am I doing the right thing by going down this path? Could he be putting Karen and the kids in danger? Should I send out that subpoena?

He knew that Simon had these guys pegged. They played with no rules and women and children were fair game. As a prosecutor, he'd handled numerous cases where the witnesses simply disappeared, only to be found weeks, months or, sometimes, years later, bound and gagged with their throats cut ear to ear. Los Zeta drug lords were equal opportunity killers, and they discriminated against no one for breaking their code of loyalty and silence.

Besides, there was more than enough evidence to convict Billups. Maybe I should let sleeping dogs lie and let the Mexicans take care of justice at their end. But that means Billups gets convicted of a crime he didn't commit and that wasn't going to happen. David was reaching for another dart when his thoughts were interrupted by a soft tapping against his partially closed door. He turned in his chair and saw the soft blue eyes of his daughter peering around the side.

"Hi, Daddy, can I come in?" Katie asked. She didn't wait for a response, and rushed over to her daddy's chair and hopped into his lap.

"I love you daddy," she said.

"I love you too, princess."

"Watcha doin?' Katie asked.

"I've been on the phone with Uncle Simon," David said.

"Uncle Simon! I like him but his beard makes my skin itch," she said.

"What are you doing?" David asked. "Aren't you supposed to be in school, young lady?"

"It's Market Days and they let us out early today. Didn't you know that daddy?"

"Yeah, didn't you know that daddy," mimicked Karen from behind the door. She walked in as David smiled and looked out his office window at the vendors that had set up their tents and booths the night before.

"Where's Luke?" he asked.

"He's walking down from the middle school with some of his friends. Too cool to ride with mom now that he's all grown up. No doubt he'll find one of us when he needs some spending money," she said. "Why the long face? You've got that serious look thing going on. I haven't seen that in a while. What's up? Is it something to do with Simon?" she asked.

"Serious look? Who? Me?" David said while making a clown face at Katie that got her laughing.

"You know what I'm talking about. Is something going on with him? You're not working with them are you? David you know I can't go through that again. Tell me you are not working with Simon," she said with a serious look of her own.

"I'm not working with Simon, okay? Now, who's hungry?" David asked, changing the subject as fast as he possibly could. "When I came back from court, there must have been twenty vendors out there selling crab cakes, burgers, and funnel cakes."

"I want some funnel cake!" Katie said.

"Me too" was her dad's response. "Let's go, I'm starving."

With that, David grabbed Katie's hand and they walked up the hall, passing Karen who stood unmoving with arms crossed and a stern look on her face.

"You were just on the phone with him. What were you talking to him about?" she pressed.

"We were just shooting the breeze. Catching up a bit. I'm not working with him, period," David said, half-whispering, half-pleading."

His wife wasn't buying it.

"C'mon, baby," he said, with a second effort wink and a kiss on the cheek. Karen refused to abandon the look but did follow her husband and daughter up the hall to where Brenda sat, draft-copy of the subpoena in her hand.

"Here it is. You sure you want to file this thing? Archie Hudgins is going to object like crazy. This is going to get folks all riled up," Brenda said. "And besides, what are you trying to prove anyway? That he ain't paying his taxes? Hell, everybody knows that cause everybody's been doin' it themselves."

"File what thing?" Karen said not missing anything, as her wifely radar was on full scale alert.

Brenda picked up quick on the tense undertone of Karen's question and attempted to backtrack on her previous comment, "Oh, it's just a routine request for some documents," she said.

"Doesn't sound so routine to me," Karen said, looking back and forth from Brenda to David.

Her husband responded fast. "Relax, baby, it's routine stuff, just like Brenda said."

Turning to the secretary that just saved his ass, he said, "Just hold on to it. I'll go over it when I get back. Can we get you anything?"

"No. I went out earlier and got a crabcake and a lemonade. I'm good for now" she said reaching for her lighter and cigarette case. "You all have fun."

Brenda then looked at Karen who was biting her lip and still glancing down at the document that lay on her desk, shook her head and walked outside to smoke a cigarette.

---

David, Karen and Katie left the office and strolled down to the old courthouse green that was filled with all the sights, sounds and smells of a Chesapeake Bay festival in full bloom. Food vendors lined both sides of the street, craft merchants were packed side by side on the court green and tourists were everywhere. A band was warming up on a sound stage that blocked off the old Court Street exit on to Main while a bunch of kids watched as one of their own got their face painted by a young lady dressed up in a clown costume.

"Mommy, can I get my face painted, pleeease," Katie begged.

Karen replied, "Ask your father. He seems to be the one making all the decisions these days."

David said "Karen, please. You're making something out of nothing."

237

Karen replied, "Okay fine, but I'm right and you know it. I won't say another word." Karen then turned to Katie and said, "Sure baby, right after you eat all your lunch."

Katie's mom then led the way and both girls decided on crab cake sandwiches while David opted for a steaming-hot Italian sausage sandwich covered in roasted onions and peppers and a couple of softshell crabs from the booth set up by the Lions Club. David wolfed his down and went over to get a funnel cake when Luke showed up with a couple of his classmates.

"Hey, Mom," he said, "Can I have a couple of bucks to get something to eat? They've got some rides over there that are pretty cool, too." Karen opened her purse and gave him ten dollars. She got a peck on the cheek as her part of the deal and then he was gone, running off with his buddies through the maze of tents and tables that had been set up in the shadow of the two hundred year-old courthouse.

David came back with a paper plate filled with the deep fried pastry delight covered in confectionary sugar and asked Karen if she'd seen Luke yet.

"Yep," she said. "He was just here. Hit me up for ten bucks and then he was outta here."

"Why didn't he stick around? Heck, I wasn't gone but five minutes," David said.

"He's getting older," Karen said. "It's not 'cool' to be seen hanging around your parents. You did the same thing when you were a kid, admit it, Counselor."

"I'm sure I did but my parents weren't as cool as I am," David replied smiling.

"I think I'm going to barf," Karen countered. She picked up the empty plates and said to Katie, "I think some little girl I know deserves to get her face painted. Why don't we go get in line?" to which Katie responded with an enthusiatistic "Yes!" and both mother and daughter walked over to the face painting booth.

Sensing a mother and daughter moment in the works, David waved bye, got up and walked around the festival, saying hello to townspeople who he recognized and trying to keep his mind off the conversation he had with Simon earlier that day.

In the meantime, Luke and his friends spent every bit of money they had on rides, soda and candy but saved enough to bet on the crab races, an annual fundraising event sponsored by the local YMCA. Luke was loving every minute of the Market Days Festival. "Growing up in Washington was pretty cool but this is great," he thought as he peeled off from his friends to go see if he could hit up his dad for some more spending money knowing that mom would be a 'no go' on the second time around.

Luke was making a detour around the back of the courthouse green so he wouldn't have to deal with the crowds when he came around the side of one of the old outbuildings that bordered Court Street and suddenly found his path blocked by four boys, all of them larger and stronger than him.

The biggest of the four shoved Luke hard up against the brick wall of the old building as the other three blocked off any possible route of escape.

The boy who pushed him spoke first, "Hey, I know you. Your old man is the lawyer that's trying to get that nigger off who killed my cousin Jimmy."

Luke was too scared to speak. He could sense that a fight was coming and his legs trembled at the thought of being beaten up by these guys who he guessed were students from up at the high school. He then looked frightfully around, hoping that some adult would magically appear from around the corner and stop all this, but it didn't look like superman wasn't coming and Luke Forbes was on his own.

The same boy spoke again, "What's the matter, you a pussy or somethin'?"

Luke still couldn't find the words that would get himself out of this and was praying fervently that his father would suddenly appear when his aggressor looked left and then right, smiled at his pals and then with as much

239

force as he could muster, drove his right fist as hard as he could into Luke's stomach.

The lawyer's son instantly doubled over in more pain than he had ever felt in his life. He thought he was going to either die, pass out or throw up when the boy followed up with a left hook to Luke's face, splitting open his upper lip and sending a splotch of blood airborne, staining the centuries old brick and adding another chapter to the rich architectural history of the old courthouse square. The second assault sent Luke to the ground. Like water from a spigot, the tears poured uncontrollably out of his eyes as he lay on the ground, curled in a fetal position, feeling as helpless and defenseless as worm on a hook.

While the other boys laughed, his assailant bent over him and said, "Look at this pussy. Now he's crying. What a wimp. Here's another lesson for you nigger lovers."

But as his aggressor stepped back to give Luke a kick in the gut, he was suddenly grabbed from behind, lifted up into the air and propelled like a battering ram into the wall where he had just pushed Luke.

The boy's body landed with a sickening thud against the brick, collapsing in a heap not far from where Luke still lay on the ground. Groaning, Luke's assailant rolled over, looked up and found himself staring into the faces of three members of the Mathews High School varsity football team, who were all very, very big and very, very black.

One football player who wore a skin tight cobalt blue Under Armor workout shirt that left no doubt that he knew his business in the weight room, spoke first.

"What's your problem, cracker?" he said, pecs and abs taut and ready for action. "Didn't your momma ever tell you not to use the N word? You want to try calling me a nigger, homey?"

In response, one of the white boys nervously stammered, "We . . . ain't got nothing against y'all. We just messing with him, not . . . .you . . . guys."

240

A second football player spoke. He was a huge, dreadlocked kid with biceps like cannonballs, skin the color of perfect espresso and was one of the guys that Luke remembered from his visit to the church. From his formidable perch at every bit of six feet, two inches, the mammoth linebacker stared downwards without mercy at all four boys and said, in a deep, baritone voice that would have made James Earl Jones proud, "You mess with him, you be messin' with us." Upon hearing that, the white kids looked like they were going to faint.

The third player, a short, stocky kid who was built like a brick shithouse with fire hydrants for legs, then said, "Look at you pieces of shit. Four on one and you're calling him a pussy? There's only three of us. You wanna try and kick our asses? We'll wreck your shit, right here and right now."

The four white boys were looking more every second like condemned men when an adult voice broke the standoff. Superman had finally arrived.

"What's going on?" said Deputy Matt Robins who had observed the gathering from across the courthouse green and walked over, knowing that something less than good was afoot.

The football player in the middle spoke first.

"These fools were beating up on our boy Luke here, calling him a nigger lover and shit like that. This one here . . . .," he said making reference to the white kid on the ground who was holding his face from getting it slammed into the wall, "punched Luke a couple of times and was getting ready to kick 'em like some porch dog when we intervened on our little brother's behalf."

The huge black athlete on the right chimed in, grinning from ear to ear, and said "Yeah, I intervened 'em all right!"

The four white boys who had attacked Luke knew better than to say a word.

Robins bent down and helped Luke up, "You okay?" he asked.

"Yeah, I'm fine," he said, as he brushed the grass off his pants and dried his tears with the sleeve of his shirt.

241

The deputy looked over at the three white kids that were standing up and then back at Luke and asked, "Do you want me to do anything about this?"

Luke glanced over at his assailants and then over at the three members of the football team and said "No. I think this is as far as it needs to go."

Robins motioned to the white kid lying on the ground. "Get up," he said. "I don't guess I need to tell you boys what's gonna happen to you if you try to pull this shit again. Next time, I ain't gonna stop the ass whippin' parade and you're gonna get what ya'll deserve, now get the hell out of here."

The four boys didn't need to be told twice and they were gone from the scene in seconds.

Robins then turned to the three football players and said, "Were you really gonna wreck their shit?" in response to which all three, including Robins started laughing. The deputy was as big as a house and was the offensive line coach for the high school football team. All three of the guys played for him and respected him.

"Nah, we just gonna scare 'em some," said the player on the left." Keep 'em away from our boy Luke here." He then looked at Luke and said, "Man, once word of this spreads around, you won't have to worry about no white kids messing with you no more. I guarantee you that. C'mon, we'll walk with you over to your folks."

Robins went back to his foot patrol and watched as Luke Forbes and the three best friends he's ever had walked together through the market days crowd until they found David and Karen at a booth watching a vendor make a small piece of jewelry out of sea glass for Katie.

Upon seeing Luke's battered face, Karen's hands went to her own and then she hugged her son and asked him what happened. Luke did his best to shrug it off but some tears still came when he felt his mother's embrace.

One of the players put his hand on Luke's shoulder and said, "It's okay, man. Let it go. That's what mommas are for. You were brave back there and don't you forget it."

Another player gave David a briefing on the incident, after which he turned to his son, put his hand on his boy's other shoulder and said, "So, I hear a few of the local boys had a little disagreement with you and some of the varsity football players showed up to lend their support."

Luke looked up at his dad and tried his best to grin despite the busted lip and said, "Yeah, we kicked their asses," which caused the three football players to laugh.

Forbes replied to his son, "Mark Twain would have liked the way you said that boy. Let's head over to the law office and get you cleaned up a bit."

David told Karen and Katie that he and Luke would be right back, said a well felt "Thanks guys" to the three football players who had helped his son and was walking toward the office with when he heard a familiar voice behind him say,

"Looks like junior don't know when to duck."

Knowing the voice was Coles Howard, he turned and faced the man who was standing, beer in hand, at the doorway to the Blue Crab.

David looked over his shoulder at Luke and said "Son, go to the office. I'll be with you in a minute." Luke sensed danger for the second time that day and said "Dad, come with me, please."

His father looked at Luke and said, "Do it!" in a tone he knew meant business. Luke kept moving down the sidewalk but could not keep from looking over at his shoulder at the tall man that was staring down at his father.

David turned his attention back to Howard who was standing alone in the doorway. The lawyer looked left and then right and when certain that only he and Howard were parties to the conversation, Luke's father spoke in a low tone and stared straight into the eyes of Coles Howard.

243

"Usually, I just ignore assholes like you," David said. "But since you brought my son into it, I'll give you a few minutes of my precious time."

"Whoa, you don't need to be so sensitive, counselor," Howard said with smirk and a gulp from his beer. "Besides, I thought we was pals. Hell, I even bought you a bowl of the best chowder you ever had, or have you forgotten my act of hospitality so soon?"

"Your acts of hospitality come with a big price tag, Howard. Jimmy Jarvis learned that the hard way, didn't he?" David said.

Howard pulled hard on his beer, looked down at David with a steady eye and said, "You watch your mouth, lawyer man or I'll crush you like this beer can, so help me and I'll love every minute of it, I swear I will!"

His threat did nothing to stop David who took a page out of his opponent's playbook and moved closer to the beer-guzzling waterman. His gaze unwavering, the lawyer decided to gamble with Simon's intel and play a bluff hand on Coles Howard.

In a soft but firm, measured voice, David Forbes delivered his message to Coles Howard.

"I know about the drug boat you and Jimmy knocked off out in the bay and I know you killed him to keep your little secret safe," he said. "But, your little secret ain't so secret anymore. You don't think the Los Zetas are gonna catch on to your scheme, but they will, trust me, they will. They always do and when they come, they're gonna kill your wife first, nice and slow, while making sure you have a front row seat. And after you've had the opportunity to watch your honey get repeatedly raped and have her throat cut, then they're gonna slice off your fucking dick, stuff it in your mouth and then cut off your fuckin' head. You're done, Howard. Fucking done. Finished. Dead man walking. Tell me, dumb-ass, how does it feel to be so stupid and so completely fucked?"

In response, Howard crushed the beer can in his hand, and David readied for a shot from one of his massive fists when six-foot-six Coles

Howard, man among men and hands down the toughest waterman on the Chesapeake Bay did the unexpected - he blinked and said nothing in response.

David smiled and whispered back, "You ever say something to my son again and I'll kill ya myself. You have a nice fucking day."

He then turned and starting walking down the sidewalk towards his office. Shaking like a leaf and completely uncertain as to whether he just hurt his client, screwed up a DEA investigation, signed his own death warrant or was guilty of all of the above. David was still kicking himself for losing his cool when he met up with Luke at his office and saw that he was with Karen in the bathroom, getting cleaned up and ready for another go at the Market Days activities.

"You sure you want to keep hanging out here?" his mother asked," Maybe we should just call it a day."

Luke replied, "No way, those guys were just a bunch of morons. I'll be okay." He then gave his mom a hug, high-fived his Dad and out the door he went.

Karen and David looked at each other and David said, "Like you said, he's getting older. He's gonna get in some fights at some point in his life."

His wife quickly countered, "Yeah, but this wasn't over some prom date. This was about one of your cases, David."

David responded, "You're right, but I don't think it's going to happen again. Luke's got some pretty big friends out there now and, unless things have changed since I was in school, he's going to be strictly hands off from here on out. Anyway, where's Katie?"

"She's over at the carnival rides with Stacey Saunders and her two daughters. I'm going to go over and check on her. I'll see you later."

Karen gave David a hug and whispered in his ear, "Don't get mad at me. I'm just a little worried. Something doesn't feel right. Promise me you'll tell me if there's something I need to know. Promise me."

David squeezed her close and said, "I will. I promise."

She kissed him and he watched as she went out the door and out into the throng of festival goers who lined the sidewalks of Main Street. David then turned to Brenda and said "We're filing that subpoena first thing Monday morning. Draw up a cover letter for the clerk and I'll carry it up there myself."

His secretary said, "You know, hell's gonna come down on us for pokin' into Howard's finances, taxes, and such. People gonna think you're saying he had somethin' to do with Jimmy's murder."

"Hell's already comin', Brenda," David replied, "and it doesn't have a damn thing to do with this subpoena."

The lawyer said nothing more and Brenda watched as her boss walked down the hallway and closed the door to his office, the soft thud of darts against the wall being the only sound she could hear as she got up, put the 'Closed' sign on the front door and left for the day, knowing that inside that office was a man who needed to be alone.

# Chapter Twenty-Four

## Baltimore

It was 3:00 a.m. and the empty tobacco warehouse on Baltimore's North Avenue stood in the darkness like a tattooed old ghost. Its pale grey concrete block walls were covered in graffiti and, in the satin light of a waxing moon, its darkened empty windows stared out like a dozen hollow eyes, the broken glass vandalized years ago by the street gangs that roam one of the worst drug trafficking areas in America.

The deserted parking lot at the front of the building was covered in decayed old asphalt which had progressively buckled over the years, leaving large chunks of gravel encrusted tar in its wake and potholes large enough to eat a tire up to its axel. Across the double doors of what was once the entrance to the main warehouse office rested a thick, heavy chain secured with a large, steel padlock twice the size of a man's fist. Weeds, briars and stands of staghorn sumac had replaced well-landscaped beds of azaleas and boxwoods and a faded 'No Trespassing' sign now greeted visitors where once tobacco brokers from across the South had conducted their mercantile affairs.

The marauding graffiti, the invading sumac and the buckling asphalt continued its assault without opposition from the front of the building to the side of the abandoned structure which ran for almost a hundred yards perpendicular to North Avenue where every thirty feet, the concrete block walls were interrupted by large metal loading dock doors that started at the bed height of the tobacco haulers and then ran upwards to trailer height, all now rusted iron red from years of disuse, frozen in place by encrusted ball bearing rollers that haven't seen grease in many a day.

Above each loading dock bay was a commercial grade domed light that hung from a large curved bracket, similar to the other lighting fixtures that were mounted at the front of the warehouse and from the nearly dozen light poles in the parking lot that surrounded the front and side of the old building. With their bulbs busted out years ago and never replaced, there wasn't a light on anywhere and there wasn't a car in sight.

At the rear of the building was a large corrugated metal garage door that was bordered by several beat up dumpsters and three abandoned tractor trailer containers. Two men wearing black ski masks stood in front of the door, both armed with Heckler & Koch MP5 submachine guns. A black Denali that had arrived just moments earlier was parked on the other side of the closed door, its passengers having joined the other occupants of the old warehouse who had arrived an hour beforehand.

The building was otherwise empty. Whatever machinery, equipment, scales, tools, tables, or furniture that once had been here to service the tobacco trade had been removed or stolen long ago and the vast vacant floor space was now occupied by a single large metal table surrounded by four vehicles - a Dodge step van, a pair of steel gray BMW's and the black Denali. The only illumination present was provided by the headlights of the vehicles which were now positioned towards each other like the points of a compass.

On the table were two large suitcases that had been unloaded by the occupants of the Denali and placed on the table that now held center stage. Together, the suitcases contained $1.2 million in heat-sealed bricks of cash wrapped in aluminum foil.

The trunk lids of both BMW's were then opened and four suitcases, two each in each trunk and similar in appearance to those containing the cash, were removed and placed next to the table.

Once that task had been completed, the men who came in the BMWs took up position next to their vehicles opposite that of where the Denali visitors had taken their stand. No one said a word and watched while a lone man stepped from behind the west side step van and walked center stage towards the cash laden table.

He, too, wore a ski-mask like the guards at the front gate and was also armed with a MP-5. He laid the submachine gun on the table and approached the two open suitcases. With a switchblade that appeared as if by magic in his right hand, he expertly sliced into each brick of cash, discarded the aluminum foil and randomly removed a bill from the brick. With a nod of his head, another masked man, similarly armed, stepped in from beyond the reach of the headlights and produced three sets of electronic devices, one designed to detect the presence of transmitters, one designed to detect counterfeit money and one designed to count large amounts of cash by weight. None of the devices were larger than a deck of cards.

The second man shouldered his machine gun, activated the first device and methodically passed it over both suitcases. Once done, he deactivated the instrument, placed it in his pocket and nodded at the first man. No bugs detected. He then took each bill the first man had removed from the bricks of cash and scanned it separately with the second device which emitted a soft ultraviolet light coupled with a laser scan. When he was finished, he nodded his head again at the first man. U.S. currency confirmed. Lastly, he placed each brick on the digital scale, and factoring in the weight of the plastic wrapping, calculated the number of dollars in both suitcases. It took him less than two minutes and the results were right on the money. As before, he signaled the good news to the first man and retreated back from the table and into the shadows. It was all there.

The first man removed both suitcases of cash from the table and quickly replaced them with all four of the suitcases removed from the trunks of the BMW's. Each case was opened and their contents displayed to the four men in the Denali. The first man rearmed himself with the MP-5, stepped back from the cases and motioned for their inspection. Two of four men stepped forward from the SUV.

Latin in appearance, they were members of the Mara Salvatrucha drug gang, MS-13 as it is better known, and were at the warehouse that night to purchase the high-grade heroin that had made the Los Zetas criminal syndicate famous for being the best drug suppliers in the business. The suitcases were packed with it. Likewise equipped with transmitter detectors, digital testers and scales, the MS-13 members did their due diligence and quickly confirmed the product was as promised. Both men then nodded their assent and retreated back to their comrades at the rear of the Denali.

Then, the first man with the mask stepped back into the center of the group, and with gun in hand, motioned for the MS-13 men to approach the table, remove the four suitcases of heroin and place them into the rear of the Denali. He spoke.

"When you leave here, you will follow the white Jeep Grand Cherokee that is waiting for you at the end of the block. The driver will take you to the parking lot of the beltway Marriott. You will wait there for thirty minutes. Once thirty minutes have passed, you may leave. If you do not follow the Jeep as instructed, you will never make it to where you think you might be going. If you leave the hotel parking lot earlier than instructed, you will face a similar certain fate. If my men are confronted in any way after you leave here, you will all be killed. Any questions?"

"No," said one of the MS-13 members.

"Then, go," he said with a wave of the barrel of the submachine gun. The garage door was raised and the Denali was gone in seconds. Once the door was closed, the man spoke again to the men on the cash side of the table.

"Well, what do you know?" he exclaimed with a laugh and another wave of the barrel of the machine gun for emphasis. "Now that the visitors have exited the premises, I guess it's time for the home town teams to do a little business. What do you say?"

"We came here to get weapons. You came here to get money," said one of the four men who arrived in the BMW's, both high end 7 series machines. "The cash is here. We did our job. Now, let's see the fucking guns."

"Easy, Jose," said the leader with the MP-5, "And you watch your tone. You're sounding a little perturbed if I may say. What's the matter? Don't you like the way I provide protection for your little drug deals or do all these machine guns make you a bit nervous?"

The man then snapped his fingers and with that seven masked men, all armed with automatic weapons came forward and encircled the heroin dealers who drove the BMW's.

"Frankly, if I were you," the leader said, "I would consider this a sign of respect. Because God only knows that I respect you. I just need to make sure that you respect me, that's all. Now, stop fuckin' around and open up the back of the van and take a look. It's all there. Signed, sealed and delivered. Just like UPS."

As the occupants of the BMWs walked toward the van, the man with the mask laughed, and stepped aside and watched as the Zetas unlatched and swung open the doors to the step van which was packed to the ceiling with crates of U.S. Government issue Colt M16A4 fully automatic combat rifles and case upon case of 5.56mm caliber ammunition.

"Madre de Dios!" he heard one of the Zetas mumble as the gang member opened one case after another.

"God's Mama doesn't have anything to do with this," the masked man responded. "Now let's get moving. You're not going to spend my precious time digging through every goddamn crate and case in that van. It's all there. Now let's roll."

On that command, two of the masked men moved quickly. They went to the front cab of the van and returned with two sets of Virginia license plates. Within seconds, the Maryland plates on the BMWs were replaced and a suitcase of cash was stashed in the trunk of each vehicle. The leader of the masked men, machine gun still in hand, then turned to the man who spoke on behalf of the Zetas.

"Key exchange time, Jose," said the man with the mask as he sent a sinister smile to the Los Zetas leader. "By the way, there's a tracking device on that van. You heard what I said to those MS-13 scumbags and same goes for you and your Taco Bell boys. Any funny business after we leave here, and its 'adios muchachos', or whatever it is you wetbacks say."

"One of these days, gringo," said the Zeta with a snarl.

"One of these days indeed, hombre," the man replied. "Now, gimme the goddamn keys."

And with that, both sets of keys passed each other in mid-flight, the garage door was opened for the last time and the old warehouse ceased once again to be a place of business. The BMWs now containing the eight masked men, backed out of the building and watched as the step van made its exit westbound on to North Avenue, loaded to the hilt with enough firepower to ensure Zeta dominance on the streets of Juarez and elsewhere in drug riddled

Mexico for years to come. The pair of BMWs then made their own escape across the same pitted parking lot, but instead took a left and headed east in the other direction towards mid-town.

Once they were on their way, the leader of the masked men spoke from the backseat of the lead BMW.

"Man, those Zetas are an uptight bunch, aren't they?" said the man as he took off his ski-mask. "They don't say a whole hell of a lot but those fuckers will kill you in an instant. Drop your guard, and they will slit your throat fast. Biggest mistake you can ever make is thinking that they like you and that you can trust them 'cause you are forever wrong on both counts and don't ever forget that. If you do, you're dead. You boys listening to any of this?"

"Man, this fucking thing is hot," he said about the mask while wiping the sweat from his forehead. "And, hey, I said . . . . are any of you boys listening to this or am I just jerkin' off back here?"

"We hear ya boss, loud and clear," said one of the men from the front seat. "When I'm around those Mexican assholes, my finger never leaves the fuckin' trigger. I'll pull it at the drop of a goddamn hat."

"You're a good man, Napoli, and they know that you'd do it, too, you crazy Italian fuck. That's why they don't fuck with us. That's why no one fucks with us. You guys remember that. Now pull in over here and let's ditch these 'Look at me, I deal dope' cars. Fuckin' morons. Don't these idiots ever learn?"

The pair of BMWs swung into an alley way just off of Baltimore Street and pulled in behind a dark green older model Dodge Caravan. The men again moved quickly, removing the Virginia tags from both cars and replacing them with the original Maryland plates. They all piled into the Caravan.

One of the masked men said to the other, "Joe, isn't this your wife's van? It smells like my cum. It must be her van."

252

"Shut the fuck up, McCluskey," the man called Joe said. "You gotta have a dick to fuck and the last time I saw you in the locker room, you didn't have a crank big enough to make a mouse happy."

"Fuck you, Joe. Minnie raves about my shit all the time."

"Guys, shut the fuck up," said the leader. "Who's got the keys to the Bimmers?"

"I do," said Napoli.

"Place 'em dead center on the hood of each vehicle. I don't want the criminals around here to have any trouble in moving these cars. Hell, with any luck they'll be out of the city before we even get home. Now let's get rolling."

Napoli did as instructed, tossed the keys on the hood of each car, leaped back into the van, drove down Baltimore Street and then headed east towards the harbor. After a few minutes, the leader spoke again.

"You guys did good work tonight. Smart and smooth. All of ya's and I really mean that. Everyone worked as a team and that's what counts. It's what counts on the street and it's what counts when we do our own thing. It's what keeps us alive. We'll get together to divide this stuff up later. Usual place. I'll text the time. Any questions? Hearing none, I declare this meeting adjourned. Nap, just drop me off here."

"Ain't you going home boss?" asked Napoli.

"Nope, too much paperwork from last week's arrests. I'm going to get an early start on my day, and besides, I can't think of a better place to secure this stuff," said Senior Narcotics Detective Donny Howard with a smile and a wink as the van pulled into the parking lot of Baltimore's 5th precinct station.

Howard exited the van, placed both suitcases into the trunk of an unmarked police cruiser parked at the far end of the lot and said, "Safe as a baby in its mother's arms. Gentlemen, I'll see you in the morning."

He then locked the trunk and watched as the Caravan pulled out of the parking lot and back on the city street. End of a long night's work. The detective went around to the passenger's side of the car, opened the rear door and retrieved a tan leather briefcase from the back seat. He opened the case and removed a prepaid flip phone that was clipped to the inside liner of the case. The phone was used for one purpose only and that was to communicate to his brother in Mathews. There had been a call while he was away on his business. It was a text message that said only two words,

"Call Mom."

Code for an emergency, Lt. Donny Howard, knew then that trouble had come to his home town.

# Chapter Twenty-Five

## Follow the Money

On Monday morning, David walked to the courthouse with the records subpoena tucked amongst the other papers in his briefcase and, with each step, he thought and re-thought the advisability of the action he was about to take on behalf of his client.

In his head, the yin and yang battle that raged over the legitimacy of the moment had reached deafening proportions when he ultimately retreated to that corner of his mind which favored the justice of it, his belief that what he was doing was lawful and right and when he reached that place, he locked down hard on what he felt, on what he *knew*, to be true.

To the other corner of his cranium he banished the plaguing thoughts of well-argued irrationality and the coming backlash that was as predictable as grass growing up and rain falling down. Motions, angry phone calls, court sanctions, negative comments in the press and the inescapable feedback from the locals. It was all there and coming hard. Reporters were following the case and were routinely checking the clerk's office for any recent filings. They would get a hold of this for sure.

Having reached maximum saturation on all fronts, David shook his head to settle the dust and quickened his pace as though *moving faster* would somehow act as a deterrent against further self-created cognitive onslaughts to his own plan of attack. But it really didn't matter how fast he walked. This man wasn't changing his mind. It was something that just had to be done. When David's feet hit the courthouse steps, he adjusted his tie in the refection from the window of the front door of the Clerk's office, looked himself in the eye and stepped inside.

Eugene Callis has been the Clerk of the Mathews County Circuit Court for over four decades and conducted affairs with the stately air of a refined southern gentlemen raised proper under the massive sweet pecans, shellbark hickories and American elms that dotted his family's estate. Soft

255

spoken and polite to a fault, he knew his business well and ran his office with the panache of a man for whom newer times meant only that there were more people for whom toleration was required, especially in the realm of manners and morality.

It was no secret that Callis was a stickler for propriety. He believed that courtrooms were places for which proper attire and proper language were *de rigueur*, no exceptions allowed. The famously fastidious clerk was also as well known for his reading of indictments that charged an unfortunate defendant with a particular sex crime, most notably certain brands of sodomy committed against young children, as he was for his well-coiffed head of silver gray hair done large in the Col. Sanders tradition. The clerk, many said, was a dead ringer for the legendary fried food king. If you threw in a matching goatee, added a string tie, and wrapped it all up in a three piece white suit, Eugene Callis could walk right out on the street corner and start selling chicken without missing a beat and make a bundle in the process.

Now, when an accused was asked to rise for the reading one of the indictments that contained elements unspeakable to the remarkable clerk, Callis would instead spell the words F-E-L-L-A-T-I-O or C-U-N-N-I-L-I-N-G-U-S, rather than be known as the kind of fellow who would speak such offensive words aloud in a public setting, most especially in the hallowed ground of the Mathews County Circuit Court, an event that was never going to happen in his lifetime, a fact upon which you could most rest assured. This oft-repeated act of linguistic chivalry probably left more than one defendant thinking that the old coot didn't know how to pronounce them 'big funny sounding words', an erroneous but nevertheless excusable conclusion given that multiple syllable Latin is typically as foreign as Jupiter to the average dirtbag charged with offenses of the morally decrepit variety.

In any event, Eugene Callis was clearly one of a kind. Highly resistant to computerizing his office, he finally yielded to high-technology some years back when the state took the element of choice out of his bailiwick, but despite the array of computers now flanking the wall in the records room and the large monitor and keyboard that occupied the credenza in his office, the clerk still wrote his courtroom notes in a lilting, long handed script that flowed like stalks of wind-tossed wheat across the arsenal of yellow legal pads that stood at the ready whenever he was riding shotgun four feet away from the large leather and brass chair where sat the Honorable Judge, Robert Paul Byrne.

Callis liked David Forbes. In his forty years of dealing with the legal affairs of an often trifling public, the clerk had seen lawyers move in to Mathews and he'd seen 'em move out just as quick. The native sons who went to law school and came back home to practice their craft would usually stick around but most of the 'come heres' wouldn't last more than a year of two before they either went out of business and started selling real estate, got disbarred for dipping one too many times into the trust funds of an elderly client or simply pulled up stakes, called it a day and drifted on to only God knows where.

Forbes, on the other hand however, was a keeper. Being organized, timely and polite at all times, the newcomer fit well into Callis's rubric of what made for a good lawyer, and David appeared to have all those qualities and then some.

First and foremost, he was married and that was a plus in the clerk's book. And he had two, well-mannered, polite young kids. This also gave David a decided edge on Callis' scorecard.

Eugene never had any children himself but always figured that any man who could fairly stand the bothersome nature of a child, and do right by it in their raising, possessed the better qualities of patience and fairness that made for good lawyering. Callis had seen attorneys who couldn't raise a worm in a box of dirt, much less raise a child and that much came clear in the way they presented their cases and presented themselves for that matter. Forbes, clearly, was not of their kind.

Callis had seen David walk in through the auxiliary entrance to the clerk's office that the public used when court was not in session. Today was such a day and the Honorable Eugene Callis had a front row seat to see the lawyers, deed filers, process servers, title searchers, marriage license seekers, concealed weapon permit applicants, reporters and everyone else coming through the door that morning to do business in his court.

"Good morning, David, how are you today?" Callis asked as he walked from the doorway of his private office that was located at the rear of a large bullpen composed of sectioned cubicles positioned to serve as work stations for his two deputy clerks.

"Morning, Eugene. I'm fine. How are you?" Forbes replied.

"Why, I'm fine too, just as long as this damn arthritis leaves me alone. You know, David, getting old just isn't as much fun as I thought it'd be. Too many aches and pains. Now how can I help you? (pronouncing it 'yew' in the grand old tidewater Virginia tradition), the clerk said while taking a studied and experienced glance at the redlined set of papers the lawyer had pulled out of his briefcase and placed on the top of the counter that divided the clerk's office proper from the rest of the world.

"I need to file a request for a subpoena *duces tecum* in the Billups case," Forbes answered. "Since the service is local, I would ask that it be served by the Sheriff. I'm sure he won't have any trouble locating the recipient. I'll drop a copy off at Archie's office as required. If you could please give me a heads up when the subpoena has been prepared and when it's been picked up by the Sheriff's office, I'd be most appreciative."

David stopped talking and waited for a response from Mr. Callis.

The clerk said nothing for the moment that it took him to read the face of the pleading, identify the custodian of the subpoenaed documents (Coles Howard), and to ascertain the array of documents requested per the subpoena which was everything that would have anything to do with the financial affairs of the Sheriff's son. Callis, nobody's fool, instantly spotted the volatility just laid on his desk.

"David," the clerk said in a mild and measured voice, "Are you sure you want me to process this today? This subpoena is going to upset an awful lot of folks around here. Have you spoken to Archie about this? I'm not one to tell you your business 'cause you certainly seem to have a good head on your shoulders, but I would certainly think this one over if I were you."

Eugene paused while he ran his well-manicured fingers along the edges of the subpoena and adjusted the solid gold link on his right French cuff. He then looked up at the lawyer through his polished silver bifocals and said, "Now what do you want me to do?"

"File it and process it, Eugene," the lawyer said. "I've thought it over plenty all ready. I appreciate your thoughts and there's a part of me that agrees with you more than you will ever know, but it has to be done. Thanks anyway. Just call me when it's been issued, that's all I ask."

"I'll do that, David," the clerk said and after a short pause, he added "Is everything all right?"

"Yeah," Forbes responded tersely, "everything's just fine as long as I don't make any waves or ask any questions about Jimmy Jarvis. But the lawyer in me won't allow me to lie that low in this case, Eugene. I just won't do it and I'm frankly getting tired of having to care about who gets pissed off about what just because I'm trying to do my job."

David knew that his words escaped his brain with a little more vitriol than the situation warranted and he immediately apologized to the old clerk. "I'm sorry Mr. Callis. I may have misspoke. My tone, if untoward, certainly wasn't directed at you, sir."

"I know, David. You've got your hands full," Callis said as he paused and watched as the lawyer snapped his briefcase closed and started walking towards the door. "David," the clerk said, "Before you go, I want to show you something."

Forbes stopped his retreat and listened as the clerk spoke. "David, I want you to look over at that far wall. See all those huge lateral filing cabinets?" The lawyer turned and looked through the doorway to his right towards row after row of beige colored metal filers that rolled silently back and forth on little railroad type tracks imbedded in the mottled brown and grey specked carpet of the filing room that held recorded deeds, wills, plats, search warrants, financing statements, tax maps and file after file that bespoke of man's endless appetite for litigious warfare against his fellow man.

"In those cabinets, David, are all of my closed cases." The clerk spoke softly but deliberately. "You need to remember that one day, this case is going to be in one of those cabinets, too, and that all of this will soon be over and done with. I think you would do well to please keep that in mind. Now, you take care of yourself. And, uh, by the way, I suspect I'll be seeing you soon in Judge Byrne's court as I have no doubt that this will not be well received by your counterpart across the courtyard."

"I suspect you're right, Mr. Callis. I'm going to go drop his copy off right now and then I'm going to come back over and spend a little time in your records room, keep your closed cases company for a while. I hope you don't mind."

"I don't mind one bit, David, you are always welcome here. I hope you know that."

"I do, Mr. Callis. And, uh, Mr. Callis?"

"Yes, David?"

"Thanks."

"You're very welcome."

And with that, David went out the door and headed back down the steps and then across the small courtyard that separated the courthouse from the offices of the Commonwealth's Attorney.

---

Archie Hudgins wasn't in so said Janice Parker his long time secretary. He was on his way back from a prosecutor's conference in Richmond but she would make sure that he got the copy of the subpoena *duces tecum* that David had handed to her, first thing when he arrived at the office. David thanked her but, as he left to return to Eugene's office, he knew with abject certainty that she was on her cell phone alerting her employer as to the filing of the subpoena. That's what Brenda would do, and he had no reason to believe that Janice would act any differently.

260

To the core of her administrative soul, Hudgin's assistant was all prosecution and she did her job with a staunch indifference to the plight of the criminally accused or their attorneys, for that matter. From her perspective, they were wholly and fully responsible for their own set of circumstances, and it wasn't for her to care one way or the other. She was polite, but her steel blue eyes and executioner's stare told you that you were inexorably on your own and if you wanted favors, well, they came hard pressed or didn't come at all. David had known plenty of "Janices" back at Justice and they were great when they were on your side but, now that the shoe was squarely secured on the other foot, the fit was a little less comfortable.

Once back in the Clerk's office, David staked a claim to one of the small desks in the records room and began to research what real estate Howard owned in Mathews County and how much he borrowed to buy it.

Forbes initially went to the county tax records and saw in the most current installment that Jimmy's employer owned, and paid taxes on, only one parcel of land, a five-acre tract of waterfront located on Horn Harbor. The tax records also referenced the deed of conveyance by book number and page. David opened the deed book to the page number identified in the tax records and saw that Howard had bought the land from the estate of one Hollis Owens four years ago for consideration in the amount of $135,000.00. David looked for any evidence of a loan or a mortgage and noted that the instrument that would secure such a mortgage, a Deed of Trust, was never recorded, meaning if Coles borrowed any money to buy the land, it for damn sure didn't come from a bank or any other institutional lender, knowing that the recording of a security instrument for a real estate loan from one of those places would be automatic.

Forbes went back to the tax records and saw that the property was reassessed two years after the date of purchase to reflect the addition of a new home which increased the property value by an additional $295,000.00. Again, as with the initial purchase, Forbes searched but could find zero evidence that Howard had taken out a construction loan to finance the building of the new residence. If he borrowed money to build his house, whoever loaned it to him wasn't too concerned with having their loan secured by the real estate. But, that's if Howard ever borrowed any money, and right now, that didn't seem to be the case.

Forbes' next port of call was to check the financing statements that would have contained instruments of indebtedness for the purchase of non-real estate items such as commercial trucks or fishing vessels. Again, just like with the real estate, nothing was recorded. No security instruments, no promissory notes, no deeds of trust and no mortgages usually means no loans, and no loans can only mean cash and carry and that's a lot of green for someone who makes a livin' catchin' fish.

On a whim, David then went to the judgment lien books and did a defendant search under Howard's name. He was rewarded when Forbes found three recordings against Coles Howard. Two were federal tax liens from six and seven years ago respectively, and the third was a judgment from five years ago and identified the plaintiff as a diesel repair service out of Norfolk. All had been marked 'satisfied' by the clerk, meaning paid in full, four years ago, and no judgments had been recorded since.

Forbes made copies of every document that he could get his hands on that bore Howard's name and returned to his desk to gather his papers and return to the office.

# Chapter Twenty-Six

## Cabell Sinclair

As he walked back down Main Street, his mind was moving at Grand Prix speed, hitting hairpin turns and breakneck straightaways, one after the other.

Howard could have borrowed all this cash from a family member who wasn't concerned with a secured method of repayment, which could explain everything, but who had this much money to begin with, nearly $430,000.00 in real estate alone if the tax records have any degree of accuracy not to mention the paid off judgment liens and the bucks laid out for the trucks and the boat? Too much, too much, too much.

When David got back to the office, things began to unravel. Brenda handed him three phone messages. The first was from Archie Hudgins who was demanding that David call him the moment he returned to the office. The second was from Judge Byrne's secretary advising him that a hearing had been scheduled for 9:00 a.m. the following morning referencing his subpoena *duces tecum* and the third was from Cabell Sinclair, a prominent attorney from the prestigious law firm of Jacobs and Rowe, one of the largest in the state, who identified himself to Brenda as counsel for Coles Howard.

As Forbes was wrestling with who to call first, a deputy came through the front door of the law office and served David with a Notice of Hearing referenced in the message from the judge's secretary.

After the deputy left, David said, to his own chagrin, "It appears that I have become somewhat popular this afternoon." He was speaking to Brenda's back as she was standing next to the open top drawer of a file cabinet, finishing up some paper work from earlier in the day.

"I'm afraid you are confusing popularity with notoriety," she said, turning around to face him and pausing momentarily to take a sip from the cup of black coffee that kept her pack of cigarettes perpetual company on the right hand corner of her desk. "There's a difference, you know."

"Oh, yeah, and what's that?" David replied, sliding down into one of the two reddish brown Chesterfield arm chairs that guarded the front lobby.

"Popularity is what gets somebody elected prom queen. Notoriety, on the other hand, is what gets the hangman's noose placed around your neck. Right now, you reek of notoriety in a big way," she said reaching for her pack of cigarettes.

"Are you saying, in other words, that I'm going to get hung tomorrow?" David asked.

"Yep. Tarred and feathered, too," she replied, now standing at the doorway, cigarette firmly in the ready position. Brenda flicked her lighter, inhaled hard and went lungs deep with the very best Virginia Slims had to offer. When she exhaled, it was like she was putting the period at the end of a really long, well written sentence.

"You know, David," she said, flicking off an ash and watching it float away like an errant snowflake. "There are some dogs that you just don't kick. You know what I mean?"

"Yeah, I know what you mean," Forbes replied. "We used to hear that stuff at Justice all the time. Don't do this and don't do that. Be careful what you look into about this Congressman or that Lt. General or this foreign dignitary or that CEO or this hedge fund manager or the Chairman of the board of who gives a shit because he's a really big campaign donor for you know who. All the time we heard that crap. And all the time, the big dogs, and I mean the really big dogs, got away with phenomenal levels of securities fraud, embezzlement, witness tampering, and stealing billions upon billions under the guise of the all mighty government defense contract."

David took a long pull from his bottle of water and continued. "Did any of them go to jail? Sure, but very, very few. But if you're a black kid on a second offense distribution of cocaine, give it up man, give it up. You are going down, hard and fast. Jails are full of young black kids while the big white dogs kick it back, light up a Macanudo, pour another McCallan and yuck it up down in Cabo."

"Look," he said. "I know I'm going to get my ass kicked tomorrow but the day I stop fightin' is the day I bar-be-cue my law license and that's not happening anytime soon. Now, where are those messages again? I might as well start returning some calls so I can find out just how big of a son-of a bitch I am in the eyes of all these people. But you know, the saving grace in all of this is that sometimes the louder the complaint, the closer one may be to that which the complaining party considers the most sensitive. So, I say it's time to have some fun. Let's consider the next twenty-four hours a 'Who killed Jimmy Jarvis?' Geiger counter of sorts and see who raises the most hell. What do ya think?"

"I'll say this much," Brenda said, "I think you're nuts but if I was in trouble, I'd want you on my side. Here are your messages. Good luck."

---

David knew that his bravado was swimming upstream against an acknowledged undercurrent of nervousness flowing like class five rapids in the opposite direction so he gathered that it would be best to get a feel for the lay of the land from a familiar face; consequently, his first call went local and that was to the Commonwealth's Attorney, Archie Hudgins.

"Hi, Archie, I got your call. What's up?" was his initial entry into the fray when the prosecutor picked up his phone three blocks away.

"What's up, my foot!" yelled the Commonwealth Attorney into the phone. "You know damn well what's up. Issuing a subpoena requiring Coles Howard, one of the most respected watermen in this county, to provide you, and I'm reading this damn thing now, - his state and federal tax returns for the last five years, all cash receipt journals for the last five years, all records as to all sources of all funds expended for all purchases of real estate, household possessions, boats, trucks and all business related equipment for the last five years, all records as to all income derived from the harvest of seafood for the

265

last five years, all records of income from all other sources for the last five years, and all records for each and every expense, personal or business, for the last five years!"

Archie Hudgins cardio-vascular was in full gear because he continued on, barely pausing to breathe. "Now do you mind telling me what the hell any of this has to do with this little murder case we have together? Do you have any idea as to what my office has been like for the last hour and a half? I've had yours truly, Coles Howard in here, I've had his daddy in here and one of the most well-known attorneys in Virginia made my goddamn day by bustin' my ass on the telephone about this bullshit subpoena and demanding to know what I'm going to do about it!"

He wasn't finished. "Well, I'm not going to do a damn thing about it. I'm going to let Judge Byrne deal with it tomorrow morning. Unless you know an awful lot about something that I don't, David, you've stepped over the line. And, I mean really, really stepped over the line."

Hudgins finally came up for air and paused for a moment, but then plunged right back as David heard some muffled conversation on the other end. Archie apparently had put his hand over the mouthpiece of the phone in an effort to limit David's share of the conversation but a garbled "Jesus Christ" still managed to seep through along with a fairly distinctly uttered "Goddamnit" that David figured was part and parcel of some back and forth between Hudgins and his secretary, Janice.

Archie quickly came back on the line at full voice. "The friggin' press now knows about it, too. Janice just walked in here and dropped a goddamn phone message on my desk from a goddamn newspaper reporter. David, tomorrow morning at 9:00 a.m., Judge Byrne is going to ask you to state your grounds in open court to support the issuance of the subpoena. May I ask what you are going to say in response to that question?"

"No," was all David said.

"What the hell do you mean "No?" Hudgins was now stammering like a misfiring machine gun. "You . . . .you . . . signed a materiality oath when you executed this subpoena request. That's a goddamn affidavit. Material how, counselor?"

"That's information confidential to the case, Archie. Strictly 'need to know' and you don't need to know." David had decided during the course of Hudgins' initial onslaught that brevity was his sharpest sword and that he had absolutely zero to lose by strapping on the Kevlar, unsheathing his saber and being a dick about the whole thing.

"We'll see about that," were the last words Forbes heard the prosecutor utter before he abruptly hung up the phone.

David could clearly feel the heat from the bridge that was burning between their respective offices. So much for down home, country camaraderie, he thought. If it ever existed at all, it for damn sure didn't exist anymore.

'Jamal Billups, what have you done to my world? he mused as he launched a dart at the board affixed to his closet door. Watching it sail like a dragonfly and find purchase with an audible 'thunk' in the black one-quarter inch from dead center red, Forbes grabbed at the other message slip that had landed on his desk that day, and again, he reached for the phone. One down and one to go.

David's call to the law offices of Cabell Sinclair was answered by a female voice so rich, so smooth and so utterly steeped in privileged, private school refinement that one had to truly wonder whether her malted barley had been smoked in peat from the Isle of Islay.

From the very first unhurried "This is the office of Cabell Sinclair. How may I assist you," the caller was immediately put on notice that the *person* on the other end was *the* Person who was *the* Gatekeeper for those lesser mortals who wished an audience with his eminency, Mr. Sinclair.

Counsel to the well-heeled and the well-funded, one couldn't open a Virginia State Bar magazine without seeing a photograph of Sinclair's big mug wedged between that of a Supreme Court Justice and the president or chairman of some lofty organization, with the accompanying article usually about Sinclair being presented an award or accolade of some sort for service above and beyond. If anyone actually paused to read half that crap, they would think that Webster himself would've lacked sufficient verbiage to accurately and completely heap the right amount of praise on the man, a fact which Mr. Sinclair himself would no doubt be in total agreement. Truly, he was a lawyer's lawyer with an expansive ass well worthy of being well kissed. And now he had been hired by Coles Howard.

As David waited on hold, he could hear the imaginary Geiger counter starting to buzz in the background. The perimeter of the enemy camp was being probed and Forbes drew his sword to the ready, knowing that his moment was at hand.

"David Forbes, Cabell Sinclair here," the voice answered. "I want to thank you for returning my call. You know, I graduated from Harvard law in the same class as did your former employer."

"I assume you're referring to Attorney General Robert McCallister," David responded.

"I am, indeed," Sinclair responded. "He was also a fraternity brother of mine during our undergraduate years at Yale. Guess you could say we followed each other academically, but parted company when it came time to leave Harvard Yard. He, of course, went public service and I chose another path. I just got off the phone with him, in fact. He says you're a good man, honest, tenacious and hardworking to a fault."

"Next time, please give him my regards," Forbes said again.

"I'll do that, and, by the way, where did you go to school, David?" Sinclair inquired, angling for the higher ground of the superior academic resume' that he knew the answer to his question would surely bring unless Forbes owned up to either being Christ in the afterglow of the resurrection or being the ghost of Abraham Lincoln.

The lawyer for Jamal Billups wasted no time in engaging the battle.

"You know exactly where I went to school," he said, sword and Kevlar at the ready. "And you know where I was born, and what my wife does for a living and probably how big my pecker is. There is a briefing paper on your desk right now that contains all of that information. You wouldn't have called me without it."

"Touché, Mr. Forbes," Sinclair stated. "Absent the dimensions of your genitalia, a rather complete bio is in fact laying here on my desk. Doesn't take all that much these days. With Google and it's ilk, the world in all of its minutia is just a click away. You were an easy find. Hard-charging assistant United States Attorney makes a right turn and heads to the country, an Atticus Finch *re dux* as it were. Tell me, David, do you miss the big stage?"

"Looks like I'm still on it, if my phone messages are any indication," David replied, gliding a washed smooth river stone edgewise across the length of his blade, while the Geiger counter went buzz, buzz, buzz.

"Bob McCallister said you were sharp, too. I left that out of our earlier conversation. Wanted to find that out for myself," Sinclair retorted.

"Now, are you going to voluntarily withdraw that subpoena you filed or are you going to make me drive all the way down to your little neck of the woods to make sure the Honorable Robert Byrne makes the right call, which he will of course. You and I both know that. It's really a simple choice, David, as it is so often, and that's whether you choose to take the path that is the most reasonable and expeditious or whether you wish to be horse drug down a wagon rutted trail strewn with rock and cactus like some cattle thief in a Gary Cooper western. Frankly, I really don't give a damn what you do."

"Have a safe drive, Mr. Sinclair," was all David said. Sharpen, sharpen, buzz, buzz.

"I'll do that. Have a good day, Sir and goodbye."

Sinclair hung up the phone and looked over at Investigator Donny Howard who was standing beside a window that ran floor to ceiling, bordered by pleated mullions of red and gold pattered silk that perfectly framed the view of the Washington monument like it was one of those images pictured on the postcards sold by the hot dog street vendors down on Constitution.

"Your retainer may not be large enough, Mr. Howard," Sinclair said. "Most of these legal beagles crawl under their beds when I call. Not him. Background check on this boy shows Marine Corps reserves while getting his undergrad at Maryland. He did his law at Georgetown, followed by four years in the FBI and then six years at Justice. His work product is obviously aimed at proving a money laundering operation. His demeanor tells me that he clearly thinks he's on to something significant to his case. It's going to take more than a phone call and a hearing or two, to rattle this guy's cage, I'm afraid."

"As to the retainer, there's more money where that came from," Howard replied, his gaze still fixed out the window like a sniper at Stalingrad, his Armani suit of gun metal blue glistening in the late afternoon sunlight that perforated the full length of the glass in long, defined diagonal rays, giving the detective the appearance of a favored apostle in a Sunday school tutorial.

"Just do your job, and things will work out just fine."

"I don't need instructions, Lieutenant," Sinclair said, rising from behind his desk like a king departing his throne. "This firm wasn't built upon the giving of bad advice and I'm not keen on being told what to do by some minor leaguer. And, now sir, this pleasant meeting is over. You will receive my report as to tomorrow's affairs once they have been concluded. Please leave as you arrived, through my private entrance. As with Forbes, I know a bit about you, too, and I think our acquaintance is best if not presented on display in the front lobby. Good bye, Mr. Howard."

# Chapter Twenty-Seven

# The Hearing on the Subpoena *Duces Tecum*

When David wheeled his Porsche into the court parking lot, he wasn't surprised to see the black Mercedes Benz SL65 AMG with D.C. plates occupying the space farthest away from the likelihood of door dings and other forms of unwanted contact.

He expected an early arrival from his Washington adversary. What did surprise him was that Sinclair's signature ride was accompanied by over two dozen pickup trucks with most sporting McCain - Palin bumper stickers, gun racks, aluminum framed dog hunting boxes, 3 inch lift kits and rolling high on huge tires, with caricature decals on the back windows of a now dead kid-like Dale Earnhardt urinating on the car number of some NASCAR rival from years gone past. More than a few had stacks upon stacks of the empty bushel baskets used to haul crabs to market.

Forbes quickly deduced that the waterman had gotten the word that one of their own was under attack and had come to court that morning not only to get a look see for themselves as to what was going on but to make sure that whoever was making trouble got the message right quick that theirs was a brotherhood and that if one of them was hurting, then they all felt the pain.

About twenty of these men were standing just outside the front doors when Forbes approached the courthouse. Crowded together in sun-bleached denim and signature Carhartt brown duck, they to a man wore the legendary white rubber boots of the Chesapeake Bay waterman and not a single one of them moved to make way for David Forbes.

Suddenly reliving the stone cold atmosphere of the now famous chowder affair at Harper's Creek Marina, David held his breath. He knew better than to try to weave his way through this kind of heavy traffic and chose instead to slowly and carefully make his way around the outer perimeter of the brined gauntlet of seafaring men built like the wind slapped trunks of very stout coast grown trees when the courthouse doors opened with the cueing punctuality befitting a Broadway premier and Deputy Matt Robins stepped outside.

The mammoth officer was working bailiff duty just inside the courthouse doors and witnessed David's predicament unfolding and unfolding badly at that. "Everyone is going to need to clear the sidewalk and the front entrance to the courthouse. If you have court business, and I assume most of y'all are here for the hearing, then come inside and grab a seat. Otherwise, y'all need to find somewhere else to just stand around. I can't have you blocking the front entrance and creatin' problems for people trying to get in and out. Thank you for your cooperation," to which Robins quickly added a, "Good Mornin' Mr. Forbes" in response to the "Thanks Deputy" David tossed his way as the crowd reluctantly parted and he stopped holding his breath, gratefully making his way past the deputy and into the lobby.

Once inside, Forbes, walked to the courtroom and found it two-thirds full of even more watermen and various other members of the local citizenry who had come to court that morning to support the home town team. David knew without question that no part of this bunch was going to be sitting on his side of the bleachers. Today it was going to be just him and Jamal against everything else that was coming through the door. Not a single black face was anywhere to be seen.

Archie Hudgins was standing up front beside his usual counsel table talking to a large, broad shouldered man who would give Clerk Callis a run for his money in the silver hair department. Wearing a hand-tailored Italian pinstripe suit of the darkest charcoal grey, a pair of flawlessly polished Allen Edmonds wingtips, a pale blue shirt with contrasting white color, a blood red silk tie and cuff links with rubies the size of grapes, Cabell Sinclair's appearance screamed legal success.

Seated in the front row just behind his attorney was Coles Howard, also well attired in suit and tie, and a quietly attractive woman adorned in ivory and dark blue was at his side who David took to be Howard's wife. Neither Hudgins nor Sinclair acknowledged David's presence as he took his place at counsel table.

David was unloading his papers from his briefcase when Robins came over and said that the Judge was going to be a little late and wanted to know if he wanted to meet with his client back in the holding cell or whether he wanted Billups to be brought out now.

Forbes told Robins to bring out his client. Might as well get his client comfortable now with the hostile crowd and delaying his arrival wasn't going to make that part of today's event any easier.

They must have had Billups just on the other side of the secured door leading to the prisoner holding area because he was in his chair at counsel table within seconds of David's conversation with the deputy. As usual, Billups looked petrified.

"What the fuck is this about?" Billups exclaimed. "Is my trial today? Tell me this is not my trial. I ain't ready for this shit. You haven't come up to see me since that preliminary hearing bullshit. You forgot about me already, is that it?"

Jamal was talking fast, nervous and loud enough to garner Lt. Carter's attention from his sentry position at the door to judge's chambers and also sufficient to cause both attorneys from the other side of the abyss that seemed to divide the courtroom to pause from their strategy session and look over at the insignificant source of the disturbance who was dead meat as far as they were concerned.

"Jamal," David sternly whispered, "Keep your voice down. This is not your trial. This is a hearing on a Subpoena I requested to get some documents to help in your defense. The prosecution objects to my subpoena and that's why we're here. That's all. So relax."

"Relax? You fuckin' relax," Billup said. "My handcuffed black ass just got walked into a large room filled with a bunch of pissed off white men who hate me and them deputies all got guns and they hate me, too."

Jamal was now glancing around furtively like a cornered, beaten dog, "Who's that big dude with the Commonwealth's Attorney? I ain't never seen him before."

273

"Cabell Sinclair," David answered. "Attorney from D.C. He's Coles Howard's private attorney."

"Why's he here?" he asked. "Ain't one lawyer enough to fry my ass? They got to bring in another one?"

"He's probably just here to advise Archie how to best defeat my subpoena request," David said. "I doubt we'll see him again after today's hearing."

"What's this subpoena thing you talkin' about?" Jamal asked. "It must be bad for them because they don't look like they like you one bit."

Billups took another long look over at the opposition and then added, "Yeah, you best be careful. Ain't nothing friendly about them folks, that's for sure, and that big guy, the D.C. dude, is trouble for you lawyer man, I can tell. He's evil through and through. As my granny would say, he done took the church pew out of his soul a long time ago."

"I can handle him," David said. "As for the subpoena, it's pretty basic. I requested all of the financial records I could think of from Coles Howard who was Jimmy's employer. Not much to it, really."

"They don't think so," his client countered. "They think there's a whole lot to it. You either done something really right or really wrong, lawyer man, cause you have hit a nerve, that's for damn sure."

Jamal slumped back in his chair and David started to make a few last minute notes when Court Clerk Eugene Callis came out from the Judge's door carrying a single file, (Commonwealth v. Jamal Billups), took his seat an arm's reach to the left of the Judges chair and smiled at David Forbes.

Although the Clerk was by definition an impartial player in the day's affairs, David nevertheless felt that maybe now, he had one person in the courtroom who, given the opportunity, wouldn't gladly run him out of town lashed tight to the cowcatcher of the five o'clock train, dripping in steaming tar and adorned with the feathers from the well plucked guest of honor at a Sunday church supper.

Forbes got up from his chair and walked over to shake hands with the stately clerk, "You've attracted quite a crowd, David." Callis said. "How does it feel to be so popular?"

"I'm not sure that popular is the right term, Mr. Callis. Brenda reminded me just yesterday that there is a distinct and palatable difference between popularity and notoriety. I think that for today, we may be witnessing the effects of the latter, if I may be so bold as to suggest"

"Well put, as usual," the clerk said. "I'll give that some thought. In the meantime, remember that people often times change the way they look at things and about the way they think about other people. These aren't bad folks in here. I've known most of them all my life. They're good people and you'll see that for yourself sooner than you think. Just don't let any of this sink too deeply beneath your skin and things will turn out just fine. And, ah, by the way, David . . ."

"Yes, sir?" the lawyer replied.

"When you get back to counsel table, you may want to hold on to your seat. And that's all I'm going to say about that. Good luck, David." And that was the last thing the clerk said as he rose and placed the Billups file dead center on the Judge's bench.

David was walking back to his counsel table when he watched a visibly anxious, some would say solidly angry, Sheriff Howard suddenly come through the entrance doors at the rear of the local hall of justice and stride like Jackson at First Manassas to the conspiratorial configuration of lawyers still huddled on the north side of the courtroom.

Like Billups upon his own entrance, Sheriff Howard now spoke fast, nervous and plenty loud enough for David to hear the word "Judge" repeated over and over again. Something was wrong, David knew it. Shoulders were now slumped. Expressions had become dire. On body language alone, Fort Sinclair was in a concerned state of mind.

For some reason, based upon the information recently delivered by the Sheriff, confidence had just slipped a notch or two in the opposite corner and strength in numbers coupled with a six figure automobile in the parking lot suddenly didn't appear so empowering. Mr. Callis's seat holding instructions now seemed to be gaining some traction.

The activities across the way weren't lost on a hand-cuffed Jamal who, though slumped in a chair and wearing a standard issue orange jailhouse one piece jumpsuit, still maintained NORAD level surveillance on the events transpiring in the enemy camp.

"What's up with those guys?" Jamal said, "They acting like someone stole their weed."

"I don't know." David replied, while taking another gander at the huddle of playmakers who were apparently reconsidering their game plan. "We're going to find out soon enough, though."

David didn't have time to comment further when a loud knock at chambers door interrupted their conversation and was instantly followed by the "All Rise" command sternly uttered by a ramrod straight, non-smiling Lt. Carter.

Joined by the shuffling and rustling of rubber shorn feet and bodies clothed in rough fabric salted stiff from a morning's tending of nets and pots, Jamal and his attorney stood together and looked on as fate played one and all with equal peculiarity.

Fortune, as Jamal learned that day, is a testy business. Some people, regardless of their good character or their good intentions, go through their entire lives without so much as a whisper of a moment that smacks of anything resembling an abiding tone.

Day in and day out, they endlessly suffer because it is in the cards for them to suffer. From their fleeting birth moment of sheer biological equality with their gestational peers (which lasts only micro-seconds until the demographics of the hut you were born in take over as the prime predictor of your fate) to their most certain and predictable end in death's waiting arms, their ticket has been cleanly punched and there's nothing they can do about it.

Then there are those certain others who relish finer air from the other end of the spectrum, who just seem to stumble happily from one grand event to the next with the path at their feet littered in precocious abundance with all of the creature comforts a person should ever want or need. For these folks, good luck frankly just washes ashore like it's legally theirs, a property right of sorts, like a description of a car on a title or of a certain piece of real estate on a deed that's got their name on it. It all belongs to them, free and clear. No liens, no encumbrances. And, all for the asking, or better yet, just automatically bequeathed without the necessary labor of a request, matriculating straight out of granddaddy's trust account, with character and deservedness seeming to almost never play a critical role in determining how or why they have become who they are.

For the less blessed and less cursed rest of humanity, there are those pioneering optimists between the bookends who remain convinced that good fortune can be erstwhile manufactured, or at least the odds of its occurrence measurably improved, by way of ones *labors*.

This struggle takes place *en masse* second by second, inch by inch, within the perimeter of the holy middle, with the less timid making occasional adventuresome forays out to the fringes but with the vast risk adverse majority overwhelmingly choosing to keep the grindstone close to home. Hard work, dedication to family, and commitment to one's chosen God are usually membership requirements for this club. Plus if you hit the gym regularly, keep the grass mowed, and act more or less like something of a financial spendthrift, then hopefully this too will increase the odds that one day fate will tip the chips in your direction.

Jamal Billups, however, was aware of none of this. Of the abundant luxury of the fortunate unbridled few or of the plight of their unfortunate opposites staked down tight on land long lost from God's "To Do" list, he really couldn't give a shit.

If it was Friday and he had a sawmill paycheck in his pocket, he had it made and the world could kiss his black, country ass. Besides, his granny always kept the light on just as she always kept his bed made in the back bedroom of her down county bungalow whose front door still bore the heel print from the boot of Lt. Jake Carter. Pinto beans and seasoned collard greens were waiting for him, steaming, simmering staples on the old woman's stove, if he could make it home in a condition somewhat less than reeling drunk. If he couldn't, the creeks were always brimming with more than enough softshell crabs and oysters for the taking if his preferred brand of good fortune rendered him enough liquor to make it an all-night affair.

This isn't to say that David's client was unappreciative of, or ignorant of, the effort expended by the middle grounders, it was just that the required tenacity of it all, the daily attention to some sort of schedule and the necessity of focusing on some measure of time beyond five o'clock was all just too much and was easily and delightfully lost in the haze of as much alcohol as a woodcutters *per diem* could buy.

But even a Jamal Billups knew enough to realize that grateful appreciation was the order of the day when the Judge's door opened and someone other than the Honorable Robert Paul Byrne walked in and sat down in the well-waxed, top- grain leather at center stage.

"Counsel, good morning. My name is Ted Powell and I'm a retired Circuit Court Judge from Portsmouth. I have a house across the river in Deltaville and I was asked by Judge Byrne last night to take over as acting judge in this case. Because of the involvement of the Sheriff's brother in the motions before the court, Judge Byrne feels, and rightfully so I might add, that he has a conflict in this case and he has recused himself from hearing any further matters as a consequence thereto. Now does my involvement in this case raise any additional issues that need to be addressed before we get to the matter noticed for today's hearing?"

David Forbes was instantly out of his chair and the words, "No, sir, we are ready to proceed," left his lips quicker than he could have shouted a "hell yes" to an offer of a free cold beer at a Redskins game. In a word, he was stunned by Judge Powell's appearance, happily so, but stunned nevertheless.

The man who came through the chamber's door that day was none other than the legendary Theodore Lincoln Powell. Born and raised in Birmingham, Alabama, by civil rights activist parents, Ted Powell knew firsthand why the choir sang so strong and the parishioners prayed so hard at the First African Assembly of God.

Powell's father was a Baptist minister who walked with King and Abernathy on a cool day in March of 1965 across the Edmund Pettus Bridge that approached Selma from the southwest. His father ended that historic afternoon with his clothing soaked like a well-used dishrag from fire hoses borne by white police officers who imparted additional doses of non-liquid violence on the marchers from the business end of billy clubs and from the snarling teeth of made vicious dogs, creating a crystal clear picture in the process to all who watched on national TV that the preferential color of a man's skin was "white" and that scant attention was going to be meted out that day as to the depth of anyone's character.

Young Ted Powell was one of many Americans watching the news from Selma that day and the grainy images of jaws wide open German shepherds, fire hoses on full blast, and fist-shaking angry white politicians became seared across his cranium like the scars from a branding iron, and they never healed until he had completed his undergrad at Howard University and went on to finish first in his law school class at the University of Chicago.

Now, if Powell had been white, big law firm jobs would have been as plentiful as olives in Tuscany when he passed the bar exam, but the 'Need not Apply' sign for African-Americans still hung huge across the pillars of Wall Street and in the hallways of corporate America, thus requiring that young Ted seek his fortune elsewhere which ultimately proved to be a very, costly mistake for his reluctant employers.

By the end of Judge Powell's long career in civil rights litigation, he had succeeded in bringing nearly every major U.S. corporation to its racial knees, extracting huge concessions for affirmative action in the process and sheparding race neutral hiring practices into the norm. Governments and educational institutions also were not immune from his attention, and he paved new inroads for the hiring of African-Americans in state and federal government leadership positions and for the admission of black students, and the hiring of black professors, in state colleges and universities.

And last, but not least, he made a bundle of money in the process, allowing him to not only be a major financial donor at historically black schools across Virginia and throughout the South, but to sit as well as a Trustee on many of their boards.

It also afforded Powell the financial leeway to step away from the practice of law and accept a judicial appointment as a Circuit Court Judge for the City of Portsmouth from a Virginia legislature still doing business in the capital of the Confederacy.

As a judge, Ted Powell quickly gained a reputation for fairness and for stark accountability and any lawyer who thought that a black defendant was going to have an easy go of it in Powell's court had misread the tea leaves.

A product of an earlier time when allegiance to family held sway over a preference for 9mm pistols and crack cocaine, Powell was merciless in the dispensement of justice. One way or the other, his Honor was going to do his level best to make sure that the endless proliferation of guns, drugs and senseless killing was going to end on the streets of Portsmouth. When he retired after twelve years on the bench, the crime rate was down, the killing had abated and it was a little harder to buy a bag of cocaine on the streets of Judge Powell's jurisdiction.

---

Having heard from the defense, Judge Powell looked over at Archie Hudgins who was bent slightly sideways at the hip, leaning over to get a whispered earful from his powerful colleague who was riding shotgun at counsel table.

"Would the person in charge over there care to respond to the courts inquiry?" Powell said, already showing that he was not amused at the fact that counsel's attentions were directed elsewhere than towards him.

Hudgins rose and said, "Ah your honor, I'm Archie Hudgins, Mathews County Commonwealth's Attorney. Its, ah, a pleasure to have you sitting in our court. I filed the motion to quash the defendant's request for this here subpoena *duces tecum* but I'm going to ask if this hearing could be continued to another day and . . . "

Powell interrupted the prosecutor,"Why? Are you lacking a necessary witness? From all appearances, that's highly doubtful. Looks like half the town is sitting in the courtroom and I'm guessing that the well-dressed man seated behind you is the person identified in the subpoena request. Plus, the defendant is present. His attorney is here and I'm here. And you need to know that it's not going to get any prettier in here after today because my ugly mug is going to be presiding over this case until this matter is concluded. Now, you are the party who filed the motion that has brought all of us together today. If you want a continuance, I'll give it to you over the objections of defense counsel, but I am not going to enter an order temporarily staying the subpoena, if that was also on your request list for this morning. Has the subpoena been served, Mr. Hudgins?"

"Ah, I don't rightly know, Judge," he said looking over his shoulder in the direction of the sheriff, who having now beaten a hasty retreat to the rear of the courtroom, deftly shook his head at the prosecutor in the direction of the universal negative.

"Ah, I don't believe it has, Judge," Hudgins responded.

"Well, unless I rule otherwise," Judge Powell said, "It will be served this morning immediately upon the conclusion of these proceedings. Is the sheriff present?"

"Yes, sir, I'm here," Howard said loudly from the rear of the courtroom.

"You heard what I said?" Judge Powell asked loudly in response.

"Yes, sir, I did," The Sheriff replied.

"Do you have any questions about my instructions?" Powell asked again.

"No, sir, I do not," Howard confirmed.

But before anyone, including the Judge, could say another word, Cabell Sinclair rose like Zeus from his temple on Mt. Olympus and said, "Your Honor. May it please the court, I would appreciate an opportunity to be heard."

"And who are you Sir?" inquired Judge Powell, a request for information that Sinclair hadn't heard in thirty years.

The ever so confident barrister took it all in stride. "Why, Your Honor, I'm Cabell Sinclair of the law firm of Jacobs and Rowe. It's a privilege to be in your court. I represent the legal interests of Mr. Coles Howard, who *is* here today as you so astutely noted."

"Fine. Now, why are you at counsel table?" Judge Powell asked.

Sinclair paused, his strategy interrupted.

'He didn't see that one coming,' David mused, who was now abiding by Callis' seat-holding instructions to the hilt. Seatbelts were fastened, trays were in the upright position and electronic devices were turned off. Ladies and gentlemen, time for takeoff was at hand and this was going to get interesting. Two great lawyers, two bulls in the same pen and each one the antithesis of the other. This was legal swordsmanship at its best.

"Well, Your Honor," Sinclair replied, "My client has been unduly and unconscionably issued legal process by this attorney over here, process that is immaterial and invasive in the least and arguably slanderous and defamatory on its face. I strenuously object . . . . "

Judge Powell was having none of it. "Mr. Sinclair, not to cut you off, but, frankly, I'm confused about the nature of your involvement here today. We have one matter on this morning's hearing docket and one matter only and that's the Motion to Quash the defendant's Request for a Subpoena *duces tecum*. The moving party is the Commonwealth of Virginia who is capably represented by the fellow seated to your right. The only other party to this proceeding here today is the defendant, Mr. Billups who, let the record reflect, is present with his attorney, Mr. Forbes. The file does not reflect that you are in any way an attorney of record to this proceeding nor does the docket indicate that a civil matter collateral to this proceeding has been filed and that a hearing pertaining thereto has been scheduled for this morning that would give you standing to address the Court."

"Your Honor," Sinclair responded with arms outstretched and hands palm up, blooming hard to recapture the initiative lost at the opening bell, "Laws are well established that place strict standards and perimeters on the legal justification for the issuance of subpoenas that require non-party citizens to turn over their private papers to be scrutinized by total strangers. It should be the right, if not the absolute duty of each and every citizen to petition the court to protect them from such frivolous intrusions, such as we have here where sensitive financial information has been requested willy-nilly simply for the sole purpose of harassing and intimidating a key witness for the prosecution in a murder case that has understandably outraged the citizens of this fine county. I am here today to protect not only the rights of my client but also to preserve the right of privacy that has been the bedrock of our democracy since Valley Forge. My standing today, my legal authority to appear before this tribunal, is thus inherent in the proceeding itself, if Your Honor please."

Sinclair remained on his feet, his pinstripes parallel with the longitudes, confident that once again his oratorical skills had evened the scorecard. But he was wrong.

"Mr. Sinclair," the judge said, "The Commonwealth's Attorney was elected to fulfill the very obligations you've so aptly described and is duly obligated to represent the interest of the citizen here today. I thank you for appearing but I find and so rule that you have no standing to address the Court or to participate as an attorney before the bar in these proceedings. You may now withdraw from counsel table and join your client in the gallery, sir."

Sinclair didn't move. He just stood there while the Earth ground to a halt on its axis, the ruling of Judge Powell resonating in his brain like a fire house Claxton, penetrating areas of his cranium previously untouched by any jurist since the man from Plains occupied the White House. The Washington attorney then looked up at Powell like a veteran bounty hunter gazing at a man across the drink laden tabletops of a Dodge City saloon whose face he had just seen on a wanted poster over at the U.S. Marshalls office next to the Five and Dime.

But the battle-proven Judge gave it back in kind and twice as tough at that, having plowed through the Cabell Sinclair's of the world in courtrooms across the United States for over three decades.

To Judge Powell, Sinclair was a well-known breed of take-no-prisoners litigators, stalwart defenders of the right of Corporate America to make sure all things go just right for Corporate America.

The showdown continued and history will reflect that the points and blades of the knives and daggers employed by South Street butchers and professional assassins alike would have proved rounded and dull in comparison to the razor-like stares that lasered back and forth that fine moment between the Honorable Theodore Lincoln Powell and the undefeatable Cabell Sinclair. Silence never sounded so loud as it did that day, a wordless cusp of haughty suspense that hung in the courtroom like thick, gray fog, dense, dangerous and impenetrable, the nemesis of watermen everywhere, as everyone held their breath and waited for Sinclair's next play. Two bulls in the same pen, indeed.

The best Washington had to offer finally spoke. "As the court wishes." was all he said, acknowledging the rarity of defeat and stepping back from counsel table like a struck out future Hall of Famer exiting the batter's box at home plate. He sat beside his client, leaving his papers at counsel table for later retrieval once this debacle had come to its none-too-soon end.

"Now, Mr. Hudgins, your motion, sir."

"Well, Judge, Mr. Coles Howard here is a lifelong citizen of this community, and, as you know, is also, ah, the son of our sheriff. He runs a fine seafood business and was the employer of the young man that Mr. Forbes' client has been indicted for stabbing to death out on Haven Beach. Now, this here subpoena just comes out of the blue, Your Honor, and requests everything but the kitchen sink when it comes to Mr. Howard's financial records. I'm talking tax returns, business records . . . ."

Judge Powell stepped in. "Mr. Hudgins, I know what is requested in the subpoena. I've read it, several times, in fact."

"Yes, sir," Hudgins said, "and well, this information the defendant's attorney has requested is just a fishing expedition and has nothing to do with Jamal Billups having murdered Jimmy Jarvis."

"How do you know?" the Judge asked.

"How do I know what?" Archie dully inquired, obviously unprepared for the present give and take in a hearing that was predicted by everyone on his side of the fence to last about three minutes with the end result a bygone conclusion. He thought he would be back in his office before his coffee got cold.

"How do you know that it has nothing to do with this homicide?" Powell inquired, Socratic Method now in full employ.

"It just doesn't, Your Honor," Hudgins said more forcefully, as he started to get his sea legs back underneath him, having fully grasped the fact that the lead pipe cinch lock approach of ten minutes ago was now dust on the floor.

"I'm well acquainted with the facts of this case and the evidence is just overwhelming that Jamal Billups killed Jimmy Jarvis. We've got the knife he killed him with, the defendant was covered in the decedent's blood, he fled from law enforcement officers, the two men had a fist fight the night before and the defendant pulled a knife on him then, too. I mean, we've got darn near everything but a confession and a video of the crime itself."

The prosecutor continued on. "In all of this, Judge, there hasn't been one iota of speculation whatsoever that any person other than the defendant had anything to do with this horrible crime. If there is such evidence, I want to see it. But nothing of the sort has been presented to my office. To my knowledge, this subpoena has not been issued to establish an alibi for the defendant, the request itself goes way beyond the scope of that defense, nor has it been issued to counter any scientific evidence that may be presented in this case, DNA and things like that. At best, and based upon statements that defendant's counsel has made to Mr. Howard at his place of business about tax evasion and things of the sort, statements which Mr. Howard is prepared to testify to here today, the defendant's only theory, which is wildly speculative and unsupported factually, is that Mr. Howard runs a cash-based business, maybe paid less than he should in taxes and that Jimmy was his employee. End of theory. And that's not enough to support the issuance of this subpoena request, Your Honor."

Archie Hudgins sat down and looked over at David. "Your turn, Mr. Forbes," Judge Powell said.

David stood up at counsel table, put his right hand on the left shoulder of his client and said, "Judge, the prosecution in this case thus far has a crime without a witness, a knife without fingerprints, a body found miles away from anywhere this defendant was ever seen that night, a defendant who, I might add, doesn't have a car and for him to have committed the crime as charged, he would have had to travel about seventeen round trip miles that night, on foot, because there isn't any evidence that anyone gave him a ride that night or that he went anywhere else after his fistfight with Jimmy Jarvis, which we don't deny happening, other than to the loft of the hay barn at Green Plains Farm where he grew up as a child."

"And let's get something straight right now. My client never took the first step to run from law enforcement until a posse of civilians, led by Lt. Carter over there, showed up armed with shotguns and crossbows, crossed the fields at Green Plains on ATVs and fired an arrow through the barn door that nearly struck my client. After that, he did indeed run for his life and took an arrow himself in his leg for his efforts. Worse than that, the mob that shot him then beat him to within an inch of his life, I've got the medical records to prove all of this, and were busy discussing his execution when the owner of Green Plains, Ms. Dorothy Hughes, leveled a rifle out of her third floor window and threatened some justice of her own if they didn't soon point their crossbows at something other than my client's chest."

Forbes continued. "Jimmy Jarvis died a brutal death, but my client didn't kill him. The decedent was an all-state linebacker in superb physical condition and for my client, whose all of 5' 8" and 140 pounds to have stabbed him to death, not shot, but stabbed with a knife on an open stretch of beach and not to have sustained a single defensive wound from Jarvis in the process is highly, highly improbable and there is zero forensic evidence that any such wound was ever sustained by my client."

"And while we're on the subject of forensic evidence, let me also advise the court that crime scene preservation and investigation in this case falls so far below acceptable law enforcement standards that it makes the O.J. Simpson case look like a textbook example of how it ought to be done. For example, no steps were taken to preserve the condition of the beach parking lot, a sand parking lot, if I may add, for tire tread analysis, as if it wasn't important for the Sheriff's department to perhaps know what other vehicles may have been in the lot on the night Jimmy Jarvis was murdered. The list of the other "un-importants" in this case goes on and on."

"As to the records requested in my subpoena, they are material to this proceeding based upon evidence in my case file which I will not reveal in open court. I swore an oath of materiality when I executed the request and I stand by it fully here today. In conclusion, the killer of Jimmy Jarvis could well be in this courtroom at this very moment but his name is not Jamal Billups who appears here today presumed of his innocence."

Archie Hudgins flew out of his chair, "Judge, I object! These comments are outrageous. These insinuations, these . . . .these poorly veiled innuendos about Mr. Howard are insulting beyond measure!"

"Mr. Hudgins, sit down!" Judge Powell commanded. "This is a first degree murder case, not a hearing on some traffic ticket. The Defendant is facing life imprisonment and aggressive representation is to be expected. The court is going to take a ten minute recess. I'll make my ruling when we reconvene. Everyone can keep their seats."

As the judge disappeared through the chamber door, Forbes was still standing. In fact, he had never moved once during the entire summation to the court and his hand still rested on the shoulder of his client.

David, who was looking down as Jamal was looking up, said, "What do you think?"

Jamal said, "I think you just kicked some ass. Man, I love you. I just hope you really believe half that shit you just said cause it's all true. Every damn word of it."

"I believe it. You don't have to worry about that. Hey, can I ask you a question?" David asked.

"Sure."

David paused for a moment and then said, "How come no one shows up to support you at these hearings? I mean I know this one was spur of the moment, but there wasn't anyone on your side at the preliminary hearing either."

"You mean, no one from my tribe?" Jamal said with a wry grin.

"Whatever, but what's up?"

Jamal looked down at his handcuffs and then said, "They just scared, that's all. Show up today, get pulled over tomorrow, that sort of thing. It's how it is, man. I really don't want nobody here if you want to knows the truth. Best for everybody if I go this alone."

David didn't reply, he just shook his head and turned to take a look around the courtroom, check out the lay of the land before Judge Powell retook the bench. Some folks appeared to have had enough of the legal festivities as there were a few more vacant seats than there were at the commencement of the hearing. But one seat had been taken since the hearing started and that was the one now occupied, again in the very back row, by Walter Taylor, who was, again, looking and smiling at David Forbes. This time, David was compelled to nod an acknowledgement towards the old man who no doubt had come this day to see just how much light the lamp he lit would throw.

And, apparently, it must have thrown quite a bit.

When Judge Powell returned to the bench, he denied the motion to quash and ordered that the subpoenaed documents were to be delivered to the clerk's office within fifteen days. Upon receipt, they were to be placed under seal for inspection only by the attorneys for the Commonwealth and the Defendant. Access by the press and the public was strictly forbidden. Hearing adjourned.

And, that was that. Howard and his wife left the courtroom before the Judge was even through his chamber's door, heading no doubt to meet his father for service of the subpoena while dodging the fevered pen of the Gazette reporter who was angling at paparazzi speed for his comments on the outcome of the hearing at hand.

Back inside, David Forbes was floored, speechless, excited, and happy beyond measure but strangely not surprised. There is expectancy in every case that justice will be done and today that expectancy was achieved by every measure. As he packed up his things, Jamal Billups managed to give Forbes the best hug a handcuffed defendant could give his court appointed lawyer before he was led back to his cell a far happier man by all accounts than when he walked in.

When Forbes turned around, briefcase in hand, to head up center aisle and get his own self out of the courtroom, he found himself staring point blank at the perfectly tied knot in the very expensive Hermes tie that was wrapped around the very expensive gullet of Cabell Sinclair.

The crown prince of legal D.C. was not at a loss for words.

"You're playing for the wrong team, David," Sinclair managed to utter through a teeth gritting smile that did nothing to hide his displeasure. "That was good work up there today. Misguided by all accounts but flawlessly presented. Be sure to let me know when you tire of this country tomfoolery, as we could use a man like you at our firm."

The ingratiating comment slid past David like Nebraska corn exiting the southern end of a tundra bound goose.

"Oh, you have plenty of men like me at your firm, Mr. Sinclair." David replied, deadpan as an executioner. "The only difference between them and me is that they're more than willing to kiss your ass and I'm not. Have a nice day."

And with that, David walked straight down the aisle, right through the lobby and made a bee line across the sidewalk to his car. Nobody blocked his path. Not in the courtroom, or in the lobby, or at the outside door way or on the sidewalk. This time, they all stepped aside. The why behind what they chose to do this time was and still is uncertain, but some folks would say that they knew that David Forbes wasn't walking around anybody, anywhere, ever again.

# Chapter Twenty-Eight

## Dinner with Walter Taylor

"So what happened?" were the first words out of Brenda's mouth when David came in through the front door of the office.

"Motion denied," was his reply as he tossed his coat on one of the Chesterfields and headed to the back to grab a bottle of water from the fridge. Brenda followed him just like the Gazette-Journal reporter had followed Coles Howard just moments ago. "You are kidding me! I wouldn't have bet a roll of lifesavers that Judge Byrne would have ruled against Archie's side of the case, especially where the sheriff's own son was involved."

"Judge Byrne wasn't on the bench," David explained. "He stepped aside and a Judge Powell heard the case."

"Who's he?" Brenda asked.

"Retired black judge out of Portsmouth," he said. "Lives up in Deltaville. You should have seen their faces when he walked out on the bench. The ghost of Oliver Wendell Holmes wouldn't have gotten more shocked looks this morning, that's for sure. I still can't believe it."

"You can't believe it?" Brenda said, smiling. "Think what the other side is feeling right about now. They are going to be some pissed off folks, that's for sure. What about that lawyer from D.C. that was calling here. Was he up there too?"

"Oh yeah," David replied, "That was a show in and of itself. Judge wouldn't allow him to appear as an attorney in the case. Told him he had to leave counsel table and go sit with his client. I wish I could paint for you the picture of how it all looked, but I just don't have enough words. You had to be there. What a morning."

"How was Jamal?" Brenda asked.

"Scared at first. Over the top happy at the end," he answered.

"You know, this isn't going to be well-received by some folks around here and you can bet that the family Howard is cooking up plans right now for retaliation. You ever think about that?" she said.

"Brenda, it's just a case," Forbes replied. "Like Eugene Callis said to me the other morning, one day, it'll be a closed file just like all the rest. I know that Archie and the Sheriff will bitch and moan some, but that'll be about it."

"I hope you're right and, by the way," Brenda said while grabbing a cigarette, "Walter Taylor came by on his way up to your hearing and invited you to supper at his house. He said to be there at 5:00 p.m."

"Well, I best call Karen and let her know she and the kids are on their own tonight." David said as he plopped into his chair and reached for the phone.

"Dinner with Walter Taylor has to be a 'can't miss' affair."

---

Framed by a gorgeous, clear sky and guarded by a westward sun that sent streaks of light bouncing off the blue green waters of Harper Creek like the reflections of tinsel on a Christmas tree, Taylor emerged onto the front porch of his home to greet David Forbes.

The old man's smile was warm and his handshake genuine. "David I want to thank you for acceptin' my invitation," Taylor said. "I know I'm takin' ya away from time that you would be spending with that pretty little wife of yours and your beautiful children, but I thought you might appreciate coming down here for a little supper with me. I won't kill ya with my cookin', I promise," he finished with a grin and a laugh.

"Walter, given the experience I had the first time I was here, it wasn't in me to refuse your kind offer. I greatly appreciate it," David said.

"Well, I greatly appreciate you and all that you're doing in your case," Taylor said. "You're a brave man to do what you did today."

"I thank you for that but I'm no braver than any other lawyer trying to do his job," David said as a steady in-bound breeze from the mouth of the harbor delivered the trademark, pungent scent of life's ceaseless battle along the shoreline deep into his nostrils.

The lapping of water where sea meets land marked the beginning and end of so much, a tale aptly told by the many shells, their hosts long dead, that lay like bleached tombstones on a sandy graveyard while endless strands of sea grass and sponge, torn asunder from their underwater moorings, dried brittle under a searing sun, bringing with it an abbreviated terminus to life's journey for the so many baby crabs, shrimp and plankton that once clung tight to the salt infused vegetation, their decaying bodies now nourishment to the plant life and sea life alike that call the water 'home'.

All the while, going in the opposite direction of the biosphere, endless schools of baitfish moved as one in the panorama of the shallow water at the shoreline, joined in the fight for survival by bunches of still living salt grass and small groups of oysters, mussels and other shellfish, all clinging fast and making their residence amongst the fists of soggy peat jutting from the sand-like ramparts against the relentless onslaught of waves of water endlessly battling the bulwarks of terra forma, a formidable community living large with each rise and fall of the bay tide.

Life begins and life ends. It all happens at the water's edge.

"I think you don't give yourself enough credit, but we'll talk more about that later," Walter said. "Right now, I'd like something to eat. Care to join me?"

"Absolutely," David replied.

"Well, come on in," the old waterman said as he opened the screen door and led David into his home.

When Forbes walked under the harpoon, he expected ramshackle. What he saw instead surprised him. Walter Taylor's residence was a study in efficiency. A one room affair by all accounts, he clearly was a man who knew what he needed and didn't have what he didn't. Against the far wall to the left of the doorway was a small twin sized bed on a maple frame that was neatly made and adorned with a faded, maroon colored bed spread and a gaudy souvenir pillow that said "Mardi Gras 1972." The bed was joined at the wall by a small chest of drawers to the left and a single wooden chair to the right that provided shelter for a pair of slippers that were carefully positioned between its feet. The wall above the bed was pierced by a window accented by a pair of pale yellow curtains that provided a million dollar view of Harper's Creek. On the remaining wall to each side of the window hung framed family pictures and a needle craft rendition of the Lord's Prayer.

The wall to the immediate left of the entrance way also was bordered by a second small chest of drawers, unmatched to the first, above which was secured a long shelf with hooks along its underside from which hung coats, jackets, overalls and hats for every season of the year. Beside this second chest were two pairs of well-worn white rubber boots, standard issue for the watermen of the Chesapeake Bay. Beside the boots was a Remington 12 gauge pump shotgun that leaned against the door frame, a location that provided quick and easy access for its owner in the event of adverse circumstances.

To the right of the entrance way was a small wooden kitchen table situated against the far wall that was bordered by a pair of tall ladder backed wooden chairs that bordered the casement window above the table which gave view to the rutted driveway that led to Taylor's house from the main highway. Plates and silverware for two sat on top of the table. A set of diner standard glass salt and pepper shakers, a bottle of Heinz ketchup and a roll of paper towels completed the ensemble.

In the far right hand corner of the room was a doorway that Forbes guessed led to a bathroom and in the center of Walter's abode was something that took Forbes by surprise.

Facing the wall directly opposite the entrance and located in the middle of the room was a comfortable, dark green leather Lazy Boy recliner. Fairly new by all appearances, the napper's chair of choice was aimed at a 42" Samsung flatscreen TV mounted on the far wall in front of the recliner. To the left of the Lazy Boy was a small table with just enough surface space for two remotes (there was a DVD player on another table located just under the flat screen), and a pair of tortoise shell reading glasses. On a shelf under the table was a set of marine grade Nikon binoculars. Both the chair and the table were sitting upon a huge oval shaped braided rug consisting of umpteen shades of beige and blue that looked warm and inviting against the salt washed pale gray of the rough- honed wooden flooring of the old man's home. Walter Taylor was becoming more of an enigma every day.

"You like my TV, David?" He said. "I see you staring at it. Bet you didn't think an old codger like me would have such a thing. I like my baseball. Sometimes watch the Playboy channel, too," he cackled as he walked over and opened a small refrigerator that sat to the right of the kitchen table and removed two plates covered in paper towels.

He set both plates on the kitchen table and said, "David, do you like rockfish? It's my favorite and I got us some soft shells to eat tonight, too. Have you ever had soft shell crabs?"

"Once before," David said, "a softshell sandwich I think it was. Delicious if I remember right."

"Well, I don't cook mine up like most folks do," Walter said. "C'mon over here to the stove and I'll show you how I do it."

Taylor walked over to a small gas cook top that shared wall space beside the refrigerator. He removed two small cast iron skillets from a shelf above the stove and then reached on top of the refrigerator and secured a small tin of lard. After placing a large spoonful of the pale white creamy paste into each skillet, he turned up a medium flame under each pan and then directed his attention to the plate containing the fillets, thick and meaty.

"Caught this morning," the old man said as he dropped the fish into the now hot lard. David watched them immediately begin to sizzle as they hit the pan and knew that he was in for treat tonight.

"I dip 'em first in a little egg and milk, then I cover 'em up with House of Autry and let 'em sit for awhile before I put 'em in the skillet. They'll be good."

Walter then picked up the other plate, removed the paper towel and showed David the six small soft shell crabs, a coveted delicacy of the Chesapeake Bay that lay like sheets of brined gold against the snow white of the old porcelain dinnerware. "I don't' bread these and deep fry 'em like most folks. I like 'em just the way they come out of the water with just a touch of Old Bay and a little garlic salt for taste."

Taylor reverently lifted each small crab off the plate and laid them shell side up, flippers and all, in the shimmering hot grease of the one hundred year-old skillet. True to his recipe, he then shook a little of the red goodness out of a large, dented can of Old Bay and then added an even sprinkle of McCormick garlic salt. On this night, the Food Channel didn't have shit on Walter Taylor. David knew that he was in the company of a seafood master and studied the old waterman's every move.

"They don't take long in the pan," Walter said of the crabs and after about three minutes, he turned each of the softshells, now white belly up against the oiled black of a skillet seasoned by seafood masters, and repeated the seasoning process that rendered a culinary vision few cooking magazines could ever hope to emulate.

Taylor then moved to his left and with a deft weld of an old wood handled metal spatula, gently flipped each of the rock fillets, now golden and delicious looking, in the adjoining skillet, giving an extra push to the legendary scent of the House of Autry breading mixture that saturated the living quarters with the same smell that has cultivated the coastal appetites of millions for over a hundred years.

The old man then picked up a large wooden spoon that lay to the left of the stove and gave a stir to the contents of a small pot that sat simmering at low heat on the right rear burner.

"I thought a little cabbage would taste good," the old man said with a smile. "But I'll warn ya in advance. It gives me gas. I'll try not to be upwind if I have to let one rip."

As Taylor grinned at his own remark and reshuffled the leaves of cabbage that bubbled softly in a glistening pool of fat yellow broth, David watched as a small cloud of deliciously seasoned steam rose from inside the pot and dissipate quickly into the inside atmosphere of the small piece of paradise that Walter Taylor called home on Harper's Creek; the resulting odor leaving no doubt that the dish had probably been baptized with both a large dollop of lard and a generous peppered slab of seasoning meat as well. No concerns about low cholesterol diet in this establishment, that's for sure.

"Grab ya a plate and I'll fix you up," Walter finally said. David did as instructed and soon was sitting at the table across from Walter Taylor with a plate of food that could only be described as, well, only of the kind that you would find in Mathews County. Unbelievable in all respects, Forbes was about to say a word of thanks but then remained silent as he watched the old man close his eyes, fold his hands and say grace:

'Dear Lord, we give thanks for this day and for every day that you allow us to be with you and our family.

We give thanks for fair weather, calm seas and for good fishin'.

We give thanks for when the weather doesn't oblige us and you allow us to come home safe to our kin.

We give thanks for allowing our children to grow up healthy and strong.

And, we give thanks for this meal that we are about to place into our bodies.

And we give special thanks to you for bringing David Forbes and his fine family into our world. Please watch over him as he's gonna need some watchin'.

Amen.'

And the two men then commenced to eatin' and talkin', but not about fishin' and cases, they instead spoke of other things. Family mostly, and mostly David's at that.

Taylor had a keen interest in why David and Karen had decided to relocate to Mathews in the first place. David explained to the old waterman that there was no real process involved. It wasn't like they had spent days and weeks visiting other locales up and down the bay. This was a once and done affair. Love at first sight. One visit and a very simple decision thereafter was all it took.

"Well, ya made a smart move, and we're glad to have ya," Taylor said while picking up the empty plates and used utensils from the table and placing them in a white drywall bucket that was just inside a small room just off the far right of Walters abode.

Taylor smiled. "If you're lookin' for a sink, I don't have one. Don't have no indoor plumbing, either. I'll wash 'em later off the back porch. If you need to pee, use the back porch, too. If you need to do other things, there's a one holer out there too. Looks like a tool shed. Built it myself. It has a ladder or two leaning against it for added decoration. If it looked like a privy, some government fool would be down here Johnny quick and condemn my house for polluting the bay. Funny how a billion fish can shit all day and the waters fine, but if a working man takes an honest crap, people think the worlds comin' to an end. Don't make sense, if ya ask me."

David just shook his head and said, "I'm fine, but thanks for the tour."

Taylor then walked over to the coat rack, grabbed a brown work coat and the same ball cap that he had on when he and David first met. The waterman then turned to David and said, "C'mon. I've got one more thing I'd like to show ya."

"Sure," David said, and both men walked out the door, off the front porch and down the dock that was bordered by the waters of Harper's Creek. The sun was just above the western horizon and the sky was an explosion of purple and gold as daylight surrendered to the dusk and Mother Nature fired a parting salute to another day well-lived. It was beautiful.

"I want to take you for a little boat ride," Walter said. "I know you're a busy man, but we'll only be gone about half an hour. You'll be glad you went."

Walter had the busy part right but the workboat was just five feet away and the water was as inviting as the next breath of air. How could he say anything other than 'Fine by me?"

So he and Taylor jumped on the boat and just as the old man was in the kitchen, so again he was a man in his element at the wheel of the primary tool of his profession.

"Ya like my boat, David?" Walter asked.

"I do," David replied. "Looks like it has served you well."

"Ya mean it looks like it's ready to sink!" Taylor laughed. "It could use a coat of paint, that's for sure. But she's seaworthy enough and her engine is tight. You can count on her to get ya to the nets and bring ya home and that's all that counts."

Taylor moved like a much younger man once his feet hit the scarred and shell scraped deck of the deadrise. Telling Forbes to stand fast to the left of the wheel house, Taylor untied the mooring lines himself, fired up the engine and pulled away from the dock like he was leaving a parking space at the Food King. Nothin' to it.

Walter was true about the engine. She purred like a kitten and gave off a soft rhythmic diesel rumble as she pushed the craft away from the dock and past the dozen or so other boats tied up on the opposite side of the water at Harper's Creek marina. Forbes noticed that Howard's boat, the 'Bay Lady' was gone.

"I wonder where Howard is today," David said, his eyes once again taking in the gorgeous view of still water meeting the small fleet of work boats tied up at the marina outfitted with net rigs, crab pots, oyster tongs and fishing equipment of all shapes and description. A few pleasure boats were tied up as well, center console fiberglass rigs and two convertible sport fisherman that gave an interesting contrast to the storm battled look of the vessels that went to sea every day, doing the work of the Chesapeake Bay watermen.

"Getting his engines overhauled at a railway up on Gwynn's Island." Taylor said. "He'll be back tomorrow."

"What's a railway, and how do you know this?" David asked.

Taylor answered part of the question. "It's a place where you take your boat to get it worked on out of the water. Two long rails are built down in the water, wide enough for the boat to slide in but narrower than the waterline. Kind of like a boat slip. Then the boat gets hauled up on the rails. Gets her out of the water. Pretty simple when ya see how its done."

Walter changed the subject. "Now, David, I want to add to your education some. See these pilings coming up at us. One has a square piece of wood on it. The other one to the right has a triangle on it. These are called daymarkers. They're like signs on a street, tell ya where to go. Square sign on the right is green and when you're heading out, ya keep it to the right of your boat at all times. The one on the left, the triangle is red. Ya wanna keep that to the left when you're heading out. Coming back it's the reverse, red on right and green on left. Stay between the signs like I just showed ya and you won't get stuck. Ya follow me?" the old man asked his student.

"I do," David replied.

"Good, now you take her and show me what you learned," and with that, Taylor stepped away from the helm and watched with an ear-to-ear grin as David grabbed the wheel and did his best to try not to show that he had no clue what he was doing but that he was thrilled as hell to have the opportunity to do it.

Taylor's eyes never left the water as he spoke, "Just watch the pilings up ahead and stay between the signs. It'll get a little shallow up at the mouth of the creek but you'll do fine. Remember to never trust how far you are from shoreline as a measure of how deep the water actually is. You can be a half mile from land and still only be in two feet of water. You best remember that."

The waterman continued. "A scientist fellow once told me that if you reduced the Chesapeake Bay in scale to the size of a football field, the average depth would be about one inch. I don't know how true that is, but you'd be wise man to pay attention to the daymarkers or you'll end up like these weekend fools who get stuck in water too shallow for their boat. Happens all the time. Stupidity and beer mixed with a disrespect for the water is a

300

dangerous combo, I'll tell ya that. Now I want ya to reach your right hand over here on this throttle and slowly push her forward, and give her some gas."

David did as instructed and the boat leaped forward, knifing through the water like she was part of the water herself.

"I built her myself in 1975," Walter said, "Bored every hole and layed every plank. She's wood but she's tight and has spent many a day out here that's for sure. Now, David, once we get to this last day marker coming up, I want ya to turn her east and head for the lighthouse. If ya never seen it before, it's quite a sight."

And that she was. Gleaming white with a weathered black observation tower, the New Point Comfort Lighthouse, located at the convergence of the York River and Mobjack Bay, rose like a missile from its island fortress of huge layers of dark gray boulders, riprap stone piled one upon the other that kept her safe from the endless storms that had swept less protected structures from the face of the Bay.

"That's one beautiful view" was all David could say.

"That it is," Taylor agreed. "Thomas Jefferson ordered her built in 1805. Although she hasn't sent out a light in many a year, she's still standing strong. Oh, the weather she's seen."

Forbes felt like he was in a scene from a National Geographic production. Setting sun, pastel streaked sky, sea gulls above, quiet water below, a Jefferson era masterpiece three hundred yards away and an old man's workboat in his hands. This was cool.

With Taylor's guidance, David did a slow 'u' turn and brought the boat west and with bow pointed towards a horizon softly aglow from a sun now gone, he steered the vessel back to Harper's Creek. Forbes was just starting to get a feel for how the old boat handled while underway when he heard a faint noise like someone talking over a walkie talkie and looked down at the instrument panel and saw a small white radio with a handheld microphone.

"That's a marine radio," Walter said, following David's eye. "Turn the knob to the 'On' position, press the button on the microphone to speak, let it go to hear and your all set. There's a small lighted screen with numbers on it. Tells you what channel you're on. Always use channel 16. That the one everyone listens to. You can go to another channel if you want too once ya get to chattin'."

"What's that red button for?" David asked, making reference to a small illuminated fixture just to the left of the on-off switch.

"That's a mayday call," Taylor explained, "means you're in danger of dyin'. Don't ever press it unless ya sinking fast. Brings out VMRC, Coast Guard, ya name it."

Forbes took it all in and asked Taylor if he wanted the wheel since the first day marker at the entrance into the harbor was fast approaching.

"David," Walter asked. "Did ya learn to swim by sittin' on the end of the dock or did ya do it by jumpin' in? You keep the wheel. You're doing fine. Just remember what I told ya about the day markers, keep your speed low and she'll take care of the rest."

Forbes did his best and marveled at how the boat was not unlike his 911. Smooth in the water, tight in the turns and solid on the deck. Not that the lawyer was any expert on boats but even a landlubber like him could quickly tell that this was a boat made right.

David now slowly passed the last day marker and was coming up on the point of land that marked Harper's Creek Marina with its array of boats tied up in the finger slips that dominated the shoreline for about one-hundred yards back up into the harbor. Taylors place was to the left, on the other side of the creek and separated from the marina by about eighty yards of water.

"Keep her to the center of the channel," Taylor instructed, "and do what I tell ya to do."

Taylor's last comment was unnecessary as David's hands were beginning to sweat. Nervous as hell that he was going to hit Walters dock, get stuck in the creek or do something else equally commensurate with his lack of boat handling ability, Forbes was wishing just a little bit that the waterman would take the wheel but that wasn't going to happen.

"Now, David," Taylor spoke again, "I want ya to give her just a little more gas, cut the wheel hard to the left and then pull the throttle back into neutral just like I showed ya. Do it now."

Forbes did exactly what the old man said and watched in awe as the boat drifted sideways and completed her arc landing parallel to the dock, with the right side of the vessel facing the old man's home. She touched the dock with barely a bump.

Taylor said, "Grab a line, David, and let's get her tied up." Forbes did as he was told and remembered that this was what Jimmy Jarvis said he was doing when he received the wound on his right arm. Now that he was doing it himself, David found it very hard to believe that an experienced mate like Jarvis would let his arm get between a mooring line and a dock piling. A screw up like that would be a hard act to accomplish even for a clueless, using the sales girls term, rookie like him. For Jarvis, it would be next to impossible. Doc Lawson's theory just gained an extra measure of credibility.

After the boat was secured to the dock, Taylor turned off the ignition and both men walked up the dock and towards David's car. One was a seafaring legend, the other was a man who now knew why Taylor loved what he did so much.

"Walter, I want to thank you for the boat ride and showing me the ropes. You've given me a great memory and I won't forget it."

The old waterman smiled, "Ya did well out there, and ya brought her in to the dock like ya been doin' it all your life. It was my pleasure to have your company, and I appreciate ya coming over for supper. I don't have many guests, so it was fun for me, too. We'll do it again sometime, I promise."

"Hey, Walter, can I ask you a question?" David said as he opened the driver's door to the 911. "Earlier tonight, I asked you how you knew that Howard's boat was up at a railway getting its engine worked on? You never answered my question."

303

Taylor didn't answer right away. Forbes let the inquiry lie there and didn't say anything more as both men looked across the creek at the vacant stretch of dock that the *Bay Lady* called home, now empty but for the glow of the one light that hung from a power pole standing twenty feet tall just to the left of the gangway that bore the brunt of the boots of Coles Howard on a near daily basis.

"David, I'm an old waterman," Walter said while keeping his stare fixed on the marina across the water. "Lived here all my life and, these days, I keep mostly to myself. But that don't mean that I don't have friends. Now, I don't have many, but the ones I got, they be finest kind and true to their word. And there's one other thing you need to know."

"Whats that?" Forbes said.

"They're your friends, too. Now go home to your family," Taylor instructed. "Ya got better things to do than spend any more time with an old coot like me. Besides, there's a baseball game on ESPN tonight, and I like my baseball. Have a good evening David."

# BOOK THREE

# JUSTICE

---

## Chapter Twenty-Nine

## The Case Comes Home

"All right, I want everyone to line up in front of the soccer goal, so that I can get a head count and find out how many players showed up for practice. Is Ashleigh here? I don't see Ashleigh. Does anyone know where she is?"

"'She wasn't at school today, coach. She was sick," said one of the players lining up at the scoring end of the field.

"Okay, what about Natalie? I don't see her here either."

"She was sick, too," came the announcement from another of the young players lining up as instructed.

"Okay. We'll it looks like everyone else made it and that's not bad. But, remember, we have our first game this coming Saturday, so we really need to have some good practices and to have good practices, we need everyone to show up."

"But, coach, how can they show up if they're sick?" asked a pigtailed ten- year old.

"Well, that's true but what I'm saying is that we just need everyone giving their best efforts to get to practice so that we can win our games! I mean, that's what we want to do isn't it?"

"My brother says we suck," said a little voice from the left side of the line. Tiny as a Londonderry waif in a Dickens novel but fast as a bullet on the field, her name was Chelsea.

"Your brother says 'what'? David asked.

"My brother is on a U-14 travel team over in Gloucester. He says you coach all wrong and that we suck," Chelsea replied as directed.

"We'll, we don't uh, stink and, . . . . ah . . . .Jennifer, where are you going?" he said to the back of a little girl who was running over to the sidelines.

"I need a drink of water!" she yelled over her shoulder.

"Coach, can I get one, too. I'm thirsty," said three more in unison.

David gave in quickly. "We haven't even touched a ball yet but, ah . . . .go ahead and come right back!"

He watched as the dehydrated foursome made a beeline for the congregation of parents who were watching from the sidelines as David Forbes, Head Coach of the Mathews YMCA girls U-10 Renegades, corralled the remainder of the team into a large circle for passing drills and ball handling practice while waiting for the water starved remnants to make their way back to the herd.

David couldn't get enough of the members of his daughter's soccer team and really looked forward to their afternoon practices. These little girls were a trip and the words that came out of their mouths were as pure as shade and as original as sunshine. The seven second delay that evolves from both age advancement and that less than pleasant experience you get from saying the wrong thing at the wrong time had yet to set in with these kids. Consequently, if they thought it, chances were that these little angels were going to say it, too. You just had to love it.

Little Chelsea's comment about her brother's opinion of David's coaching skills probably had a ring of truth to it, but so what? The local Y needed coaches, and volunteers for the position were in short supply. Forbes couldn't quite understand that because insofar as the application process was concerned, there was nothing to it. As David quickly learned, all you had to do was sign up, pass a background check, get the right size t-shirt with the word "COACH" stenciled on it, grab a net bag full of balls, cones, a bunch of yellow pinny practice jerseys; throw a whistle around your neck and you were all set. Accessorize the outfit with a game schedule and a 'Coach' was born; experience optional. In other words, damn the torpedoes, full speed ahead. Daughter's team needs a coach? Daughter's teams gonna get a coach.

There were, however, rules.

Coaches were never responsible for the wins (all credit goes to the kids), but they were completely responsible for all the losses (your team only loses because you, as the older brother said, suck as a coach). Plus, all teams always came equipped with a steady supply of 'assistant coaches' at the ready who, standing with hands in pockets or otherwise plopped into shoulder slung, folding fabric chairs armed with cup holders and NFL-insignia sun shades, remain ever on the alert to remind you that their precious daughter *has* to be played at forward or she is *just going to die.*

These 'assistants' are also called 'parents', a vicious species whose habitat is the sideline of soccer fields everywhere and who primarily feed on the derrière of any coach not bright enough to always recognize the unquestionable wisdom of their good judgment.

Welcome to the game.

Once the team had regained full troop strength, David had them do three laps around the field and then settle in to some triangle passing drills while he also tried to work in the goal with the tallest of the girls who looked like the best fit at keeper. Things quickly got out of hand in a good way. The girls were kicking the balls in every possible direction, laughing each time it sailed past their intended target and he soon found himself running all over the grass, retrieving missed shots, and trying to keep the girls focused all at the same time. A herculean task at best for a one coach team.

On one such adventure to grab an errant shot that had rolled into the woods, David turned around after retrieving the ball and saw that a man about his age, shorter and stockier than he with a raft of red hair had taken the field and was working with his choice at goalie. Forbes walked over to meet the new helper.

"Hi, I'm Sean Simmons." the man said, with a broad smile and a thickly British accent. He greeted David's outstretched hand with a strong, friendly shake, "I'm Jennifers's granddad. That's her over there. She lives with us. We have custody and all that. Don't mean to intrude, but it looked like you could use an extra set of legs out here."

"Sean, I'm David Forbes. I'm Katie's dad. I think she's in Jennifer's class and you bet I can use a hand. I can't thank you enough, and, from your accent, I suspect you also know a thing or two about the game."

"Rugby, mostly. Wife and I are from New Zealand. But I know enough to tell a soccer pitch from a cricket bat if you know what I mean."

"That I do. Think you can turn this young lady into a future Olympian?" David asked while smiling at the lanky, freckled ten year-old girl who was sitting on the soccer ball beneath the goal posts listening to the men speak.

"I think we can give it a go," Sean replied, looking at his new assignment. "Raw material looks right. C'mon young lady, off the ball and into the keep. Let's see what you've got."

And with that, David worked the other girls up and down the field and they ended the practice with a half-field scrimmage that could not have gone any better. In the twenty minutes that Sean had to work with his young protégé, she went from unsigned draft choice to franchise player. She simply looked great in the goal and it became evident to David that Sean was the key ingredient that could make the Renegades one hell of a team. A job offer was in the making.

"Hey Sean," David called out as he gathered up the last of the balls and cones. "I really don't know a damn thing about soccer, to be perfectly honest. If you've got any time on your hands, I could sure use you out here. You've got a knack with the kids, too. What do you say?"

"I say I'm on board, mate. I was the second I walked out here today. I'm retired, so I've got the time. Plus, coaching makes you an instant hero in your kid's eyes. Time well spent, as I see it. Besides, it sure beats grousing around on the sidelines watching you have all the fun. Next practice is Thursday, same time?"

"It is and I'll see you then."

"We'll both be here. You can count on it. C'mon Jen, off we go," he said to the brown haired youngster standing next to Katie beside a pile of yellow practice jerseys. They were whispering and pointing at David and Sean.

Forbes smiled and watched as his new assistant coach and his granddaughter walked over to the row of cars parked at the far end of the practice fields that bordered the west side of the middle school. Katie walked over to her dad, still looking in Jennifer's direction, and said, "He talks funny."

David replied "It's called an accent. We all have one. It's how you sound when you speak your language. He sounds different because he's from another country called New Zealand. It's near Australia in the South Pacific. If you were in New Zealand, they would say that you sound funny, too."

"Okay, I get it," Katie said. "We have a new girl in our class from Alabama. I think she has an accent, too. She really talks funny. She kinda talks like *thee*-is" Katie giggled, sounding the long 'e' and doing her best to mimic the butter sweet tonality of the Deep American South.

"That's an accent alright," David said, laughing as he picked up the last of the gear and headed in the direction of the parking lot.

"Hey, Daddy," Katie said.

"Yes, pumpkin," David replied.

"What's custody?" she asked. "I heard you talking to Mr. Sean. Is he Jennifer's daddy? He looks kinda old."

"Well, um . . . . He's ah, not all that much older than me, pumpkin," David uselessly reminded his daughter, "But he is Jennifer's grandfather and she lives with him."

"Why doesn't she live with her mommy and daddy?" Katie asked, her question accented by her big brown eyes that looked for answers to questions that were as old as time and as complex as the Big Bang Theory.

"I don't know baby," her dad replied, "lots of things can happen. I guess her mommy and daddy thought it best that she live with Mr. Sean for the time being."

"I guess," Katie said. "I don't want to live anywhere except with you and mom. Can we go to New Zealand some time?"

"Absolutely, baby. That's a great idea. But right now we have to go to the grocery store and grab some stuff for dinner," David said as he dropped the equipment bag at the rear of Karen's 4Runner (She had the Porsche for the day) and rummaged for his keys in the pockets of his cargo shorts.

"You better grab some stuff for dinner because I'm starved!" shouted Luke who suddenly sprang up from behind the vehicle parked adjacent to theirs in an attempt to scare his sister.

"You didn't scare me. I saw your backpack next to the front door," Katie confidently declared, hands on hips and a smirk on her face that only a sister can deliver to a brother.

"I'll get you next time, you toad." Luke countered, heaping a dose of brotherly love back on his little sis.

"Daddy, he called me a toad," she responded with pursed bottom lip that reaped zero response from her dad.

David mutely smiled, exercised the right to remain silent and tossed the equipment into the back of the SUV. He then climbed in, yelled a "Let's go," and listened with a well-trained parental ear for the reassuring snaps from the seat belt buckles doing their business across the laps of both kids. They were soon heading east back into town and into the lot of the local grocery store.

––––––––––––

Karen was working late at the school that night. She had scheduled a couple of parent-teacher conferences on top of her usual work day so David volunteered for dinner duty and had the evening menu well in hand. With the adrenaline from yesterday's hearing having finally made its way out of his plumbing, David was ready to kick back and knew exactly what was on deck in the dinner department - Italian sausage over bowties. The family favorite required lots of fresh garlic and olive oil with fresh herbs from the garden all blended into a perfect marinara. He thought he'd grab a nice bottle of red wine, maybe grab two. Whip up a great tossed salad and top things off with a warm loaf of garlic-buttered crusty bread to mop up the sauce. With plan in hand, culinary nirvana awaited as the family Forbes crossed the threshold of the Food King and headed stage left to the produce department, list in pocket and cart at the ready.

"Hey Dad, "Luke said, sensing the festivity of the moment and having decided to probe his dad's level of generosity, "Would you like some ice cream?"

"Sure, I would," David said, "And you both can pick out a flavor for me. Take your time, don't run and I'll meet you somewhere in the middle."

"Thanks, dad" Luke said, and both kids disappeared to the other end of the store leaving David to solo shop for dinner. That boy's going to be a better lawyer than me one day, he thought. That was a really slick way to get a 'yes' to the ice cream question.

Forbes moved quickly to complete his own shopping mission, and, in no time at all, he had all the ingredients for the feast and was five steps from the checkout register when he was intercepted right at the end of the aisle by a cart welding woman living somewhere in her 70's, who wore dark red slacks and a light tan jacket layered over a white blouse trimmed at the collar and sleeves in embroidered flowers of soft pink and aquamarine. Her hair was steel blue and looked beauty parlor rigid. A beige leather purse the size of a

311

Craftsman tool box was occupying every available square inch of the fold out kid's seat with the remainder of the cart's bullpen half full of bread, milk, canned goods and various other items that bespoke of the limited diet of someone who lived alone. Resting on the bridge of her nose were thick glasses, with lenses encased in oval frames of muted silver, which gave cross-hair like focus to the senior citizen eyes that bore a serious hole straight through the noggin of the lawyer come coach.

"You're that attorney, David Forbes, aren't you?" she shouted accusingly, "the one representing that colored boy who killed Jimmy."

The woman spoke in a voice of such volume that it reached from aisle one to aisle five, inclusive of all points in between, and she just as well could have been announcing the daily coupon specials over the store's P/A system. She was just that loud.

David didn't instantly respond. The shock of the unexpected confrontation left him momentarily mute as a door knob and frozen fast in his tracks like the taproot of a redwood.

In his mind, he was actually miles away when Nirvana was interrupted. He was home, in his kitchen, dicing garlic and sipping a glass of the Chianti in his cart. Karen had just put on his favorite radio station, the Tide out of Williamsburg and a marinara was slowly simmering on the Viking cooktop, sending aloft aromatic evidence of the spicy, wonderful culinary sex that can only be found when perfect sauce meets perfect Italian sausage. The kids were quiet, life was good but here this woman was, defiant, intrusive, and immovable in the breech and deftly creating a crowd by blocking the shopping cart traffic going back and forth between the end of the aisles at store front and the entranceway to the checkout registers. It was after work, the grocery was busy and the log jam of people on both sides of her self-created barricade was growing by the second. But that didn't appear to be of any concern to her at the moment.

In fact, an audience was just what she wanted.

David was frantically looking around for Katie and Luke when the woman spoke again. This time, her voice was even louder.

"You don't have to answer me! I know that's who you are! I recognize you from the papers and I just want you to know that Coles Howard is my cousin's boy. I've known him since he was a baby. And Jimmy Jarvis went to my church and how dare you . . . ." she said, tears bubbling up in her eyes as she reached deep for a tissue buried in the confines of her enormous handbag that was wedged in the cart within easy reach that kept all necessary things close at hand for its carrier.

She continued on, dabbing the tears from her eyes to great effect, as the crowd of distracted store employees and momentarily suspended shoppers grew in number around the head-to-head carts that sat like opposing tanks in an alleyway, barrel to barrel, treads locked, with no room to give.

This time she added a pointed finger to the onslaught and decreased the volume of her words not one bit.

"How, how dare you accuse Coles Howard of murdering that boy!" she exclaimed. "You don't know him, you didn't know Jimmy and you don't know us! Coles loved Jimmy. I saw it with my own eyes! Every day, I saw it and so did everyone else!" a comment to which there were multiple murmurs of agreement from the onlookers gathering like a breaching force at David's flanks.

The woman paused, drew a breath and then resumed her attack with the crowd around her nodding their approval at every word. All David could think of was that hopefully, Luke saw what was going on, sized up the situation and got Kate out to the car quick. This could get ugly, fast. The woman's words seem to have no end and there was no back door out of this one. He was roped in tight. She continued.

"You have no business here, with your fancy lawyer talk and your evil ways, accusing good people of murder. Murder!" she railed. "Leave us alone and go back to wherever it is you came from, you . . . .you . . . ."

David was fast running out of options when welcome words hit his ears.

"Now, Ms. Hudgins . . . .!", came the timely intrusion of the store manager who came flying around the corner, looking in all respects like a high school principal who just got word of a gang fight in the cafeteria. Having run from the offices at the rear of the store where he saw the events initially unfold on the security video monitors, the man in charge was flushed of face and clearly feared the worst, a mob contagion spurred on by the words of a local matriarch. Once he caught his breath, the hostage negotiations began in earnest.

"Now, Ms. Hudgins," the manager said again, "I've got a business to run here and lots of busy people are trying to finish their shopping and get home to their families so if you could please let this gentlemen get on with his business, I'd be right much obliged."

"I'll be right much obliged when he rots in hell!" the lady loudly replied, her chin so jutted and firm that you could have used it to split wood. "I'll move my cart. You don't need to tell me twice, but I'll tell you something Mr. Manager, I'm not shopping in any store that he does, so you can take this cart, too. I'll take my business elsewhere and you just wait and see if some other folks don't feel the same way as I do! We have ways of taking care of our own around here. You'll see, you'll see!"

And then she left the store, purse on her arm, money in tow and leaving a crowd behind that had plenty of supporters. If she were running for local office, the election would be all over. She would easily be the hands down winner as the favorable ballots for the opposition wouldn't be enough to wallpaper a shoebox.

The manager took David by the arm and whispered, "You...ah...finished shopping, ah, Mr . . . .ah . . . ."

"Forbes." David said. "And, yeah, I'm finished. Sorry for the disturbance. I certainly didn't plan on bringing that into your store. I'm looking for my kids. You didn't happen to see them did you?"

"Well, yes, I did," the manager responded. "And....ah....I sent them outside when I saw what was happening. I hope you don't mind. They have their ice cream, it's on me. So don't worry about it. Let's get you over to a register and you can get out of here."

"I wonder what set her off? This case has been going on for a while so something new must have happened to get her this upset," David said as much to himself as he did to the manager who was still riding shotgun at his elbow as they made their way to the nearest checkout register.

"I guess it's maybe the headline on today's paper," the manager replied, barely looking over at Forbes as he spoke. "Everybody's been talking about it all afternoon long."

"What headline?" David asked, who by now was feeling like he was in another dimension and on another planet. All that was lacking was a narration by a Rod Serling look alike wearing a 'Men-in-Black' suit and smoking an unfiltered Lucky.

"This one" the manager said, as he reached over to a stack of papers and tossed a copy down on the conveyor belt at the checkout just inches ahead of the sausage, the wine and the rest of David's cart

Forbes stared at the two inch tall headline that banner blared across the top of the Gazette-Journal. "Jesus Christ, that explains it," he said.

## 'COLES HOWARD ACCUSED OF JARVIS MURDER; BILLUP'S ATTORNEY SWEARS CLIENT IS INNOCENT.'

"Yep. It sure does," the manager said in agreement. "Mr. Forbes, I . . . . ah, appreciate you and your family coming in here to shop and all, but I'd be very grateful if you took your business elsewhere for the time being. I'm sure you understand. Have a nice day and sorry for the inconvenience."

# Chapter Thirty

# The Phone Call

David left the store and walked quickly to his car, bags in hand, and was relieved to see Luke and Katie waiting on the far side of the 4Runner, clutching half gallons of Dutch chocolate and French vanilla and looking anxiously for their daddy.

"That lady was insane," Luke said to his dad as they got into the car. "Who the heck is she and why was she acting like that? She's nuts!"

David didn't immediately reply, he then just shook his head and said "I don't know, boy. Never met her before. She just isn't happy about how I'm handling the Billups case. One upset woman, that's for sure."

Katie didn't say anything. She just sat quietly in the backseat and obliquely stared out the side window, as the long lost look on her face reflected on the rear view mirror that David had aimed at his little love.

"You okay back there pumpkin?" David asked as they exited the parking lot and got up to speed on the highway heading home.

Katie replied in a soft voice barely audible over the muted hum of the engine mixed with the subtle whisper of fifty mile an hour wind gliding over well-waxed, sound-dampened, four door steel.

She said, "Daddy, I was scared."

Her words ricocheted through David's heart and ripped sideways through his soul like an errant rocket, pole-pitching after a misfire at liftoff. Right at that time, and for that moment, he hated himself for doing what he did and for being where he was. He had brought this upon himself and the spillover had seeped like rank sewage into that part of his world that was off limits to all things negative and bad. Karen and the kids. What had he done?

"I'm sorry, baby. I had no idea that lady was going to say those things. Did you get the ice cream you wanted?" David clumsily asked, as if changing the subject was going to give a quick turnaround to this quagmire. Slim chance of that happening was the foregone conclusion but the bigger issue, by far, was how Karen would take all of this.

David was more than aware that his wife was pins and needles sensitive about everything having to do with this case and her instincts, as usual, were dead on. Uncanny how she had picked up on Simon, and David knew that the impact the headline had on the grocery store crowd had to of made its way across town to the middle school. That was as unavoidable as the next high tide and God only knows what heat she's taken from that.

He was half-inclined to ask the kids to keeps things quiet about what had just happened at the store but that would be the wrong thing to do for a plethora of really good reasons.

First, it wouldn't work and, second, Karen would just be all the more upset if he tried to engage the kids in some sort of blood oath to not tell their mother who was already correct in her opinion that her husband was not giving her the full briefing as to all of the particulars of the Billups' case. Any more evidence of secrecy and she would have damn good reason to be really pissed at her husband and that was something to be avoided at all costs.

The smoother path was to just let recent events play themselves out, hope good judgment takes siege of the higher ground and stay ever mindful of Mr. Callis' reminder that this case too will soon be among the ended causes of the court.

Forbes ultimately didn't get an answer from Katie to his ice cream question, just an unblinking stare at the floor boards that was matched in kind by a now silent Luke who rode in the seat next to his father. David decided to give the topic a rest and focus instead on just getting home and making a good meal. That was why they went to the store in the first place. Best to stay on course, keep to the game plan and that's exactly what he did.

---

The sound of tires crunching against the beige pea gravel of the Forbes family driveway was a welcome sound indeed as David hit the garage door opener and pulled in tight to the left, leaving plenty of room for Karen to dock the Porsche. The kids were in the house and fast to their rooms before the garage door made its way back down to the tarmac and David was left to fend for himself in the bringing in of the groceries.

Normally, a part of the chore list for which kid involvement was mandatory, David was letting that kind of stuff slide for the evening. Katie and Luke needed to have some time to themselves to sort out the recent events, so he went it alone, hauled in their purchase and got busy in the kitchen, whipping up the evenings repast. After all, a plate of great pasta, *al dente*, has marvelous medicinal properties, and is known the world 'round for its ability to smooth over the roughest of edges and take the bite out of the daily dogs that snarl at one's feet. Given that, and given everything else recent and near, tonight's fare could be just what the doctor ordered.

David glanced at the clock and immediately started chopping cloves of garlic and mincing a small yellow onion. He knew that Karen would be leaving the school fairly soon and wanted to make sure that home smelled like home when she walked through the door.

He married the onion with the garlic in a medium sized sauce pan, added a large splash of olive oil, set the flame to low heat and moved sideways to a cutting board where sat six long links of fresh, sage laden Italian sausage, ready for slicing into bite sized hunks of pure culinary pleasure.

David moved through the kitchen like a hungry man cooking a favorite meal should be expected to move - quick, efficient and supremely focused on the end product - but, of course, pausing now and then to sample the wine that he had decanted at the start of the evening's adventure. After all, a wine infused chef was a happy chef and tonight of all nights, Mr. Forbes needed a little happiness.

He slid back to the onion garlic medley, now nicely sautéed and added two cans of San Marzano plum tomatoes, a small pinch of anise seed slightly ground between forefinger and thumb, a larger pinch of sugar, a splash of the Chianti classico, and a minced potpourri of herbs from the small garden

318

adjacent to the front deck. David turned the heat up a notch, bringing it all to a slow, bubbling simmer. He then launched the sausage into a shallow pan, added more garlic and olive oil, cranked up the heat and let the magic happen.

He tossed back another sip of the Chianti, turned on some music and then walked back to the end of the hall where the kids had their quarters and found both Kate and Luke sitting together on his bed, watching a video on the older child's laptop. David let them be and spun back to the kitchen where he grabbed a small hand held blender and was just about to puree the simmering tomato mixture into something beautiful when the phone rang.

"Hello," David said, fully expecting the caller to be one of the kid's friends who always thought that dinner time was the perfect time to initiate a telephone conversation.

"Do you love your wife?" was all the caller said. The voice was male, rough, muffled, sinister and clearly violent.

David didn't know immediately how to respond. "Yes" was the literal answer but the question was not delivered with that reply in mind. All the lawyer could do was gape at the phone as a second go at near speechlessness in less than an hour's time had his head once again reeling. His mind instantly became disheveled and dark as every hair on his body started to stand at full attention as pure fear rolled in like the tide on a beach, sending streams of adrenaline that had every nerve primed for action.

His muscles trembled and he felt his mouth go parchment dry as he uttered the words, "What did you say?"

"You heard me," the caller said. "Now, go open the door. She's home." And then the line went dead, words of terror now replaced by the mocking neutrality of a dial tone.

David threw the phone down and ran like the scared husband he was from the kitchen to the mud room door that opened out to the garage, taking a microsecond in the process to glance out the windows that bordered the large kitchen for any sign of Karen's car pulling into the driveway. The Porsche was nowhere to be seen. David paused in mid-flight, giving some thought to grabbing the pistol he kept on the top shelf of the bedroom closet, when he opted instead to go it unarmed and get to Karen first. Head exploding and heart racing like Secretariat in the sixth furlong at Churchill Downs, David was reaching for the door knob when it suddenly pulled away from him and a body appeared in its path causing Forbes to jump back like a mouse from a prematurely snapped trap.

It was Karen.

"David, are you okay? What's going on? You look like you've seen a ghost." Karen said, as she walked in, handed him the keys to the 911 and dropped her folder of homework to be graded on the L-shaped granite bar top that gave a double sided perimeter to the cooking area.

"I . . . .ah . . . .just didn't hear you come in," David stammered, as he took a quick look past her into the now full garage and closed the door.

"Well, I guess you didn't with the music this loud. Rocking out, are you baby? Don't lie to me, bottle of wine tells the tale. Got a glass for me?" she said with a wink. "By the way, kitchen smells heavenly. I'm going to go change. You can bring my glass upstairs to me if you want," she said, adding another, more suggestive wink to the conversation.

"And the kids are where . . . ?" she said as she headed up the steps to the second floor master bedroom.

"Ah . . . down the hall." David signaled with a thumbs up directional twist of his wrist. "Chilling out in Luke's room."

David watched as Karen took the corner at the top of the stairs. With his breath coming in deep, drawing gasps, he turned to stare at the phone. It was the one part of this new enemy that he could see, that he could touch. Forbes wanted to smash it to pieces as his mind flew through the options as to what to do next.

Tell Karen, lock the doors, get his gun, call the sheriff, move the kids to the upstairs bedroom, do all the things that needed to be done and do them now. To wait, to delay could be fatal.

But instead of moving like Eastwood, David just stood statue still in the kitchen like a snowman in the front yard. A carrot for a nose, lumps of coal for teeth, he felt frozen and alone as the icy cold truth crawled up his spine.

There was no one to call. No cavalry was going to come today to rescue the family Forbes. He was on his own. Like Luke against four, now it was his father against an unknown enemy who had the upper hand. The helplessness of overwhelming odds knotted his gut. He looked upstairs where his wife was changing and then down the hall towards his children's bedrooms. Forbes took a long deep breath, and then another and then he moved.

Grabbing a sausage flavored six inch piece of well-honed Chicago Cutlery steel off the cutting board, Forbes quickly turned off both burners on the stovetop, locked the door to the garage and slapped his hand across the wall switch plate turning off the downstairs lights.

He was heading back to Luke's room to get the kids when the phone rang again.

Stopping his stride mid-way down the hall, Forbes turned around and picked up the phone but this time said nothing. He just listened.

The same voice spoke again.

"I know you're there, counselor. I can hear you breathing. And you can turn the lights back on, that'll only work in the movies. The dark actually makes my job far easier. I need you to listen to me, but first I need your respect. I have a gift for you. It's on top of the left front tire of the pretty little car your wife just drove into the garage. Now go get it."

With that, the line again went dead, the dial tone humming like a vibrating vein of angry electricity with no place to go.

Forbes hung the phone up and glanced around the house like a caged rabbit surrounded by starving wolves. In a house built to satiate the appetite for a water view from every room, glass was everywhere. Damn these windows, he thought. He can see my every move and there is nothing I can do about it.

Checkmated from his game plan, the husband and father followed the caller's instructions and walked to the door to the garage. With knife in hand, he turned the door knob and slowly moved towards the silver Porsche parked a 4Runner away on the far side of the garage.

David's grip on the oak handle of the razor honed blade was vise-like as he moved slowly, cautiously, in a space that once was as familiar and friendly as a first cousin but now seemed foreign and strange, with the voice on the phone screaming from every shadow and unknown horrors lying beneath the chassis of each vehicle. The boogeyman of childhood lore had returneth indeed, but this time, the boogeyman was real.

Forbes made his way to the left front of the 911, and, after checking the perimeter of the car for all points of attack, he knelt by the wheel and slowly ran his sweating, trembling palm across the top of the low profile run-flat Pirelli.

The tire was smooth. Nothing was there.

David panicked and looked over his shoulder. He feared a ruse had been set to get him out of the house. He visualized the slamming shut of the garage door, him being locked out of the house, and hearing the screams of his wife and children while they get butchered one by one by the madman who had his telephone number.

His nightmare suddenly became real when he heard a loud noise in the kitchen and Karen calling his name. Moving like Ripley saving Newt from alien creatures with acid for blood, the spring of a meal pursuing cheetah had nothing on the speed with which David Forbes bounded from his crouched position at tire side to the two-step elevation from garage floor to mudroom entrance.

He was one step past the doorway when David thanked God he had foolishly left the knife next to the car. Karen was in the kitchen pouring wine into a glass she had just taken down from a cabinet beside the refrigerator and the shutting of the cabinet door must have been the noise he heard. God only knows that if he had flown into the kitchen looking like Rambo with blade at the ready, his wife would have gone nuts. David tried to look as calm as possible, and prayed the phone would not ring so soon.

It was silent for now.

"Since when does a girl have to serve herself around here?" Karen said. "And why are all the lights out? And what are you doing in the garage? And who was on the phone?"

"Ah, sorry, baby." David said. "Bob called from two doors down and wanted to know if he could borrow some vise grips and, ah, some plumbing tape. I was just checking to see if I had what he needed. And, ah, I just didn't light the candles yet."

David hated lying but right now, telling the truth would just make things really get out of control. Adding another layer of emotional chaos to this situation, in addition to his own, would just be one big bad idea and that wasn't what he needed. What Forbes needed was time, and to get it, the callers game had to be deftly played.

"Why don't you go check on the peeps, and I'll grab some candles and get the pasta water on," David added.

"Great idea. Did you have everything that Bob needed?" She said over her shoulder, back turned and walking down the hall.

"Maybe, need to check my tool box one more time."

Forbes quickly returned to the garage and ran his hand again across the top of the tire and was straining to get a visual when he heard something hit the cement and start to roll. It was a coin, a penny in fact, and it ceased its locomotion at the heel of David's right foot. He picked it up and hurried back inside

Karen was still down the hall with the kids, no doubt getting an earful about what happened at the Food King, when the phone rang again.

"Got it?" the voice asked.

"I do," David replied.

"The date on the penny is 2006." The voice responded. "The questions you need to ask are not how do I know that or how did that penny get on the top of your tire. Those answers are stark and obvious. Rather, the question you truly need to ask yourself is whether you respect me. I submit the answer to that question should likewise be stark and obvious by now. Don't you agree?"

Rubbing the correct date coin back and forth between his fingers, David said nothing because there was nothing to say. The caller was right on all counts and he knew it.

"Listen carefully, Mr. Forbes. There is ample evidence with which to convict your client and which would easily justify the entry of a plea agreement. You will call Archie Hudgins tomorrow before noon and advise him that your client will be pleading guilty to second degree murder and will be accepting of a twenty-year sentence. I have every confidence that Mr. Hudgins will begrudgingly accept your offer. However, if you do not call him as I've suggested, I will then have little choice but to feel, well, disrespected. You know, I could have easily killed your wife tonight. My fingers actually brushed over the nape of her coat as she traipsed by in the dark. Good night, Mr. Forbes and enjoy your dinner."

# Chapter Thirty-One

# The Next Day

David Forbes never woke up on the worst day of his life. To wake up would require some period of sleep and that didn't happen. With his eyes frozen open and the sound of the caller's words echoing endlessly through his brain, David saw nothing but ceiling with each tick of the clock, as Karen slept beside him, her breathing rhythmic, and her body warm.

———————

Last night's attempt at dinner was a strange affair, surreal in all respects for the lawyer who just had his entire family threatened to be killed unless an innocent man pleaded guilty to a crime he didn't commit.

David remained steadfast and didn't tell Karen anything about the phone calls when she returned from her pre-dinner visit with the kids. To tell her would create more problems than it would solve and more problems was not what Forbes needed. What he needed was a plan and that was the key item looming largest on the big list of things in short supply.

But a plan required thought and right now, his mind was spinning too fast to think. He had to slow down, get a grip on the situation. Clear his head of all that which was clawing at his skull. Karen, Luke, Katie, violent men in his garage, a penny on a tire, threats called in and the feigned guilt of an innocent man.

And, the helplessness. Forbes hated that feeling the most. The feeling that there was nothing he could do about any of it, checkmated again in a sad, sick game of murder, drugs and money. In the end, the bad guy was going to win and that, more than anything else, stuck deep in the lawyer's craw like a too large chunk of thick, broken glass.

After the last call, as David stood sentry duty in the kitchen and waited for Karen, he noticed a strange calmness about himself and suddenly realized that oddly, he didn't feel scared. Despite everything that had happened in the last twenty minutes, he wasn't worried that his family faced an *immediate* danger. Forbes knew the caller was no amateur at this game, and professionals usually pursued persuasion prior to committing promised acts of violence that often prove to be tedious and complicated, especially where women and children are involved, as is the case here.

Tonight was indeed the persuasion stage, a finely tuned blend of cold elementary logic coupled with a distinct display of the capacity to deliver as promised. Forbes' instincts told him that nothing would be done unless David acted otherwise than as instructed. He had until tomorrow at noon, of that he was certain. After that, if he did not do what was asked, his family's jeopardy was his gamble, their fate a roll of the dice that the caller had placed in his hand. Until then, *he still had time.*

Forbes took a sip of the Chianti and hoped that his wife would brush off the grocery store encounter as a small town thing, remote and superficial, but that was not to be.

When Karen came back into the kitchen, she topped off her wine glass, grabbed a seat on one of the stools that bordered the island bar that separated the kitchen from the living room and said, "Well, the fun never ends. Luke gets beat up at Market Days and then you get accosted by Grandma Moses in the canned goods aisle. What's next? A public lynching at the gas station?"

"David," she asked, "When the hell is all of this going to be over? I'm tired of it. I really am. We moved here to get away from all of the high pressure D.C. crap and now here we are once again, up to our eyeballs in case-related bullshit."

She threw him a glance, tossed back a healthy gulp of wine and then fixed her gaze back down the hallway where the kids had yet to emerge.

"Ah, we can't shop at the Food King for a while," David muttered while he gave the sauce a quick stir and dumped a box of pasta into the pot of salted, boiling water.

"What do you mean we can't shop at the Food King?" Karen said, turning her attentions back to her husband and ramping up the intensity of her voice in the process.

"The, ah, manager asked us not to shop there for a while, until, I guess, the case is over," he responded, now more focused than ever on preparing the meal at hand rather than meeting Karen's inquisition head on. At this point, mundane distractions from the evening's events were welcome and David was giving the boiling bowties all the attention he could muster.

"David, you are kidding me!" Karen exclaimed, "Now, we're banned from the goddamn grocery store? Jesus Christ!"

Karen got up off the stool and went over to a couch facing the wide windows that looked out over the small cove that was so pretty, so serene. It was this view that made them fall in love with the house. It was this view that allowed the voice to see David's every move. Karen sat with her back to her husband, wine glass in hand and didn't say another word.

Forbes let it be. The damage was done and nothing he could say was going to turn things around tonight. It was going to take something more than verbal Band-Aids to fix this mess. This one required big medicine and between watching the steam float off the pot of boiling pasta, and the steam float off the gorgeous shoulders of his boiling wife, Forbes' mind for the moment was as empty as the inside of a balloon as to just what that might be.

Lost in a middle zone of inaction, a place of crippling stasis for those incapable of doing for want of not knowing what to do, David took another sip of wine, looked out the windows for what he knew he would never see and then walked back to the kid's room to tell Luke and Kate that it was time to eat.

———————

At 4:30 a.m., David surrendered to the inevitable and got out of bed, having given up all hope of ever getting any sleep before embarking on what he knew was going to be one hell of a day. He went downstairs to the kitchen, loaded up the grinder with some Starbucks French Roast, got a pot of coffee brewing and then headed back upstairs to throw on some work out gear. Best to hit the morning head on and an hour of pumping iron would help to get things off on the right foot.

Having replaced boxers and a t-shirt with some sweats and a favorite pair of road proven Mizunos, David made his second trip back down the stairs, grabbed a cup of steaming coffee and was heading in the direction of a small flight of stairs on the other side of the kitchen that led to the bonus room when he paused to look at the phone.

At that moment, the caller's voice echoed in his mind and David shook his head as if to send the killer's words back into an orbit that would take it far, far away from his beloved home. He then set his coffee down and walked to the door that led from the kitchen to the garage. Holding his breath, he opened the door and looked inside.

The garage was noiseless as a crypt, both vehicles sitting like caskets, surrounded by shovels, rakes, hoses, ladders, bikes, a garden tractor, soccer balls and all the other things that sat on floors, leaned against walls and hung from hooks that witnessed the intrusion of the night before. Forbes exhaled, then closed and locked the door. Clear your head, he said to himself. *Clear your head.*

David turned around, grabbed his coffee and took a healthy slurp of the steaming brew. He reveled in its warmth and gained some measure of strength as the dark roasted caffeine, strong and bitter, made its way through his veins.

They will not beat me. They will not win. They will not beat me. They will not win.

He said this to himself over and over as he drank his first cup of the morning and stepped outside on the deck at the front of the house, the pre-dawn breeze light but steady. David could make out the lights on a container ship heading north up the shipping lanes of the Chesapeake Bay and he thought of Jimmy Jarvis, and what he saw and how he died.

A drug robbery on the high seas and a double-cross against Los Zeta trained curriers was something so far beyond that poor kids comprehension that David was almost certain that Jimmy played no part in its design or execution. Howard wouldn't have taken that risk. A high stakes gambit like that required split-second ruthlessness coupled with a natural instinct for killing and Jimmy didn't have any of that. He was just a country boy through and through, but one smart enough to know that there was no coming back to who he was once that drug boat slipped beneath the water. Life as that boy knew it was finished. The dream was over and the nightmare had become real. A line had been crossed and he had become a criminal, an accessory to capital murder with robbery as the motive. He lost his soul that night and Coles Howard knew it and killed him because of it.

David's mind rolled on as the visions appeared in his head, frame by frame. Jimmy's death must have been gut-wrenching in its insanity. He had to know his killer. Did they talk for awhile? Did he ever see the knife? Did he ever have the chance to tell Cassie goodbye and that he loved her? How long did he live after being stabbed? Did he beg his assailant to let him live and did he cry, knowing that he was dying, as the life in him bled out on the sands of Haven Beach?

Forbes finished his coffee and went back inside to get rearmed with a fresh cup. He grabbed a hand towel from the rack in the downstairs bath room and then cruised over to the other side of the house, walked up the three steps to the gym he had in the bonus room, loaded a P90X video into the DVD player and let Tony Horton put the hurt on his body while David built the plan in his head.

They will not beat me. They will not win.

# Chapter Thirty-Two

## Counterattack

David tore through the gears of the 911 as he pushed the accelerator to the floor and crested the hill at Freeport Landing going a lot faster then he should. It just felt good to have steering wheel in one hand, gear shift knob in the other and gobs of horsepower rumbling at his back. He needed the speed, to feel the power, to have something under his own control going where he wanted it to go, where he needed it to move. The fact that he was exceeding the speed limit by more than forty miles an hour didn't mean a damn thing to him. It was just how it needed to be.

He was on his way to see Jamal Billups at the Middle Peninsula Regional Security Center, and, for this meeting, there was no script nor planned agenda for what they were going to discuss. David's brain hadn't gone that far. It was still far too full of heinous things that had turned his cognitive processes into a scattered hodgepodge of 'now what's' and 'what if's', devoid of rhyme, reason and anything remotely resembling an answer. His thoughts were buzzing around in his skull in a thousand different directions like the random, elliptical flights of a thousand angry bees protecting a disturbed hive, when what he desperately needed instead was a cold hard line of statistical oneness, like the bright blue line of a highway shown on an interstate road map. Start here. End there. You're done when you reach the gas station in Sedona. Geographic simplicity would feel so good right now. He needed to quiet his head down. The car helped and for added reassurance, he reached for the phone and called Simon.

He got his friend's voicemail message in return, "Hi, this is Simon Epstein. Leave a message and I'll call you back. If you're as gorgeous as you sound, also send a pic. Thanks!"

David couldn't help smiling when he heard his friend's voice. Good old Simon. The big yid was always good for what ailed him and today, he was ailing big. Forbes left a message.

"Simon, this is David and I need some help. Need to know what you can find out about a drug cop with the Baltimore PD by the name of Donny Howard. His father is the sheriff down here and he may have something to do with this murder case I've got going on down here. Some things have happened that I need to talk to you about. Call me back ASAP."

Forbes hung up just as he approached the Route 17 intersection, dropped into second as he hit the green light, went right onto two lanes of northbound traffic and headed into Middlesex County without ever touching his brakes. He couldn't tell Karen about any of this but he was for damn sure going to brief Simon, who was as expert in his world as last night's caller no doubt was in his.

While in his teens growing up on the cocaine heavy streets of Miami, Simon Epstein had watched his older brother and sister succumb to the drugs and the violence and he swore at their funerals that his vengeance would be relentless and he held true to his promise.

After college, Simon couldn't join the Drug Enforcement Agency quick enough, and, once in, he volunteered for every high risk undercover assignment he could get. Tough and aggressive, the young agent soon developed a legendary reputation for delivering as many dead bodies to the morgue as he did live ones to the D.A.'s office for prosecution.

Epstein was brutally efficient in his work with not only a rather well-defined sense of right and wrong, but the agent also held fast to a simple equation as to whether someone deserved to die.

If you dealt in narcotics, Simon Epstein was your grim reaper.

With him, drug dealers had two choices - go easy to jail or go home in a box. It didn't matter one way or the other to Simon. He was game for both. The man from Miami carried hell on his hip in the form of a H&K P30 in .40 cal S&W and delivered justice with hands and feet well trained with three black belts in Okinawa karate, judo and in Grav Maga for added measure. Epstein knew his business well, and right now, David was really glad he was his friend.

With five miles to go before he got to the jail, Forbes put the Porsche on cruise control and centered his thoughts on what he was going to say to his client. How do you tell someone that their lawyer's family has been threatened and may be hurt or worse, killed, unless he agrees to serving a twenty year sentence in a state prison for a crime he did not commit? Or do you not tell the client any of that and simply roll over like a beaten dog and instead *explain* to the client that you have reviewed all the evidence and now feel that it's in *their best legal interests* to work out some agreement with the Commonwealth Attorney so that they avoid a life sentence and all that crap.

Sad to say, defense attorneys, especially court appointed ones for indigent clients, have that conversation with criminal defendants all the time. 'Listen man, suck it up, take the twenty, give up your skin to retain your bones and don't bitch when the sentence comes down, don't bitch when you can't see your family and don't bitch when the sound of steel clanging against steel and the smell of cold wet concrete and the sound of screaming, yelling men becomes your every day, your every hour reality. Better for you that you say "yes" and a damn sight easier for me without a doubt. No case to try and no risk of a verdict with a life sentence that will require appeals and all that goes with it. A sellable bargain, is it not? Sure. Trade your innocence for a murder conviction and twenty years of confinement at the Sussex Correctional Center. With hard core violent men for bunkmates and a brutal rape a day as entertainment, life should be just great for Jamal Billups.

David felt sick and swallowed back the well tied knot that was trying to disgorge itself from his stomach. "How fucked up," he said to himself, a thought succinctly measured as the first bit of rationality that had emerged since this nightmare began.

---

He was passing by the West Marine store located just south of the county seat which was advertising a season-end clearance sale featuring a bevy of kayaks and towables that adorned the front entrance of the establishment with long, slender crafts of molded plastic and taut fabric, round platforms bearing eye-catching shades of bright orange, cobalt blue and the ever popular sea grass green. It was so colorful that it looked like a Disney theme park. All that was needed to complete the scene was a larger than life caricature of Goofy standing over the lobster red, ocean going two seater leaning against the front entrance wall.

As he rolled past the store and headed slightly above the legal limit towards the jail, David was thinking that some kayaks around the house would be a nice make up present for all that the kids had been through over the last several days, when suddenly another thought came out of nowhere and took center stage. It rolled in quick and struck fast and deep like the bite of a razor edged ax into a log of well-aged black oak.

This was the moment he had been waiting for. The bees had stopped buzzing.

Forbes quickly checked his watch and saw that he had time for a quick pitstop. He threw the 911 into a wheel screeching u-turn and headed back to West Marine. There was business to be done.

---

David wheeled the Porsche into the parking lot, weaved his way around the display items he saw from the road and entered the store. It was quiet, not unusual for an early weekday morning and he walked to the right side of the store where there was an array of GPS navigational units and fish-finding electronics. Forbes was unaccustomed to marine equipment, and he viewed in awe the amazing clarity of the various screen projections for both navigating the Chesapeake Bay and finding where the big ones were swimming on any given day. The amount of detail was incredible.

"Can I help you?" came a voice from over his shoulder.

David turned around and stared into the face of a girl who was in her late teens, maybe early twenties. With short brown hair and pale blue eyes that threw a stare like Nolan Ryan threw a fast ball, she rounded out her appearance with the standard uniform of the day - navy blue West Marine polo, tan khakis, Sperry Docksiders - and stood with her hands on her hips, ready for the sale.

"I think maybe you can," David said, haltingly. "I'm not frankly interested in purchasing one of these things but I need some information as to how they work, kind of."

"You don't own a boat, do you?" the young woman asked.

"Ah, no, I don't and how could you tell?" Forbes asked.

"Well, because you don't look like a boater or a fisherman for that matter and you don't talk like one either," she explained.

"How does a boater talk, if I may ask?" David responded.

"They all try to act like they know what they're talking about even if they don't," the girl replied.

"And I talk, ah, how . . .? Forbes asked.

"Clueless but that's okay. Clueless, I can deal with," she said. "These other folk, who roll in here with a Bass Pro catalog in one hand, a Cabelas flyer in the other and talk to me like I'm five cents short of a dime, are the ones I can't stand. Come back Saturday, and you'll see what I mean. We get chock full of 'em. Now you need to know exactly what about what, again?"

David was taken by the young salesgirl. Full of spunk and a way with words, she was a welcome distraction from the debacle that was the previous twenty-four hours.

"Well, let me put it this way," David tried to explain, "What if someone had one of these navigation units on their boat, one of these top-of-the-line expensive models, and what if that someone wanted to find out where they had, ah maybe been some time ago. Like to a favorite fishing place or something like that. I mean, if they had entered data into this machine so that they could get from, say, a marina to some place out in the Chesapeake Bay, how would they be able to find out where they had been, if they wanted to, like maybe a couple of months after they had been there. Am I making any sense?"

"Yeah, you want the way point history," the salesgirl said.

"Yes, that's it," David affirmed.

"You don't have any idea what I just said," she replied, deadpan as a door knob.

"Well, I think maybe I do," David replied.

"No you don't. You're not becoming one of those Bass Pro catalog dumbasses are you?" she said, her fastball stare now at 92mph and climbing fast.

"Oh hell no," David quickly said. "But, I can only look so stupid for so long. I'll risk a fake if it'll get me out of the woods, so to speak."

"It didn't work. By the way, I know who you are," she said, dropping her voice down a notch.

"You do?" David said, looking quickly around for anybody close within listening range.

"Yeah," the girl answered. "You're that lawyer who represents the black boy they say killed the Jarvis kid over in Mathews. My brother works up in the jail in Saluda. He sees you going in to meet with your client. My daddy was a waterman. He died last year."

"I'm sorry to hear that," David said.

"I thank you for that," she replied. "He was a hard-working, honest man and he hated Coles Howard with a passion. A lot of watermen do. I read the local papers, too. I know what you said about him in court. Now let me show you what you need to know about downloading way point history. It's easy and I'm going to sell you a portable GPS unit and a USB cord that will do the trick."

"I'll take one of those kayaks, too," David said, "the dark green single seater out there. I'll need a paddle to go with it."

"You're gonna need a hell of a lot more than that, the kind of thing that we don't sell in this here store, to do what you're going to do," she replied, the stare from her eyes now nothing short of radioactive. Like an x-ray, she was seeing right into his brain and Forbes swore she knew what he was going to do.

"I'm gonna give you my cell phone number. Something tells me you might need some technical assistance. Call me if you need me."

"Can I ask you a question?" David asked. "Why are you doing this? Everyone else within a hundred square miles of this place hates my guts and wants to kill my client. You help. What's up?"

"'What's up?' is none of your damn business," she said, switching to an inside knuckle ball that hit the corner of the plate like the horsehide had eyeballs. "Let me ask you a question. Has a waterman done you wrong since you took this case?"

"Well, no, but they come to every hearing and look imposing as hell," David said. "That's one tough bunch."

"Why do you think they come?" she asked.

"To show support for Jimmy Jarvis I would think. Maybe Coles Howard, too. Hell, I don't know," David said, looking lost under the cross examination of West Marine's best.

"Did you ever think that maybe they come to show support for you?" she said. "They're not blind you know. Their eyes see, too."

"It sure didn't look that way to me but maybe I'm just missing it. What did you say your name was again?" Forbes said, his brain spinning like the earth on its axis from the twist in the road this case once again had put in his path.

"I didn't. I'll help you but only if you do one thing for me," she demanded, hands still on hips.

"What's that?" the lawyer asked.

"You make damn sure that you get that son of a bitch," she said. "Now let me show you how this stuff works."

# Chapter Thirty-three

# Jamal and the Plan

At 10:15 a.m., Forbes parked in a Visitors Only space and walked towards the entrance to the Middle Peninsula Regional Security Center a few dollars lighter than when he left home that morning. Roped to the top of his car was a new kayak and laying on the passenger side seat was a mobile GPS unit, a bag with a USB cable and an instruction booklet just in case he needed a refresher course to the already abundant amount of information provided by the salesgirl at the West Marine. She knew her product well and taught David fast on the particulars of downloading navigational histories from Garmin GPS units and other similar devices. True to her word, she wrote her cell number on his receipt but he left without ever knowing her name.

A deputy who was leaving the jail passed him on the way out and said "Going fishin' Mr. Forbes?"

"Well something like that I suppose," David responded, and turned around to take a last look at his new rig that looked like a silver bullet with a big green pickle tied on top. The sight eked a brief smile out of the worn weary lawyer as he presented his credentials to the officer manning the front desk, cleared the metal detectors and headed back to the attorney meeting room where Jamal was already seated, clothed in the standard issue orange jumpsuit and handcuffed to a small u-bolt held fast in the cement seat opposite the table and chair that awaited his attorney.

"You look like shit," Jamal said.

"You don't look so good yourself," David replied. "But, then again, orange jumpsuits and handcuffs for bracelets don't exactly bring out the best in anybody."

"Don't give me that shit. We all buddy, buddy at the end of that last hearing but good things for me never last but so long and they always, always get followed up by bad shit. It's how it's always gone down and now here you are. You got more good news or are we all done with that?"

"I don't know," was all David said.

"So why are you up here, lawyer man?" his client asked. "I read the paper and saw the headline. I know you be takin' some shit for that hearing. And you have, haven't you? You don't have to answer. I can see it on your face."

"Look man," Billups said. "I know my town. I grew up there. You scored big in that courtroom throw down but that's the only place you scored. Everywhere else, you lost. True, isn't it? And that's why you're up here now. To sell me some shit cause you tired of taking shit yourself. Getting' old, ain't it? They done wore you down. Yeah, I know and now we be at that part of the movie where Jamal gets fucked. I've seen this show before. Lawyer walks in with hound dog look on his face and says, while deepening his voice, "*Well Mr. Billups, it's best if we accept this here plea agreement so take my pen and sign your name right motherfuckin' here.*"

Jamal laughed at his own lawyer imitation and said, "Yep, just sign right motherfuckin' here. My black, country ass goes to prison and everybody else goes to lunch. Is that how it's going to be today, lawyer man?"

David said nothing and just stared at the floor the same way his client had when they first met so many months ago in this same room. Jamal in his jumpsuit, Forbes in pinstripes and a thin file on the table.

How things have changed since then.

David finally looked up at Billups, rubbed his sleep-starved, bloodshot eyes and asked, "Do you trust me?"

Billups replied, "Man, I don't trust any fuckin' lawyer."

"I didn't ask that," Forbes shot back. "I asked if you trusted me. Do you?"

This time it was Billups' turn to lend a muted eye to the battleship gray of the holding cell floor, chipped and marred by the soles of the shoes worn by attorneys and defendants alike who had shuffled back and forth over the years while discussing justice in all of its blind and balanced actualities. An honorable cause, if you truly believed in it. Horseshit made sweet if you didn't. Jamal Billups was a man on a fence.

David's client raised his head after about a minute of silence and said, "Do I really have a choice?"

Forbes said, "No, not if you want to stay out of prison. But you need to trust me and I mean really trust me. Now, for the last time, do you?"

Jamal and David locked eyes and seconds passed without either man saying a word when Jamal finally nodded his head up and down and said, "Yeah, I trust you. But you got to tell me the truth and I mean everything. Shit has been happening and I need to know what and who is trying to fuck me up. You do that, and then you get my complete trust. I'll do whatever just as long as we straight up on that. Deal?"

"Deal." David said and the two men shook hands like one just bought a car from the other.

"All right," Jamal said, "now that we got that over with, what the fuck is going on?"

———————

Fifty-two minutes later, David put both hands flat on the table, pushed his chair back and stood up. He had told Billups everything. He told him about his initial conversations with Simon about a drug boat gone missing off the Mathews coast around the same time of murder. He told him of his talk with Walter Taylor and everything the old man had told him about Howard's seafood business, about the overabundance of apparent money and the nighttime journey of the *Bay Lady* two nights before Jimmy Jarvis was repeatedly stabbed on Haven Beach. He told him about the records search at the courthouse and how it confirmed the old waterman's tale. He told him about the beer cans and shoes seen at the beach and how they mysteriously failed to appear in any of the crime scene photographs taken by the sheriff's office. He told him about his conversation with a clearly terrified and obviously pregnant Cassie Thompkins and the beating he took from the hands and feet of her beyond angry step-father and new best friend, Coles Howard. He told him about the assault on his son at Market Days and the keying of his car. He told him about the street corner conversation with Doc Lawson and the wound to Jimmy's arm. He told him about the standoff with the customer in the Food King and about the three calls he received at home, of a penny on a tire, and the *quid pro quo* for the lives of his family. He told him about the comment made by the sales girl at the West Marine and then he told him his plan.

Forbes looked at his watch. "I've got to be at the Commonwealth's Attorney's office before noon. That means I've got to leave here in less than ten minutes. It's your call, Jamal."

Billups asked, "If I do what you want, am I going to prison for this bullshit?"

"No," David said.

"But you want me to plead guilty?" Jamal responded.

"Yep," said his lawyer.

"And say 'sure' to a twenty year sentence?" replied his client.

"Yep," David said again.

Jamal squinted hard at his attorney and said, "That sounds like prison to me."

"It'll sound like prison to them, too." Forbes answered. "That's the point. We need their guard dropped. This will do it."

Billups smiled and said, "You know, you are one crazy nigga."

David smiled back and said, "Takes one to know one, Jamal. Thanks for the compliment."

"Oh, man, I'm crazy alright," Jamal said. "Okay, I'm in. Let's do this. Just don't fuck it up and, ah, one other thing, lawyer man. You need to watch your ass after I do this plea agreement business."

"Yeah, why's that?" David asked.

"You're a witness," his client explained. "They know you know. After they think all this shit is said and done, they gonna pull your white ass over one night when you all by yourself, make you step out of the car and shoot you dead. Throw a bottle of liquor in your car, stuff a bag of weed under your seat and call it resisting arrest. Don't think that thought won't cross their minds, 'cause it will. Oh, yes, it will. That's the way evil thinks and these folks are pure evil through and through."

"That thought has crossed my mind, too," Forbes replied. "But it's a risk I'm ready to take. They fucked up when they threatened my family. Now, I've got to roll. We straight?"

"Very. And like that salesgirl asked, you gonna get that son of a bitch?"

"You can count on it. I'll talk to you later Jamal."

————————

David was on high alert as he headed back into Mathews County. This was no game. It was warfare at its most earnest, and he agreed with his client that his own days were numbered once Jamal signed that agreement and headed west to Powhatan Correctional Center for processing. Forbes would be a loose-end for sure and they weren't going to let him dangle for long. Walter Taylor's son had been a loose-end, too, and the Sheriff shut him up good. Doing it once as a deputy took some balls. Doing it a second time now that Junior Howard wore the big badge would be as easy as breathing.

Forbes stopped by his house on his way towards the courthouse, dropped off the kayak and at 11:45 a.m., walked through the front doors of the office of the Mathews County Commonwealth's Attorney.

"Hi Janet," David said, "I need to see Archie. His car is parked out front, so I'm assuming that he's in."

"He is but he has two visitors with him right now."

"Well, he's about to have a third," David said as he walked past the secretary's desk and opened the door to Archie's office without a knock or invitation. There was none needed. He was expected and David knew exactly who the other two guests were.

Archie Hudgins tried hard to look both surprised and not nearly as uncomfortable as he really was. The other occupants of the room had no such concerns.

Sheriff Howard sat with legs crossed and wore a smug look that reeked of victory, his face a study of sinister triumph; him having inside knowledge of the mechanisms by which it was obtained. Forbes was under his boot, and it felt good.

In the other seat sat Coles Howard who was working a tooth pick harder than a hummingbird flapping her wings and grinning from ear to ear.

"Counselor, we meet again!" Coles said with a laugh. "I feel so lucky I'm gonna go buy me some lottery tickets. You want me to buy you some, Mr. Forbes? Happy to do it, my treat."

"Shut up, Coles," Sheriff Howard said.

Archie Hudgins chimed in, "David, this is a bit unexpected. I would say come on in but you already availed yourself of that opportunity. Usually Janet gets the pleasure of announcing whose next on the appointment list but that bit of protocol doesn't seem to be working today. So, ah, what can I do for you?"

"Cut the crap, Archie," David said. "You know exactly why I'm here and what I'm about to say. Billups will plead to second degree and do twenty. Give me the plea agreements and I'll have them back here, signed, by end of business tomorrow. I want the first available court date to get this matter before Judge Powell and close the file."

"Well, David, I need some time to consider all of this." Hudgins said, doing his political best to sound, well, political. "After all, I am an elected official and not too few of my constituents are going to be hopping mad that Billups isn't getting life for what he did to Jimmy Jarvis. Even if I did agree to your terms, it will take a while to get the agreements drawn up for your client to sign."

David walked towards the front edge of the prosecutor's desk, leaned forward until his hands were resting squarely on both sides of Hudgins' brass nameplate, then looked him straight in the eye and said, "Archie, there are two big differences between you and me. For starters, I lie a hell of a lot better than you do. And second, I'm nowhere near to being as big of a pussy as you are. Those agreements have already been typed and they're in the yellow manila file that's sitting on the right side of your desk. Your eyes locked on it the second I came in here and your right hand has been resting on it ever since. Now give me those fucking things before I forget my manners."

Archie Hudgins didn't say a word. He reached for the folder and handed it to David Forbes who walked out of the office, leaving the door wide open and garnering in the process a look on Janet's face that was one for the ages.

"Game time," David said to himself as he hopped in the 911. "Now it's our turn and payback's going to be a bitch." As he settled into his seat, he instantly checked his cell phone for a call back from Simon but no such luck.

"It's all right," David reassured himself as he settled into the leather and started the engine. "Probably vacationing with some super model babe on some exotic beach. He'll check his messages sooner or later and he'll call. He always does."

They will not beat me. They will not win.

344

# Chapter Thirty-Four

# Mexico

In the rugged hills southwest of Sinaloa, a pair of Jeeps followed each other along a worn and rutted path that wound its way from flatland to mountainside, getting more narrow and rugged with each passing mile. The higher altitude air was cool and the sky was dark. It was 3:45 a.m. and the sun was still asleep.

There were three men in each Jeep. Two up front and one in the back. The men riding in the rear of each vehicle were carrying M-50 sub machine guns. Those riding up front packed side arms. All were dressed in black tactical gear from head to toe.

After two hours behind the wheel, the driver of the lead vehicle told the occupant in the passenger seat that they were getting close to their destination and motioned ahead with his right hand towards a concrete wall approaching in the distance that spanned the canyon wall from side to side. Two feet thick, approximately eight feet high, and topped with bundles of razor wire that were stretched like skin-slicing slinky toys across the top of the wall, the formidable structure was divided in the middle by an electronically activated gate that was ten feet wide and as tall as the wall. As the Jeeps approached, the gate opened, and they drove in, coming to a stop just inside the wall. The men remained in the vehicles until the gate slid back into position. They were enveloped in darkness, not a light could be seen.

The driver of the first Jeep spoke several words into the microphone that was attached to his headset and from out of the darkness came four men, all outfitted in black, night raid tactical uniforms and carrying automatic weapons, each one equipped with a silencer.

The front passenger in the first Jeep stayed in his seat and said, "Any problems?"

"None," said one of the men who came out of the darkness. "These five over here went down before they knew we were here, the rest of the hostiles back at the base are out of commission as well. I understand four were left viable for questioning. No casualties or wounds for the good guys."

The passenger looked over to the right of the gated wall and saw the bodies of five men, all Mexican and all very dead. Four of the bodies displayed the telltale signs of a well-played assault, each having one shot to the chest and one shot to the head. The fifth body suffered a different kind of fate. He had been gutted from his groin to his sternum by what must have been a very sharp knife because nestled inside his now eviscerated body was also his now detached head.

"Hmmm, looks like Dishman came along for the ride," said the passenger.

"At your service," a voice said from amongst the pack of four.

The passenger smiled. "Alright, good work. We're out of here in thirty. Stay sharp."

Both Jeeps then lurched forward and drove another two hundred and fifty yards until the vehicles came to a staging area constructed deep into the side of the mountains that provided cover for what was, until approximately forty-five minutes ago, the largest heroin distribution center for the Los Zeta drug cartel.

The staging area itself was about half the size of a football field and clearly built to accommodate both medium-sized delivery trucks and to also act as a helicopter landing site. The area was bordered on the far side by two large single story metal buildings, each painted in a mixture of patterned colors perfect for camouflage in the Desert Mountains of northeast Mexico. Several trucks, with paint jobs to match the buildings, were parked adjacent to each structure.

Standing next to one of the buildings was a group of six men, all dressed identical to the others at the gate. The Jeeps drove in their direction and parked. The passenger got out and looked around him. In the glow of the

346

desert moon, he could see that the staging site was littered with bodies. Just like at the gate, all were dead and all were Mexican.

Formed in 1999 as a private army for the Gulf Cartel under then leader, Osiel Cardenas Guillen, the core of the Los Zeta Cartel was comprised of former elite military soldiers from both the Airmobile Special Forces Group (GAFE) and the Amphibian Group of Special Forces (GANFE.) who chose to lend their talents to the importation of heroin and cocaine into the United States. They gained their power by earning a reputation for merciless slaughter and relentless violence. Drug competitors from rival cartels, law enforcement officers, innocent civilians. It didn't matter to the Los Zetas. They killed them all.

But on this day, this band of narco-terrorists were no match for the serious hell that descended from the nighttime sky. Parachuting in from a plane too far up for anyone to hear or see, ten elite members of the CIA Counter-Terrorism Unit came calling to teach these drug runners the same lesson that had Taliban warlords and Al Qaeda terrorists hiding under their beds.

An all-volunteer group consisting of former SEALS and Marine Force Recon, these unit members were the best mercenaries in the world and easily eliminated the Los Zetas garrison at the staging area with surgical precision.

"I understand you kept four of these pig fuckers alive. Where are they?" the passenger inquired.

"Inside," said one of the men, taking off his night vision goggles and securing them on his hip. "But there's something you need to see over in this other building first."

Both men then walked over to the adjacent building, opened the door and went inside. The interior was illuminated by rows of overhead fluorescent lighting and walking space was at a premium as the floor was literally covered by over a dozen wooden pallets upon which were stacked kilo after kilo of plastic wrapped bricks of Afghanistan heroin.

"Impressive," the passenger said. "Looks like we hit the mother lode just like Intel predicted."

"That's not what I brought you to see," the man said. "The heroin itself is a nice haul but this over here is the really bad news."

And with that, the soldier walked to the rear of the building and pulled aside a large brown canvas tarp that provided cover for over fifty crates of Colt M-4 fully automatic assault rifles. "Ammo is in those boxes over there," he said pointing to row upon row of smaller metal cases stacked beside the guns.

"It gets worse," he said as he made his way around the weapons and boxes of ammo.

"Over here, we've got enough C-4 to level half of Los Angeles," the soldier said. "Sir, it's all U.S. government issue. They're killing us and a lot of others with our ordnance, sir."

Simon Epstein initially said nothing. He picked up one of the M-4's out of an opened crate and held it like a just born baby in his hands. A beautiful weapon, without a doubt, and brand, spanking new. He continued to survey the scene, quietly taking it all in, thinking before he spoke.

"Photograph the rifle crates, ammo boxes and the C-4," Simon finally commanded. "Get all of the serial numbers and other tracking data that you can from all three. Secure two of the rifle crates for extraction with the team. Make sure your men get all the electronics that they can. Cell phones, hard drives, lap tops, you know the drill. And, make good use of the C-4. Ten minutes after liftoff, I want this place and everything in it vaporized. Any questions?

"No sir," the man replied.

"Now take me to these assholes," Simon added, "time for a little chat. I'll be brief with them. Call the removal team. I want to hear rotor blades in T minus fifteen. Understand?"

"Yes, sir," came the response.

Simon and the team leader walked back over to the first building. The four prisoners had been brought outside and were now kneeling side by side about ten feet from the front door which had been left open.

Looking in, Simon, with the M-4 rifle still in his hand, could see an array of disheveled bunk beds, old stuffed chairs, and wide shelves filled with food and soda. A couple of beat up refrigerators and a freezer ran along another wall. There was a table with a microwave. Another table held a TV screen that showed the image of a video game in progress. Beer cans were scattered everywhere and the place reeked of marijuana.

Simon turned his attention back to the four prisoners, now bathed in the soft florescent glow that emanated from the open door to the housing unit. They were dressed in jeans, cheap sneakers, t-shirts and had their hands bound behind their backs by nylon wire-ties. Three of the men said nothing and stared in silence at the dusty floor of earth that was now well soaked with the blood of over thirty of their dead colleagues. The fourth man stared instead at Simon and sent him a grinning snarl through teeth rotted black from the daily use of methamphetamine.

"Get him up," Simon instructed one of the CIA operatives.

The man with the snarl was quickly yanked to his feet and moved apart from the others with his back to the broad open space that would soon serve as the tarmac for the CIA stealth copter that was now inbound for extraction.

"You're smiling. You must be happy," Simon said.

"Fuck you," the man growled back.

"Where did you get this?" Simon asked, holding up the M-4, which he then handed off to one of the soldiers.

"From your fucking mother," the man shot back.

"My mother doesn't sell guns to little kid cocksuckers like you," Simon said. "Now, for the last time, where did you get that rifle?"

"I speak only to Mexican police, not to Yankee pigs," the man responded.

"Fine," Simon said, "Have it your way." The DEA agent then pulled his HK P30 and in the blink of an eye, sent a .40 cal round of Smith and Wesson's finest through the drug smugglers temple, snapping his head back in the process as the two hundred grain bullet exploded from the rear of his skull, leaving in its wake a bright pink mist of atomized brain and blood as the hunk of brass and lead flew helter skelter into the parched Mexican hills.

The CIA men gathered around the scene took it all in with the dispassionate glare a rattlesnake reserves for a just fanged rabbit. They had seen Simon in action before, and it didn't bother them one bit. Besides, these worthless pieces of shit were only getting what they deserved.

Simon then turned his attention to the remaining three and pointed to the next one in line.

"Him," was all he said.

After the man was brought to his feet and placed downrange, Simon again pointed to the M-4 and said, "Where did you get that?"

"I don't know," the man said, eyes to the ground.

"Okay," Simon said, "who around here would know?"

"Ah, you just shot him," the Mexican replied.

"I don't believe you," Simon said and fired off another round from the P30 that struck the man in his left thigh. Blood gushed instantly from the wound as the handcuffed man tumbled to the ground, screaming in pain while he rolled in the dirt like the drug running maggot he was.

Simon, with pistol still in hand, walked over to the other two Zetas and while staring at the kneeling men, he noticed that one of the men had a pool of urine on the ground between his knees but the other did not. Simons experience told him that the pisser would be the first to talk so he approached him first.

"You," Simon said, while lifting up the man's chin with the toe of his boot. "Look at me. You now know what I will do to you if you don't answer my questions. I will kill you. Now, where did that rifle come from?"

"I work here only," the man responded, his accent thickly Hispanic, his words wrapped in fear. Beads of beer infused sweat poured down his face in buckets and gathered together in large drops at the base of his chin until, feeling gravity's pull, they fell, one by one, through the remaining two feet of air, landing soundlessly in the piss-stained mud.

"I never go north," he continued, "but the guns, they come from up north."

"Shut up!" the Zeta beside him suddenly screamed, "you tell these dogs nothing!" he added as he hockered deep and sent a large wad of spit that caught Simon on the leg.

Simon didn't react to the actions of the man who spit. Instead, he continued his conversation with the man who never went north.

"What's your name?" the agent asked.

"Diego," The man replied.

"Listen to me, Diego. Your friend here is a dead man, but it doesn't have to be that way for you. Now, I know that you know more than you're telling me. You're a smart guy, I can tell that. And, you hear people talk when they come back here with things like these rifles. Now tell me, what did you hear them say?"

Diego paused for a moment. This time, his partner said nothing, having been convinced into silence by the muffled barrel tips of two M-4's that were now pressed into the back of his skull.

"I hear that they sell lots of drugs to MS-13 and use the money to buy the guns," the man finally said.

"From whom do they buy the guns, Diego?" Simon asked.

"I don't know, man, I don't," the man said, "but I do know where they go to get them."

"And where's that?" Simon responded.

"Baltimore," Diego said.

"Thank you, Diego," was Simon's final comment to the prisoner who immediately collapsed into a puddle of piss and sweat as the DEA agent holstered the P30, left his presence, walked over to the side of the building and gathered the soldiers around for pre-departure instructions.

"C-4 set?" Simon asked.

"Yep. Primed and ready to go," replied one of the CIA operatives as the sound of distant rotors brought a welcome hum to the cool morning air.

"What about them?" another of the soldiers asked, motioning in the direction of the three surviving Zetas.

"Secure the pisser and the wounded fuck to the crates of the M-4's back in the shed," Simon ordered. "They at least deserve a ringside seat when everything goes boom."

"What about the other guy who loogied your leg?" the same soldier asked.

Simon cast his eye's over to the one remaining Mexican who was still on his knees, defiant to the end, and then looked down at the goblet of thick marijuana stained spit that had moved its way earthbound, leaving a snail like trail of saliva from mid-calf to the top of his boot.

The DEA agent thought for a moment and then smiled as he spoke. "Let Dishman know that we have someone waiting for him who seriously doubts his skills with a knife. Tell him he has two minutes to convince the man otherwise. Now, as to the rest of you, grab your gear, pack the intel and let's get the hell out of here."

# Chapter Thirty-Five

## The Girl from West Marine

The second David was sitting in his chair behind his law office desk; he picked up the phone, called Karen and told her that Billups was pleading guilty to second degree murder and that the case was, for all practical purposes, over. The relief in his wife's voice was as palpable as that of a cancer victim getting an "all clear" from their oncologist, as this case, for Karen, had become a horrible disease that had infected her entire family and she was tired of it.

"David," she said. "I know you believed him but the evidence just said otherwise. You did the best you could and that's all anyone expects you to do. Billups knows that but he also knows that he killed that young man. And, when is the sentencing? I need to know when this case will really be over."

"Tomorrow at 9:00am," he said, taking a drink of water while flipping through the stack of phone messages that had piled up over the last several days. "It should be a quick proceeding. I'll call you when I finish up so that you'll know that its finally a done deal."

"David?" she asked.

"Yeah, baby?"

"I love you," Karen said.

"I love you, too, baby." David replied. "Now, I gotta run. I need to get back up to the jail, get these agreements signed and brief Jamal on the sentencing procedure he'll face when Judge Powell hits the bench tomorrow morning. Burgers on the grill tonight after practice?"

"Sounds great," Karen said. "You cook, I'll clean."

"It's a deal and baby," David said with a smoother tone to his voice. "If I do a really good job on those burgers, what else will you do for a chef of my proven expertise?"

"Anything you want, sugar," Karen replied, sending a wink over the phone lines. "Anything you want."

---

David was heading back out to his car when Brenda stopped him and handed him a message slip.

"This girl called while you were on the phone. She wouldn't give me her name. Caller ID said West Marine. Do you know what she wants?" his secretary asked.

"Maybe," Forbes replied.

"Are those the plea agreements in that folder you've got stuffed in your briefcase?" Brenda asked.

"Well yes, and how do you know that?" David inquired, having not told Brenda a thing about his morning's visit with both Jamal and the Commonwealth's Attorney. Again, he was amazed by how little remains quiet in this town.

"Janet called me from Archie's office." Brenda explained. "She wanted to make sure that you were really going to get them signed before she called Judge Powell to tell him about the sentencing for tomorrow. Is Billups really going to sign them? Guys like him are famous for changing their minds at the last minute, you know."

"Something tells me that I don't think we're going to see a mind change on this one," he answered.

"Would that something have anything to do with that West Marine phone call?" Brenda asked, tossing a stare like he tossed one of his darts in his office.

"Ah, no," David said, caught off guard by the spot on accuracy of her question. Jeeze, the women around me are quick, he thought. They don't miss a thing.

"I bought a kayak from them this morning," he explained. "I probably left some warranty information on their counter. I'll call her on the road and find out what she needs."

"She didn't sound to me like she was calling about some warranty paperwork on a kayak. You want me to call her and find out?" she suggested, turning on the high beams in the process. Brenda was now looking at David like a veteran homicide cop looks at a lying murder suspect who is so guilty even his own mother would slap the cuffs on him.

"No," Forbes replied, briefcase and keys at the ready. "Thanks but I'll handle this. I'll call you when I leave the jail so that you can give Janet the thumbs up."

"David," she said, as he opened the front door to leave, "It's just a case. Don't do anything stupid."

"Don't worry, Brenda," he lied on his exit. "It's all going to be just fine. Jamal goes to prison tomorrow, and Eugene gets another closed file, just like he predicted. And, for us, life gets a little more normal. See you later."

And, out the door he went. David wasn't on the road five minutes before he kicked into action and called the West Marine number on the message slip. A familiar accent answered the phone.

"Hi. Welcome to West Marine. This is Tiffany. How can I help you?" the voice said.

"Well, now I at least know your first name." David replied. "Tiffany, this is David Forbes. You called my office. Thanks for your help earlier this morning. I appreciate it. What's up?"

"You know my first name but you don't know my last name," the girl called Tiffany said. "It's Thompkins. Cassie's my first cousin."

Forbes let fly a spontaneous 'Holy shit' as Tiffany continued.

"Our daddies were brothers," Tiffany explained. "She and I are close and we talk a lot. I know what happened that night on Haven Beach. Cassie told me the whole story. You probably want to hear it from her, but she ain't ever gonna tell you. She's so scared of Coles Howard and the sheriff that she can barely breathe. She wanted to tell you that day you came to the trailer but she figured she get killed for it if she did. You saw how her step-dad is. He's a real piece of shit. Treats Cassie and her momma the same way he treated you. God has a special place for him, and it's not up top if you know what I mean."

"I do know what you mean," David said, his mind reeling once again. "Tiffany, can you tell me what Cassie told you about that night?"

"That's why I called you," the girl replied. "I'll tell you but my mind will go silent as a clam if you subpoena me to testify at some trial. That I can't do. I've got a little boy at home who needs his momma. He ain't gonna have one anymore if anyone finds out we talked. You understand that?"

"I do," David replied. "This conversation stays here. No notes, no letters and no subpoenas." He could hear a soft touch breeze against the mouth piece of the phone and guessed that Tiffany had stepped outside to gather in a little more privacy.

She began her tale.

"Cassie told me that after the fight, she locked up the store and she and Jimmy went out to the beach. They had sex and all and were walking back to his truck when two men came towards them from the parking lot. One was Coles Howard. The other one she hadn't ever met before. Coles told her to keep walking on to the parking lot, that he and this other fellow had some business they needed to discuss with Jimmy. Cassie said that Coles was laughing and smiling, and so she did what he asked her to do. She said she was about to get in Jimmy's truck 'cause it was a little cold out when she heard him scream her name. She turned and ran as fast as she could back up the beach in the direction of Jimmy's voice. It was pitch black out but as she got closer there was just enough moon where she could see that Jimmy was on his knees and had his hands on his chest while the other man stood off a ways, just

356

looking at him. She tried to get to Jimmy but Coles headed her off, grabbed her by the arm and drug her through the sand back up to the parking lot. He put her in the back seat of his truck, told her to lie down and if she looked up, he said it would be the last thing she ever did. She did as she was told. After a few minutes, she heard the other man get in the truck but said that he and Coles didn't say anything to each other and the next thing she knew, she was at her parents' trailer. Coles walked her up the steps of the front porch and told her if she said anything about tonight to anybody, that he would kill her mother just as sure as night turned to day. She didn't doubt one word and that's why she couldn't talk to you."

"But she did talk to you," David said.

"Yeah," Tiffany said, "Like I said, we're cousins and close cousins at that. She made me swear not to tell anyone, and I kept that promise until just now."

"Did she tell you anything about some beer cans and leaving her shoes at the beach?" David asked.

"Yeah," Tiffany again replied. "She said she'd brought a six-pack from the store and that she'd left her shoes in the sand next to where they'd been before Jimmy was killed. She told me that Howard brought her the shoes the next day when he came to drink beer with her step-father."

David was floored. "Tiffany, let me ask you one thing. Why are you telling me this stuff and why now? Why not just keep this to yourself and let it all go away on its own terms. Telling me isn't going to bring Jimmy back and it's a foregone conclusion that innocent or not, Jamal Billups doesn't stand a chance of being found not guilty unless Cassie takes the stand which we both know isn't going to happen. So, again, why are you telling me this?"

"Because you went to Cassie's house that day to learn the truth," Tiffany answered. "And, because you gave her the CD case with her ultrasound that you found at the beach, and because you treated her with dignity when she was on the witness stand, lying about what took place and because you came into the West Marine this morning wanting to know about equipment that I know you weren't going to use for yourself. I knew that you knew the truth when we was talkin' and I could tell that you were not going to let that black boy go to prison for something that he didn't do. That's why I told you what Cassie told me."

David knew he needed her help to free his client and save his family. "Jamal Billups is going to plead guilty tomorrow to second degree murder and receive a twenty year sentence. You'll read about it in the papers. Can I trust you?"

"There shouldn't be any doubt about that by now," was her reply.

Forbes agreed and told her his plan. When he was finished, she said, "Do you still have my cell phone number that I gave you at the store this morning?"

"Yep," David replied. "Sitting right in the console of my car."

"Text me the approximate time and I'll be ready to go," she said.

"You got it," David replied. "And, Tiffany?"

"Yeah?" she said.

"Tell Cassie I'm going to bring some justice back into her world real soon," David answered.

"She knows that Mr. Forbes," Tiffany explained. "I told her that you were in the store this morning. I called her right after you left. The reason I called your office is because she asked me to call and to tell you what I just did. She's scared but she believes in you. Please help her."

And then the line went dead. Tiffany went back to work, and David went to go see Jamal.

---

After he arrived at the jail, the lawyer told his client about the phone conversation with Cassie's cousin. They then reviewed the plea agreements which Billups signed without hesitation. Jamal handed the signing pen back over to his lawyer and said, "What that West Marine chick said kind of seals the deal, don't it, lawyer man."

"What do you mean, Jamal?" David asked.

"I mean the doubt is gone," his client said, "cause now we know that we're right and I mean really right. It's no more like *'I gotta believe Jamals tellin' me the truth'*. Now it's *'I know he's been tellin' me the truth'*. There's a difference, ain't it? You know it is, for sure!" Billups crossed his arms and looked at David like he had never done before. David was searching for some response words of his own when Billups delivered the rest of what was on his mind.

"You don't have to say nothing, lawyer man. It's okay. I know how it is. I mean you had your big case theories and all that shit, but there was still a smidgen of doubt in that head of yours over whether ol' Jamal here been tellin' the truth. Ain't that right?" Jamal asked.

"No, that's not right," David countered. "The way things added up, I didn't think you were guilty."

"Yeah, but did you think I was *innocent*?" Jamal asked. "There's a big fuckin' difference, man. Being guilty requires all that proof beyond a reasonable doubt bullshit. Look at O.J. Cut his wife's throat ear to fuckin' ear. But the police fucked up his case and the jury found him not guilty. Now that may be the case in the eyes of the law, not guilty and all, but that don't mean he's an innocent man. That's why I'm saying that the West Marine chick sealed the deal. Meaning, in your eyes, she finally made me an innocent man."

David smiled and said, "True."

Jamal smiled back and said "Alright then, lawyer man, now repeat after me . . ."da nigga been tellin' the truth!"

Forbes started laughing and his client joined in, causing a guard to peek inside the holding cell to see what all the commotion was about. Seeing the guard with his face against the window just made the two men laugh even harder.

Jamal then held his hands up like a maestro directing an orchestra and said "okay now, keep your white ass still cause I been waiting a long time for this here moment so don't fuck it up. One more time. Here we go, let's say it together, and a one, and a two and a three…"

"Da nigga been tellin' the truth!"

The chorus of the two so loudly came from inside the cell that the guard was caused to look in for a second time and what a scene he saw.

David was laughing so hard that he slipped off his chair, taking some of his file with him to the floor which just made Jamal's body shake that much more from so much laughter, his smile now a mile wide as he helped gather up the pages of the plea agreements that had tumbled to the floor while the guard at the door just stared at the two men, totally confused as to how an all but convicted murder suspect and his court appointed attorney could find so much to be happy about in this goddamn place.

David finally got his papers together, clicked his briefcase shut and said, "It's been quite a ride, Jamal."

Jamal responded, "Ride ain't over yet, lawyer man."

"It will be by tomorrow night." David said. "Tomorrow morning, however, Judge Powell will wonder what the hell you're doing pleading guilty after we all but stood on the table professing your innocence at our last little hearing, so expect some raised eyebrows and a few questions when the Commonwealth's Attorney tells 'em that you can't wait to go to prison for twenty years."

"Don't you worry about that there Judge," Jamal countered. "I can hang my head, shuffle my feet and look like a road gang coon with the best of 'em. You just do your thing. I'll do my thing and together, we're gonna to bring this shit to an end. In two days lawyer man, and I mean in just two fuckin' days, we'll be havin' dinner at my granny's. You can count on it. Chicken and dumplings, fried oysters, collard greens, black eyed peas, fuckin' awesome cornbread and a mason jar of the best peach shine you ever tasted. We're gonna get well-fed and tore up something good. You and me together,

Jamal style! Now you need to get your ass outta here and take care of business."

As David got ready to open the cell door, he said "You know, in the church parking lot, your granny said that her prayers would show me the way to set you free. I'm beginning to think there may be some truth to that. She must be one special woman."

"If you think her prayers are special, just wait till you try her cornbread." Jamal said. "Now roll, lawyer man. Tomorrow is our day."

# Chapter Thirty-Six

# Twenty Years for Jamal Billups

His Honor was not amused. Judge Powell held the plea agreement in his hand like a southern slave owner would have held the Emancipation Proclamation and glared down at the two lawyers who stood before him in a courtroom that was all but empty save for the defendant, the clerk, a bailiff, a court reporter and the two folks who sat together on a bench two rows behind where Jamal Billups was seated beside his lawyer.

The Reverend Terrance Covington and Jamal's grandma sat side by side in a courtroom usually filled to the brim with watermen and the lynch mob looking regulars who did little to hide their impatience that the gallows couldn't be built quick enough for David's client. Even Coles Howard and his eminency himself, Sheriff Howard, didn't show up ringside for the main event.

Forbes quickly took note of the drop in attendance. It surprised him in some ways and in other ways it didn't. There was an undercurrent of activity going on in this case that he couldn't define or even really explain. It was just there, palpable and pulsing, gliding through his world like whispery ghosts, specters from the past and present, all teeming around him like so many fish.

David knew that the family Howard had plans in the making for his demise and there was something as well about Walter Taylor and Tiffany from West Marine that stuck in his head. Those two were clearly more than the sum of their parts. They both gave off an impression, an aura as it were, of knowing more than they were willing to communicate, but it wasn't an unwillingness in the negative sense, rather it was like they measured each dose of information like a wise physician meted out medicine to a sickly soul. You got what you needed at the time you needed it. No more and certainly no less.

When Forbes entered the courthouse that morning, after parking in a lot devoid of the usual accompaniment of pickup truck after pickup truck, he encountered the Reverend Covington and Jamal's grandmother in the lobby just outside the doors to the courtroom. All three had arrived early that morning well before the hearing was scheduled to begin.

The reverend wore a crisp white banded preacher's collar, a solid black shirt and a pressed to perfection dove gray suit. A four-point, black pocket square and tasseled loafers of a darker gray rounded out the ensemble. Ms. Billups wore her standard Sunday attire, a maroon two-piece suit with brass buttons, an ivory blouse, a string of pearls, earrings to match and pumps the color of hand churned butter. Standing there together, they gave the appearance of made to order figurines from some documentary about African American church goers in the great American South. In a word, they looked superb.

David didn't know exactly how he would be received by the two. The fact that Jamal was going to plead guilty to second degree murder in a couple of minutes would not be received by these folks as good news, and David approached the pair with some degree of apprehension. The Reverend Covington, however, quickly put the lawyer at ease.

"Good morning lawyer Forbes," the Reverend said in his deeply toned greeting as he warmly shook the hand of Jamal's attorney. He then put his hand shaking arm around the shoulders of Ms. Billups and lowered his voice. "I had a pastoral visit with Jamal up at the jail yesterday after you had left. They let us meet in the library so he and I had the opportunity to talk without our conversation being recorded like they do in those telephone-to-telephone meetin' rooms. He told me of your plan and of the burden now borne by you and your family. Ms. Billups and I come here today to support you and to let you know that God is with you and Jamal every step of the way. Of that you must have no worry or concern. Do you believe me, Mr. Forbes?"

"Today, I do Reverend," David replied. "Today, I truly do."

"Good. Then let us not hinder you further in your labors," Reverend Covington said. "We shall sit quietly and witness in confidence that you are the one truly chosen to do His work here today. God be with you, sir."

"Thank you Reverend" was all David got the chance to say before his was embraced by the steel strong arms of Jamal's granny. "Please save my

363

grandson," she whispered into his ear as she quickly stepped back, wiping away the tears that had stained David's cheek in the process with a deft touch from the Kleenex tissues that were clutched in hands both left and right.

"I will," David promised as the woman said nothing more and, following the lead of the Reverend, turned and headed into the courtroom where her grandson would soon get to serve twenty years in the state pen if David Forbes failed to do His work as the Reverend expected.

Forbes followed them into a courtroom that was as empty as an unused coffin. David took out his file, arranged the few papers that would have any bearing on the events set for hearing before Judge Powell and waited for the required players to arrive.

It didn't take long. Archie Hudgins and a young lady providing court reporting services for this morning's docket arrived a minute later and walked together down the center aisle, with Hudgins looking like a perturbed father who was about to give his daughter's hand in marriage to a less than desirable future son-in-law.

Archie peeled off to his right and stood at David's left elbow for a full four seconds before the defense attorney felt obliged to acknowledge his presence. Forbes looked up as Hudgins looked down and spoke his mind.

"For what it's worth," the prosecutor said, "Jimmy's family is some pissed off about this agreement and have collectively promised that they will vote for a Labrador retriever before they cast their ballot ever again for my re-election. With that being said, they have also agreed not to oppose its entry and will not be joining us today. I thought you would find that of interest."

"Which part, Archie?" David asked, "That they aren't opposing the plea agreement or that they intend to vote for a dog next time you run."

"Both, I suppose," Hudgins mumbled to himself as he turned and walked over to his table facing the Judge's bench from the southwest.

Hudgins' entrance into the courtroom was followed soon thereafter by the bailiff and Mr. Callis who were both barely situated at their duty stations when a knock on chambers door signaled the arrival of Judge Powell.

The learned jurist took the bench, received the file from the court clerk, swore in the court reporter and then turned his attentions to both attorneys.

"Counsel, I have been advised that my presence was required here this morning to hear proceedings involving the entry of a plea agreement. Is that correct?"

"Yes sir, your Honor," came the refrain from both attorneys in a jumbled harmony of collective concurrence.

"Well, I have to admit to being a bit surprised by this particular development, Mr. Forbes," the Judge said, sending his comments in David's direction. "Given the particulars of the last hearing, you would have thought Jesus Christ himself was going to take the stand and profess your client's innocence. But now, instead of salvation, we have guilt and severe punishment. My intent this morning is not to delve into the subtleties of your case, but the court is compelled to make inquiry into what exactly it was that has rendered this abrupt change in adjudicatory demeanor, as it were."

David stood and addressed the court, "If Your Honor please, this has been a most challenging case. I would like to think that my file would reflect that a 'no stone unturned' approach has been fully implemented by my office and, as a result, all evidentiary avenues have been thoroughly explored. Because of this effort, the width and breath of the case is no longer an unknown, and when viewed from this perspective, the totality of the facts make it difficult to believe that a jury of twelve would ultimately return a verdict of other than guilty. This plea agreement cuts my clients potential losses considerably and gives him some hope of living the remainder of his life, at some point in time, somewhere else other than behind bars. As a result thereof, we ask today that the court enter the plea agreement as presented."

"Have your received the documents that were the objective of your most fought over subpoena *duces tecum*?" the Judge inquired.

"No, sir, the response date is still several weeks away," David replied.

"Then how can you make the statement you just did when we both know that you do not have all of the evidence necessary to reach that conclusion?" Powell asked.

"Well Judge, like I said just moments ago, I . . ." David began to say before he was cut off in mid-sentence by a clearly unconvinced Judge Powell.

"Well Judge nothing," Powell abruptly countered, "You want me to accept a plea agreement that puts a man behind bars for twenty years with you having acknowledged here today in open court that your investigation is unfinished? How can you ask me to do that and what the hell is so magical about 'now'? Why must this be done today? Why is it that all of this cannot wait until after the documents have been returned pursuant to the subpoena, reviewed by counsel and then, if so compelled by the totality of the evidence, as you phrase it, then ask me to put this man in prison? I will tell you that I am not comfortable with this one bit and I'm half-way inclined today to appoint another lawyer to represent this man. I've seen far too many cases of half-baked justice to let something like this have my fingerprints on it and I'll say one more thing and that's...."

"Your Honor," said an interrupting voice that had yet to speak a word. It was Jamal's. He rose to his feet and stood side-by-side with a lawyer who this time needed a helping hand from his client.

"It's my decision to plead guilty, not my lawyer's. I told Mr. Forbes that I wanted to do it, and he's just doing what I asked him to do, sir."

Jamal's utterances on his own behalf took some of the wind out of the judge's sails so Powell dialed down the attack on Forbes and, instead, directed his inquiry towards David's client.

"Mr. Billups, you no doubt have heard my comments to your attorney. There is a wealth of evidence that has yet to be reviewed that may well have a positive bearing on the outcome of your case. My concern here today is that all of this is a bit premature given the still open status of the investigation that was initiated on your behalf. Why a plea of guilty cannot wait until all of the facts are available for review is frankly a question that should not be the subject of debate among persons sincerely interested in the administration of justice. If my comments offend anyone here today, the court extends its apologies but that's just how the court feels about the position of this case as it has been presented here today."

"Judge," Jamal said. "I appreciate everything that you are trying to do. You're a good man, but the fact of the matter is that I done killed that boy that night out on Haven Beach. I stabbed him and I stabbed him good. I was mad that his girlfriend wouldn't sell me no beer that night. I was mad that he done hit me so many times out in front of that store that I bled like a gelded mule. I was mad when them white boys showed up in them fancy trucks, all jacked up an' shit, and pulled baseball bats and come at me with smiles on their faces, knowing that they were gonna beat my black ass. And, I was mad 'cause they been doing that to me my whole life. This time, Jamal wasn't going to lie down and take it like the porch monkey he's been called since kindergarten. This time, Jamal was going to do things his way and I been waitin' my whole life to settle up and that's what I done. I tracked that Jarvis boy down and gave him what I been gettin' and I ain't sorry that I done it neither. My point is, I'd be most appreciative if we could please just dispense with all this search for justice shit, and get this over with so that I can get the hell out of here."

Jamal's averments to his lawyer that he could shuffle and roll with the best of 'em were right on target and Judge Powell entered the plea agreement without further comment. "Good luck to you, Mr. Billups" were the last words the jurist spoke before he took leave of the bench to the tune of the conclusive instruction of the bailiff that court was adjourned.

Billups shook his lawyers hand and headed back to the holding cell where two decades of hard time commenced per the papers that rested comfortably on the clerk's desk, still warm from the judge's touch. With the ink barely dry from his Honor's endorsement of the plea agreement that now bore his signature, Eugene Callis carefully paper clipped the document to the file and began to make his way back to his office when Forbes cast a comment in his direction. They were the last two people in the courtroom.

"You were right, Mr. Callis," David said.

"How's that, David?" the Clerk responded.

367

"That one day it would be a closed case like all the rest," David said. "And, today is that day. A closed case it finally is."

"David, I thank you for the compliment as to the accuracy of my projection but that didn't take being right, it was just knowing how it had to be. It couldn't end any other way. Just like life itself, we all know how it, too, ends. No accuracy needed in predicting that now is there?" the stately clerk suggested.

"No sir, I guess there isn't," David acknowledged as he started his own exit from the courtroom.

"Ah, David," The clerk said, stopping him in mid-stride, "The case is, ah, over, isn't it?"

Forbes stared over a turned shoulder at a man for whom he had great difficulty in being less than honest in his reply. He chose his words carefully. "I'm afraid I can't answer that right now Eugene. Time will tell. All I can say right now is that Judge Powell was spot on when he said that justice in this case was not being served by an incomplete investigation."

"Well, David, if you agreed with him then why did your client plead guilty?" asked Mr. Callis.

"He didn't plead guilty Eugene," David said. "Billups told the court what the court had to hear in order to do what needed to be done here today. There's a difference."

"Are you saying that he's not guilty?" the clerk asked as he adjusted his glasses that had slipped from the bridge of his nose due to his eyebrows going skyward from his reaction to the comments of the lawyer who just stood beside a man sentenced to twenty years in prison.

David uttered his last comment to the clerk as he took a step towards the door, "All I can say right now Eugene is that if I were you, I'd keep that case out of that lateral file cabinet of yours just a little while longer. Let it sit on your desk a spell. Just like you said about life, this case, too, has a predictable end and that didn't happen here today. You take care of yourself Eugene. I'll be seeing you soon."

And with that, David Forbes headed out the door.

# Chapter Thirty-Seven

# The Devil's Den

David sat in Karen's 4Runner at the far end of the rutted road that led to Walter Taylor's house and watched as the *Bay Lady* tossed gently against her mooring lines, the large workboat going up and down in rhythm with the waves that had picked up in their intensity in the twenty minutes he had been parked with a clear view of Harper's Creek Marina his sole objective.

The weather report of overcast skies with a chance of severe thunderstorms was coming true in its prediction as the SUV was already being pelted with rain, and David could hear the far off rumble of bass drum thunder getting closer with each passing minute. The marina was battened down for the storm and there was no activity of any kind at Howard's boat.

Still, the lawyer sat and watched. Tonight was a one-shot deal and it all had to be done by the numbers.

If he pulled it off, his client would go free and Coles Howard would get life for the murder of Jimmy Jarvis and lethal injection for the double murder and robbery of the drug runners in the Fountain.

If he messed it up, Forbes was beyond certain that life as he knew it would be over. His career would be trashed. He in all likelihood would be disbarred, potentially arrested, probably convicted and understandably divorced.

David checked his watch. It was 2:10 a.m. and time to move. He did a last minute check on his equipment. He put on an Under Armour black stretch fabric cap that covered his ears and the headset that was hard wired to his cell phone which was set on redial and secured in a zippered waterproof pocket of his fatigue jacket. In another pocket was the portable GPS unit and USB cable that he had purchased from Tiffany at West Marine. All electronics were on full charge. In his left cargo pants pocket was an MF Tactical 350 lumen LED flashlight. In his right pants pocket was a SOG Trident knife. He was set. David switched off the interior lights to the Toyota, got out of the vehicle and softly closed the door.

Once his feet hit the ground, Jamal's attorney was instantly greeted by rapidly increasing  taps of rain water against the coarsely woven nylon fabric of his fatigues and he paused a moment to enjoy the cool rush of the moist night air. He filled his lungs with it as he took another look over at the *Bay Lady* where she sat approximately two hundred and fifty yards south towards the mouth of the harbor, bathed in the single light from the lamp pole to her left. The boat, as well as the marina, were devoid of any inhabitants, with everyone apparently home and weathering out the storm, tucked and warm in their beds.

David moved to the side of the 4Runner, unlatched the newly purchased kayak from its Thule roof mounted carrier and walked it silently down the bank of grass and sand to the narrow gut of creek water that bordered the old man's driveway. Resting the craft half on solid turf and half with its nose wedged among the stand of cattails and reeds that grew in abundance along the water's edge, Forbes returned to the truck, quietly lifted the rear gate and removed a paddle and a large dark beach towel that was rolled length wise and secured at both ends with a couple of his daughters elastic hair bands. He returned to the slim plastic boat, slid the rolled towel down into the shell, got in, grabbed his paddle and pushed the kayak from shore. The mission was on.

---

The law office had a different atmosphere about it when David returned from court that morning after Jamal's sentencing. Inquisitive as a cat, Brenda didn't ask him one question how the hearing went when he walked through the front door. The absence of inquiry surprised him a bit as cigarettes and case details were an expected part of their usual post-court debriefing. However, on this day, David's secretary just kept sipping her coffee and looking over her paperwork as he made his way past her desk and down the hallway to his office.

David assumed that Brenda's courthouse communication network being what it is, that she had already gotten the play-by-play and wasn't going to bother him with the details. That was fine by him. But there was also something about the case being over that brought a quieting effect of its own to the small country law office that had lived and breathed intense legal intrigue for far too long.

The Billups file was, in many ways, like a big carnival that had come to town. For a while there were lots of rides, and games and strange, colorful people doing odd, magical things all under one big tent. But that tent was now folded, the balloons were all gone and as the wagons rolled up the road and on to the next town, the silent conjecture of that which is the normal and the usual moved in to fill the void. The vacuum so abhorred by nature was now gone, its emptiness erased save for the stench and stain of that which had once been.

Karen and the kids were quiet, too. David thought that an odd similarity, until he paused to realize that what was for him sheer professional excitement, an anxiousness of the positive, productive kind, was a burden of a dissimilar quality for his family. They were clearly glad and obviously relieved that it was all over. Karen floated around in the kitchen like a just born butterfly soaring on gossamer wings above a sun warmed field of sprouting wildflowers. The chains of her worry were now gone and happy for that she was.

It was the same for both Luke and Katie. For them, the future was bright as day now that Daddy was no longer going to get yelled at by handbag wielding ladies in the Food King, Luke didn't have to worry about getting beaten up by boys he didn't know because of some case his dad was involved in and for Katie, her mommy was now happier than she had been in a long time and that was all that mattered to her. As in the office, here too in the house of Forbes, the normal and the usual had moved in to fill the void.

For the evening meal, his burger idea got shelved because the kids wanted BBQ from the Blue Crab and David was more than pleased to pick up as much take out as he could carry. A light sprinkling of rain nixed any idea of eating on the deck so they all just grabbed a stool around the island bar in the kitchen and laughed and talked their way through piles of steaming pulled pork and racks of ribs done right.

After dinner, the kids obliged their parents by an early bedtime and David and Karen retreated to their second floor bedroom and became lost in their own world of sweet, stirring love and strong, impassioned embrace. Several hours later, as David sat up in bed, he looked over at the soft, flowing mane of Karen's dark brown hair and wondered if, after tonight, all of this would be gone.

As he got up to change, doubt, hesitancy and fear continued to make their case, but ten minutes later, as he stood in the downstairs kitchen and stared at the phone that had brought threats of hard violence into his most perfect world just forty eight hours ago, all of the doubt, the hesitancy and the fear went south fast.

Forbes wrote a note to his wife that he couldn't sleep and that he was going for a drive. 'Be back soon was the time frame for his return. He left it on the kitchen counter and headed for the garage with a penny in his thoughts and a cold sense of justice in his soul.

———————————

It took David three strokes of his paddle to cross the narrows of the upper tidal channel and reach the marina side of Harper's Creek. Not a star was visible in the sky and the kayak disappeared quickly once it reached the opposite bank of reeds and grass, its dark green color morphing into an odd shade of gray in the muted twilight as storm clouds befuddled the moon and turned everything into shadows within shadows. David's choice of black tactical gear added to the disguise as man and boat glided as one towards the first of the vessels that called Harper's Creek Marina home.

Most of the boats tied up at this end of the creek were smaller pleasure craft, mainly center consoles, a few deck boats and assorted day sailers. As Forbes paddled past these initial elements of the fleet, he kept a sharp eye and a fine-tuned ear on the ready for any sign of trouble and for

David, trouble meant Coles Howard. So far, all was good. The weather was perfect for what he needed to do and the parking lot of the marina was as empty as a crater on Mars.

But the storm continued to gather in strength and by the time Forbes' kayak reached the mammoth bulkheads where the larger workboats were berthed, the rain was hitting him hard in wind driven sheets that first slapped his face from side to side and then went downward, with the drops resonating off the topside of the kayak like a thousand little drumsticks all drumming at the same time.

David pulled hard on the paddle and took shelter from the downpour as he worked the kayak underneath the dockage, weaving between thick pilings that looked like the legs of barnacle encrusted elephants in the murky, watery dark. This was an unexpected bonus as the bulkhead provided excellent coverage in terms of both weather and visibility, and he was able to make his way to the bow of the *Bay Lady* without ever bringing the kayak into open water.

Once he was close enough to Howard's boat to touch it with his paddle, David checked his watch and then reached into the hull of the kayak and took out a ten foot long piece of 3/8" braided nylon line. He tied one end of the line to a small cleat he had attached to the upper side of the kayak and wrapped the other end around a salt water soaked wooden joist spanning the ten foot gap between two of the outermost barnacled pilings that supported the bulkhead that ran parallel to Howard's boat.

Once his kayak was secured, he adjusted his headset, pulled out his cell phone, made sure the headset jack was plugged in tight and pressed redial. After two rings, Tiffany answered the phone.

"Where are you?" she asked.

"Right beside Howard's boat," Forbes responded, "under the dock actually. I called you a little earlier than planned. I guess I wanted to make sure you were still on deck for tonight's festivities."

374

"You knew that I would be," the girl responded. "You just called earlier than scheduled because you're a little bit scared, a whole lot nervous and if my front porch is any indication, really wet and really cold."

"You are correct on all counts," David acknowledged.

"Yeah, I know," Tiffany said, "Cassie is with me. She's spending the night. I thought that might be a good thing. Never know what might happen."

"I know what you mean," David said. "I'm going to get in position to board the boat. I have to do something first and I can't talk while I'm doing it, but I don't want to call you back, so just hang on, okay?"

"Okay," Tiffany said. "Do what you gotta do."

"Good, here we go," David said as he reached down into the hull of the kayak and removed the rolled up beach towel that he had stowed away back at Taylor's driveway. He slipped off the elastic hair bands at each end and slowly unwrapped the towel from around the Crossman air gun that he had bought Luke for his eighth birthday.

Already loaded and pumped, Forbes put his arm through the leather sling of the rifle and lifted himself carefully out of the kayak and on to the plank that acted as a perch that afforded Jamal's lawyer an excellent view of the light pole that stood less than eighteen feet from where his head was now positioned level to the dock.

David positioned the gun against his right shoulder and resting the barrel on the uppermost portion of the bulk head, he took careful aim and slowly squeezed the trigger.

The result was not what he expected.

He missed the bulb completely and instead hit the large saucer shaped metal shade that reflected the light from the target bulb directly to the *Bay Lady*. The anticipated whoosh of compacted pneumatic air pushing a BB through a twenty inch barrel was quickly followed by a loud '*PAH - TWAANNG!* the classic ringing sound of rifle shot metal ricocheting against metal.

Forbes immediately ducked down behind the bulkhead and could swear that his heart was beating hard enough to drive nails into cement. He had never heard anything in his life that sounded louder than that ricochet, and he swore that he could still hear the sound of the missed shot echoing amongst the rain drops that poured down around him in uncountable abundance.

"What was that?" Tiffany said.

"Shhh," David cautioned.

Forbes reached into his left lower jacket pocket and took out another BB. He loaded the rifle with a shaking hand and slowly pumped the gun for the next shot. He carefully poked his head above the bulkhead and looked around for a sign that anyone had taken an interest in his lack of marksmanship.

As before, the parking lot was still empty and all of the lights in the store were still off. Forbes again took aim and slowly squeezed the trigger, asking in the process for the blessing of any and all gods from any and all religions that would be kind enough to offer a helping hand. His prayers must have been answered because this time his aim was dead on and all that was heard after the trigger did its work was the soft puff of an imploding tissue thin bulb and the resulting tinkle as shards of shredded glass landed against the hard lay of the crushed oyster shell parking lot.

The *Bay Lady* was now as dark as the sky. David made his way back into the hull of the kayak, stored the rifle beneath his legs and untied the nylon rope from the plank.

"Tiffany, you there?" David spoke into the headset. "I'm ready to roll."

"Yeah, I'm here," she responded. "What were you doing?"

"Making my rifleman instructor at boot camp think I'm an idiot," he answered.

"You can explain later," she replied. "Now listen. Once you are on board, make your way to the very back of the boat. You will see a second set of controls. Steering wheel, throttle and transmission. All of this stuff is mounted on a small console that is attached to the right side of the boat. The bottom of the console is uncovered. Look underneath the console. On the left side is a hook with a set of keys. The smaller key unlocks the door to the wheel house. The larger key starts the boat and activates the electronics, just like a car. Get those keys and get in the wheel house fast. Is your GPS powered up and did you bring the USB cable?"

"Yep," he said.

"Good boy," she replied. "Now move. Let me know when you're in."

David kept the paddle inside the kayak, choosing instead to pull the boat hand over hand down the length of the network of joists securing the pilings under the bulkhead until he was midway along the waterline of the *Bay Lady*. He then tied up the craft as before, wrapped the beach towel around his neck and using the joists, again laddered his way up the side of the bulkhead until he was dead level with the *Bay Lady*.

From where he was perched on the side of the dock, Forbes was directly beside the wheelhouse of Howard's boat which lay about three feet from the side of the bulkhead. David looked over towards land. The rain was still pouring down. The lot was still empty. He looked back at the boat, stretched his right arm out as far as he could and got a cold, wet grip on the upper rail of the deadrise. David reached with his left arm, pulled hard, pushed up and over and was soon laying with his back against the deck of the *Bay Lady*.

"I'm on," David said into the mouthpiece.

"Stop talking," Tiffany commanded. "You need to move and move fast."

Forbes did as instructed and pushed with his feet until he had slid across the water soaked surface and had made his way to the far right rear of the boat. The control console was exactly where Tiffany said it would be.

377

David rotated his body until he could see under the unit. Feeling with his right hand, Forbes found the set of keys, then rolled over to his stomach and quickly crawled to the wheelhouse door. Using the smallest of the keys, he reached up, unlocked the door and went in.

Once inside, he felt less visible and stood up. It was good to be out of the rain. The storm was still trying to find its peak and the *Bay Lady*, though expertly tied to weather the gale, was still pitching up and down in her berth with a growing intensity as the weight of the storm now sent wave upon wave towards the mouth of Harper's Creek.

Forbes took a moment to survey the full measure of his surroundings. The interior of the wheelhouse was finished in a mixture of polyurethane treated pine, white fiberglass and polished stainless steel. Now dark from the absence of light from sources both natural and from BB shattered glass, David was nevertheless able to appreciate the activity of the place from the blended musty scent of diesel fuel, salt water and dead fish that filled his nostrils.

As his eyes adjusted to the shadowy interior, a large instrument panel came into focus that was accompanied by an array of switches and gauges surrounding a stainless steel steering wheel that was bordered on the right by a set of controls similar to those at the rear console from where David took the keys.

To the left of the instrument panel on the far wheelhouse wall were a mounted fire extinguisher and an adjacent wooden rack stuffed with gloves, hats and half a dozen rolled up maps and chart books. Underneath the rack and the extinguisher were two pairs of white rubber boots that sat atop the non-skid rubber matting that covered the width of the wheelhouse floor. David Forbes was now clearly in the domain of Coles Howard.

"Talk to me Forbes. What do you see?" said Tiffany's voice over the headset.

David turned his eyes to the polished flat wooden surface above the set of gauges on the instrument panel where sat a Garmin GPS.

"I see the GPS unit. It's a Garmin." he said. "I've got the key in the ignition switch. I'm turning on the power now."

"Remember to turn the key to the first position only," Tiffany reminded him. "If you go any further, you'll make the engine turn over and that'll cause all sorts of racket. Did you bring the beach towel?"

"Yep," he responded.

"Good," she said. "Don't forget to use it 'cause when those gauge lights turn on, it'll look like Christmas inside that wheelhouse at this time of night."

David unfurled the large beach towel from around his neck and laid it like a tent over his head and positioned it so it covered both the instrument panel and the screen of the GPS. He then took the second key and inserted it into the ignition. He slowly turned it to the first position and closed his eyes knowing that if he didn't he would lose what night vision he had when the gauge lights fired up.

The key now turned, darkness was replaced by the soft glow of iridescent light and Forbes slowly opened his eyes and stared at what was now a fully functioning GPS, its touch screen ready to go.

He reached into his jacket pocket, and removed the handheld portable GPS and the USB cable. He powered up the handheld and spoke into the headset.

"Tiffany, the GPS on the boat is on," David said. "I'm putting the USB into the ports of both units. Take me through this fast. It's getting rough out here. This boat is going up and down like crazy."

"Go to the 'main menu' icon on the boat GPS and press it," she replied. "When the window opens, press 'History'."

"Ok, that's done. What's next?" he asked.

"See the icon that says 'download'?" she asked.

"Yes," David answered.

"Press it," she instructed. "A window will open that asks where you want to store the data. Press the 'external device' icon. That will send it to the handheld."

David did as instructed. "Done," he replied.

"Good," she said. "Now you'll see a percentage meter at the bottom. Once it reaches one hundred percent, you're done. Unplug, lock up and get the hell out of there."

"I'm only at thirty percent," he said. "Moving slow."

"It must be a shit load of data on there," Tiffany replied. "I'm guessing he never deleted any of his waypoints which is good news for you and your client."

"Hopefully. Right now I just wish this would go faster. Getting rougher out here," David said as a sudden violent pitch of the boat made him grab on to the steering wheel to keep from being tossed across the wheelhouse.

Seconds of silence passed and then Forbes spoke next, "Looks like we're almost there," he said looking at the upload percentage meter at the bottom of the screen. "Ninety percent, ninety-five percent, one hundred percent. Done. I'm gone. Talk to you later."

"Move fast and get out of there," Tiffany said. "He's dangerous. Good luck."

David turned off the power to the boat, removed the key from the ignition and once again surrounded in darkness, he wrapped the towel back around his neck and secured the evidence loaded GPS in his jacket pocket.

He then took a last look out the wheelhouse window that faced the parking lot and the general store. Peering through rain streaked glass and seeing nothing but cold wet emptiness, Forbes knelt on the floor of the wheelhouse, slowly opened the door and crawled outside. He was instantly hit by howling wind and wicked water, but the lawyer didn't care. The cold and the wet felt good, exhilarating, in fact, as his work was nearly done and soon he would be back home, warm in bed with his wife and an early morning call to Simon on the agenda.

The attorney then reached up and with key in hand, locked the wheelhouse door and turned to crawl towards the console at the rear of the *Bay Lady* when he saw movement to his left. He turned his head to see what it was and it was then that the face of David Forbes suddenly met the massive leather boot of Coles Howard.

The waterman unleashed a viscous kick that caught the lawyer square on the underside of his jaw, shattering four of his teeth and sending lightning blasts of pain through every inch of his body. Paralyzed by the force of the attack, Forbes collapsed on the deck of the *Bay Lady*, blood pouring from his mouth.

Howard stood above him in the howling wind and pouring rain and said, "With there being a storm and all, I thought I'd walk down here to check on my boat and what do I find?"

"First thing I see is that some damn fool done shot my light out and then I find the damn fool who done it on my boat and in my wheelhouse."

"So I ask myself, 'Now what do ya suppose is so interestin' about my boat that would make somebody want to go through all this much trouble, particularly on a night like this?'"

Howard continued on. "Then I think to myself. Why, could it possibly be that damn lawyer whose been fuckin' with my life for the past six months? If anybody would know better than to do a damn stupid thing like this, it would certainly be a highly educated fellow like Mr. Forbes but then maybe again it wouldn't. Maybe, he would be just the sort to try some dumb fuckin' thing like comin' on my boat and doing exactly what I don't know but I'm about to find out. Now let's see what you got here."

The waterman reached down, turned Forbes over on to his back like a ragged bloody doll and drove his right fist into David's stomach with all the force he could muster. Forbes' body instantly convulsed upwards into a sit up position that was immediately reversed by a full force backhand to his face from Howards left paw that sent David's head crashing against the deck.

With Forbes more helpless than ever, Coles started rifling through the pockets of David's jacket and found the Garmin handheld.

"Well, well, a portable GPS and some sort of fancy cord," Howard exclaimed. "What's you been up to, boy? Screen on this thing says something about a history download. Oh me, oh my."

Howard started laughing to himself. "Forbes, you smarter than I give you credit for, boy. Ya got balls, too. No doubt about it. Goddamn waypoints. I never thought about deleting them, myself. Kind of feel like a fool I have to admit. Almost as big of a fool as you must feel right about now yourself."

"You almost got me, Mr. Lawyer. Yep, you came right close but that's as close as you're ever gonna get. Say good-bye to your little GPS here," Howard said as he sent the handheld unit spiraling though the darkness to be forever lost in the sand and silt under the waters of Harper's Creek.

"Now what to do about you," he asked, turning his attention back to Forbes. "I could call my daddy. But that would just make for more people in the know and we don't need to be waking anybody up at this time of night, now do we. Besides, I think that you and I can handle this little matter ourselves."

Unable to say a word or to think of any thought other than that he had seen the last of Karen and the kids, David just stared up at the source of the voice. He knew his fate was a done deal and he had the image of his family in his mind when Howard suddenly lifted him off the deck by grabbing him by the front of his jacket with one hand and then unleashed a thunderous punch to his head with the other that rendered him an unconscious heap on the deck of the *Bay Lady*.

Coles inspected the body at his feet, and it was at that moment that he saw the headset. His last bit of work had knocked off the black cap that David was wearing that night and the waterman followed the headset cord to the phone in the lawyer's pocket.

382

It was still on.

Howard put the headset on himself, listened for a moment to the silence coming from the other end and then spoke.

"Hey, I'm okay'" he softly mumbled into the receiver, trying to mask the voice of the man who was about to kill David Forbes.

Tiffany didn't bite. She knew Forbes was in trouble. She also knew that Howard now had her number on caller ID. His dad could trace it to her in a minute. Nothing further to be gained by staying on the line, she hung up, turned to Cassie and said, "We gotta go."

Howard heard the click of the disconnected call and correctly guessed that his little ruse didn't work. No matter, whoever this person was, they too would be taken care of in due time. He pushed Forbes' bleeding, unconscious body away from the wheel house, went in and started her engines. While she warmed up, he went over to the bulkhead, untied Forbes' kayak, hoisted it aboard with one hand and then walked back to the wheelhouse.

"Somebody is about to have a boatin' accident," Howard said with a laugh to the motionless body as his feet. "Yes, sir, a man ought to know better than to go out in water on a night like this in some skinny little piece of shit like that. Yes, sir, a man should know better, that's a fact."

Howard laughed again as he untied the lines and eased the *Bay Lady* out into the center channel of Harper's Creek. The screen on the Garmin was blank. No GPS waypoints needed this time. Howard knew the course he was going to take all too well and besides, this trip was going to be their little secret, shared on the way out, Howard's alone on the way back in.

In less than sixty seconds from the dock, the *Bay Lady* had slipped away from view, enveloped in the long, dark curtain of rain soaked blackness as she exited the headwaters of the creek and began the rough passage into the pounding waves of Mobjack Bay.

It was at this moment that Walter Taylor put down his binoculars, left his front porch and picked up the phone.

# Chapter Thirty-Eight

# The Fight on the *Bay Lady*

David wasn't unconscious more than fifteen minutes when he awoke and found himself against the rear transom of the boat, looking up at the console where just an hour ago, he had found the wheelhouse keys.

Initially, he didn't move. Shocked to still be alive, he just stared at the scene in front of him with the one eye he had left that wasn't swollen shut from the rocket blast he had taken from Howard's fist. Things had gotten obviously worse after they had left the dock. The weather had become extreme. As Tiffany had so accurately surmised when they first met that day at the West Marine, David Forbes did not know a damn thing about boats. He was a maritime amateur in all respects. But he knew enough that night, as he lay bleeding and battered on the deck of Howards boat, to realize one true thing.

The *Bay Lady* was in trouble.

Hard rain and big wind while docked at Harper's Creek was one thing. It became something entirely different once you leave the shelter of the harbor and motor towards open water. What David now saw before him eclipsed every definition of bad weather he had ever known. The nor' easter he had sat through on the shores at Haven Beach now had all the relative intensity of a spring shower as David gritted his shattered teeth and watched as the bow of the workboat plunged down into a fifteen foot deep trough of gray green water that sent shudders through its keel and David's body crashing against the other side of the deck.

As Forbes braced for the collision, he noticed for the first time that his feet were tied together with the same nylon rope he had used to secure the kayak. He instantly thought of the SOG but when the *Bay Lady* climbed out of the trough and skated onto the side of a mountain of a wave so steep that David literally was looking over the side of the boat and straight down into the belly of the bay. All he could try to do was hang on, but gravity again did its work, and his body was slammed at full speed against the bulkhead of the opposite side of the boat.

David almost lost consciousness again. He knew one more shot like that to his head and he was done for. Forbes looked up and saw the steering wheel of the console. He grabbed the wheel and held on tight as the boat once again plunged bow forward into the hell that had become Mobjack Bay.

The storm had clearly gathered in fury and the rain had become irrelevant as the whipping, angry water created a precipitation all its own as the tops of each wave exploded where its thinning peak met gale force wind, sending their salty residue into the air like infuriated swarms of watery marauding bees. The roar of the wind overcame David's senses and seemed a part of something that was alive, something far greater than just water and wind gone mad. The grainy blackness of the sky had long since disappeared, replaced now by a pelletized gray green haze of oxygenated water that surrounded the boat like a life form in and of itself, one determined to rip apart the boat of Coles Howard and kill all aboard who dared venture into its domain. Mother Nature was clearly pissed.

Howard had powered up two massive flood lights mounted on the front of the wheelhouse and Forbes watched from the stern of the boat as the *Bay Lady* went bow first into a massive illuminated wave that covered her decks in sea water.

Forbes understood now why he was still alive. Howard couldn't leave the wheelhouse long enough to kill him. David's thoughts went back to the knife but his pocket was empty. Howard must have found the knife when he went through the rest of his gear after that last punch that took him out of the game. Forbes looked at the knotting around his feet. Expertly tied, it wouldn't be undone quickly, so David ditched that thought from his head and focused on the man in the wheelhouse who had oddly become salvation for them both.

The door to the wheelhouse was closed and the soft glow from the electronics gave Howard's body a ghostly outline as he threw the wheel first one way and then the other as the best captain on the Chesapeake Bay was giving it all he had to keep from meeting his match. Out here, water always held the upper hand and Howard knew that this time, he would be a lucky man to ever again walk in his white rubber boots across the crushed oyster shells of Harper's Creek Marina.

The captain of the *Bay Lady* took a look over his shoulder and saw through the rear window of the wheelhouse that David was awake and holding on to the steering wheel of the console. Howard powered down the boat, opened the wheelhouse door and stepped outside. Holding fast to grip rails on the side of the wheelhouse, he screamed above the sound of the wind at the man laying at the rear of his boat.

"You're a lot of trouble, Forbes," Howard said, "but all that's gonna end soon I can promise ya that. Once this shit settles down, I'm goin' to toss you overboard and let you do a little underwater sightseein' for a while. We're gonna see how long you can swim with just your arms and then when ya get too tired to do that, we're gonna see how long you can hold your breath. Notice that I didn't tie your hands. Thought rope marks on the wrists of a dumb ass kayaker might look a little funny."

Howard leered at Forbes from his grip hold at the wheelhouse door, while David just stared back at the man who held his fate in his hands and didn't say a word as wave after massive wave made misty green from the two floodlights pitched the *Bay Lady* further into the mouth of the maelstrom where the intersections of the Mobjack Bay and the mighty York River join forces with the waters of the Chesapeake Bay.

"Ya ever think you'd meet your maker by drownin', Mr. Forbes?" Howard yelled again over the noise of the wind. "Horrible thing, drowning. First, ya know that you're gonna die and then being awake while your lungs fill with water. Scares the shit out of me just thinkin' about it. How 'bout you Forbes, scare the shit out of you, too?"

Again, David, said nothing. He was too cold, too wet, too beaten and in far too much pain to engage in conversation with the all but proven killer of Jimmy Jarvis.

"Cat got your tongue, boy?" Howard said, hanging on to the grip rail with both hands as another wave violently rolled the boat from side to side and then up and over the cascading roller coaster of water that seemed to have taken over the world.

"Aw, hell, I'd probably be the same way if it was me back there instead of you." Howard yelled with smile. "Lost in my thoughts, I would be. But I'd want some last words. You got any last words, Mr. David Forbes, attorney-at-law?"

This time David looked up and spoke.

"Yeah," was all he said.

"And what might they be?" Howard asked.

Forbes managed a slight grin across a face ripped with pain and yelled back, "Say hello to Thomas Jefferson."

Howard looked at Forbes like the lawyer had lost his mind and said, "What the hell kind of thing is that to say?"

They were the last words to come from the mouth of Coles Howard as David wrapped both hands around the steering wheel and watched as the flood lights of the *Bay Lady* brought into sharper focus fifty-eight feet of storm proven resiliency, the New Point Comfort Lighthouse.

David remembered it from his after dinner voyage with Walter Taylor and here she was again, emerging from the darkness like a Colossus with her heavily rip rapped shoreline ready to guard her from any and all comers.

The *Bay Lady* crashed bow first into the large boulders and Coles Howard had no chance of hanging on. His body slammed into the wheelhouse door and then was flung backwards like a ragdoll sent airborne and David watched as Howard hit the upper rail of the rear transom face first, with pieces of teeth, gum, nose and lip flying everywhere.

This time it was Howard's turn to bleed and it flowed in abundance, with red tinged water of his own making now washing by the gallon full across the fiberglass of the now impaled *Bay Lady*.

Wedged on the rocks, the boat became lifeless prey for the waves that now mercilessly pounded her flanks. No longer needing to hang on, David moved from the console and crawled across the now slanting deck to the body of Coles Howard who was bleeding profusely from the nightmarish wounds to his face.

The king of the watermen, with nose smashed, teeth gone, gums shattered and lips torn asunder now looked ghoulish, and he flailed his arms and legs on the deck as pain took over, rendering him a speck of the man he once was.

David immediately started his search for the SOG as the boat continued to get raked by the waves and the wind when he finally found the knife in the inside pocket of Howard's jacket. Forbes opened the knife and put the blade to good work, cutting the ropes off his legs while keeping enough length to return the favor to Howard.

He then kneeled on the deck, gathered up the rope and was reaching to tie Howard's hands behind his back when the bleeding waterman suddenly kicked Forbes in the chest, crashing him against the console and sending the knife flying from his hand.

Horribly injured as he might be, no one was going to tie the hands of Coles Howard on his boat.

The massive waterman struggled to one knee and then lunged at David, slamming his shoulder against Forbes' chest. David responded with a left hook straight into the waterman's badly wounded mouth and Howard let out a primal scream that pierced the wind like it came from the all mighty himself. Forbes followed up the first punch with a second, and then a third as his feet moved furiously to free himself from the weight of Howard's body.

But the waterman was relentless. Although he was able to scramble a few feet at a time away from the proven power of Howard's fists, David was repeatedly drug back towards the battle as Howard's powerful hands grabbed at his legs and clothes, pulling him closer and closer until Howard had managed to put both of his hands around David's throat and began to squeeze.

389

The waterman's grip on his neck was like a large tourniquet made of wet, flesh warm coiled steel, and as saliva mixed with hot blood poured down on David's face, his world became a disoriented haze of flashing bright light and screaming pain as the capillaries in his eyes began to burst.

He was being strangled to death.

Forbes was losing consciousness fast and knowing that he had only seconds to live, the husband of Karen and the father of Luke and Katie fought with every ounce of love and hate that he had left.

He kicked and he punched and he grabbed and he clawed and he moved his body every way that he could but Howard still hung on, his hands like vise grips around the neck of David Forbes.

Time was up. Forbes was dying and the lawyer's arms and legs started to flail wildly on the deck like some live insect impaled by a stickpin welding nine year old, when his flapping right hand found the SOG.

In one flick, the blade was open and David drove the knife as hard as he could into the chest of Coles Howard.

For the second time that night, Howard's screams pierced the wind as the waterman rolled to his side, clutched his chest with both hands, turned and faced his adversary, looking all the while like a mortally wounded wolf at the end of the chase.

Howard got to his knees and looked down at his hands that were now fingers open and palms up. They were covered in fresh blood and David could see that the knife had found its target as the waterman's life pumped from the wound like water from a hose.

Coles Howard was finished and he knew it. But with one last attempt at taking with him the enemy who had proved to be his only match, Howard lunged at Forbes with what strength he had left but the lawyer moved fast and again drove the blade of the SOG deep into the waterman's chest.

Howard collapsed against the knife, but this time, instead of pushing him away, Forbes held Howard close in his arms and spoke into his ear which was just inches away from David's face.

"How does it feel, Howard?" he said as he twisted the blade of the knife, the waterman's weakening body convulsing against his own with each movement of steel against flesh.

"How does it feel to be so completely fucked? Remember what I told you I was going to do if you ever threatened my family again? I told you I was going to kill you myself. You should have listened to me, you really should've."

Forbes continued his hold as the waterman's still beating heart continued to pump fresh blood on the deck of the boat.

"You know Howard," David said. "The first time that blade went into you, that one was for Jimmy Jarvis. And the second time, well, that one was for my wife and kids. But this time, pal, this time it's all gonna be just for me."

"Now, it's my turn to ask the big question. You got any last words, asshole?"

David then held Howard's bloodied body upright with his left hand and stared at the waterman's shattered mouth, its homeless tongue flopping around like an agitated snail without its shell.

"I didn't think so," Forbes said with a smile as his right hand drove the blade of the knife low and deep into Howard's stomach, and the attorney didn't stop slicing upwards until he hit solid bone. Even then, Forbes didn't withdraw the blade until Howard's eyes rolled back into his head and his life ceased to exist.

David released his grip, pushed Howard away and watched as the waterman's body slid to the deck of the boat, where wave after wave washed the blood of the Captain of the *Bay Lady* through the scuppers on her deck and into the waters of the Chesapeake Bay.

# Chapter Thirty-Nine

## Walter Taylor takes the Helm

Karen was deep asleep when the booming knocks began to land on her back door, one right after the other.

When she awoke, she instantly knew something was wrong. David was not in the bed and it was 3:45 in the morning. She threw on a robe, walked downstairs and through the windows could see three men standing on her back porch. All were wearing rain gear. The man knocking on the other side of her door was as big as a house and he started a second round of announcements as his massive fists rapped on storm door aluminum. Karen paused for a moment before answering. Her eyes then spotted David's note on the kitchen table and feared that something had happened to her husband. She opened the door.

"Ms. Forbes," the knocker said. "I'm Randy Callis. I apologize for disturbing you at this hour, but I need to talk to you. I know that your husband is not home, but you have nothing to fear from us and that's the God's honest truth. Can we come in? It's right gnarly out here," the large waterman added as the storm sent airborne buckets of cold stinging rain against the backs of the men who were huddled together under the overhang of the small porch roof.

Karen opened the door wider and stepped aside as the visitors came in and stood dripping wet and cold on the foyer floor.

"Where is my husband and why are you here?" Karen asked.

"Them's real good questions, ma'am," Callis said, in response as he took off his hat and nervously rolled it in hands as large as country hams.

"All I can say is that I think that Mr. Forbes is on a boat right now with Coles Howard. Where that boat is right now, I can't rightly say."

Karen's stomach started to twist in knots as her fears began to build. She looked down again at the note from David and said, "My husband wrote me that he couldn't sleep and was going for a drive. How do you know that he's on some boat with Howard?"

"Ah, Capt. Taylor saw your husband get on Captain Howard's boat and then saw Howard get on the boat and then saw the boat leave the creek."

"In this weather?" she asked.

"Yes ma'am," he answered.

"My husband is in danger, isn't he?" Karen asked.

"Yes ma'am, probably so," the waterman replied.

"Why are you here?" she asked.

"Because Capt. Taylor thinks you and you children might be in danger, too. He called me up and asked me to round up some of the fellows. So that's what I done. This here's Charlie Morgan. This other fellow over here is Kevin West. They're finest kind and you and your children will have no worries tonight I can assure you of that."

"Worries about what? What's going on?" Karen said, casting a glance down the hallway to the kid's bedrooms, as the tears started to well in her eyes.

"Ma'am, all I can say is that your husband kicked a hornet's nest that's been buzzin' for many a year," Callis explained.

"Some folks don't cotton to what he's done at all. Others like us, well, we see it differently. Now, Charlie here is gonna sit out in his truck and block the driveway. Kevin and I are gonna keep a close eye on the front and back of the house if that's all right."

Karen didn't say anything at first. She went to the phone hanging on the wall across from the island bar and called David's cell phone number. It instantly went to voice mail and the sound of his recorded greeting made the tears flow even more.

She grabbed a paper towel from the dispenser on the bar, wiped away the streaks that now lined her face and said, "Okay, I guess it makes no sense to call the Sheriff, am I right."

"Very much so ma'am," Callis replied. "That won't do no good at all. That's one reason why we're here."

"What's the other reason?" Karen asked

"Because we respect what Mr. Forbes' done," Callis said. "He's right about Howard. That's why we been comin' to court when we could, to show support and let Howard know we weren't gonna let your husband stand alone on this."

"I'm not sure David felt that your presence there was to show him support." Karen replied. "I think he always felt that you were there to intimidate him, scare him, something like that."

"I understand," the waterman replied. "As a group, I guess we look a little rough around the edges to folks who don't know us real well. But that's okay. We'll get it straight with your husband when he comes home and he will be home, don't you worry about that. Now if you could oblige us with some coffee, we'd all be very appreciative because it's going to be a very long night."

---

The massive storm was doing all it could to rid the lighthouse of her unwelcomed guest as wave after wave continued to pound the *Bay Lady* that was still wedged among the boulder like rip rap that surrounded its 1805 architecture. The lights of the deadrise were still on and as David made his way up the inclined deck towards the wheelhouse, he felt like he was trapped in some bizarre dream, one of violence, pain and death all wrapped together in the surreal scene of a two centuries-old lighthouse illuminated by a storm ravaged boat covered in blood.

Forbes managed his way into the wheelhouse, shut the door and paused while his body adjusted to the shelter from the elements. For the first time in the eternity that was the last two hours, there was no rain and no wind, just a warm, muffled welcoming silence. Weakened by exhaustion and overcome by relief, he couldn't stop his legs from buckling and with his back against the wheelhouse wall, he slid to the floor and did nothing as the rain continued to rain and the wind continued to blow.

Once his strength started to return, Forbes started to take inventory of what he had left from the original equipment he brought aboard the *Bay Lady*.

David went through the pockets of both his jacket and his pants and found nothing. His phone and headset were gone as was the GPS. The USB cord was missing, as well. The only piece of equipment that was going to make the round trip if he ever made it out of here was the SOG knife, and that was somewhere in the back of the boat keeping company with the body of Coles Howard.

Looking up, Forbes reached for the steering wheel and slowly, painfully pulled himself to his feet. His entire body ached as though it were one giant muscle that had been beaten like a rented mule. He hurt from top of head to tip of toe.

Just like the after effects from the assault by Cassie's step-father, David's chest was ripped in pain from Howard's shot to his stomach. The waterman's foot and brick-like backhand also had done their work as parts of the lawyers face were numb and swollen while other parts felt like they were on fire.

Grimacing from the pain, David unintentionally gritted his teeth and two of the shattered four sent bolts of electricity into his brain, buckling his knees for a second time and nearly causing him to pass out.

Forbes tightened his grip on the wheel and breathed deep to clear his head from the rocket blast that had just emanated from his jaw. It was then that David felt the back of the boat began to lift and slightly sway from side to side.

Something was happening that was loosening the grip of the rock and David began to panic. Being stuck on the rip-rap until daylight was something he could handle. Being thrown back out on the water was something he knew he couldn't survive. Forbes was well aware that his options were limited and that Mother Nature held all the cards on this one.

Another wave suddenly lifted the boat and David felt the keel beneath his feet slide ever so slightly off its perch on the rocks. Whatever he was going to do, Forbes knew he had to do it fast and the words of Walter Taylor came back to him just in time.

"That's a marine radio," the old man had said. "Go to Channel 16 first. That's the frequency everyone monitors. Then switch to another frequency once ya got your conversation goin'."

David, feeling the boat lift again to the rhythm of another wave, turned the radio on, reached for the microphone and went to channel 16.

He pressed the button on the mic and spoke, "This is David Forbes. I'm on the *Bay Lady*. Can anybody hear me?"

Forbes released the talk button and listened as whispery electronic static filled the wheelhouse. No one replied.

After about twenty seconds, David spoke again, same words as before and awaited a reply. Still nothing came back his way. He brought the mic to his battered mouth to speak a third time when a familiar but unexpected voice spoke to him through the radio.

"This is Sheriff Howard. Where are you and why are you on my son's boat."

Forbes paused for a moment and then replied, "I'm at the lighthouse. Your son's boat is stuck on the rocks."

"Where is my son?" the Sheriff asked.

"He's here with me on the boat," David replied.

"Put him on, now," the Sheriff demanded

396

"Ah, that's not gonna happen," David countered.

"You listen to me you son of a bitch, you put my son on this radio right now!"

"Your drug running son is dead, Sheriff. His body is in the back of this goddamn boat. He killed Jimmy Jarvis and tonight he tried to kill me. This time, it didn't quite go his way. Sorry for your loss."

"You bastard! You murdered my son! I'm pulling the warrants myself . . ." the sheriff screamed when another voice, this one expected and so very needed, cut across the frequency.

"David, do ya remember how many softshell crabs we had for dinner the other night?" Walter Taylor asked. "Now go to that channel."

Forbes quickly turned the knob to show '6' on the LED channel indicator, and said, "Walter, are you there?"

"Yeah, boy," The old waterman said, "I'm here. Where are you?"

"Howard's boat hit these big rocks around the base of the lighthouse." David said. "Been stuck here for about an hour, I think, but now the boat is moving. I think she's coming loose. It's crazy out here. I don't know what I'm going to do if this thing gets back out into the water."

"Listen to me," the waterman instructed. "Tides comin' in. Nothing you can do about it. The boat is gonna come off the rock so ya best be ready. When she comes free, keep her bow to the lighthouse, start her engines and slowly put her in reverse just like I showed ya. By the way, your wife and children are fine. Several of New Point's best turkey hunters are making sure of that."

"Walter, I can't thank you enough," were the words David was speaking into the mic when a large wave rolled under the *Bay Lady* and lifted the workboat off the rocks.

She was free.

"Shit, Walter, the boat's moving," David said frantically into the mic. "I'm floating, what the hell do I do?"

"David, do what I tell you to do. Turn on the engine and put her in reverse. Do it now."

Forbes's hands were shaking like a condemned man's three feet from the gas chamber when he turned the key and the engines fired to life.

Taylor heard the sound of the engines over the mic and said, "Now pull the lever back towards ya and move away from the rip-rap. Do it fast before the sea gets another shot at ya. Once you're clear, turn her 90 degrees starboard and . . ."

"Ninety degrees starboard?" David exclaimed "Walter, please, I don't understand this crap. Give it to me in English."

Walter laughed and said, "Relax boy, turn the steering wheel like ya be making a right hand turn in that pretty little car of yours and once you've turned, go straight and count to fifty. Once you've reached fifty, turn the wheel like you're making another right hand turn, then keep straight and then I'm thinkin' you should be headin' back into the Mobjack and towards Harper's Creek."

"How the hell can you tell?" David asked. "I can't see shit out here."

"Storm came from the North," the old man replied. "I'm figurin' that she blew ya onto the rock with your bow pointin' south. I'm taking you west and then north. Should work out fine if the hull to the boat holds. The storm is movin' past us so the water should be calming down a bit. I've got two workboats comin' out to bring ya in. Watch for their lights. You'll see 'em in about fifteen minutes. Match their speed and follow them in. Sun'll be up soon enough so you should see some light from the east. When you get to the dock, bring her in like I showed ya and you'll do just fine."

"Walter, I can't dock this goddamn thing." David said.

"Least of your worries as I see it." Taylor replied. "Your bigger problem is that Sheriff Howard will be greetin' ya when ya come in. He'll be none too happy about his boy laying dead in the back of his boat. Not hard to guess what he'll be inclined to do so watch yourself when you hit dry land. Now, I'm getting off this channel . . ."

"Walter, don't get off the radio!" Forbes pleaded.

"David, this is your time," the old man said. "Do what I said and you'll do fine, just like a nine-year old boy did so many years ago. Like I told ya, the sea giveth and the sea taketh away. This time, she gave you your life when she could have took it like she done so many others. If you weren't meant to make it home, you'd have been dead long since."

And then the radio went silent. David kept it on channel six but the airwaves were silent and Forbes counted alone. Two right hand turns with fifty counts in between had him creek bound up the now quieter waters of the Mobjack Bay, and true to his word, fifteen minutes later, Walter Taylor's promised convoy of two workboats appeared out of the northwest and guided him up the channel to the *Bay Lady*'s berth at Harper's Creek Marina.

# Chapter Forty

# The Showdown at Harper's Creek

Unlike its storm rendered emptiness when Forbes first boarded the *Bay Lady*, the parking lot at the marina was now crowded with watermen as David slowly brought the boat from the mouth of creek and down the channel, passing the osprey nest on the day marker that was empty, the chick now grown and feeding on its own from the abundance of stripers and blues that occupied the colder water of the late fall.

The sun was now creeping over the horizon and the gathering light of day, piercing through skies clear and rainless, recreated for David Forbes the timeless beauty of the first time he had laid eyes on Harper's Creek General Store.

A pristine relic of days gone past, this monument to the working watermen of the Chesapeake Bay was still a glorious sight to behold. The pastels of the moment were layered with the grace of Monet against a canvas of oyster shell gray and storm washed skies of blue and as he brought the workboat starboard to the bulkhead, he feathered back, dropped briefly into reverse, went into neutral and glided her in like he'd been doing it since he was nine years old.

Except for the fact that this wasn't his boat and that its owner was lying face first on the back deck, stabbed and dead, this would have been a perfect day.

The second the *Bay Lady* touched the bulkhead, two watermen jumped on board to secure her lines while a dozen more lined the dock to stare at the body of the great Coles Howard.

In some ways it was like an old fashioned western, where the bounty hunter rides into town and the townspeople gather around to see who was the poor soul trussed up and riding face down on the back side of his pack mule.

One of the watermen helped him to step off the boat and David was finally standing on dry land. With one eye swollen shut and the rest of his face bruised and mauled, he walked past the dockside onlookers and towards Harpers General Store.

But like Taylor said, getting this far was the least of his worries. Walking towards him from the other end of the parking lot was Sheriff Howard, Lt. Jake Carter and four deputies, including Matt Robins, and they were all armed with shotguns.

Forbes walked towards the gang of law enforcement officers and held his hands in the air.

"I have no weapon, and have committed no crime," David said loudly to the approaching officers and to the audience of watermen who were forming a ring around Forbes and Howard's band of deputies.

"I suspect you will take me into custody anyway," David continued. "In front of these witnesses, I swear that I will go peacefully and without resistance. You may handcuff me anytime you please."

To David's surprise, Howard walked right past him and proceeded directly towards the *Bay Lady*. "You hold this piece of shit right here till I get back," the Sheriff said to Carter who obliged the directive by sending Forbes to his knees with a swift kick to the back of David's legs.

"Move from that spot and you're one dead lawyer, you got that, boy?" Carter whispered out of earshot of the ring of onlookers.

David kept his hands in the air, spit on the ground and said in a voice of equal tonality, "Go fuck yourself Carter. Your days are numbered, too."

Carter was about to respond with a second threat of his own when the voice of Sheriff Junior Howard boomed over the crowd.

"Get that sack of murdering shit to his feet," Howard instructed and Forbes was instantly yanked skyward and turned around so that he was facing the approaching Sheriff who now had a pistol in his hand and was pointing it at David's chest.

"You killed my son!" The sheriff screamed to the crowd. "In    cold blood, this no good goddamn lawyer killed my son! That's him back there in that boat, stabbed to death just like his nigger client stabbed poor Jimmy. Learned somethin' from him, now didn't you boy?"

"Yeah," David said in a voice as loud as the Sheriff's. "I learned something all right. I learned that Billups didn't kill Jarvis. Your son did to keep him quiet about a drug robbery that took place the night before Jimmy was murdered."

"You shut the fuck up, boy!" Howard yelled back, waiving his pistol in David's face. "There weren't no robbery and there weren't no killing. You are making shit up now that Howard and Jimmy are both dead and can't defend themselves. That's what lawyers do best - tell lies and such. And now we got ourselves a lawyer who is willing to commit murder to get his client off from a murder charge himself!"

"I'll admit that I killed Coles Howard," David said to the Sheriff and to the crowd. "Your son found me on his boat late last night. I'll admit that, too. I went on the boat to get his waypoint history from his GPS. I knew it would show where his boat had been the night of the drug robbery. Howard caught me doing it. He kicked and punched me in the face and shattered four of my teeth. He was going to drown me when the storm blew us on the rocks at the lighthouse. We ended up fighting, and I killed him in self-defense. That's the God's honest truth."

"The truth is that he caught you committing a crime on his boat and you killed him because of it!" Howard roared. "You're a no-good lawyerin' son of a bitch who breaks and enters onto people's property and tries to steal their belongings. My son loved Jimmy Jarvis like the boy was his own son! And now you've killed him!"

"Jimmy Jarvis was a first-rate boat hand," Forbes countered with the most important closing statement he had ever done in his life, "everybody here knows that. Remember the wound on his arm? He told Doc Lawson that he'd got it caught between a mooring line and the piling. Jimmy was lying. He was too good at his job for something stupid like that to happen. The wound to his arm actually came from an AK-47 round fired by one of the drug

402

runners they shot that night on the other side of the bay. Doc Lawson will testify to that. The fact is, Sheriff, that your son was running drugs up and down the Bay and making a fortune doing it. You know it, I know it and so do all these men. It's over, Howard."

"This ain't over, boy," the Sheriff said, his voice growing louder and angrier with each spoken word. "It ain't over until I say that it's over! I am Sheriff Junior Howard, and having been duly sworn to protect the citizens of Mathews County, it's my job to dispense the justice around here and that's just what I am going to do!"

Howard had his gun pointed dead center at David's chest and was pulling the hammer back on his Colt .357 magnum when a third voice came to be heard in the arena of watermen that had gathered in the morning sunrise on that oyster shell parking lot.

"Sheriff Howard! You killed my son! You took him from me and now the sea shall taketh you away from this place. May you forever be damned for what you did!"

The sheriff knew the voice well and turned to face his accuser.

It was Walter Taylor but it was not the voice of a Walter Taylor, 89 years of age, the sheriff heard that day. Rather it was the voice of a much younger man, thirty five years less off the clock, who had stood by his son's body as it lay on a stainless steel gurney at the funeral home and saw how the .357 magnum bullet fired by the then Deputy Howard had entered the chest of his only child just below the sternum and had exited directly through his back bone, leaving a hole of torn flesh the size of a billiard ball.

It was also the voice of a man who for the next thirty five years had waited patiently for this moment and for this time.

Just like when it was his time as a nine year-old child to step into the shoes of his father, now, again, it was his moment to right the wrongs and settle all things.

For too long, he had watched from his porch as drugs came in and money went out, day after day, year after year, until the same poison that had

403

killed his son three and a half decades ago had killed another poor boy in the promise of his youth. When Jimmy was found dead on Haven Beach, Taylor swore that it wasn't going to happen ever again, and most importantly, not now, and not on this day, to David Forbes.

Then, with the strength of the younger man he once was, and with the aim of a nine year old boy who listened so very well to the whale hunting stories of his grandfather, a child who only wanted to be like the man shot down so many years ago on a long forgotten dock on Maryland's eastern shore, Walter Taylor reared back his arm, and with the love of a father for a son taken from him so long ago, he let that harpoon fly.

The barbed and rusted killer of whales that had hung above the door way to Taylor's home for over three score was already airborne and half way to its intended destination when Sheriff Howard completed his turn away from David Forbes and leveled his gun instead at the figure of Walter Taylor, who stood back to the sun like Josie Wales facing down murderous Union army redlegs and savage comancheros.

It was the last thing Howard would ever see.

Weighted and designed to puncture deep into the thick fatty hide of five ton whales, the blade of the harpoon not only tore easily into the sheriff's chest, but hit him with so much power and impact that the man who would be king staggered backwards three steps before falling to his knees, the gun still in his hand.

In the moments before he died, the sheriff never said a word nor was he able to muster the strength to fire off a round at the old man who stood thirty feet away, watching him die. He just stared down in bewildered silence at the iron and wood instrument of his death that projected four and a half feet from the front of his shirt, the point of its entrance just a few inches to the right of his well-polished gold badge. Surprisingly, he bled very little and finally fell over on his right side, looking to all the world like a toothpick impaled cocktail wiener awaiting a hungry guest.

Sheriff Junior Howard was dead.

No one moved until Lt. Carter unholstered his weapon and started walking towards Taylor.

The big man with the shotgun, however, had other plans and Carter quickly dropped his sidearm and raised his hands after Robins shucked a round into the twelve gauge and pointed it at the Lieutenants head.

Like Taylor, Robins was a patient man and had a file some two inches thick that would soon send Mr. Carter away for many a year.

After Howard's second in command was taken away, the deputy walked over to David and said, "Rescue squad will be here in about five minutes. Like it or not, you're going to the hospital."

"Matt, I don't care where I go," David said with the best attempt at a smile that he could render all things considered, "just so Karen and the kids are alright."

"Your family is one hundred percent safe," Robins said. "They'll meet you at the hospital, I promise."

David Forbes needed to hear no more. Here was truth, here was justice and here was redemption. And as the pairs of white rubber boots softly made their way to the side of the man who had become one of their own, and as his shoulder felt the embrace from an old man's arm that had so few minutes ago brought justice for a son lost so many years past, David Forbes finally surrendered.

Becoming hopelessly lost in the love for his family and losing all hold he was able to maintain on the moments that had brought life and death together as one, the lawyer who was no longer in a fight for his own life or for the life of his family, or for the life of an innocent man, could do no more. David Forbes, a man for whom life itself seemed again reborn, collapsed to a bended knee and cried.

# EPILOGUE

## Five Days Later

"Jamal, you know I don't like it when you bring your liquor into my house. We have guests here for dinner, and I want this to be a special time and if you start to drinkin' it will ruin it for sure."

Jamal looked up at his granny from where he was sittin' on the front porch of the old woman's home and took another sip from a mason jar filled to the brim with moonshine mixed with canned peaches.

"Now, granny," he said, wiping a drop from his chin, "First of all, we out here on the front porch so we're not technically bringing this shine into the house and I promise that I'm going to watch myself this time. Just a few sips for Jamal, that's all and besides, I've got my lawyer here to keep me straight, right lawyer man?"

"Jamal," David said from his seat on the porch step opposite of Jamal, "keeping you straight is too much work for just one lawyer but I'll see what I can do."

"Well let's see what you can do with some of this peach goodness and then we'll settle down to some chicken and dumplings," Jamal said with a smile as he handed the jar over to Forbes who took a sip and handed it back to his host.

"That's, ah . . . good stuff," David managed to say as Jamal's homemade concoction warmed him right up.

"I'll keep an eye on them, Ms. Billups," Karen said with a smile from her perch on the porch swing, as she rolled her eyes at David and added, "Boys will be boys".

"My, oh my," Ms. Billups said, "lawyers and colored folk sipping liquor on my front porch," she exclaimed as she turned to go inside. "What's the world comin' to?"

Both men laughed and shared another round of Jamal's finest. "You know Jamal, you're a lucky man," David said. "Had Coles Howard killed me out there that night, you wouldn't be sittin' here right now, that's for sure."

"I heard that," Jamal said, "and I appreciate all that you did and I just want you to know that I'm going to clean up a bit. Know what I mean? Cut back on the drinkin' and shit like that."

Both men stared at the jar of shine sitting between them and laughed again. "You mean you'll cut back right after dinner, I suppose?" Forbes asked.

"Yep, right after dinner," Jamal noted, "Which, if my nose is any indication, is about to begin any minute."

As if on cue, Ms. Billups came to the door and said, "All right now, you men put that jar up and this time I mean it. Mr. Forbes, don't be encouraging him now. He don't need no encouraging when it comes to stuff like that."

"No ma'am, no encouraging from me," David replied to the mild good-natured scolding.

"Hmmm, you men all alike," she said, "now Jamal, please show Mr. and Mrs. Forbes where they can wash up before dinner and then come help me set the table. And where are those children?"

David went go round up Luke and Katie as Karen brushed by, giving him a quick peck on the cheek as she headed to the kitchen to give Jamal's granny assistance in getting the table set for dinner.

When Forbes entered the small living room that adjoined the kitchen, he saw that there were place settings for five at a dining room table that had a matching hutch holding holiday dishes behind wood framed glass doors and for two more at the small table in the kitchen. He then noticed that Jamal's granny had twice gone to the front door as though looking for a yet unarrived guest for dinner.

"Expecting someone?" David asked.

"Well, I was hoping so, but I guess he couldn't make it," she was saying when a dark blue BMW pulled in front of her house. It was Judge Theodore Lincoln Powell.

"Holy cow, it's the judge," David said.

"I asked him to dinner," Ms. Billups explained with a smile. "It was only fittin' that he be invited to sit with the rest of us."

Jamal's granny and David Forbes walked out to meet the noble jurist at the top of the steps to the front porch.

"Thank you for coming Judge," said Ms. Billups with a slight curtsey. "I appreciate it so much."

"Well, I thank you for the invitation," Powell replied. "You are very kind. You know, I usually don't do this kind of thing but as you can imagine, my opportunities to enjoy cookin' as fine as I know yours will be are somewhat rare. As such, it was impossible to resist coming here this evening to your lovely home."

"Oh, thank you. Now if you'll excuse me, I'll get dinner on the table," she said as she left the porch and made a beeline for the kitchen.

"Good to see you again, Judge," David said.

"Good to see you and tonight, it's Ted," the judge said, who then looked left and right and spoke with a lowered voice, "but I will hold you in contempt if I don't get a sample of that peach shine you been drinking. I can smell it five miles away and there's nothing better in this world."

"Ted," Forbes exclaimed, "some of Jamal's finest coming right up."

And so it was. Ted Powell, David Forbes and Jamal Billups, with family in attendance, all joined forces in the same room where a tear stained gray dress and pages torn from a family Bible once bore witness to man's inhumanity to his fellow man, with the new hutch being a replacement for the busted chiffarobe that had fallen prey to the boot heel of the now incarcerated Jake Carter.

Both David and Ted had expected culinary greatness, and Jamal's granny was not one to disappoint. Steaming bowls of collard greens, seasoned cabbage and spoon bread from heaven acted as supporting cast members to the peppery chicken and dumplings and fresh fried oysters that Jamal had shucked that morning. Sweet potato pie along with another blessing of Jamal's favorite beverage provided the encore and all that was life was good.

———————————

Four miles north of Salisbury, Maryland and two hours' drive time from center city Baltimore, a black GMC Denali and a dark gray seven series BMW followed each other down one of the many rutted hard-scrabble roads that laced across the farm lands of coastal Maryland. It was noon and the vehicles cast nary a shadow as they drove under the sky high sun.

Finally, they came to a halt along a stretch of road that was a straight shot in both directions for well over a mile, giving the occupants of both vehicles a clear view of any cars approaching from either the front or back. There wasn't a building or house in sight.

In less than three minutes, a third vehicle, this time a Jeep Grand Cherokee approached them from the opposite direction at a high rate of speed. Coming to a stop approximately one hundred feet from the BMW, the occupants of the Jeep, three men, emerged and approached the BMW.

They were met by two men who had exited from the Denali long before the Jeep had come to stop. Both men carried sub-machine guns and were standing guard next to the BMW.

The fact that the men were carrying weapons didn't seem to faze the other three men one bit.

"Okay, where is he?" asked one of the men from the Jeep.

The two armed men looked at each other, and nodded as the man on the right tapped the glass of the right front passenger door of the BMW with the barrel of the machine gun and stepped aside as Simon Epstein exited the vehicle.

"So you are the famous Epstein?" said one of the occupants from the Jeep.

"I am. And you are Carlos Morales, lead asshole for Los Zeta East Coast, correct?" Epstein asked.

"Except for the body part reference, your statement is accurate," Morales replied. "You asked for this meeting and I graciously consented even though your butchery of our employees is well documented. How strange it is that there are never any survivors when your men descend from the skies to attack our shipping centers? No arrests, no trials, just death. You are not good for business, senor."

"I'm glad you brought that up. Let's talk about business," Simon said. "Four months ago, your people sold 1.5 million dollars of high grade Afghanistan heroin to an MS-13 cartel operating out of D.C. and then used the cash to buy a shitload of Colt M-4's from a bunch of dirty Baltimore cops. All this took place in a warehouse on North Avenue. You know this because you were there. In fact, you drove this same BMW that is parked behind me right now. Don't deny it. My information, as you can tell, is very good. If you do deny it, I have instructed my men to kill you right here, right now. You are also aware that we found the majority of those weapons when we crashed your little party in Sinaloa. I'm sure that your heart broke over that one, as there were lots of guns there and lots of ammunition, too. We enjoyed killing your men."

"How did we learn about this, you may ask?" Epstein continued, "We have our sources, of course, but one source was better than all the rest. He ratted you guys out big time. That's how we knew about the money, the drugs, the weapons, the whole fuckin' enchilada. But it didn't end there. This guy was ripping you off and you didn't even know it. You know that huge drug shipment that went missing off the coast of Mathews about five months back? All his work. This hot shot set up his brother and his old man in the distribution business and then skimmed the butter from your cream every which way he could and his name is Detective Donny Howard. He also happened to threaten a friend of mine which did not make me happy at all."

Simon wasn't done. "You know, Carlos, one of these days, I'll come for you and we both know what's going to happen when I do. But, until that much anticipated day arrives, you can buy yourself some very precious time by making sure that I know, in advance, all of the drug movements of MS-13. You help me there, and I'll hold off on the inevitable hunting expedition with one exception. If I hear of you ever again attempting to buy U.S. military-grade weapons, I'll track you and your family down quick and not a single life form with your DNA attached will walk on this Earth after I'm done. Comprende'?"

"I understand," Carlos said.

"Great," Simon said. "Things always go better when people understand each other, don't you think? And, ah, by the way, you can have your car back. Keys are in the ignition and there's a gift for you in the trunk. Have a great day."

The Los Zetas didn't move until the Denali had turned around and sped off into the distance down a road bordered on both sides by tall stalks of ready to harvest yellow corn. Once the danger that was Simon Epstein had disappeared from sight, they removed the keys from the ignition, went to the rear of the vehicle and slowly opened the trunk of the BMW.

Wedged in the floor of the trunk and wearing the same Armani suit that he wore for his visit to the offices of Cabell Sinclair was a bound and gagged Lt. Donny Howard.

When the lid went up, Howard's eyes clamped shut as the darkness of the trunk was replaced by rays of blinding sun. Once a few seconds had passed, he slowly opened his eyes and looked up at the men staring down at him, his face becoming a mask of sheer terror when he gazed upon faces last seen in an east Baltimore warehouse.

"Gringo, we meet again!" Morales said, "but this time, it's just you, me and, ah, what was it you said, my 'Taco Bell' boys?"

The Mexicans laughed while Howard struggled like a roped calf. He tried to speak, but the gag, like the nylon wire ties around his feet and hands, was just too tight.

"Isn't that what he said to us last time?" Carlos said to a round of "si's" from the Zetas flanking him on the left and right, "Taco Bell?"

"But last time, you had a machine gun in your hand and lots of friends and they had guns, too." Carlos said with a grin on his face. "This time, however, you have no gun and no friends to help you out. But we are good guys and we will help you out, out of the car that is."

All three men then lifted the detective out of the car and dropped him hard with a sickening thud like a heavy sack of potatoes on the side of the road.

"I'm afraid that this is the end of our relationship, Mr. Howard." Carlos said as he kneeled beside the detective's tethered body, reached into his coat pocket, flipped open a razor sharp switchblade and cut off Howard's left ear and then his right ear, as well. Blood poured from the wounds as Howard went ballistic against the unforgiving nylon, twisting left, and then right as spasms of pain ripped through his body. His eyes went wide as headlights, begging, pleading not to be cut anymore but Carlos was not even close to being finished.

"That's for not listening," Carlos said, throwing the pieces of Howard's ear into the weeds that bordered the shoulder of the road.

He wiped the blood off the blade of his knife on the lapels of Howard's suit, and said, "This is for not keeping your mouth shut." Howard's eyes followed the knife's every move and started shaking his head from side to side as the blade approached its target. One of the other men grabbed Howard's hair, pulled back tight and watched as Morales took his blade and with practiced, surgical precision cut off the gag and then sliced off Howard's cheeks and lips.

The man then released his hold and all three watched as spasms of pain raked the detective's body, the killing ground of sand and asphalt turning

412

dark red as Howard's blood went everywhere. Skin now gone, Howard's face below his nose looked like an acid soaked skull. With his gag removed, Howard tried to talk but he had no language today, just the garbled animalistic sounds of a man trying not to choke to death on the blood that flowed down his throat.

Carlos stabbed at a piece of Howard's cheek that was lying on the road and held it up for Howard's examination. "You like this, cop? I do because you've been a very bad boy." The detective was looking up at the head Zeta like he was expecting some sort of explanation, when Morales smiled, flicked the piece of flesh off his knife and drove the tip of the blade deep into the center of each eye.

"And that, my friend, is for telling people what you see."

In pain beyond description, Howard went insane as thick, grayish white fluid seeped from the wound in each eye and his skinless jaws clicked open and shut like a Halloween skull toy.

Carlos stood back and surveyed his work. Howard's earless and lipless face was covered in blood. But the bleeding was from the non-lethal wounds by design and he was still very much alive.

"Howard, can you hear me?" Carlos now yelled, which caused his two comrades to laugh hysterically. "Have you suffered enough? You tell us when you want to be put out of your misery. Just nod your head and we will end it by cutting your throat. Until then though, my friends and I shall have our fun with you."

"Gentlemen," Carlos said as the two other Zetas flicked opened their switchblades right on cue, "It is time to go to work."

And so they did. As seagulls played across a pale blue sky and as a soft breeze made its own music, flowing across the top of the corn field, stirring the stalks into a funeral symphony, dried husk brushing against dried husk, Carlos Morales and his 'Taco Bell Boys' drove their knives into every body part that detective had.

Six minutes later, Lt. Donald Howard, runner of guns, killer of Jimmy Jarvis, placer of pennies on tires in garages, crooked cop extraordinaire and the kid who never took a knee when he injured a competitor on the football field, finally, nodded his head. Morales then obligingly cut his throat from ear to ear and the three men watched like vultures as what was left of the detective's life bled out under the warm Maryland sun.

**The End**

# ACKNOWLEDGEMENTS

There is no one that I am indebted to more in the writing of "A Silent Tide" then my wife, Katrina Johnson. Without her love, support, encouragement, editing prowess and sense of discipline, this work would not have been possible.

Many others contributed to this work. I wish to thank John Corrigan, English teacher at Mathews High School and writer extraordinaire, for the incredible amount of time and energy he expended in editing "A Silent Tide". If this book achieved any measure of refinement, it is because of his good work and I am forever in his debt. A special thanks is also extended to Sandy Beamer, guitar instructor, voracious reader and great friend, who contributed not only her editing skills but also her listening skills, tolerating well my habit of reading each chapter aloud. These "reading sessions" proved to be an invaluable tool and I attribute much of the books readability to her involvement. I also owe much to Ginger and David Vuich for their assistance in getting this book across the finish line. Ginger's excellent editing and David's excellent martinis, coupled with his professional advice to" just get the damn thing done" helped immeasurably in completing this project. A sincere thanks is also once again owed to my friend, Bruce Nelson, for his outstanding photography and cover layout design. He is one of the best in the business and I am glad he is on my team.

Thanks are also in order to friends and drug task force officers, John Mattis and Eric Vanfossen, for their technical assistance in writing this book. Investigator Bill Riley of the Mathews County Sheriff's Office also assisted as one of my review readers and I cannot thank him enough for his insight. Friend and school board colleague, the Rev. Kevin Smith, was an invaluable asset in shaping the book from the African-American perspective and the character of "Jamal Billups" owes much to his involvement as do the scenes from the First African Assembly of God.

This acknowledgment would not be complete without reference to the people of Mathews County who have impacted my life in so many wonderful ways. Credit here goes first and foremost to my beloved neighbor, Marian Gray Trusch. Fate brought us together 22 years ago in the little hamlet of Bavon and I am the better man for it. Second, this book would never have been written were it not for the incredible friendships that I was blessed to earn with the working watermen of Mathews County. I first met Walter Coles Burroughs in 1991 when a much younger and very broke, country lawyer attended a waterman's association meeting at the local Ruritan hall to drum up a little business. From that day forward until I carried his casket in 2004, 'Walter Coles', as he was known, allowed me the honor and privilege of becoming part of his world and in my gratitude, I have endeavored to honor him through the character of Walter Taylor. Mention of the family Burroughs would not be complete without reference to Walter's son, Ronald Coles Burroughs. Waterman tough, but with a pony tail, a beguiling smile and toothpick at the ready, 'Ronald Coles', as *he* is known, contributed much to this work, simply by being the great and interesting individual that he is. The late Dr. Toney Reed also deserves mention. Friend, client, physician and great storyteller about all things Mathews, his presence lingers hard in my memory and, hopefully, I captured a little bit of his warmth, wit and incredible intelligence in the character of Dr. Robert Lawson.

My legal career as a small town country lawyer had an indelible impact on this work and I am grateful for having had the opportunity to work with so many exceptional people in our local courts, particularly former Mathews County Circuit Court Clerk, E. Eugene Callis and Commonwealth's Attorney, Jack Gill, both of whom had occasion to tolerate my presence more than most and I thank them especially for their ability to retain both their sense of humor and their conversant abilities during the heat of battle, so to speak. Thanks is also due to the Sheriffs of Mathews County, Hugh Jordan, Danny Howlett and Mark Barrick, none of whom bear any resemblance to arch villain, Junior Howard. These brave men, and the deputies who have served them well, have made Mathews County the safe place to live that it is and much is owed for their great service.

Lastly, I am grateful beyond words for the love of my five children, Eric, Jacob, PJ, Caleb and Katie. My memories of reading aloud each chapter of "A Silent Tide" as it was completed while they sat around me in the living room of our Bavon home are some of the most incredible moments this father has been blessed to have. I thank you every one. - W.J.

# About the Author

"A Silent Tide" is Mr. Johnson's first novel. His first published work was the critically acclaimed non-fiction, "A School in Pennsylvania," a copy of which is on file at the U.S. Department of Education. Of additional note is that his short story, "The Death of Redemption" won an award for adult fiction at the 15th annual Chesapeake Bay Writers Conference.

Mr. Johnson has been practicing law for over twenty years, he was the featured defense attorney on the CBS program "48 Hours Mystery - The Taylor Behl Murder" and has twice been proudly elected to serve on the Mathews County School Board. Mr. Johnson, his wife and their five children, live in Bavon, Virginia, among the watermen, at the southern tip of Mathews County.

To read more about the author and his other books, visit his website at www.williamjohnsonbooks.com.